DISCOVERY
OF THE SAIPH

Book 1
Of
The Saiph Series

PP Corcoran

ISBN: 978-1-912327-00-3
Paperback Edition

Published by Castrum Press
c/o PP Corcoran Ltd, 138 University Street
Belfast, BT7 1HJ, United Kingdom

Visit www.castrumpress.com

"the good must associate; else they will fall, one by one, an unpitied sacrifice in a contemptible struggle." – Edmund Burke

~

"Suit, call Alonso." A pause followed by a double tone informed Alec that his suit couldn't establish a link to Alonso, instead it automatically searched for the next active ranking marine.

"Go for Semple." The voice sounded strained and distracted. Alec's face paled as he did a quick mental calculation. Semple was something like tenth in the chain of command.

"Sitrep, Sergeant?"

"The situation is… let's call it fluid at the moment Sir… Wait. Jonas on your six! Two enemy on… Shit!"

On Alec's display Marine Jonas' name flashed red then disappeared as Semple came back on the link.

"Sir I have fifty-three KIA and virtually everyone else has an injury of some sort. The initial entry went as planned but as soon as we cleared the airlocks we were assaulted by enemy marines in full-up armor. They were using some sort of plasma grenade. The suits can take a lot of damage but plasma in a confined space you can imagine…" Semple paused, Alec heard the stress in his voice.

"Sergeant! Can you hold?"

– From Discovery of the Saiph by PP Corcoran

Books by PP Corcoran

The Saiph Series:
Discovery of the Saiph, book 1
Search for the Saiph, book 2
Hunt for the Saiph, book 3
Legacy of the Saiph, book 4

The K'Tai War:
Invasion, book 1

Anthologies:
The Empire at War: British Military Science Fiction
Explorations: Through the Wormhole
Explorations: First Contact
A Fistful of Credits

Science Fiction (shorts):
Beyond Apollo

Ghost Soldiers (shorts):
The Province

Most books also available in ebook and audiobook.

Sign up at www.ppcorcoran.com and get 'Beyond Apollo' free!

Table of Contents

CHAPTER ONE

DOORWAY TO THE GALAXY

SENATE OF THE TERRAN REPUBLIC - GENEVA - EARTH

Senator Gillian Rae, representing the Boreland habitats on Titan, listened to the grey haired scientist who was concluding his testimony before the Senate's Science and Technology Committee.

"The ion drive is our most advanced light speed technology," the scientist said. "It is capable of speeds of up to one quarter the speed of light, which means it will reach the closest stars within twenty-five years, a vast improvement on previous attempts. The probe can gather images and data from the stars' planetary systems and send those images and data back to Earth by radio. My peers and I agree this is our best hope of identifying other worlds suitable for human habitation, thus ensuring our continued survival. Thank you."

As the scientist took his seat, Gillian glanced at her fellow senators. Many were nodding their heads in approval. She waited a beat, and then another, and then rose from her seat and got the attention of the president.

"Does Senator Rae wish to be recognized?" Bartholomew McMullen asked.

"I do, Mr. President."

"Very well. You have five minutes."

Gillian took a breath and began. "Mr. President and fellow

Senators, I need not remind you of the consequences of fully autonomous machines with insufficient programming and little or no human override. Many of you know I was fortunate to have survived an incident involving one such machine."

Gillian paused to let her comment sink in. As most of her colleagues knew, she was one of the few survivors of the 'Boreland Blasts', a disaster triggered by a prototype of a fully autonomous mining machine undergoing trials on Titan. The machine mistook a fuel line for a mineral vein and used a laser cutter on it. The resulting chain of explosions and rapid decompression of living quarters killed 104 men, women and children.

Gillian heard murmurs of recognition and saw nods from many of her peers.

"Who knows what these probes will discover when they reach their destinations?" she continued. "Who knows how they will react to their findings in the face of unknown variables, which may be beyond their programming? Such autonomy may result in the loss of vital data, missed opportunities, or worse, the loss of life."

Gillian paused again. She saw more nods but also some puzzled faces. Behind her, she heard whispers.

"I propose we send out manned probes. I understand this increases development difficulty a hundredfold. It requires the expansion of our deep space environment technology program, and it will delay the probe deployments. Nevertheless, the benefits of having a human on the spot to make critical decisions will be worth the added time and expense. I hope my colleagues will agree the risks to our people are too great to ignore. Thank you."

Bartholomew McMullen, the twenty-third President of the Terran Republic, stood to address the Senate. "Thank you, Senator Rae. Senators, we are all aware of Senator Rae's personal and professional experience in this field. She is a devoted member of the Science and Technology Committee, where she has put her engineering degrees to good use, and I know she speaks with knowledge and expertise in this field."

The president paused and glanced around the chamber before continuing. "I call for a vote on Senator Rae's motion – the deployment of the unmanned probes suggested by our learned senior scientists should be delayed at least until the feasibility and practicalities of sending a human crew are investigated."

The holo cube in front of Bartholomew flashed as the senators' votes were recorded and counted. A few minutes later, a bell signaled the end of the voting. Bartholomew studied his screen before rising to announce the results. "Senator Rae's motion is carried."

Unbeknown to the president and the Senate, Gillian Rae, the former engineer from Titan, had just ensured the continued existence of the human race.

#

HASLETT RESEARCH STATION - ASTEROID BELT

Doctor Jeff Moore was having another bad day. He had decided his state of the art computer enjoyed driving him mad, and he was seconds away from reducing it to a heap of rubble when an incoming call tone sounded. Jeff turned away from the offending machine and answered the call, immediately regretting it when the smirking face of Valerie Hayes, Director of the Vega Star Probe team, appeared.

"The bad computer laughing at you again, Jeff?"

"What can I do for you, Valerie?"

"I was going to offer you breakfast in the staff canteen."

"The thought of breakfast in the staff canteen just made me lose my appetite."

"How about a cup of coffee instead?"

"What's the occasion?" Jeff asked.

"One of my engineers, Danny Dunlewey, pulled an all-nighter studying the data from the last Improved Ion Engine test, and he's come up with a few anomalies the computer disregarded."

The Improved Ion Engine was the reason Jeff was having a spate of bad days. He theorized a field of gravity waves projected in front of a steadily accelerating spacecraft would act like the bow wave of a prewar oceangoing ship and allow greater speed and less resistance. It was a great theory, but it seemed to work only at limited velocities. Whenever the test probes accelerated to two-thirds the speed of light, they exploded. At least he assumed they exploded. The last anyone saw of them was a flash of light, and they were gone, obliterated into particles too small to be picked up by optical or electrical equipment – or so he surmised.

Adding to his frustration, the cryogenics team at Caulfield Research Station in New South Wales had made rapid advances in techniques to ensure the safety of the Vega probes' human crew. Meanwhile, his efforts to reduce the probes' travel time to Vega had stalled.

"Is it real coffee?" Jeff asked.

"As real as the recycled air you're breathing," Valerie said. "See you in five."

Jeff left his office and took the lift two floors up to Valerie's office. He wondered what Danny Dunlewey had found—perhaps a way to track the larger pieces of his exploded drive.

Twenty minutes and a second cup of coffee later, Jeff felt as though his world had turned upside down. The data on the holo cube in front of him seemed to prove the impossible. Yet there it was, evidence of faster than light speed travel, a way to fulfil man's quest to travel to the stars.

Jeff moved his gaze from the screen to Valerie. "Where's Danny?"

"He's outside."

"Would you please get him?"

Valerie frowned. "Look, Jeff, I hope he hasn't led you on a wild goose chase. I know he hasn't been here long, but he does show a lot of …"

"Ask him to go to Conference Room One and set it up to present his data to the heads of departments, will you?"

"Oh. OK. Sure."

Jeff stood up. "I'm off to the Communications Room. I need to make a few calls to Earth."

OFFICE OF THE CHAIRMAN OF THE SCIENCE AND TECHNOLOGY COMMITTEE - CANBERRA - EARTH

Gillian Rae admired the sprawling city through the glass wall of her office, which towered 160 floors above Canberra.

Humanity had worked hard to reclaim the nearly destroyed Earth after the wars. Australia had escaped the worst of it and recovered more quickly than Europe or North America. As a result, it had served as the capital and base of the fledgling Terran Republic until Geneva became habitable again. The Science and Technology Bureau had sunk its roots deep in Canberra and, when the rest of the apparatus of government moved to Europe a decade earlier, Sci-Tech stayed behind.

Gillian had come to appreciate Canberra as a second home, so different from her original home on Titan, and now promoted to chair of the Science and Technology Committee, she felt even more at home. Australia provided another advantage, one Gillian had just begun to appreciate. With the president and the rest of the Senate tucked up in their beds half a world away, she had an extra few hours to get a grip on what the scientist and engineer perched on the couch in her office were trying to explain to her.

Gillian turned from the view of Canberra and faced Jeff Moore and Valerie Hayes. Jeff appeared even younger than his eighteen years as he sat alongside Valerie in one of the comfortable chairs. Valerie was chosen as the Director of the Vega Star Probe Team not only for her exceptional mind but for her political savvy, both proved to be invaluable assets when you push for, and get, authority from those in the corridors of power to employ young, fertile minds straight from university rather than choosing scientists and engineers with more… experience.

When Gillian received the urgent request for a face-to-face meeting, she immediately queried the necessity for the five day inter-system shuttle trip by Valerie and Jeff, instead of the usual holo cube communications, but Valerie had refused any explanation and insisted on the in person meeting. Now Gillian knew why.

"Explain this to me again in simple terms, please. I'm only a humble politician." Not entirely true, but her double first in Spatial Engineering from Cambridge hadn't quite prepared her to understand completely what Danny Dunlewey had discovered.

Valerie took a deep breath and began. "As you know, Senator, we at Haslett Station are trying to develop an improved ion drive for the Vega Star Probe mission. Since Vega is more than twenty-five light years from Earth, our current best estimate is thirty-eight years travelling time, minimum. Accounting for the time required to survey the system and radio the data to Earth, it would be some sixty-six years before we heard back from the Vega mission."

Jeff continued. "The effort expended to get our probe there at near the speed of light would save at least thirteen years, well worth it we all thought. And so, for the past five years we," he indicated Valerie, "have been out in the asteroid belt building and testing the best engine ideas humankind can think up, but we reached some kind of wall, a hurdle we couldn't clear. We'd been unsuccessful getting beyond two thirds the speed of light before our probes exploded. Or so we thought." Jeff took a breath. "Our engineers put a failsafe on the engines. If, for whatever reason, the engine test beds lose continuous communication with Haslett base for two seconds or more, a cut-off switch is engaged, the engine is powered down and they begin transmitting a recovery beacon. We, as it turns out, wrongly assumed the previous four test engines were destroyed, thus, the computer ignored any transmission on their recovery beacon frequency. Dunlewey was analyzing the data from the fifth test engine before it too was destroyed when he noticed an anomaly. Remember the computer had been told to ignore, not delete, the recovery beacons from the destroyed test beds, and Danny found beacons from three of the five probes. They hadn't been destroyed at all."

"But why was their signal not detected before?"

"Because it's taken the first signal two and a half years to get back to us,"

"Hang on, are you saying our test engines are all in one piece somewhere out there?" Gillian gave Jeff an incredulous look.

"No, Senator. So far we've only identified the beacons from engines two and three," Valerie interjected. "If engines four and five survived, then we expect to hear from engine four in another year, and five seven months after four."

Gillian took her seat and peered across the low coffee table at Jeff as Valerie continued. "All telemetry received via the beacons indicates the engine shut down at the planned two seconds after the lost contact marker."

"But if the signal took two and a half years to reach us travelling at, err…" Gillian tried to drag the figure for the speed of light up from memory.

"290,792,458 metres per second," Jeff added helpfully.

"Thank you, Doctor Moore. So you're telling me your engines are sitting two and a half light years from here and covered the distance in two seconds?"

"Those're the facts as we read them, Senator," answered Jeff with a nervous laugh. "Our engines are half way to Proxima Centauri and if we figure out what we did right the Vega Star Probe will arrive at Vega in under seventeen seconds."

Gillian sat stunned for a few moments then faced Jeff and Valerie squarely. "But how? Short answer please, I may have to explain this to the public."

Jeff turned to Valerie. "Would you like to demonstrate?"

"OK," said Valerie moving into tutorial mode. "I need a piece of paper," her eyes searched the ultramodern office.

Senator Rae rummaged in a nearby drawer and pulled out a battered little diary, promptly ripping out a blank sheet and handing it to Valerie. "Sometimes it is useful to keep some old tech to hand." She smiled.

Valerie continued with her demo and scribbled on the page. "A good way to imagine this is by using this paper. See I've marked one end A and the other B?" Valerie showed the senator before placing the paper on the coffee table in front of her. Senator Rae nodded in acknowledgement.

"Now imagine an ant crawling across the paper from A to B.

15

If you leave the paper flat on the table, it might take a little while. Now…" Valerie picked up the paper and folded it while she narrated. "If I pick up the paper and fold it so A and B are right next to each other, just so…" She demonstrated this to Gillian. "Now, imagine the ant moving from A to B."

"Of course, Doctor Hayes." Gillian nodded her head, slowly as realization dawned. "Fold space theory…"

"Exactly, Senator." Valerie continued. "Travel time is exponentially reduced. Essentially, this is what Doctor Moore's Gravity Drive has done. Completely by chance it has given us the means to explore the galaxy in our lifetime and at our leisure."

"This may change things slightly," said Gillian wryly. "Now my next question. How soon will a practicable vessel be ready?"

Jeff responded with the eagerness of a puppy, glancing from Valerie and back to Gillian. "Well with the ability to travel, for all intents and purposes, instantly, I would think the current research at Caulfield could be scaled back. Give us their environment researchers and engineers and we could probably produce a test bed within a year. We could be ready for a full scale launch within three."

"Make plans, Doctors. I think you will get everything you might ever need. And good luck." Gillian smiled and stood. She held out her hand. The two doctors, taking this as their cue, also stood before shaking the Senator's hand. They made their way out of the Senator's office.

As they left, Gillian placed a call to the president's private residence. The last Jeff and Valerie heard was Senator Rae's charming, playful, voice saying to a presidential aide "Well, wake him up gently then. But wake him up!"

CHAPTER TWO

FIRST FLIGHT

TDF MARCO POLO - DEIMOS DRY DOCKS

TDF *Marco Polo* gracefully released the mooring clamps securing it to the dry docks orbiting Deimos. The Terran Republic's first interstellar manned ship lit off its reaction drive and slowly pulled away heading for the freedom of open space.

Its captain, David Catney contemplated the past five years. Doctor Jeff Moore had estimated three years to produce a ship ready to go to Vega but his estimation proved a little optimistic. Figuring how to build the automated recovery probes, which made it half way to Proxima Centauri to recover the original engine test beds had taken eighteen months alone. Analyzing their data fully and beginning to design the *Marco Polo* had taken a further two years, all the while sending out more and more unmanned probes ensuring the jump to such phenomenal speed would not turn the crew into paste on the rear bulkhead.

However, as Valerie Hayes pointed out, "If my precious computer circuits can survive the jump into fold space and back to normal space, so can you."

Yeah, fills me full of confidence, thought David. All the same, here he was, along with his bijou crew. A carefully selected crew, as each displayed excellence in their respective fields.

David took time out to consider his command team: Executive Officer, commonly shortened to XO, Lieutenant Commander Roger Cromie, and Chief Engineer Susan Harper. They had become friends over the past six months of training on the *Marco Polo* and had come to trust each other's judgment implicitly. Also on the bridge were two civilian scientists: Doctor Walter Kernaghan and Doctor Amanda Allenby, physicist and xenobiologist respectively. Although they too trained alongside the Command Team, they had both remained a bit of mystery to David. There was no questioning their knowledge and expertise, but often science got in the way of real life and neither had really engaged with the rest of the crew as human beings, albeit there was mutual respect, friendship was out of the question.

Five years, David mused, *five years, the best minds humanity has to offer, a bucket load of cash and here we are, humankind, is about to take its first tentative steps into the unknown...* David said, "All ahead one third, Chief."

"All ahead one third, aye," responded Susan. The *Marco Polo*'s reaction drive pressed them back in their seats. The gravity sump, a spin-off of the Gravity Drive taking them into fold space, was not entirely effective at negating the acceleration forces.

Mixed emotions welled, excitement, trepidation even a touch of fear of the unknown. David pushed these aside, conscious he and his crew had an important mission to complete. He was also conscious if he felt this way, his crew likely was too.

"Everyone, it has been a pleasure training and working with you on the buildup to this mission. I regard you all as experts in your fields and as colleagues. Some of whom have become my friends, others I regard with the utmost respect." He glanced at the doctors as they sat by their control panels. "To each and every one, I thank you for your hard work and dedication in making this possible. Rest assured I will do everything in my power to ensure a successful mission and ensure we all return to friends and family having made history." David did not wait for a response, he took a breath and said in his best command voice, "OK. Let us make it look good for the press folks. Stand by on the sensors, Doctor Kernaghan, Doctor Allenby." Both of their indicators went to green on the captain's repeater display, "Very well, Chief. Take us to all ahead two thirds."

"All ahead two thirds and three, two, one... fold!"

David felt a slight tremor run through the ship and then a second tremor as the computers automatically cut the Gravity Drive. "External view ahead." On command, the view ahead of the *Marco Polo* was projected into the main display Holo Cube to the front of the bridge. He let out the breath he did not realized he was holding. "OK, people. We're here." Under his breath he said, "Wherever here is...

"Commander! Position fix – computer and manual if you please. Chief! Rotate ship and bring us to a dead stop. Doctor Kernaghan, Doctor Allenby, full sweep all sensors. But passive only, no need to let anyone know we're out here."

The doctors exchanged exasperated glances.

"But Captain..." began Walter in protest, his thirst for knowledge outweighing his concern for his own and the ship's safety.

"No, Doctor Kernaghan. Passive only. Until I personally give orders to the contrary. Clear?" David addressed Amanda too.

"Yes, Captain," they announced in resigned unison.

David gave a nod and thought scientists could be such children. He operated the internal communications system and barked at his engineer, "Lieutenant! Are you still with us down there? And more importantly, how are my engines?"

"Give me a few minutes to do a complete system check, sir." Glendinning's reply was tinny and a little muffled.

"Very well. Report to the Chief on completion."

"Aye aye, sir."

David observed his chief. He knew she would double check all Glendenning's results, not because she didn't trust him, but the old adage of 'two heads are better than one' sat well with David too, especially when you were two and a half light years from home.

"Commander, thoughts?" asked David of his XO.

Roger raised his gaze from his console and said deadpan,

"Sir, so far we successfully carried out phase one of the mission. We're still alive."

David smirked. "And phase two?"

"Navigation computer puts us within the margin of error for the fold transit. Sensors report no contacts within passive range, and Engineering shows a green board." The news satisfied David as Roger continued, "All data has been downloaded to the courier drone, as per Standing Operating Procedure, and the drone is ready for launch."

Roger referred to the courier drone. Despite the huge scientific leap in technology borne out by the capabilities of the *Marco Polo*, still the most efficient means of communicating over these vast distances was by courier drone. It was fitted with an individual Gravity Drive and travelled from the ship's current location through fold space before docking back in the Sol System. Its aim was to bear news of the *Marco Polo*'s location and status of the crew and ship, and it allowed for the manual downloading of all data gathered during their mission. An effective system, a bit like a carrier pigeon really. As long as you had drones, you had communications. Thankfully, *Marco Polo* carried the standard twenty.

"Very well, Commander, launch the drone and plot our next Fold. I want to arrive at least ten AUs outside the Proxima Centauri System." David planned to exit fold space some 1,490,597,871 kilometers from the edge of the system, close enough for the passive systems of the *Marco Polo* to scan the whole system and far enough away to allow the *Marco Polo* sufficient warning of any danger.

"Understood, sir. Calculation running. Standby. Ready, sir."

David turned to Susan "Ready, Chief?"

"Ready, Captain."

"Very well, rotate ship to..." David glanced at the navigation repeater in front of him, "three one five decimal seven degrees by negative zero decimal seven degrees galactic and ahead two thirds."

"Three one five decimal seven degrees by negative zero decimal seven degrees galactic and ahead two thirds, aye aye," repeated Susan "Rotation complete and three, two, one...... fold!"

This time the slight tremor went virtually unnoticed and the main display Holo Cube showed a dim red dwarf star, Proxima Centauri.

David reflected on the importance of this maneuver. They had done it! The first humans to visit another star. Damn, he felt good!

Back to business. "Same again people, confirm location, sensors on passive only. And bring us to a dead stop relative to the system primary."

A chorus of "Aye aye, sirs" greeted David, and he began to relax as he watched his people go about their business. Suddenly he realised he was hungry, a small snack wouldn't go amiss. After all, he had travelled a long way he thought, with a wry smile. Out of the corner of his eye, he caught one of his scientists frowning at his sensor suite, punching new commands in as quickly as results were being displayed. "Problem, Doctor Kernaghan?"

"I'm not sure, Captain. I'm getting some strange readings here."

David sat bolt upright in his chair. "Explain strange." David felt an uneasiness creep over him. Unbidden, he saw his XO downloading the ship's logs into a courier drone and readying it for launch. Walter was still querying his computer.

David said "Now, Doctor!"

Walter shook his head slowly. "Well I'm seeing what looks like a... a..." He grappled for a word to describe the abnormal readings he could not believe he was seeing. "A power source," he finally settled on. Walter directed his next words straight to David. "It's from one of the inner planets, Captain. However, it is no natural source. It must be machine generated."

Without a second thought, David began to recite the ritual he had practiced so long and hard. A ritual he had hoped never to complete. "Computer, Alpha X-ray six four two initiate,"

A pause, then a flat emotionless female voice replied. "Voice print confirmed, Captain Catney. On your authority Alpha X-ray

21

six four two is activated, courier drone launched. Bio readings indicate Lieutenant Commander Cromie is alive and unharmed. Does he concur?"

The two civilians regarded the captain in stunned silence. What was happening? Why was he communicating directly with the ship's computer? What was this gibberish?

"Computer," said the XO. "Bravo Yankee five three one, I concur."

Amanda had been virtually silent until this point, but now her face was flushing red with frustration and anger at the lack of understanding of events on the bridge.

"What the hell is this military double talk, Captain?"

David ignored her and instead addressed his explanation to the bridge. "On my command, all our logs were downloaded to a courier drone, this drone has now folded to a location held by the ship's computer. I have no idea of its destination. Only the computer knew. I say knew, past tense, because as soon as the courier was launched the destination was erased from the computer memory." There was silence on the bridge as they took in this information.

"When our return to the Sol System becomes overdue, a data chip will activate at Survey Command headquarters. This chip holds 200 possible locations of our courier drone. A recovery drone will be deployed to search and retrieve it." The civilians' faces paled. "If in the next sixty minutes the computer does not receive the correct coded halt cipher from two of this command team, Commander Cromie, Chief Harper or myself, then the computer will activate a fusion device hidden somewhere on board the ship."

"Are you serious?" Amanda's outburst was rhetorical.

David contemplated each of his bridge crew before resting his gaze on Amanda. "It's very simple, Doctor. Your colleague stated the energy source detected is mechanical. Meaning alien intelligence, potentially hostile alien intelligence. Humanity is vulnerable while our star travel is still in its infancy. We are all located in one star system. We…" He gestured to them all, "cannot afford to leave a breadcrumb trail back to Earth. The result could be the extinction of our very race. So, Doctors. You now have some fifty-five minutes to prove to my satisfaction this alien intelligence is no threat."

#

TDF MARCO POLO - PROXIMA CENTAURI
4.22 LIGHT YEARS FROM SOL

"Well, Doctor Kernaghan?" asked David,

"In a minute. It takes time to narrow the location down at this distance," replied a harassed Walter. Beads of sweat visible on his forehead.

"A minute is about all we have," muttered his fellow scientist, Amanda.

"Twelve to be precise," said Roger tightly.

"Enough! Ladies and gents," said David from his command chair. "Doctor?"

"OK, I have it. Planet Three. There's a lot of background radiation but I have it isolated to within 200 square kilometers."

"Computer, display Planet Three region as specified by Doctor Kernaghan."

The Holo Cube lit up with what could have been a view from the orbit of the moon, if not for the red tinge of the system's red dwarf primary. Crater upon crater filled the Holo Cube.

"What am I looking for, Doctor?" asked David.

"Is this scene at all familiar, Captain?" asked Walter.

David stared harder. Yes, just like the cratering on the moon. Before he could answer, his Chief spoke.

"It's like the Midwest plains of North America, or the Urals of Russia after the nuclear strikes of World War Three."

Then David saw it, a strike pattern… There was nothing random here.

"Do you want the good news, Captain?" asked Walter.

"Yes please." David thought the doctor was enjoying this now, but their personal countdown to destruction was still ticking,

"I would calculate using radiation decay rates this happened at least 700 years ago. It's old news."

"Are you positive? We can't afford to be wrong here."

Walter replied confidently, "Yes, give or take twenty years. The system is reasonably accurate even at this distance."

"What about the power source, Doctor?"

Walter ran through the data in front of him again. "There is no indication of any change in the level of output since the time we detected it."

"Very well." Turning to address his XO, David enquired, "Commander. Thoughts?"

"Given the doctor's calculations, I think it's safe to say whoever or whatever did this is long gone. As far as the power source goes, the fact our presence has caused no reaction leads me to believe it is not a weapon or detection system of any kind. I think we can assume we, and therefore, Earth, are in no immediate danger."

"I concur. Computer, Romeo Charlie Nine six three, execute."

A pause, then the computer replied, "Voice print confirmed, Captain Catney. On your authority Romeo Charlie nine six three previous auto destruct can now be countermanded. Bio readings indicate Lieutenant Commander Cromie is alive and unharmed. Does he concur?"

Roger spoke aloud, "Computer. Whiskey Zulu one eight seven, I concur."

"Auto destruct aborted, fusion weapon deactivated," the computer confirmed.

The relief on the bridge of the *Marco Polo* was palatable.

"OK, Commander. Plot us a course to Sol and take us home. You have the con. I'm going for a coffee while I think about what I tell our lords and masters."

CHAPTER THREE

CROSSING THE RUBICON

INNES BASE - PLANET III - PROXIMA CENTAURI

Robert Ignico considered the red dwarf that was Proxima
Centauri, through the clear steel dome protecting them from the
bitter cold, a touch above the average noon temperature on this
scarred rock – minus 112 centigrade.

He searched for the reflection of TDF *Ferdinand Magellan* in
geostationary orbit above the base, he knew it was futile, even
though it was by far the largest interstellar craft humans had so
far built. It was some 1300 metres long, 250 at the beam and
weighed in at 110,000 metric tonnes. It carried the essential parts
and personnel who initially constructed Innes Base on the surface
of Planet III of the Proxima Centauri system. TDF *Ferdinand
Magellan* had then shuttled back and forth to Earth, bringing
more scientists and engineers and materials as Innes had
expanded to become the current home to some 630 men and
women, all of whom were searching for the elusive source of the
power spike found by TDF *Marco Polo* six months before.

The engineer in charge of the drilling had promised Robert
today was the day. He had been promising this for the past week.
Although the source of the power spike had been located quickly
enough, it was found to be some five kilometers underground.

One of the first groups to arrive on the *Magellan* had been mining engineers. They had been digging ever since.

The crackling in his earpiece returned Robert to the present.

"Doctor Ignico?" called the disembodied voice of the duty controller.

"Go ahead."

"We're approximately ten minutes drilling time from the target"

"OK. I'm on my way thanks." *Time to go to work*, thought Robert as he headed off to his office in the control center.

#

Robert was seated at his desk facing the holo cube that filled the center of his office trying to figure out what his eyes and his chief structural engineer were telling him.

"Sorry, run that past me again?"

"Radar on the drill head is reporting a cavern some seventy-five metres across and at least four, possibly five buildings. We must wait until we learn more from the robot sled after it arrives at the bottom of the drill shaft in another thirty minutes or so." Sarah repeated herself while tracing the display on the holo cube.

"What's new?" said Robert. "Best tell them to start widening the shaft. I want to get down there as soon as possible."

"Yes, sir." Sarah began making the necessary calls to the drill team.

#

FIVE KILOMETERS BELOW THE SURFACE
PLANET III - PROXIMA CENTAURI

A long week of Robert's team trudging under the artificial lights illuminating the cavern and casting conflicting shadows around it. Mapping and measuring the squat, box like buildings arranged with one at each corner of a square and, what Robert and his engineers were assuming, was the power plant in the middle. None of the buildings showed any obvious doors or other access points — assuming, of course, whoever or whatever built this

26

cavern had the same thought processes as humans. Now, with baited breath came the moment of truth.

"OK, Sarah. Let's do it."

Sarah Boone, Robert's chief structural engineer nodded and signaled to her cutting crew. Plasma torches flared and Robert began making his own door.

The walls had turned out to be two metres thick. This place had been built to last! All the evidence pointed to some form of nuclear bombardment on the surface. The five kilometers of rock had provided protection but whoever had built this place was obviously not taking any chances.

The plasma torches should have cut through the walls like a hot knife through butter but instead it took forty-five minutes to make a hole large enough for a human to fit through. *Well, the moment of truth*, thought Robert. "Rank has its privileges," he said. "Recorders on and let's go see what was worth all of this protection." Robert entered the building.

Robert circled where he stood. He stared at the walls covered from floor to ceiling in storage racks holding small crystals, no bigger than a finger, crystals of every colour. In the centre of the room was a small raised podium with something similar to a lectern upon it. The lectern had a small keypad on the right hand side and a slot on the left. Robert mused, "If I'm not mistaken the slot is about the size of one of those crystals."

Sarah's eyes widened incredulously, "You're not thinking what I think you're thinking, are you, sir?"

"We are here to find out everything we can about this place, and this seems to be the next logical step to me."

Sarah pronounced slowly, "You're the boss..." glancing apprehensively at Robert as he selected a crystal at random and carefully placed it in the slot in the lectern.

Nothing.

There was a collective sigh, as much of relief as disappointment. Then Sarah reached over with a wry smile, glancing at Robert who was watching her every action, she carefully removed the crystal and reinserted it the other way round.

A million sparkling pinpoints of light encircled the podium.

"Oh my God!" Sarah exclaimed.

"Whoa," said Robert.

"Now there's an understatement," commented Sarah. She was not sure where to look or what she was looking at.

Robert flung her a shriveling look before returning to stare at the lights. "Are these familiar, Sarah?"

Sarah paused to re-examine the lights, trying to focus on an image, writing, something familiar… "Eh, no I don't think so. Random light, a visible language maybe?"

"You diggers. Try looking up now and again. These, unless I am mistaken, are stars. This is a map of our galaxy. We, Sarah, have hit El Dorado."

#

Robert compiled a hasty report and forwarded it to the *Magellan* for onward carriage to Earth by courier drone. Finding himself overcome with exhaustion, he realised he had been on the go for thirty-six hours.

Stimulants could only keep you going so long, so with strict instructions to the scientists, who were virtually salivating at the mouth to take the other Block Houses apart, to touch nothing until he returned, he left for the surface and his quarters to grab a few hours' sleep. His head seemed to just touch the pillow when the incessant beeping of his Comm woke him. "Yes, what is it?" he barked.

The face of his chief xenobiologist stared at him from the Comm. "Sir, I think my team may have found something quite interesting. Would you come back down here please?"

Robert rolled himself into an upright position "With what I've seen in the past two days, this wants to be good, Ivan."

"You need to see this for yourself, Robert. Trust me."

Robert let out a grunt. "OK I'll be there within the hour Ignico out." Robert headed for the shower in the hope it would infuse some energy into his tired body.

Thirty minutes later Robert found himself inside Block House Five. "Alright Ivan what's up? I would have thought the astronomers and physicists would, if anyone, have been the first to come up with something."

Doctor Ivan Kulibin smirked. "We do what we can to play our small part, sir."

Robert smiled back. "Get on with it Ivan." Robert noted he had the 'cat who just got the cream' air about him.

"Didn't it strike you as strange how you were able to stand at the lectern?"

The penny dropped for Robert. The position, the size of the lectern – he had not paid much attention at the time *Damn!* He thought, aloud he said, "Of course. Why would an alien race construct a lectern which fits the human form and posture so closely?"

"Well it was Sasha from ergonomics who first noticed it. She practically fell on her rear end, peering at the lectern's control panel, when she stood back up she naturally placed her hand onto the keypad and discovered the keypad is designed for five fingers. Five!"

Robert stood in stunned silence, trying to let his logical, scientific brain process the implications. Eventually he recovered the ability to speak. "Are you telling me whoever or whatever built this was approximately the size and shape of a human, even down to having five fingers?"

"It would certainly appear so, sir."

Robert closed his eyes in concentration for a moment then. "Alright, Ivan. I want your team to work on that assumption. Split your team in half: the second half will play Devil's Advocate and try their best to find fault in your logic. There is no way we are telling Earth about this 'til we can firm it up, understood?"

"Yes, sir. I'll get on it right away. May I make a suggestion which could speed things up?"

"You know all suggestions are welcome,"

"Well we could open one of the other Block Houses in case this is just a one off."

Robert thought for a second. "OK, so authorized. Get Sarah back down here. Pick a Block House at random and proceed. I'm

going back to bed. I can feel a long few days ahead for all of us."
Patting Ivan on the back, Robert headed back to the drill shaft
and bed.

#

INNES BASE - PLANET III - PROXIMA CENTAURI

"Ivan, you look like crap. When did you last sleep?" Robert
regarded the figure slumped in the chair in front of him.

Ivan smiled and replied, "In another life, sir."

Robert smiled back and cast an eye over Sarah Boone. She
was perched on the arm of the other chair in his spartan office
located beside the control room on the surface of Planet III, or
Rubicon as it was fast becoming known. Named after the Roman
river which legend said if an army ever crossed it then nothing
would ever be the same again. Nothing would be the same again
if the snippets of information Robert was getting where anything
to go by.

"Sir," Sarah began, indicating the holo cube in the corner of
Robert's office where a diagram of the cavern located five
kilometers below them appeared. "As per your instructions, we
divided into two teams and began to assess the data from
opposing views. With the opening of the second then, with your
permission, the three remaining Block Houses, we found the raw
data was forcing the two teams to reach the same inescapable
conclusion. If I could briefly go over the relevant points?"

Robert nodded and the image in the holo cube changed to
show the internal layout of Block House One.

"As you know, the basic layout of each Block House is the
same." Sarah described the images displayed in the holo cube.
"Four sides with floor to ceiling racks full of the data crystals and
a lectern on a raised podium located in the center." The holo cube
image changed to show the location of each of the Block Houses.
"Working on the assumption of this layout being replicated in
each of the buildings, we entered Block Houses Three, Four and
Five from above, keeping any possible damage to the data
crystals to a minimum." The Holo image rotated and settled on a

30

3D rendering of a single story Block House, with a smaller cube directly below the center of the structure.

"Each Block House is independently powered from a source located below its structure, here." Sarah pointed toward the smaller cube in the image, and then continued. "And each structure appears to contain specific information. The easiest Block House to decipher was the one containing the Sciences – some things are a given constant, such as the composition of the atom – so once we identified the key, things gathered pace."

The holo image expanded to show the other Block Houses, each numbered. As Sarah described each Block House, the holo cube highlighted each image in turn. "Block House One was the first entered. Two seems to contain what we are assuming is art and music by the images and sounds. Three appears to hold enormous amounts of written data. Four is of a similar nature though it seems to contain more graphics, it appears to be planetary mapping but not all showing the same layouts, a bit confusing at the moment but we're working on it. Using the data from Block House One as a common cipher, like our very own Rosetta Stone, the computers are slowly but surely beginning to identify key points. But the sheer volume of information is staggering." Sarah took a deep breath. "That leaves us with Block House Five." Sarah paused again, which caused Robert to search her face rather than the scrolling data in the holo cube.

"Go on, Sarah," said Robert.

"Sir…" Sarah began hesitantly, "upon examining the lectern in Block House Five, one of the technicians noticed a subtle difference in its keypad make up. It's subtle but it's there. Therefore, we decided we had pushed our luck far enough for the moment. As you know, we have been randomly trying a crystal from one Block House in another Block House's lectern and they all seem interchangeable." Sarah paused. "All except those from Block House Five. No crystal from there will play in the other four lecterns, and we have been too afraid in case we damage them to try the modified lectern in Block House Five. In conclusion, sir, I would say we have found an entire civilization's reference library."

"Thank you, Sarah. Ivan?"

"I think Sarah's conclusion is correct, Robert. We have enough data here to keep every scientist and researcher from every field of study on Earth busy for the next decade."

"But not from Block House Five?" said Robert.

"Not yet, sir," replied Ivan.

Robert jumped to his feet, startling the tired Ivan. "Well, let's see what we can do about that, shall we?" He headed out of his office toward the shaft to the underground cavern, followed by Ivan and Sarah.

Robert stood in front of the podium in Block House Five, staring at the seemingly innocent keypad on the raised lectern, with Ivan and Sarah standing behind him.

"Are you sure you want to do this, sir?" asked Sarah.

Robert smiled. "Well if it all goes wrong, Sarah, you get an instant promotion." Without another moment's hesitation he stepped onto the podium and place his hand over the keypad while inserting a data crystal (chosen at random) from the surrounding wall racks.

He felt a faint tingling and a large, contorted shape appeared in front of him. No, not contorted. A spiral. With the groove on the left of the spiral being much larger than on the right, he heard Ivan gasp behind him but was too entranced to turn around. Then it came to him, Ivan was a medical doctor by training, Robert was not, though he still remembered the image from biology.

He was feasting on a DNA helix – his DNA helix – and, as he watched, whatever computing machine drove the lectern highlighted sections of the helix. One area... two... three... eventually some ninety percent of the helix was illuminated. But this was not possible. *How could this machine identify so much of the human DNA helix so quickly?* At this thought, the image disappeared. For a brief second there was nothing...

Then images began to appear. Soon they were all around him, replaced every few seconds by another.

"Schematics!" Sarah blurted, "Complicated schematics. Where's Taylor?" Activating her wrist Comm, she shouted, "Control. Sarah. Find Taylor, tell him to report to Block House

Five immediately!" Without waiting for a reply, she signed off and returned to examining the schematics. She was a structural engineer but these were not building schematics. Taylor was a design engineer, he would be clued in to what these were. Where is he? She asked herself impatiently.

After a few minutes, an out of breath Taylor arrived. "Yes, ma'am?"

At last! "What are those? Best guess will do," Sarah indicated to the still changing images.

Taylor watched intently for a few moments then shook his head and watched for a few more moments, turned to Sarah and said, "Ships, ma'am. Not just any ships. I would say warships… Pretty big ones!"

#

OFFICE OF THE PRESIDENT OF THE TERRAN REPUBLIC - GENEVA - EARTH

Bartholomew McMullen, permitted by a special act of Senate to run for a consecutive third term as president, had won a landslide victory. In these rapidly changing times it seemed the voters wanted someone familiar to trust their fate to, and that someone was Bartholomew McMullen, twenty-third President of the Terran Republic.

Bartholomew sat at the base of a horseshoe shaped table, with his cabinet and trusted advisers arranged on either side of him. A holo cube easily ten metres across directly in front of him. He watched Robert Ignico's follow up report for the second time, having viewed it in private earlier in the day, describing the contents of Block House Five.

He took the opportunity to gauge the reactions of the group assembled around him as the report played out. Faces showed a multitude of reactions from enthusiasm at the prospects for the scientific advancement the new information provided to apprehension as to why there was such detail on weaponry.

At the realization that the final lectern required human DNA to activate it, an air of thoughtful silence settled around the table.

The report concluded and heads turned toward the president, waiting for him to speak. *I knew I should have retired*, Bartholomew thought.

"Well, ladies and gentlemen," he began. "Your faces look just as mine did when I first viewed Doctor Ignico's report a few hours ago. It's a lot to take in so let me hit the highlights as I see them." Bartholomew stood up and slowly walked around the back of table with his hands clasped behind his back. He summarized the salient points as he saw them. "Firstly, this seems to be an alien race's complete reference library. Everything they have ever done or been is stored here." Bartholomew paused his slow pace and brought his hands to his front, posing in a thoughtful manner. "Secondly, what is the significance of the massive and detailed military database? If I consider this with the obvious nuclear bombardment on the surface, I begin to wonder – is this library a last ditch attempt to preserve what was the accumulated knowledge of an entire civilization? If so, preserve it for whom?" Bartholomew walked back to his seat at the base of the table and sat as he contemplated aloud. "Was it a threat from factions within their own society or some external force? And thirdly, Block House Five." He regarded in turn each of the people sitting at the horseshoe table, catching the eyes of just a few who were brave enough to look directly at him, "How did the lectern in Block House Five recognize human DNA so quickly? And why did it trigger the release of the apparently encrypted information?" Bartholomew broke his gaze from those in the room and rested it downwards on the table. He shook his head slightly, before raising his eyes and addressing the room again. "This causes me the most concern and I am sure it will be the source of the most consternation and worry amongst our people."

Nods around the table assured Bartholomew he had hit the proverbial nail on the head.

"The only saving grace I can see, at this moment in time, is – according to the *Marco Polo*'s initial assessment and subsequent work by the *Magellan* — the nuclear bombardment on the planet's surface occurred some 700 years ago. This point must be emphasized to the general population, to allay fears of any immediate attack. Whatever disaster overtook this unfortunate civilization, we can rest assured it is not about to visit us tomorrow."

A gruff "We hope," sounded from Bartholomew's right.

Bartholomew eyeballed the source of the comment. Admiral Olaf Helset of the Terran Defense Force. Standing at a 180 centimeters tall, broad shoulders tapering to a narrow waste, blond, close cropped hair and chiseled jaw with grey eyes the colour of the North Sea (which his Viking ancestors traversed with impunity those centuries before). Helset was a man who spoke his mind and hated politicians of all ilk, in the way only a military man could.

"Do you have something to say, Admiral?" enquired Bartholomew with a smile which failed to reach his eyes.

"I am a military man, Mr. President, charged with protecting the Terran Republic. But for these past 150 years the only threat to the Republic has come from the odd pirate attacking merchantmen plying their trade within the Solar System. The Defense Force is more like a coast guard than any sort of standing navy. There has simply been no requirement for such a force. So I truly hope, and I mean this with all my heart, this civilization destroyed itself. If it didn't, and whoever did this comes calling on us, then it will be a very short, one sided fight."

There was a stunned silence for a moment before the room filled with a cacophony of noise as each cabinet member attempted to voice their concerns. Bartholomew banged his fist on the table and called, "Enough!" The room fell silent once more. Scanning slowly around the room, Bartholomew said, "Ladies and gentlemen, I think we all agree without more information any statement to the public at this time would be precipitous. I suggest our course of action is to wait until we have examined the data more thoroughly before we release any statements to the public. As I speak, our scientists at Stickney Base on Phobos are working on deciphering the Rubicon data, including Block House Five."

There was a general murmur from the room. "My decision is final: we wait."

CHAPTER FOUR

OUR ROSETTA STONE

STICKNEY BASE - PHOBOS - ORBITING MARS

Stickney Base was located in Stickney Crater on the Martian moon of Phobos. Phobos was only seventeen by fourteen by eleven kilometers in diameter and Stickney Base was five kilometers across. The base filled the entire crater, making the base seem even larger than it actually was.

With an orbital period around Mars of only zero point three two Terran days it did have the effect of causing seasickness on many new arrivals to the base, but not Patricia Bath. She had been on Phobos for what seemed most of her adult life.

Stickney was her first choice on graduating top of her language course at MIT, and she had never looked back. As head of department, she was intimately involved in interpreting the data brought back from the Rubicon cavern so many light years away orbiting Proxima Centauri.

Patricia shook herself out of her melancholic mood as her Comm beeped for attention, "Bath."

"Patricia, I've been running the new interpretation cipher of yours…" It was Vince Kealey, a few years older than Patricia but content to let her be the boss. It allowed him to get on with the more serious work of decoding everything and anything he could get his hands on while avoiding the spectrum of paperwork

Patricia dealt with on a daily basis.

"Yes, Vince?"

"Well, I made a few tweaks and I think we've cracked it! We've significant matches across the board and should be able to start producing good translated copy by early tomorrow."

Patricia smiled. "Not bad for an old man, Vince. Even one whose brain clouds over with old age every now and then."

Vince laughed down the Comm. "You're not too old to be put across my knee, young lady," replied Vince. "So get your behind down here and take over so an old man can get some well-deserved rest."

"Yes, Granddad. Be there shortly." Taking one last look at Mars whizzing past only 9000 kilometers away, Patricia turned and headed back toward her lab and the mass of data awaiting her.

#

OFFICE OF THE PRESIDENT OF THE TERRAN REPUBLIC - GENEVA - EARTH

After a soft knock, the door to Bartholomew McMullen's office opened. An aide ushered Admiral Olaf Helset through the door. Olaf marched in, halted short of the president, who rose from his seat at the head of the small round conference table, and saluted him.

"Please join us, Admiral." Bartholomew indicated a seat at the table where two others were already seated. "You know Senator Gillian Rae and Senator Thomas Crothers, my Secretary of Finance."

Olaf nodded toward both politicians by way of greeting. When requested to meet with the president, he had assumed it was about the Rubicon Cavern (as the area of the discovered Block Houses was now known). It would explain why Senator Rae was here. But what was the Secretary of Finance doing here? Well, the only way to find out was to get on with the meeting, Olaf supposed.

"Admiral," began Bartholomew. "I've invited both Gillian

38

and Thomas to join our little discussion today. We're just waiting for two more guests before we begin."

Olaf remained standing and addressed the president. "Sir, with all due respect, perhaps you'd like to tell me why I'm here and what the meeting is all about?" Olaf's intonation conveyed he had better things to do than shoot the breeze with a bunch of politicians.

"Patience, Admiral, I beg you. Now, please take a seat."

With an audible sigh, Olaf sat down, somehow managing to sit as far from the three politicians as the table allowed. *Should be an interesting meeting!* Bartholomew thought.

Another knock on the door. The same aide ushered in a reasonably tall woman and a willow wisp, slightly greying and overweight man into the room before closing the door behind them. Bartholomew stood and approached the woman. "Ah, thank you for coming Doctor Bath, and you Professor Ballantine. Perhaps we could get started. Please be seated."

As his new guests found seats, Bartholomew composed his thoughts. *Damn, I should have retired when I had the chance!* "If you'd like to begin Doctor Bath, I don't know if you have met all my guests before, so I'll do the honors - this is Senator Rae," he indicated Gillian then moved on to Thomas, "and Senator Crothers and finally Admiral Olaf Helset."

"Thank you, sir." Patricia directed her gaze around the table as she continued, "I am Doctor Patricia Bath, head of linguistics at Stickney Base on Phobos, and this," indicating Ballantine, "is Professor George Ballantine, head of xenobiology here at Geneva University." George nodded around the table at the introduction. "OK… eh… well I'll cut to the chase" Patricia paused "since successfully interpreting the language found in the Rubicon Cavern…"

Olaf interrupted her flow with a strangled "What! What did you just say?"

Patricia regarded him steadily and repeated herself "Since successfully interpreting the language…"

Olaf turned a brilliant shade of red "Just what I thought you said, Doctor!" Throwing Bartholomew a glare capable of stopping elephants in their tracks, he addressed Patricia. "And when did this happen?"

"Some five months ago, Admiral," replied Patricia.

If Olaf could have gotten any redder, he would have. He stood and approached Bartholomew. "Why wasn't the TDF informed? Who decided to withhold this vital information? It could mean the life or death for Earth –"

Without rising from his seat, Bartholomew cut the Admiral off in mid flow. "I did, Admiral. Now, sit and let the doctor finish her brief."

Olaf hesitated, and for a moment, Bartholomew thought he was going to continue. Instead, Olaf retook his seat and sat there like a volcano on the brink of erupting.

Bartholomew took a breath before turning to Patricia. "Please continue, Doctor."

Patricia glanced from Bartholomew to the admiral and back to Bartholomew, took a deep breath and continued. "Thank you, Mr. President. Now, as I was saying, having successfully interpreted the alien language we began cycling through the accumulated data brought home by the *Magellan*. The sheer volume of information is staggering. The original estimate of a decade to translate everything may not be far off, there is just so much of it, but finding the index to each Block House has made our life much easier. So far, we have managed to translate five percent of the data, but we have been able to make some reasonably good assumptions."

"WAGs, you mean, Doctor?" interrupted Olaf. Patricia looked confused. "Wild Ass Guesses" said Olaf helpfully.

"Ah, well yes, Admiral. But we think we have the data to support our guesses," she replied pointedly. "It seems pretty obvious this alien civilization was more advanced than ours. They had already explored parts of the galaxy. We have discovered at least seventeen different planetary maps from their astrological database, some of which we have been able to verify using our own known data. I think it is safe to assume they managed to colonize some of these worlds. Their medical databases also reveal insights into their physical make up."

This time Gillian Rae interrupted. "You mean we know what they looked like?"

Patricia's face broke into a large grin. "Yes, Senator." An image appeared in the holo cube in the center of the table. All eyes in the room fixated on the 3D image of an alien being.

It was approximately one meter forty centimeters tall. Covered in light brown hair, not quite as thick as fur, two round eyes were set in a slightly pointed head with the ears mounted higher up the head than a human. The mouth and nose protruded slightly, a short thick neck leading to a barrel chest with two arms bending at an elbow and two legs with knee like joints. All in all, it could easily be mistaken for a relative of Earth's monkeys.

After a moment, Patricia continued, "That's right, ladies and gents. This image is very familiar to us and we may be forced to reassess our theory of evolution." Patricia could have heard a pin drop in the room.

"Doctor Ballantine and his team at Geneva are sure the DNA similarity between our alien friends and ourselves is not a coincidence. How could two species evolving in two different parts of the galaxy have so many points within the DNA helix that match? The odds are astronomical." Patricia paused for a second to allow the minds of the others in the room to grasp the implications of what she had just said, "It's our belief we have a common ancestor."

Olaf was going that shade of red again. "Whoa, stop right there, Doctor. Are you saying we are descended from aliens? Because I didn't realised today was April Fool's Day."

Patricia turned to the president. "Perhaps Professor Ballantine would be better at explaining this, it is his field after all."

With a nod from Bartholomew, Professor Ballantine stood up and cleared his throat. "Mr. President. Twenty-five or so million years ago, for some reason we still can't explain, the rhesus monkey broke away from our particular chain of evolution. It has, also for an unknown reason, ten markers in its DNA helix which really should not be there. We have been at a loss to explain them."

"Some 3,000,000 years ago the chimpanzee also broke away from our evolutionary chain. It is our closest DNA match with something like ninety-five percent duplication of human DNA. I have concluded both the rhesus monkey and the chimpanzee were failed attempts to produce an intelligent creature. I believe the aliens millions of years ago manipulated our DNA to produce as near a version of themselves as possible but tailored to the Earth's environment." His conclusion met with a deafening silence. It hung in the air.

Bartholomew's voice sliced through the silence "Thank you Professor Ballantine. Perhaps Doctor Bath, you would continue?"

"Mr. President, the data is still sketchy but it would appear these aliens originated in the constellation of Orion, from a planet orbiting the star we call Saiph, some 2200 light years away."

"A hell of a long way to travel just to experiment with our DNA, don't you think?" asked Gillian. "Surely there's a more suitable planet closer to their home star?"

"Senator," replied Ballantine. "We are working on the premise the seventeen planetary maps so far discovered in the Saiph database are also locations where they experimented with the DNA of indigenous life forms."

"But why?" interjected Olaf. "If their goal was colonization, why not just send a ship full of – what did you call them – Saiph? It's certainly a lot quicker than waiting for a new species to evolve."

"Because they wanted to leave something behind, Admiral. A legacy if you will," said Patricia.

Olaf regarded her in puzzlement. "I'm sorry, Doctor, leave something behind? A race that advanced doesn't just vanish overnight," he looked around the room at the others, "for all we know they are probably still out there somewhere."

Patricia looked directly at the Admiral and knew that what she was about to say would change the future path of humanity. "I doubt that, Admiral, because they were at war... At war with a foe who was not out to conquer them but to annihilate them. To erase the Saiph's very existence from the galaxy. And the enemy was winning."

As the aide closed the door behind him, Bartholomew turned to his remaining guests. The two scientists had left, leaving the two Senators and Helset. Thomas was staring intently at his coffee cup

"Penny for them, Thomas," asked the president. Thomas had been noticeably silent throughout the briefing. Glancing up, Thomas paused, then said,

"Mr. President, although the contents of the briefing have my head swimming, I keep returning to the same question."

"Go on, Thomas," urged Bartholomew gently.

"It's not why the Saiph manipulated life on Earth and other planets, or even how such an obviously advanced race could lose a war… Its why am *I* here? I understand the admiral represents Defense, Senator Rae – Science and Technology. But me? All I do is manage budgets."

Bartholomew began to chuckle, to the amazement of the others in the room, "Oh Thomas, you are probably the most important man in the room." Thomas seemed completely perplexed, Bartholomew continued. "Without you I can't carry out my plan."

"Which is… sir?" asked Gillian, Thomas' puzzlement reflecting in her own face now.

With his best vote winning smile, Bartholomew answered, "Why, simply to build a fleet of survey ships, in complete secrecy of course, to explore and find out what happened on the other seventeen planets." He beamed at the occupants of the room, before resting his gaze on the Admiral. "Olaf, here, will provide the requirements and crew." His eyes moved to Senator Rae. "Gillian has the technical wherewithal to build them." Bartholomew brought his gaze back to Senator Crothers. "But you, my dear Thomas, will need to provide the millions of Feds to finance them. All without the Senate or our citizens finding out. Simple? Wouldn't you agree?"

Thomas dropped his coffee cup onto the carpet. Staring open mouthed at the smiling president, who had just declared himself as, potentially, the biggest embezzler of government money… ever…

CHAPTER FIVE

OPERATION MINERVA

CHARON BASE - ORBIT OF PLUTO - SOL SYSTEM

John Radford stopped to get a look of his surroundings as he exited the shuttle door. "Now this is the quintessential middle of nowhere."

"Sorry, did you say something, Captain?" asked the ensign assigned to meet this shuttle.

"Nothing, Ensign," John sighed, "Just remarking on the location my lords and masters at the Admiralty have decided on as my new assignment. I'm now wondering who I pissed off to be sent this far off the beaten track."

The young ensign impatiently expressed the 'I've heard it all before' look. "Your orders, sir?"

"Yes, sorry. Here." John handed over the data chip containing his orders and personal records. The ensign inserted them into his PAD. He confirmed John was indeed Captain John Radford and he was indeed posted to some unheard of Joint Service working group on the logistical requirements of establishing and maintaining manned bases outside the solar system.

A friend of John's had remarked the posting sounded like a barrel of laughs as he bought John a consolation drink on the last night of his shore leave, shortly before John caught the inter system shuttle which would deliver him to his home for the next three years.

Perhaps, his friend pointed out, John needed a few years to grow into his new rank after his recent accelerated promotion and the media circus which followed him. The press had sensationalized John's actions during the 'Alexandria Incident' and brought unwanted, and John felt unwarranted, attention to him and the Admiralty. John wholeheartedly agreed with him. Without a doubt this was the Admiralty's way of getting him 'outta sight, outta mind' for a while. John's face formed an unhappy scowl. With his experience he should be out there exploring the galaxy and setting up those bases, not sorting out how many packets of toilet rolls it takes to support them.

As the ensign returned the data chip to John, he said, "If you follow me, sir. The Admiral is expecting you. You're the last to arrive."

Oh great, thought John, *last to arrive. Hope the Admiral is in a forgiving mood or this could be a long assignment.*

As the ensign escorted him to the briefing room, they passed down corridors bustling with Navy, Marine and civilian personnel. All seemed to be moving in a hurry and with a definite purpose. This struck John as odd, but when the ensign stopped at a doorway with armed marines guarding it he decided something was definitely not right here.

The ensign turned to John and indicated a state of the art retinal scanner mounted on the doorframe. "Press your right eye to the retinal scanner, sir. You'll be met on the other side."

"You're not coming?"

"No sir. I'm not cleared." The ensign turned on his heel and headed for his next task.

An ensign not cleared for a logistics meeting? Forgetting himself he thought aloud, "What the hell?" He shook his head before placing his right eye in front of the retinal scanner. The door popped open and he stepped through. A greying female lieutenant commander wearing the insignia of Naval Intelligence confronted him.

She scanned him up and down and without a word of greeting

46

said, "This way, Captain. Admiral Vadis is expecting you."

John stopped dead in his tracks. "Admiral Aleksandr Vadis?"

The lieutenant commander had already taken several steps, she stopped and turned with a knowing smile. "The one and only."

John's mind raced. Aleksandr Vadis… the spook's spook. He had been immersed in the black side of intelligence work for some forty years until he was implicated in a corruption scandal, what – three years ago? He had been forcibly retired in disgrace. A sad end to a lifetime of service. What the hell was he doing way out here at the edge of the solar system? Better still – if he retired in disgrace – why was he in charge?

Full of questions John was led along a corridor. They reached another door, again guarded by marines. These ones seemed even nastier than the pair guarding the building's entrance. Another retinal scan, however, this time the lieutenant commander also presented her right eye.

As the door opened, the lieutenant commander led the way and they entered the room. It held an oval shaped table with four chairs on either side and two at the top. Already seated were three Navy captains, two men and one woman, along with four Marine majors, paired off – navy, marine, navy, marine. John's escort indicated the empty seat beside, what seemed like, an overly tall marine while she walked to the head of the table and took her seat beside, damn – it was him. Admiral Aleksandr Vadis.

"Welcome, Captain Radford," said Aleksandr with a smile suited to a fox about to thieve a few chickens. "I have no doubt you're wondering what the hell you're doing here, as I'm sure are the other men and women seated here."

Scrutinizing the faces around the table, John could see he was not the only one who had no clue of what was going on.

"This briefing," Aleksandr paused, "is so sensitive anyone who knows about it is either on this godforsaken rock, and will stay here for the rest of their natural lives, or in key positions within government. Not even all of the cabinet know about us."

John's stunned face reflected the others around the table.

What the hell?

"As is general public knowledge, the discovery of the Rubicon Cavern proved once and for all that we are not alone in the universe. It may be the library of a long dead civilization but the odds are, sooner rather than later, we will run into a living, technologically advanced civilization. Do we all agree?" There was a general nodding of assent around the table. "As I said, the Rubicon Cavern and the existence of its creators is now public knowledge. What is not is how this particular civilization came to its demise. The government has encouraged scientists to expound theories on the subject, but we have known almost from the start the Saiph were wiped out by a technically inferior but numerically superior race. They were outnumbered, not outgunned."

John thought he heard the jaws of the people gathered around the table hit the floor.

Aleksandr's smile resembled a fox. "Oh it gets better, ladies and gents. We have since discovered the Saiph knew they were losing the war and so set out to tinker with the evolution of worlds, to ensure part of them survived. One of those worlds was Earth. So we," he glanced around the table, "are the evolutionary result of their tinkering."

Silence filled the room as minds raced to comprehend Aleksandr's words.

"Now you understand why this has been kept a secret. From the Saiph's library, we have identified seventeen other worlds where they have... 'Tinkered', for want of a better word. It is your mission to find out what happened on these other worlds. In complete secrecy we have, over the past three years, designed and constructed four stealth survey ships. We have incorporated as much Saiph technology as we presently understand."

Aleksandr pointed toward each of the Navy captains. "You will each command one of these Vanguard class ships. The marines will be inserted onto the surface of any planet deemed worthy of further reconnaissance. It is imperative you all understand the covert nature of our mission, both here at home and out there amongst the stars. At home, we cannot anticipate people's reaction if they find out an alien race manufactured them. Out there, we may make first contact with another intelligent species – peacefully we hope. But what if the race that destroyed the Saiph is still out there?" Aleksandr paused, making eye contact with each of the personnel gathered around the table. He continued in a tone he hoped relayed the gravity of his words. "We launch in six months, and you…" Aleksandr again slowly caught the eye of each of them, "have a lot to learn. I now turn you over to Lieutenant Commander Elizabeth Wilson, my chief of staff, to continue your introductory brief."

John appraised the Lieutenant Commander with fresh eyes. To be the chief of staff to Admiral Vadis you had to be something special. Before him stood a sixtyish, grey haired, slightly chubby woman who had the appearance of someone more at home playing with her grandchildren than helping to run a secret mission.

"Good morning, ladies and gentlemen, and welcome to Operation Minerva. Before we begin, I must emphasize the covert status of this mission. Few are aware of this operation and those participating are chosen carefully. You are amongst the chosen few, as am I. To give you a little of my background: I retired from active service seven years ago. I enjoyed civilian life, I was enjoying watching my grandkids grow up," With a quick glance and a smile at Aleksandr Elizabeth continued, "Until Admiral Vadis approached me and not so politely told me my commission had been reactivated. My mission was to go to the asshole of the universe and supervise the mining of some worthless rock. As you can imagine, I was full of the joys of spring at the prospect." Chuckles emanated from around the room. "I didn't actually know what my real mission was until I was on the transport out here and the Admiral arrived at my door with a briefing pack and a strong brandy in hand. Sorry, I've no brandy for you!" Elizabeth smiled. "But I completely understand how you feel right now. So, to business." She touched a control on the panel in front of her.

An image of a ship appeared above the center of the table, slowly rotating to give everyone a three sixty degree view. All the naval officers at the table lent forward for a better view, including John, who heard himself let out a low whistle. It was nothing like anything he had seen or heard of before. The marines tried not to show any interest in mere navy stuff – the Navy was only there to provide them transport after all – but John could see out of the corner of his eye the marine beside him intently studying the small ship. Small but… elegant.

The ship was the black of darkest night, making it hard for John to make out details, as they seemed to merge. A blunted off wedge shaped bow morphed into a smooth rounded off superstructure. John only just discerned the stern where again it was wedge shaped. As the image rotated, John made out more details, sunken engine protrusions in the rear wedge. Spread along the length of the beam from bow to stern where small clusters. They appeared remarkably like small laser turrets. Mounted just after the wedge at the bow, top and bottom, there was mounted a shallow turret holding twin cannon with the same design of shallow turret mounted above and below at the stern. This ship may be small but it seemed she could handle herself.

"This," Elizabeth continued, "is the Vanguard class survey ship the Admiral mentioned earlier, weighing in at 15980 tonnes and with a crew complement of 135 naval and eighteen marines. She is only 325 meters long and twenty-one at the beam..."

"Seriously?" John thought, then realised the word had actually come out of his mouth.

"Yes, Captain?" said Elizabeth. "You have a question?"

Foot in mouth again thought John as the whole table turned to him. *Oh well here goes. Deep breath.* "If I heard you correctly Commander, you said the ship was only 325 metres long. With a crew of 135. Only four years ago, TDF *Marco Polo* was the best technology we had. The engines alone were something like 200 metres long and massed 600 tonnes each with a crew complement of 2100."

"If I may, Commander," interjected Aleksandr, "You are correct, Captain Radford. The difference between the *Marco Polo* and the Vanguard class is," he pronounced slowly and definitively, "RE-MARK-ABLE... I must point out something you said yourself. The best our technology had." He paused. "My staff have been moving heaven and earth to reverse engineer the Saiph's engineering library. It helps that it seems the Saiph knew whoever found and accessed their library had to be led by the hand. Therefore, our people have been racing ahead. We feel confident the Vanguard incorporates the best Saiph technology we currently understand. Does that answer your question Captain?"

"Yes, sir. Thank you," replied John.

Aleksandr turned to Elizabeth, "Please continue, Commander."

"Sir. Full technical specs are available in your briefing packs, but to summarize the high points, the Vanguards design is not for head-to-head combat. They are primarily stealth covert survey ships. Engineered to get you in and out of your objectives without alerting anyone to your presence. Each Vanguard incorporates the latest version of our chameleon stealth units, employing active optics to project whatever is behind the vessel onto the part of the vessel viewed by an enemy – effectively making the vessel invisible."

"Not everything is perfect, there is always the chance of failure. An enemy may not be deceived or may possess technology which may defeat the chameleon system. To mitigate the risk, we have armed the Vanguard with four dual turrets of particle cannon. From the image you will see: two forward mounted above and below the hull, and two to the rear again above and below the hull. Spread across the hull, for close in defense, are Laser Area Denial weapons which should kill anything that gets too close for comfort. Also embarked are two Tanto class covert insertion shuttles for use by the embedded marines."

"In relation to personnel. In your briefing pack, you will find the manning lists for your crew. They are the best the Navy has to offer. There are some... um..." Elizabeth and Aleksandr exchanged a knowing look, "unorthodox individuals amongst them, but both the Admiral and myself decided that for a mission of this importance we needed the best. Whatever their previous commanding officers may have said. I strongly urge you to read between the lines when you read their personnel jackets. Now, let me turn to the marine contingent."

At this the four marine officers sat up a little straighter, as if everything they had heard so far was just a preamble to the important bit, the Marines.

"As you will have no doubt noticed, ladies and gentlemen, sitting to your right is a Marine major."

John turned to his right and took his first proper look at the Marine officer beside him. It was then he noticed he was not the atypical marine. The haircut was there, tight to the skull, but he did not have the expected massive body builder bulk. It was then he noticed his eyes: dark blue and unblinking, like an eagle. Lacking any emotion while displaying complete concentration. An unbidden shiver ran down John's spine, *the sort of man you do not want to meet in a dark alley*. The marine looked at him as if he were working out where to strike him, and then much to John's surprise, he stuck out his hand.

"Alec, Alec Murray," a thick Scottish accent softly rolled the 'r's and was accompanied by a small smile.

"John Radford," John shook the outstretched hand and held Alec's eyes briefly before flicking back to the main speaker in the room.

"Each of these marines command your marine detachments. You have quite a bit of leeway while on your missions and you may decide a ground reconnaissance is required. In consultation with the marine detachment commanders on board, you have the resources to plan and execute any such ground reconnaissance." Elizabeth paused. "The key to mission success is information. This is not a guts and glory job. Earth badly needs to know what we are facing out there. The only way to do so is to explore, record the findings and get the information home. To this end, each Vanguard has a complement of courier drones embarked to allow each ship to get its information back to us for evaluation and dissemination. It is our intention to share all relevant information gathered by each Vanguard with the other Vanguards. As the mission is covert, the plan is for you to drop a stealthy communications relay buoy at your point of entry into each system. An incoming courier drone will hit it with a whisker laser to pass its messages. In turn, your ships can hit the buoy with a whisker laser and download any messages stacked there for you. If, however, we do not hear from a ship within a seven day window, it will be classed as lost and no further attempts will be made to communicate with it." Elizabeth took the time to regard each of the men and women sat around the table. "Understood?"

There was consensus from the gathered officers. "At this point, I'd like, with the Admiral's permission, to call a halt for today. Your senior officers will meet you tomorrow at zero nine hundred hours in the designated briefing rooms. An ensign is waiting for each of you at the outer doors to escort you to your accommodation. Admiral?"

Aleksandr stood. "Ladies and gentlemen, be under no illusions. You have the complete resources of the Terran Republic at your disposal. We must ascertain if there is any threat to humanity out there in the stars. Your mission is to locate, identify and return home without any one, or anything, knowing you have been there. Good day."

The officers stood to attention as the Admiral left the room. John picked up his briefing chip, turning he was startled to find himself staring straight into the face of a smiling Alec Murray. "I don't know about you but I could do with a beer. What say we pull rank on the ensign and get him to take us to the Officers' Club?"

John gave a wary smile of his own unsure of Murray's motives "Sounds like an idea," John led the way to the door and punched the activator, he motioned Murray through "Lead on"

"Typical Navy, Let the Marines lead. Bet you don't have any money either."

John sniggered aloud and Murray smiled at his own joke. *A killer with a sense of humor? A novel thought!* John decided the marine might not be a bad lad after all "OK, first one's on me, Alec."

"Right answer! You're too easy, are you sure you're not

English?" the smile reached Alec's eyes.

#

Watching the departing officers on his desk display Aleksandr looked up as Elizabeth entered the room, he gestured for her to take a seat as he stood and made his way to the small bar in the corner of his office. He poured two double bourbon on the rocks before placing a glass in front of Elizabeth and retaking his seat. Aleksandr took time to savor the bourbon's aroma. The Russian in him still rebelled at the thought of drinking bourbon rather than the traditional vodka. He inwardly reminisced, how he, as a shiny new ensign, had boarded his first ship all those years ago and was introduced to a dyed in the wool Kentucky CO who'd promised Aleksandr he would disavow vodka by the end of his tour and would have converted to bourbon. Surprisingly, his CO had been right. Aleksandr took a small sip of bourbon allowing himself a final moment of pleasure before returning to work.

"So what do you think of them Elizabeth?"

Elizabeth tilted her head slightly as she considered his question savoring a sip of her drink, it gave her more thinking time.

"As far as the Marines go the Corps has done us proud. You could not ask for a more professional and dedicated group. Of course, marines are not my area of expertise, it's the ships captains who are. As we've discussed before, Admiral, the final selection of the Vanguard Captains is entirely your choice and…"

A raised hand from Aleksandr stopped her mid-sentence.

"I asked for your opinion Elizabeth, don't beat about the bush."

She frowned, she hated being put on the spot and Aleksandr knew it. Sometimes she wondered if he did it just for his own amusement. Taking a deep breath she let it out as an audible sigh she.

"Captain Lewis is the most experienced. Having read his personal file it shows he has turned down promotion on more than one occasion until the time came when the Admiralty just

54

stopped offering it. It explains why at fifty-six he is still only a captain. He is a born explorer, but take into account his Command Course results you will see he came top of the tactical phase. In my opinion he should've been forced to take promotion… If this all goes wrong and we get into any kind of shooting war out there we'll need his experience in fleet command."

Aleksandr made a mental note to drop a line to his old friend and fellow admiral, Ai Jing about Lewis. Elizabeth was right some people should not be given the choice to avoid promotion.

"Captain Papadomas is a student of history and its societies, he's also a devoted family man. He joined as a seaman before making such a good impression on his commanding officers he ended up being offered a commission as a mustang. He is perfect for the role of exploration. A man with a keen thirst for knowledge but tempered by the need to return to his family, so… unwilling to take undue risks with his own or his crew's safety."

Elizabeth paused to take another sip of her bourbon.

"Captain Witsell, on the other hand, enlisted as a commissioned officer. Top of her class at the Academy she has not put a foot wrong in her career and is without doubt a rising star on the command track, thus her place on this mission. My only concern is she has not been tested in a combat situation. Not that we are expecting the Vanguards to go into combat but this is her first command of a major vessel. I'm afraid I must reserve judgment on her at the minute."

Aleksandr eyed Elizabeth over the rim of his glass. Noting they both needed a fresh drink he lifted Elizabeth's glass from her hands and went to the bar, still with his back to her he said "I see you have left our young Captain Radford to last. Impolite of you considering he is senior to Witsell."

A harrumph emanated from Elizabeth and extracted an un admiral like grin from him, he quickly recovered before turning to Elizabeth and passed her the now refilled glass.

"Unlike you Admiral, the exploits of Captain Radford do not impress me and you know fine well the only reason he is senior to Captain Witsell is because they appeared on the same promotion list and the letter R comes before the letter W."

Now it was the admiral's turn to buy himself some time by taking a sip of his drink. "Radford may be young for his position but the decisions he was forced to make during the 'Alexandria Incident' show when push comes to shove he puts the greater good and his duty first. Being responsible for deaths under your command so you can ride to the rescue of civilians could be seen as making a tough call or…"

Elizabeth locked eyes with her admiral. "Putting your crew in danger to satisfy your own need for glory hunting."

CHAPTER SIX

THE JOURNEY BEGINS

CHARON BASE - ORBIT OF PLUTO - SOL SYSTEM

John Radford sat back in his seat on the command deck of the new Vanguard class survey ship, the *Henry Hudson*. It was so new his seat still squeaked. The last six months had flown past. From his first sight of what was to be his new ship still shrouded by the cradling arms of a construction dock to the myriad of briefings led by Lieutenant Commander Elizabeth Wilson and her underlings. Where did that woman get her energy? She seemed to be everywhere and had an answer for everything. If she did not know, she knew a man who did.

No wonder Admiral Vadis had dragged her out of retirement to be his right arm.

John glanced around the bridge, taking in the officers and ratings preparing the ship for launch. The Admiral had not been joking when he said John and his fellow captains were getting the best the Navy had to offer. His comment about reading between the lines of his crew's personnel jackets was so true. Taken at face value, the majority of his crew were the cream of the crop, but some appeared to receive strangely low ratings from their past commanding officers. Unless you read into it. You really could not blame their COs. The TDF was not a large force. Split into its composite parts of Ground, Marine, Navy and Survey it got even smaller. It would not be the first time, or the last, John was sure, a CO would write a neutral, if not slightly shaded, report on one of his subordinates in the hope of keeping them. Frustrating for the subordinate but good for a lazy CO.

John's own navigator, Lieutenant Carlo Danino, was a prime example. Before Vadis seconded him to Charon, he had been working out on the asteroid belt doing traffic control for the endless amount of freight traffic plying back and forth to the inner system. On his arrival at Charon John met him at the shuttle, as he had with each of his command crew, to get an initial feel for him. Danioni arrived with the expression of a beaten man, resigning himself to another tour of another humdrum asteroid. John was not impressed. That evening while having dinner with Alec Murray, who had become not only a friend but also a good sounding board, he expressed his concern. "You should have seen him, Alec, he got off the shuttle and couldn't even look me in the eye."

"Well I don't know about you, John, but if I'd just finished a tour shuffling freighters around for three years and was told I was going somewhere even more remote for another three, I'd certainly wonder who I had pissed off."

"Yeah... I suppose your right. If he is such a shit hot navigator why don't we see what he's made of?" John tapped his communicator.

"Control?" a disembodied voice said.

"Control, can you tell me if any of the Vanguard simulators are free?"

"Wait one, Captain... Yes, sir. Simulator Two is free till zero eight hundred tomorrow morning."

"Thanks. Can you book it in my name for zero one thirty hours till zero four thirty hours and load a level four navigation scenario for me?"

There was a short pause on the other end of the link. "Sorry, sir. Did you say zero one thirty till zero four thirty and level four?"

"That's correct. I feel the need to push myself a little, brush off the rust, so to speak."

"At level four, sir, I hope you're on the top of your game."

So do I, John thought. "Radford out."

Alec sat back and raised his beer glass. "I salute a fellow humanitarian, a man who cares for his crew and thinks of their every need. So when do you give the good lieutenant the news of his make or break simulator test?"

"Oh," a large grin appeared on John's face, "about zero one ten hours," and sipped his own beer.

A very harassed and out of breath Danioni came running round the corner at the end of the corridor holding the entrance to Simulator 2. John glanced at his watch. "Zero one twenty-five, Lieutenant Danioni. What took you so long?"

"Sir, I only arrived on the base this afternoon."

"Which has given you adequate time to check out the basic base schematic, has it not, Lieutenant? I don't expect excuses from any of my crew."

Surprise ascended Danioni's face "Crew, sir? I thought I was here to do traffic control?"

John looked him square in the eye "That, Lieutenant Danioni, is what we are here to decide. Follow me." Radford entered the simulator with Danioni in tow. There was a sharp intake of breath behind him as Danioni took in the view. A complete replica of the command deck of a Vanguard class survey ship. John smiled. "Close your mouth, Lieutenant. You're not catching flies." Danioni's mouth closed with an audible click. "Sit down over there, Lieutenant." John indicated a seat surrounded by monitors against the left hand bulkhead and then took his own seat in the center of the command deck. "Until I am satisfied you're up to the job, we will run simulations. If, however, you do not come up to scratch, I think freighter controlling will be your calling. So do we understand each other, Lieutenant?"

Danioni did not even turn around as he busily tried to familiarize himself with the controls around him. "Yes, sir. Clearly, sir."

John sat back in his chair. "Then let us begin."

Three hours later and John's head was pounding. On the first two simulations John had beaten Danioni to the correct navigation solution but as the lieutenant became more familiar with the control system of the Vanguard, he was able to beat John by a greater and greater margin. If John did not know better, he would have sworn Danioni was cheating. He was able to do complex math in his head and cut out the need to input the information into the nav computer. He did not have to wait for the results, and therefore missed steps out of the final computation... truly amazing.

After the final simulation, John saw a different side of Danioni. As the lieutenant turned to face him, he was smiling from ear to ear. His whole body seemed to have come alive with raw energy, eager for the next challenge. John regarded him for a moment. "Well done Lieutenant. I stand corrected. Welcome to the *Henry Hudson*."

Giving John a quizzical look, Danioni said, "Thank you, sir. But, eh... what is a *Henry Hudson*?"

John laughed aloud, nearly falling off his seat in the process. "Briefing room, zero eight thirty sharp and all will be revealed. Now go get some sleep. I know I plan to."

TDF HENRY HUDSON - CHARON BASE - ORBIT OF PLUTO SOL SYSTEM

A call from the marine at the outer hatch informing him Admiral Vadis had just boarded and was on his way to the command deck broke John Radford's train of thought. A few moments later, the Admiral strode through the hatch followed by Lieutenant Commander Wilson, his chief of staff.

"Admiral, a pleasure as always," John said in his best upbeat tone. Vadis saw right through him.

"You're such a poor liar, Captain. Nevertheless, ten out of ten for trying. You know and I know I only interfere when I have to. Most of the time I send my henchman – woman," he nodded toward Wilson, "to do my dirty work, but not this time. Could I ask you to assemble your senior staff in your briefing room in say... thirty minutes? Until then, why don't you show Lieutenant Commander Wilson and me the comfy chairs in your cabin?"

John glanced over at Commander Bill Talbot, his Executive Officer, seated at the other side of the bridge. Bill nodded and started making calls. "If you'd like to follow me, Admiral." John was not getting a good feeling about this.

The *Henry Hudson* was a small survey ship. The captain's quarters consisted of only one cabin and a small office attached to it. With John, Vadis and Wilson ensconced in it, it was not exactly spacious. John stood behind his desk. The Admiral took the other most comfortable seat and indicated for the others to sit.

"Well, John. As I said, we have had a slight hiccup. As you are well aware, I have been banging on about the covert nature of our mission and of Charon base. We have managed to keep the whole thing secret for nearly four years – a small miracle in itself. When President McMullen first authorized Operation Minerva, only the then Chair of the Science and Technology Committee, Gillian Rae, the Secretary of Finance, Thomas Crothers and Admiral Helset were even aware of its existence. When I was brought on board, I had direct contact with Admiral Helset only, the theory was simple. If I didn't know anyone and they didn't know me then leaks are kept to a minimum. In the spy business, we call it compartmentalization. When President Coston took over..." Vadis referred to Rebecca Coston, the new 24th President of the Terran Republic. She recently replaced the popular outgoing President McMullen. He had reached the end of his fifteen-year presidential term and, too much disappointment, was forbidden from standing again. After all, the permitted maximum term is fifteen years.

Vadis continued. "She was briefed by McMullen of our existence. Rebecca Coston agreed to keep not only the operation secret, but to keep key personnel such as Crothers and Rae in place." Vadis chuckled. "I would love to have been a fly on the wall when she told her party officials she was retaining two senators from the opposition party in their posts! Unfortunately, the president's party insisted on replacing Admiral Helset. He apparently made some of them feel uncomfortable. I can't imagine why..."

This time Wilson giggled like a schoolgirl. "He always had a knack of annoying politicians," she said.

"True, Commander, but I digress. It is with his replacement that our problem lies."

John was confused "But surely his replacement is General Joyce? A marine through and through. You couldn't get a secret out of the man with an explosive charge."

"Quite right, Captain." Vadis exhaled sharply. "General Keyton Joyce will make an outstanding leader of the Defense Force. However, somehow, and I am personally investigating the reason, the eyes only briefing pack on Operation Minerva was delivered to the wrong office." Vadis was clenching and unclenching his fists as he spoke his words through gritted teeth.

This was not going to be pretty, thought John.

Vadis continued. "How do you deliver a sealed, eyes only, briefing pack inside a secure briefcase, attached to the wrist of an armed marine, to the wrong office. Accept the wrong ID for it and walk away happy as Larry?"

Uh oh, thought John. Some poor marine officer was going to be in charge of chipping small flakes off an asteroid with an ice pick for the rest of his career.

"Anyway, to the point." Vadis physically calmed himself again. "The clerk who accepted the pack had no way of knowing its contents, just the code name — Operation Minerva. When the marine came running back into the office to recover the pack, he apparently threatened the clerk with a fate worse than death if he ever mentioned the name 'Minerva' again."

Wilson turned to John, "And what do you think happened next?"

"Not funny, Commander," Vadis growled "Over a drink the same evening with some..." The Admiral screwed up his face in disgust, "... reporter, he told the whole story. Said reporter did some snooping and spoke with a source in Finance, who being a good citizen told him all about some project being run directly out of the Secretary's office... In addition, it appeared to be swallowing up significant portions of other projects' budgets.

The reporter in question intends to run the story tomorrow with the bare minimum of facts and the maximum of conjecture."

"It would seem, Admiral," said John, "the cat is out of the bag. Where do we go from here, sir?"

Vadis looked at Wilson. "Commander, if you would."

"Yes, sir. The plan, Captain, is to bring the launch of all the Vanguards forward. Instead of launching two ships at a time to their respective destinations, the ships will launch as and when they are ready."

John thought for a moment before answering. "Well, we could be ready to go in seventy-two hours, sir. We were scheduled to launch in six days anyway."

Wilson nodded. "About what I thought. Over the next fourteen days we intend to launch all the Vanguards. The *Vasco De Gama* and Captain Witsell will take the longest to prep as they've been having some technical difficulties with their navigation systems, but the yard dogs have assured me they will be able to rectify any problems before launch."

As Wilson finished, Vadis stood up. "We will not delay you any further, Captain. You have a tight enough schedule. You need to be meeting with your staff and sharing the good news."

It was John's turn to smile. "Yes, sir. I'm sure they'll be overjoyed."

The Admiral and his chief of staff headed through the hatch, toward the outer air lock connecting the *Henry Hudson* to the dock, escorted by a marine. John headed for the briefing room a few doors up from his cabin, his brain doing flip flops as he considered how to squeeze six days of work into seventy-two hours. John paused at the briefing room hatch and smiled as he recalled that on any ship the XO handled the bulk of any task. Talbot was going to love him. He pressed the hatch release and entered the briefing room.

#

Commander William 'Bill' Talbot was attempting to cat nap while he waited for his computer to finish checking, what seemed like, an endless list of supplies and equipment: from rations to fuel to computer gel packs which the ship's supply officer, Lieutenant Kessler, had assured him were now safely on board the *Henry Hudson* and stored correctly. The last seventy-two hours had been ones of frantic activity. He was sure the captain had been smiling at him when he told the assembled staff of the quote, 'small change in plans', unquote. Ha! Talbot's well thought out detailed plans to be ready in five days were flung out the airlock. Instead, he created new plans off the top of his head. No wonder he was going bald!

The computer made an attention tone. Talbot opened one eye to see if the list was complete. It was still running. The noise was the hatch entry tone. Talbot reluctantly pressed for acceptance and wondered what problem was about to disturb his well-deserved snooze. Talbot stood up a bit too fast and swayed a little as he realised the captain was standing in the hatchway. "Steady now, Bill," John said with a grin.

"Sorry, sir. Just having a little cat nap while the computer finishes."

"Have a seat, XO." Talbot flopped back into his chair. "I bring a peace offering." From behind his back, John produced a bottle of cold – there was even frost on the bottle – Australian beer. "I believe you are partial to some of the amber nectar? Seeing you have managed to keep my promise to Admiral Vadis – I do appreciate it when my minions make me look good – I thought a small reward was in order. Not forgetting," as John produced a second bottle from behind his back, "a reward for myself for having the good sense to employ such a useful minion." Both men laughed as John passed over the beer and took the only other seat in the office.

Talbot took a good long pull of his beer and let out an appreciative sigh. "You know, sir, that was almost worth all the hard work... almost!"

"Enjoy it, XO. It's going to be our last for a while. Are you happy we're ready to go?"

Talbot paused for a moment before replying. "Yes, sir. The crew have worked their guts out to be ready. Every department head has got a green board and I have complete confidence in them."

"Well, XO, if that's your opinion, then it's good enough for me. I will inform Admiral Vadis the TDF *Henry Hudson* is ready in all respects for launch. After I finish my beer, of course."

Talbot looked back at him "Of course, sir."

#

John Radford sat, once more, in the conference room in which he had first learned of the real reason for his posting to, what he thought at the time, a logistics assignment.

John was accompanied this time by his own command staff: Commander Bill Talbot, Lieutenant Commander George Taylor, his Chief Engineer, Lieutenant Commander Albert Remberts, Chief Medical Officer, Lieutenant Alexandra Falconer, Tactical Officer, Lieutenant Cai Tingkai, Communications Officer, Lieutenant Alfred Kessler, Supply Officer, and last but not least Lieutenant Carlo Danino, Navigation Officer. Also present was Major Alec Murray, CO of the Henry Hudson's Marine contingent – a man whose judgment and common sense John had learned to trust over the previous six months.

A side door opened and all present stood at attention. Admiral Aleksandr Vadis entered, followed closely by his right hand man, Lieutenant Commander Elizabeth Wilson. "Please be seated, ladies and gentlemen," said Vadis as he himself sat at the head of the conference table. "I know you have accomplished a minor miracle in the last seventy-two hours, Captain, preparing for launch. No doubt your XO and supply officer are suitably harassed." Vadis smiled and nodded toward Talbot and a face reddening Kessler. "But now to business. The initial targets of the Vanguard ships will be those stars identified from the star charts recovered from the Rubicon data. We know the Saiph have visited at least seventeen star systems. It is prudent to believe these star systems were not chosen at random but were part of their greater plan to seed indigenous species, such as ourselves, with the physical and mental makeup to develop into advanced civilizations. We have no idea how well this seeding has taken root. It is your job to go out there and find out. But…" Vadis paused and allowed his eyes to rest on each person in turn, "your overriding priority is not the discovery of new life, it is the preservation of life on Earth. If, for whatever reason, something does not seem right to you, Captain, you turn tail and head for home. Do you understand?"

All present stood to attention once more as Vadis reached out and grasped John's hand in his.

"Good luck, John. I wish it were I going. Do us proud."

"I'll do my best, sir," replied John.

The Admiral left with Commander Wilson in tow. John turned to his staff and noted their expectant demeanor "Launch in three hours, People, so let's get those last minute checks done and be on our way."

Vadis watched John dismiss his staff from his office adjacent to the conference room before turning to Wilson,

"Well?" he said.

Wilson consulted her PAD. "*Henry Hudson* launches at fifteen hundred hours, Captain Papadomas and the *Jacques Cartier* is due to launch at zero nine hundred hours tomorrow with Captain Lewis and the *James Cook* at seventeen hundred hours tomorrow. Which only leaves Captain Witsell and the *Vasco De Gama*. The techs are still having problems with her navigation computers but assure me she should be ready for launch by twenty-three hundred hours."

Vadis was quiet for a moment as he thought. Four small ships representing man's first true attempt to explore the surrounding stars. All accomplished in utter secrecy... until that idiot went to the wrong office. He unconsciously scowled as dark clouds of anger entered his thoughts. *Enough!* He thought. *I have better things to worry about than things that have already passed.* The press and the general population would get the whole story in a matter of hours when President Coston broadcast the details of Operation Minerva to the public.

Vadis preferred the survey ships were launched and returned safely before entering the public arena, but so be it. At least all the interest in Minerva had ensured the second prong of Operation Chimera had remained hidden from prying eyes.

"When is Admiral Jing due to arrive, Elizabeth?"

Wilson consulted her PAD. "He should be here by eighteen hundred hours today, sir."

"Good. I'm anxious to hear how he is progressing. I pray we never need Chrysaor, but we have no idea what's out there." Vadis paused as his thoughts wondered amongst the stars.

"With the Admiral's permission?" Wilson interrupted, hinting at her wish to leave the office.

"Yes of course, Elizabeth." Wilson left Vadis alone with his thoughts.

CHAPTER SEVEN

FIRST ENCOUNTER

TDF HENRY HUDSON - ORBIT PLANET II OF 70 OPHIUCHI

John Radford studied the unimposing planet suspended in the Holo cube. By his survey's reckoning it was one-third water and two-thirds land. Most of the landmass was desert wasteland, the planet orbiting just a little bit too close to its sun.

On arrival in the star system, John had held the *Henry Hudson* at maximum range while his crew searched for any possible signs of energy sources in the system and deployed the communications buoy and courier drone to inform Charon Base of their safe arrival. When no artificial energy sources were detected, John had instructed Danioni to plot a spiral course, gradually bringing the *Henry Hudson* in system to the only planet within, what humans would consider to be, the life bearing zone. If the Saiph had meddled with the DNA of an already indigenous species and, if they had gone for a similar type of planet to Earth, then John was betting this was the place. John frowned as he stared into the Holo cube. Too many ifs for his liking.

"Penny for them John?" John glanced to his right and there stood Major Murray, his Marine Contingent Commander.

"Jesus Alec! Are you sure you're not part ninja?"

Alec grinned. "No, just very sneaky."

68

Even with the tension John could not help but grin back.

"So what do we have Commander?" John asked his XO. Talbot was closely studying the information fed to him by the ship's computer and the dedicated biosciences section.

"Well, now we're in orbit and able to use our active sensors..." On arrival at the star system John had stuck rigidly to Standard Operating Procedure and hung out system using only passive sensors until a threat assessment was completed. Better to be safe than sorry where the safety of the ship, the crew and Earth was involved.

"... Our initial ideas are firming up nicely. What life there is, is mostly located around the dense tropical rain forests, around the equator of the planet. There are no obvious signs of civilisation of any kind, no detectable power sources, and no clusters of artificial structures. Nothing in the way of pollution in the atmosphere to indicate industrialization or contamination. The air is thinner than on Earth, by some eleven percent, but still capable of supporting life, which does appear to be thriving. I suggest our next step is to send a survey party to collect some plant and animal samples for analysis and to check for any evidence of Saiph influence."

John considered for a moment, "Agreed, XO. Prepare a survey team. Full biohazard gear. Alec, provide a protection detail. No need to take chances."

Both men chorused "Aye aye, Captain," and left the bridge.

John took one more look around the bridge and stood to leave, "Lieutenant Danino, you have the bridge."

"Aye aye, sir. I have the bridge."

John made his way toward his cabin, thinking he could do with a few hours' sleep before listening to Murray and Talbot's plans for their planetary landing.

Without warning, the Battle Stations alarm began its steady wail throughout the ship and the computers automated voice called "Battle Stations, all hands to Battle Stations."

John spun on his heal and ran back toward the bridge, scattering crew members with his shout of "Make a hole!" as they too ran for their stations.

Striding through the bridge hatch, a scene of organized chaos greeted John. His crew swiftly and efficiently brought the ship to full readiness. "Report, Mr. Danino, if you please." John said in his calmest voice.

Without turning, the young lieutenant replied, "Sir, a few moments ago active sensors detected a neutrino surge from a point just beyond the system's Kuiper Belt, approximately thirty-five AUs from our current location. As per your standing orders, I immediately sounded Battle Stations and have moved the ship into the shadow of the planet. There is now no direct line of sight between ourselves and the location of the neutrino surge."

John was assimilating this information when the XO and Alec Murray arrived on the bridge. Alec had his sidearm strapped to his leg – a pulsed energy projectile infrared laser pulse-emitting pistol, which creates a rapidly expanding plasma on contact with the target. The resulting sound, shock and electromagnetic waves stun the target and cause pain and temporary paralysis.

"Expecting boarders, Alec?"

Alec looked at him incredulously as he tapped the PEP in its holster, "better to be prepared."

"I bet you were a great Boy Scout," murmured Talbot moving off to his console.

"Sir," Lieutenant Falconer at Tactical called. "All departments report at Battle Stations. All plasma cannon and Laser Area Denial weapons are online. Marines report armed and standing by to repel boarders. Engine Room reports ready to fold on your order."

John turned to the XO. "Anything more on what caused the neutrino surge, Bill?"

Talbot was staring at his display and trying to make sense of the masses of information displayed there. "Sir, it appears Lieutenant Danino's initial reaction was correct. If I'm reading this data correctly, there is some sort of vessel at the spot where he detected the neutrino surge." All talk and movement on the bridge stopped as Talbot turned to his captain before continuing. "The Saiph database has made a tentative identification of the ship as one belonging to the enemy they were fighting."

My God! John thought. *They are still out there. Have they seen us?* "XO, download all data to two of the drones and get them off. Make sure their initial flight path takes them away in the shadow of the planet and they fold before they come out of the shadow. I want at least three folds per drone before returning to Earth."

Talbot nodded his head in understanding: John intended the drones to make multiple folds in case whoever was on the unknown vessel was able to track their initial flight path.

"OK people," John addressed the bridge crew. "If this vessel does belong to the enemy of the Saiph, I see it as our first priority to alert the Admiralty to their existence, hence the drones. Second priority is to gather as much information as possible on this potential threat. To that end," John turned to Danino, "Navigator plot me a course away from the planet which will keep us in its shadow as long as possible, putting us above the ecliptic plane. When we clear the planet's shadow I want the ship rigged for silent running. I want us to be a hole in space. Understood?" John scanned the bridge and a series of nods from his officers greeted him. "Good, then let's get to it people and let's find out who's out there!"

#

TDF HENRY HUDSON
TWENTY AUS ABOVE THE ECLIPTIC PLANE OF 70 OPHIUCHI

Captain John Radford sat at the head of the table in the small briefing room on board the TDF *Henry Hudson*. For the past five days, the *Henry Hudson* had pretended to be a hole in space as it ever so slowly climbed above the ecliptic plane of 70 Ophiuchi in an attempt to get a good eyeball of the unknown vessel which, in a burst of neutrinos, had appeared near the system's Kuiper Belt.

The past few days had been tense for the whole crew.

Had they been observed as they left the shadow of Planet II? Had the two message drones John launched on their multi fold flight to warn Earth been detected?

At least the passive sensors of the *Henry Hudson* had shown

71

no obvious reaction by the unknown vessel to either the presence of his ship or the departing drones. *A good sign, right?* John contemplated as the heads of department gathered around the table. He cleared his throat to get their attention.

"OK people. What do we know? XO if you could bring us up to speed."

"Yes, sir," Commander Talbot began. "It appears Bogey One, as we're calling the unidentified ship, is making steady progress in system. Not moving swiftly and we are occasionally detecting strong electromagnetic activity. We suspect this is a sort of detector sweep which seems to be concentrated on the ecliptic plane rather than above it. We believe our chameleon system is so far obscuring our existence from Bogey One. It has made no move to intercept us after any of the sweeps. Either Bogey One doesn't know we're here or it's not interested in us." His comment elicited a smile from a few gathered at the table. "According to Lieutenant Danino, Bogey One's course should take it to Planet II. I agree it appears to be its most likely destination, as you can see by the display."

The Holo cube in the center of the briefing table showed a schematic of the 70 Ophiuchi system with the tracks displayed of the course of both the *Henry Hudson* and Bogey One.

"We have been able to gather quite a lot of useful information by using only our passive sensors. We estimate the ship to be around 1700 meters long and some 400 meters at the beam, weighing in at around 220,000 tonnes."

"A big beast. Bigger than anything Earth has built to date," remarked Falconer.

"Correct, Lieutenant," said John. "Please continue, XO."

"Sir, one of the most interesting things, though, is we believe we have discovered Bogey One's source of propulsion."

John sat up straighter. "Really, XO?"

"Yes, sir. If the Chief Engineer would explain." Talbot motioned toward Lieutenant Commander George Taylor and sat down as the Henry Hudson's chief engineer stood.

"Ladies and gentlemen, without turning your poor command brains to mush..." A ripple of laughter ran through the

72

assembled bridge officers. The friendly, and sometimes not so friendly, rivalry between the command line officers, engineering and science officers was a well-known fact – had been since before man had entered space. Stretching back as far as the wet navies. From the view of the command line, they saw themselves as the decision makers while the engineers and scientists were there to make things work. On the other hand, the engineers and scientists saw the command line as, to be polite, stuffy, strutting marionettes who thought they ruled from Mount Olympus. Deep down, both lines knew they could not do their jobs without the other to rely upon, so the friendly rivalry persisted and the work was done.

Once the laughter died down, the chief engineer continued. "Sir, it appears Bogey One is employing a form of Alcubierre Drive. It contacts space in front of the ship while expanding space behind it. The net effect is faster than light travel. It explains the neutrino effect as they slow to below the speed of light. I know researchers at Haslett Research Station seriously considered it before the discovery of the Gravity Drive but I don't know how far they got. Whoever this Bogey One is, they seem to have perfected it. I reckon for travelling in system, as they are now, the drive can also use the Mach Effect doubling as an impulse engine to move them around at sub light speeds. What I find concerning is the velocity advantage at sub light speeds they have over us. On the other hand, our Gravity Drive permits almost instantaneous travel between the stars while they are restricted to multiple of the speed of light to get between the stars." John mulled it over for a minute before asking,

"So, Bogey One, in your opinion, has a tactical speed advantage while we have a strategic one?"

"Yes, sir. That's my take on it."

"OK thanks, Chief," replied John. "XO, anything else?"

Again Talbot stood. "Yes, sir. Having had some time to think over what the Chief thinks propels Bogey One, it brings us to another tactical point – which I think will have a bearing on our future options. Bogey One's power output and its threat envelope."

John was beginning to see where the XO was going with this, the sort of power required for an Alcubierre Drive could also power a formidable weapons package. The *Henry Hudson* was severely out gunned.

"If I could ask Lieutenant Falconer to carry on the briefing, sir?" John nodded his assent and Falconer took the floor.

"Sir. This new information, as the XO has pointed out, certainly gives me pause to think. When I consider the sort of reach and strength of any power generated weaponry Bogey One may employ against us. I don't think it is much of a reach to say they could defeat our ablative hull armor without a second thought and, as they out mass us by some fourteen to one, I'm willing to bet they can take a lot more hits than we can."

John looked around the table at the fallen faces, solemn at the realization of what they truly faced if Bogey One became aggressive toward them. John turned his attention back to Falconer as she continued.

"On the brighter side, sir, as the XO said, it appears our chameleon system is worth its weight in gold. Though I advise we get no closer than our current distance to Bogey One. If they get a sniff of us and come investigating, I can't guarantee we can avoid their sensors."

Now that is food for thought. "Thank you, Lieutenant. Now, last, but by no means least, could you give us a quick supply run down, Alfred?"

The diminutive German stood up. "As of zero eight hundred this morning we have sufficient perishable supplies for another fifteen days of operations. At our current level. This increases to twenty-two days if we employ rationing with immediate effect." There was a general groan from around the table at the thought of reducing the fresh food and replacing it with ration packs, and worse still reducing showering time. Everyone loved a nice long hot shower.

Kessler continued as if he had not heard the complaints. "Our tactical ordnance is at full strength. No ordnance, to date, has been expended. Our spares for critical systems are still at ninety percent. This is no doubt due to the exceptional maintenance performed by the Chief's crew rather than my own department's foresight as to system requirements." John cast a quick glance at the Chief who was doing a very good impression of a kettle about to boil. People forgot Kessler had a very sarcastic side and for a mere Lieutenant to take the hand out of the ship's third in command took some serious balls, but it still made John laugh. He could only imagine how the Chief would extract his revenge.

"Thank you, Lieutenant." John looked around the table. "Thank you all for your hard work to date, and please pass on my gratitude to your various departments. I shall not hold you back any longer. XO and Major Murray, join me in my quarters immediately after this. That is all." All around the table echoed "Aye aye, sir," as John stood and left, heading for his quarters.

John sat behind his desk while Talbot and Murray sat in the only two remaining seats in the cramped quarters. This was John's inner circle. He had confidence in these two men and knew they would give him good council. "Well, Bill. Options?"

Without a second thought Talbot said, "We break contact with Bogey One while we still remain undetected. Dogleg through a couple of Folds to ensure no one is tailing us and head for home with the information that whatever destroyed the Saiph is still out here. Albeit we've seen only one ship, we've no idea if he has any friends out there who could arrive right on top of us."

John had similar thoughts though he wanted to explore his options. "Alec?"

Alec looked from John to Talbot and back again. "To give you a good balance, I think I'll have to play Devil's Advocate here. If we continue to shadow Bogey One in system we can confirm their final destination is in fact Planet II. It also gives us the opportunity to possibly observe their modus operandi when it comes to landing on planets and maybe give us a visual of them." Alec looked at Talbot and could tell he did not like the idea one bit, but Alec's job here was to give his captain options, and that was what he was doing. There was a long pause as John weighed up both options.

Head home and tell them the news, the enemy of the Saiph still lived.

Stay and take the chance the *Henry Hudson* would remain undetected and be able to give an invaluable insight into the operations of whomever Bogey One belonged to. Well, he supposed, this is why I get the center seat. John made his decision and stood up. As he did, so did Talbot and Alec. "I don't like it but for once I think I'll have to go with the Devil's alternative. The information we could glean is invaluable if we end up facing these people in a slugging match. Bill?"

"Sir?"

"I want fifty percent of the crew stood to at all times. We need to be ready to fight or flee at the drop of a hat. The remaining fifty percent go on enforced rest. Tell the Chief no routine maintenance is to be carried out and tell Alfred to institute rationing forthwith."

Talbot nodded his understanding. "Understood, Captain."

"Goes for you too, Bill. Either you or I are in the center seat every minute. Bogey One's tactical speed advantage means we cannot afford any critical delay in making a command decision. If you see something developing, use your own judgment — do not wait for my confirmation. You know I have complete faith in your judgment."

"Thank you, sir,"

"Alec."

"Sir?" replied the marine.

"Same goes for yourself. I want your marines armed and dangerous in every critical section, ready to fight or offer assistance as and when."

Alec gave that smartarse grin of his. "At your command, my liege."

All three men smiled before John ushered them out. "Make it happen, minions, while I compose a message to Admiral Vadis detailing our daring and courageous plan."

All three men laughed before Talbot and Murray headed off and John returned to his desk.

#

CHARON BASE - ORBIT OF PLUTO - SOL SYSTEM

Lieutenant Commander Elizabeth Wilson entered the office of Admiral Aleksandr Vadis. He was leaning into his holo pickup with a finger pointed like the barrel of a plasma rifle and she could hear him shouting at some unlucky soul.

"No, I don't think you do understand! Look at my face and tell me you want me to visit you in your nice plush office in Geneva and kick you so hard up the ass that my boot comes out of your mouth! Do you understand me now?" Vadis waved Elizabeth to a seat, his hand out of view of the pickup. Elizabeth sat, patiently waiting. She barely made out the mumbled apology from whoever was at the receiving end of the Admiral's displeasure.

"Good! Now if I have to speak to you again about this matter it will be in person and my voice will be the last human voice you hear, because for the rest of your living, breathing days all you will hear is the sound of penguins mating!" He cut the connection.

"Motivating the troops again sir?"

Like night turning to day Vadis' face broke into a large smile. "Commander, I would never motivate someone under my command in such an overbearing fashion. A political weasel, on the other hand, is in need of much more of a... hands on approach. So to business, Elizabeth. Has anyone in intelligence been able to make any headway with the information the *Henry Hudson* has provided us with?"

"Sir, it is their considered opinion, and I must agree with them, the ship Captain Radford encountered and subsequently identified as the alien race which the Saiph were at war with, is indeed what it appears to be."

This came as no surprise to Vadis. Having examined the data from the Henry Hudson's courier drone, the images had been unmistakable.

"The fact we now have indisputable proof this group of aliens are still out there, taken alongside the Alcubierre Drive, with its potentially massive energy output for weapons systems, the boys and girls down in intelligence are having kittens."

Again, this came as no surprise to Vadis. He may be an admiral working out of an office, but over the years he had gained a healthy respect for a potential enemy's weaponry. "Has Doctor Moore's team at Haslett Research Station been able to give any insights into this Alcubierre Drive's performance?"

Elizabeth consulted her PAD. "As Chief Engineer Taylor stated in his initial brief to Captain Radford, Haslett had been working on a drive of the same principle but it was all shelved with the discovery of the Gravity Drive. Doctors Moore and Hayes are reviewing our research and using it to try and get a handle on the technology used by these aliens."

"What of Doctor Bath at Stickney? Has she not been able to at least give us a name for this group of aliens yet?" asked Vadis,

"It would appear, sir," replied Elizabeth, "the Saiph only seem to refer to them as 'The Others'."

"What the hell does that mean, Elizabeth?" said Vadis. "How more cryptic can the Saiph get? No home star system? Not even a general location?" Vadis let out a deep sigh. "They were fighting these Others for hundreds, if not thousands, of years and the best they could come up with was the Others!"

Elizabeth waited as Vadis calmed down. "Seems so, sir. I remind you Doctor Bath has so much data to go through in the Saiph database – even when it is organized for ease of access – that she is simply swamped and her research is going to take time,"

"Time, Commander," Vadis said almost to himself, "is something which we may find ourselves in short supply of if the Others are able to pinpoint Earth." Vadis sighed again. "Please ensure courier drones are dispatched to the other Vanguards bringing them up to speed on what the *Henry Hudson* has found and our conclusions at this time."

"Yes, sir." Elizabeth stood up and left.

Once the door closed, Vadis sat still for a few minutes contemplating his next move. Coming to a decision he pressed a control on his desk. The face of a young ensign appeared in his Holo cube.

"Communications, sir. Ensign Davies."

"Ensign, get me a secure priority link to Admiral Jing." Time to bring Chrysaor up to speed.

TDF HENRY HUDSON · 4 AUS ABOVE PLANET II OF 70 OPHIUCHI

Radford sat in his command chair as TDF *Henry Hudson* sat still in space, four astronomical units or 598,400,000 kilometers from Planet II of 70 Ophiuchi. It had taken another ten days of shadowing Bogey One before it settled into a geosynchronous orbit around the planet. The orbit obscured Bogey One from the *Henry Hudson* for half the planetary day but, as promised, the gathered intelligence was worth it.

From their position, the crew of the *Henry Hudson* had a great view of Bogey One sending its shuttle equivalent to the surface of Planet II. Sensors had identified four shuttles used almost continuously, moving between Bogey One and the same spot on the surface. Within hours of the first shuttle landing sensors detected independent power sources on the surface. Tactical surmised the crew of Bogey One were setting up a permanent base on the planet. *A fair assumption*, John thought. A call from Lieutenant Alexandra Falconer at Tactical interrupted John's musings.

"Neutrino surge, 275,000 kilometers to starboard,"

Too close, thought Radford. *They cannot fail to see us.* "Battle Stations, Lieutenant."

As the wailing alarm sounded throughout the ship, Falconer continued, "Second vessel emerging. Designating Bogey Two. Initial sensor readings indicate a vessel of similar shape and size as Bogey One. Wait, wait, wait… Heading change. Bogey Two has changed heading. It is on course directly for us. I am getting strange power indications. The computer assesses Bogey Two is powering up weapons."

John displayed the characteristics that had gotten him selected for this mission. Thinking on his feet he said. "Engineering, stand by to fold. Navigation, randomly select a destination from my prearranged list. XO, get the message drone away and a backup if you get time."

"Chief reports ready to fold. Coordinates locked, Navigation ready."

John spared a glance in the direction of Carlo Danino, all those hours in the simulator when he first arrived had been worth it for this situation alone.

"In your own time, Carlo." Danino did not even acknowledge John instead he kept his eyes locked on the XO until he got the nod, message drone departed.

"Three. Two. One. Fold!" The *Henry Hudson* vanished from the 70 Ophiuchi system.

CHAPTER EIGHT

FIFTY THOUSAND LIGHT YEARS

TDF VASCO DE GAMA - CHARON BASE - ORBIT OF PLUTO SOL SYSTEM

Ruth Witsell could not, by any stretch of the imagination, be said to be in a good mood. The Captain of TDF *Vasco De Gama* was only five feet two inches tall and of slight build, however, at this precise moment, her bridge crew were avoiding her gaze as if she could strike them down in an instant.

"Lieutenant Winters, have we rectified our small navigational error yet?"

Her navigator, the aforementioned Lieutenant Winters, checked his board again before taking a deep breath and replying. "Yes, Captain. Our angle of departure is good. The engine room reports ready to fold."

Ruth knew it was not really her navigator's fault –on leaving the dock at Charon Base the ship decided the holding orbit of twenty kilometers should be twenty-five kilometers instead. The *Vasco De Gama* seemed plagued by a fault in her navigational computer. Neither the crew nor the yard dogs had been able to find the source. If time had been on her side, Ruth would have requested Admiral Vadis to delay her mission to Gama Leporn, some 29.25 light years distant, until the whole navigation system was replaced. However, Ruth was already three days behind schedule.

Ruth had watched President Coston's announcement, explaining to the citizens of the Terran Republic the mission parameters of Operation Minerva – to visit the seventeen known systems in the Saiph database. Ruth also observed the news media's clamoring to get to Charon Base, to see for themselves how billions of Feds had been spent. It only reinforced her decision to lobby Admiral Vadis to release the *Vasco De Gama* and send it on its way.

Ruth glanced across at her XO, Commander Ronald Hopkins, who gave her a silent nod of agreement. Ruth addressed her navigator. "Very well, Mr. Winters. Let's be on our way."

"Aye aye, ma'am. Fold in three, two, one... fold." The Vasco De Gamma ceased to be in Sol space.

The transition into and out of fold space should have been seamless, but it certainly was not for Ruth. She suddenly felt groggy, the ship seemed to have bucked like a wild horse. The entire bridge crew appeared shaken in a similar fashion. The sound of an alarm blared into her consciousness, the proximity alarm. "Navigation. Report!"

Winters was, just now, beginning to react. "Ship is tumbling. Correcting now. Large object near, portside 52000 kilometers, moving away from us now."

Ruth's mind raced. They had been due to come out of fold space some twenty parsecs from the edge of the Gama Leporn system. So what could be out this far? Some rogue comet perhaps? She noticed Winters was still working furiously away at his station.

"Problem, Mr. Winters?" Winters appeared to ignore her. Ruth raised her voice and pointedly announced "Mr. Winters! Is there a problem?"

Winters turned toward her with a shocked face. Before he could say anything the urgent voice of Lieutenant Alice Balerno at Tactical rang out,

"Captain! Passives are picking up energy readings, lots of them!"

Ruth spun to face the holo cube "Bring it up, Guns." Ruth used the ancient nautical term for her tactical officer without thinking. Immediately, the holo cube filled with a primary, the system's sun and eleven planets orbiting. Two in the life zone on opposite sides of the primary, one close in, closer than Sol's own mercury. *Wouldn't that be a nice place to visit?* And eight more extending out from the life zone to just beyond the orbit of where Pluto would be.

The two planets in the life zone were scattered with red blotches indicating artificially generated energy and, more interestingly, there were red dots orbiting both planets.

Artificial satellites perhaps? Hold on – was that one moving? By God, it was! Ruth realized. One of the energy signs was undoubtedly moving between the two planets. *This civilization is spacefaring!*

"Captain?" the XO called.

Ruth turned to face him, but Hopkins only pointed toward where Lieutenant Winters was, still staring at his Captain with a pale face.

"Mr. Winters, report!"

Winters hesitated for just a moment. "Captain. This is not Gamma Leporn," he hurriedly added, "I have checked and double checked: this is definitely not where we should be." Winters noted Ruth's doubtful expression. "Captain, according to the Saiph database this system should only consist of seven planets."

Ruth studied the holo cube and the eleven planets it was undoubtedly displaying again. Damn, why hadn't she noticed the obvious? "Continue, Mr. Winters," she said.

"All I can put it down to is the error in the navigation computer which we couldn't track down, it must be exponential. When we left the dock it took us twenty-five kilometers to a parking orbit instead of twenty kilometers... Ma'am if I work on that ratio it means instead of traveling the 29.25 light years to Gamma Leporn, the navigation computer has travelled an extra five kilometers for every twenty we've travelled, twenty kilometers becomes twenty-five kilometers, sixty kilometers becomes 144 kilometers and so on," Winters paused, seeing his captain now worried.

"Go on, Mr. Winters," Ruth said with more conviction than she felt.

"Ma'am if my math is correct, we are actually somewhere in the Messier 54 Cluster. Some 50000 light years from home."

The stunned silence was broken by a small gasp from Lieutenant Ben Leopold at communications. Years of training did not fail Ruth. She had not been chosen for Minerva for her lack of decisiveness.

"Navigation! I need an exact fix soonest."

Winters responded as though struck with a cattle prod. "Yes, ma'am."

"Tactical I need to know A, your best guess if we have been detected, and B get together with Bio and Mechanical Sciences – I want an estimate in comparison with Earth on the level of technology of this system.

"Aye aye, Captain."

"Engineering, complete system wide check. 50000 light years is a long way to come and I want to know if we did any damage."

"Aye, Captain."

Finally, Ruth turned to Commander Hopkins. "Ronald, coordinate the department heads. I want answers and I want them quickly. Not at the expense of mistakes: more speed less haste. When navigation have a good fix on where we are exactly, I want you to plot a series of folds to get us home. Plot them manually, so you better dust off those navigation brain cells I know you used to have."

Hopkins's facial expression showed just how much work manually plotting folds takes. *The yard dogs would answer for this,* Ruth thought, *if Hopkins didn't get to them first.*

"XO, I'll be in my cabin." The bridge erupted into action. Ruth stood and headed through the bridge hatch. The marine on duty was standing smartly to attention, as if he could fail to notice the activity on the bridge.

"Thank you, Marine," said Ruth as she strode down the corridor to her cabin. A second marine came to attention as if on a parade ground. "Marine, give me ten minutes then I'd like to see Major Egnorov."

"Aye aye, ma'am." Ruth entered her cabin and sat herself down on the chair behind her desk. 50000 light years. An unknown civilization. A crew demanding her leadership and direction. Ruth smiled. This is why she loves command. Now, if only she knew what to do next.

#

All told, the majority of the answers demanded by Ruth of her crew took the better part of three and a half hours. Now she was here, gathered with her department heads in the briefing room of the *Vasco De Gama* ready to hear those answers.

Ruth addressed Commander Hopkins "XO?"

Ronald Hopkins cleared his throat. "Captain, before I start I would like to point out the departments are working with the minimum of data. I decided on variables which were used in some decision making processes and some of those variables are only my best guess."

Ruth smiled at her haggard second in command, "Understood, Ronald. I consider your best guess to be better than some peoples facts so please continue."

Hopkins gave Ruth a tired smile of his own before continuing. "As you know, ma'am, due to an error in the navigational computer we are some considerable distance from where we should be." This brought a nervous chuckle from those around the table.

"Mr. Winters, using a hand comp and some math I was never taught at school…" Ruth could see young Lieutenant Winters reddening slightly around the cheeks. "… Was correct in his original estimation of 50000 light years. He has narrowed it down to 48975, but I wouldn't hold 1025 light years against him."

At this point Winters' whole face went red and it appeared something on the deck at his feet had him completely engrossed. Ruth could not help let a small laugh escape from her. "I think we shall forego the keel hauling on this occasion, XO."

Hopkins said in deadpan seriousness. "The Captain is too lenient." This time there were various snorts from around the table, and, if possible, Winters turned an even brighter red. "But I digress, Captain. We appear to be just outside a solar system consisting of some eleven planets. We know two are inhabited. Our current position puts us about sixty-one degrees above the ecliptic plane, we are in a very good vantage point to observe the system. As best as we can tell, there has been no reaction to our presence yet. In the three and a half hours since our arrival, we have noted some forty-six vessels moving between the two planets displaying energy sources. From the speed of the vessels, we estimate a traveling time in the region of eleven months between the two inhabited planets. Further, we have noted planet Messier A, as we have designated it, currently the planet furthest from us has substantially more energy sources than Messier B. Bio Mechanical Sciences theory states either planet B is less advanced than A or, and I will explain my thinking, planet B is a colony of A."

"Your thinking for this, Commander?" asked Ruth.

Hopkins paused for a moment gathering his thoughts. "The emissions of planet A, although more numerous, are of varying strengths and types. Some are more efficient than others, whereas on planet B, all are virtually of the same strength, type and efficiency." Ruth nodded her understanding. "Those on planet B are similar in manufacture and being more efficient than the vast majority on A would indicate newer manufacture to a higher standard, i.e. you would send your best most efficient to a startup colony." Hopkins smiled. "That's how I see it, ma'am."

Ruth looked across at Major Egnorov who had the smile of a cat who had just caught the mouse with the cheese. Hopkins, slightly perplexed by the exchange between his captain and the marine, continued. "Considering the type and efficiency of the energy sources. The apparent transit timescale between planets A and B. The spectrographic analysis of the respective planets' atmospheres for pollution, radiation and so on, along with electronic eavesdropping of broadcasts in the electromagnetic band, I believe we could safely place this civilization as equivalent to pre-World War III Earth." As Hopkins studied his captain's reaction, he could not help but notice the small smile crossing her lips and, if possible, the smile on Egnorov's face got bigger.

"So you would rate any threat to ourselves from the planets as…?" asked Ruth.

"In our current location I would have to say negligible, Captain."

"Thank you, XO. Engineering?"

"A level one diagnostic shows no damage to either the ship or more importantly the Gravity Drive. The momentary dizziness we experienced was due to the time spent in fold space. No one has ever spent so long in transit before and the Chief Engineer..."

Ruth glanced down the table to Lieutenant Commander George Lee. He had studied under Doctor Jeff Moore, and to say Moore had been slightly upset when Lee was collared for Chimera would be an understatement. Moore saw Lee as a protégé the Navy stole from him. "... Has assured me if we can keep the folds to under 5000 light years each in the future, then the engines shouldn't even notice it."

Now this was news. The rating for the engine was folds of only fifty to sixty light years. Ruth addressed Lee directly. "George, anything you want to tell me?"

"Captain, while running our drive checks I reviewed its performance in detail. I was able to identify the elements of a theory I had been working on with Doctor Moore before leaving Haslett Research Station. Our prolonged unplanned journey has given me empirical data to collaborate the theory and I believe with a few alterations, with your permission of course," Lee gave Ruth a lopsided grin, "I could extend the range of each fold to a comfortable and more importantly, repeatable 5000 light years."

Ruth thought for a second. "How long to make the alterations and what would be the downtime on the drive?"

Without hesitation Lee replied, "The software alterations can be completed offline then uploaded into the engineering mainframe with no disruption. The physical engineering alterations will take a maximum of thirty-six hours, with the drive offline for about seven of those hours."

Seven hours with no means of getting out of here in a hurry if needs be. *A big gamble*, thought Ruth. Hopkins lack of conviction was enough for Ruth.

"OK, prepare the software changes but do not install them. Same for the physical changes. Keep the XO up to speed on your progress. When you are ready to go, we will reassess."

The crestfallen Lee replied. "Aye aye, ma'am."

Hopkins looked happier. The idea of being dead in the water for seven hours did not appeal to him either.

"Anything else, XO?"

"Yes, ma'am, just one more thing." At this, Alice Balerno, the tactical officer, and Lieutenant Ben Leopold, the Comms officer, both seemed to sit a bit straighter.

Hopkins continued. "During our evaluation of the inhabitants of the planets, we covered their electromagnetic emissions." Hopkins paused. "Lieutenant Leopold, if you please."

Leopold switched on the holo cube in the center of the table. A biped, possibly 168 centimeters tall, wearing a tan and brown uniform with some emblems at the waist, a small circular mouth with what appeared to be three slits either side of where a nose should be and two eyes set widely apart above the slits. There seemed to be no ears, or for that matter any hair apparent on the body.

"Captain," said Hopkins with a flourish. "May I introduce the sentient species of Messier 54?"

Ruth stared at the image for a few seconds before saying, "Ronald, your flair for the dramatic is never ending"

"But Captain," said the XO, "I saved the best for last. May I draw your attention to the arms?"

Ruth examined the image once more. Two arms, but where the elbow should be there was a joint which didn't look quite right. Ah, double jointed! The elbow could bend in two different directions. A shorter forearm and a hand with, *I'll be damned!* Ruth turned to her XO and then to Egnorov.

Vladimir Egnorov matched her gaze and said simply, "When do I leave?"

UPPER ATMOSPHERE PLANET B
MESSIER 54 CLUSTER - 50000 LIGHT YEARS FROM EARTH

Major Egnorov glanced around the Tanto covert insertion shuttle and then at the heads-up display projected into his left eye by the Wraith Combat Suit.

Issued to Force Recon Marines, the Wraith Combat Suit was composed of ultra-strong shock absorbing material. Constructed from inorganic nanostructures – five times stronger than steel – the Wraith Combat Suit, commonly simply called 'Wraith', remained highly elastic and provided a complete range of movement for the wearer. The assimilated exoskeleton provided immense strength through the servomotors utilizing high gauss permanent magnets and step down gearing to provide high torque, responsive movement in a small package. The combat suit was, therefore, unrestrictive to the wearer, allowing them to access even small surface areas. Power, provided by miniature solid oxide fuel cells, was easy to replace in the field and would sustain the suit at maximum power output for eight hours or with normal use, thirty-six. The suit was capable of use in a vacuum for short time periods – enough time for a planetary assault, for instance.

One of the key elements of the suit, for any Force Recon Marine, was its ability to communicate with not only other suits but also with ships in orbit. Comms was established by either suit to suit/ship radio or more covertly by use of whisker laser – a point-to-point communications system which could not be intercepted unless one happened to stray into the path of the laser — deemed a highly unlikely scenario.

An equally vital element of the suit was the Chameleon unit, a stealth system integral to each suit. It was a compact version of the stealth systems used by Navy ships. Chameleon used optics throughout the Wraith Combat Suit, effectively projecting whatever was 180 degrees behind the suit to 180 degrees in front. If the enemy peered at the wearer, they effectively saw right through them. The wearer became indistinguishable to the naked eye and undetectable to any known electro optical systems. The Force Recon Marine became, essentially, invisible.

Egnorov's Wraith was counting down the altitude of both him and the shuttle as they descended through the atmosphere of Planet B. Egnorov and six other marines similarly suited in Wraiths were providing close protection for the ten Navy types commanded by the *Vasco De Gamma's* XO, Commander Hopkins. The mission was to collect as much material from soil, plant and animal samples as possible without discovery by the 'Baldies'. Egnorov chuckled. Some midshipman had christened the sentient species on Planet A and the colonizers of Planet B the irreverent nickname, but it had stuck.

Egnorov and Hopkins had been planning this mission for three weeks, as the *Vasco De Gamma* crept slowly in system, continually checking for the tiniest indication of detection as it closed on Planet B. It became quickly obvious that not only were the Baldies on the planet, but mining operations were also in progress within the asteroid belt. A steady flow of traffic had been observed between the belt and what appeared to be orbital facilities around Planet A. This same traffic provided a navigational headache to Lieutenant Winters, but the young navigator had proven his worth, spending endless hours at the helm. Eventually, caught fast asleep in his chair on the bridge, Captain Witsell ordered him to his bed, along with strict instructions not to return for at least forty-eight hours.

The plan Egnorov and Hopkins devised was a variation of one the marine and Captain Witsell had deliberated long before leaving Charon Base.

Admiral Vadis spoke of the probable requisite for surface reconnaissance at his initial briefing on Operation Chimera, so, while Witsell prepared her ship and crew for their mission, Egnorov and his marines investigated potential scenarios warranting their own surface mission and identified their parameters.

When the captain had called him to her quarters and briefed him on their current predicament on arrival in Messier 54,

Egnorov had been able to warn his small planning section to begin prepping for a mission. By the time Commander Hopkins briefed the captain, Egnorov knew he was going to command the first marines to visit a planet controlled by an alien species.

When he filled Hopkins in on this after the captain's brief, Hopkins understood the reason for the smile on Egnorov's face.

The jolting of the shuttle brought Egnorov back to the present. The pilot was bringing the shuttle in on an oblique angle, mimicking the trajectory of a meteorite. Although the shuttle was the stealthiest yet produced, Egnorov saw no reason to take unnecessary risks. He and Hopkins had chosen a landing site far from any detected population centers.

The planet sunrise dictated the night landing – land one hour after dark and leave one hour before sunrise. A quick in and out mission. His instructors at Marine Force Recon would have been proud.

Egnorov relished in happy memories of those long tiring days and nights at Recon School – maybe happy was not the right word. The highest praise Egnorov had heard out of the mouths of those marine gunnery sergeants was "Satisfactory, Egnorov." By the end of the course of 160 initial candidates, only Egnorov and two others qualified as Marine Force Recon. As Egnorov graduated, his gunny instructor shook his hand and said "Satisfactory, Egnorov." His instructor paused and, with a hint of a smile, tagged his comment with, "Sir."

Egnorov reminisced back to his arrival on Titan Base, shortly after his graduation, when he took up his post on Titan Base as Team Commander. A fresh faced lieutenant.

He recalled his arrival interview with the commanding officer as... brief. The CO was a long service naval admiral with a reputation of running a tight ship. He did not suffer fools gladly. Titan Base was the front line where they waged the fight against asteroid belt piracy. Marine Force Recon teams deployed from Titan to rocks thought likely to harbor pirates. They carried out surface reconnaissance in non-existent gravity and hard vacuum. Only the best were sent to Titan Base, which was why the 'satisfactory' Egnorov was slightly perturbed at his posting there.

He recollected the conversation.

"Lieutenant Egnorov," the Admiral had said.

"Yes, sir," a nervous Egnorov had replied.

"I see here your gunny instructor was Gunny Bates."

"Correct, sir."

"I've known Gunny Bates for more years than I or he would care to remember. As a young ensign, I carried out a boarding action with him on a pirate ship out past Ceres. Messy business. The pirates kidnapped the crew and passengers from a cruise ship and murdered most of those not worth ransoming. They knew it was the gallows for them if they were captured, so they fought like animals." The Admiral let out a short snort. "My pistol ran out of charge eventually. I was left facing two of them with the civilians behind me. Son, if anyone ever tells you your life flashes in front of you at times like that, it is a lie. I was too busy being scared. The only thing I had to hand was my survival knife… and survive I did. The pirates never reached the gallows. The Navy in their wisdom decided to give me a medal."

Egnorov stood a bit straighter as he noticed for the first time a small blue and white ribbon on the Admiral's chest. The Terran Medal of Honor. The highest award a military man could receive, awarded only by recommendation of the entire Joint Chiefs and the consent of the Senate.

"Son, I managed to sneak a peek at the after action report years later written by Gunny Bates. Gunny rated my performance: 'Satisfactory. This officer has potential'. Beside it was a handwritten note from the then Chairman of The Joint Chiefs. It read: 'Recommended for the TMH on Gunny's say so'. Now, if The Joint Chiefs think a satisfactory rating from a mere gunnery sergeant is something to stand up and listen to, then who am I to disagree? If Gunny said you were 'satisfactory', then I am damned glad to have you. So welcome aboard!"

The admiral stood up, shook Egnorov's hand and escorted him to the door. "Now get out. I've got work to do." So started Egnorov's career with Recon.

Whoa! Egnorov screamed back to the present, kept in his seat only by the restraining ties locked onto his suit as the shuttle made another wild maneuver.

"Thirty seconds," called the pilot. Egnorov did a brief team check via his suit's onboard computer. Bio readings of his marines were nominal, damn! He studied Gunny Alison Chew's readings again. If he did not know any better, he would swear she was asleep. *Are all gunnies the same?* He thought and shook his head making the helmet of his Wraith move slightly.

"Touchdown! Doors opening!" Egnorov and his marines were out in a heartbeat and moving off to a distance of 300 metres in every direction to form a secure perimeter around the Tanto. The Navy personnel moved off next and formed a second perimeter close to the Tanto, ready to re embark at the first sign of trouble. Egnorov stood by the Tanto's boarding hatch. Using the Wraith's link to his Marines he quickly and efficiently completed a threat assessment. None of his marines detected any danger and it seemed they were down unnoticed.

Egnorov enabled his whisker link to the *Vasco De Gamma.* "Team down and undetected as far as I can tell, Captain."

In geosynchronous orbit, Ruth Witsell sat on the edge of her chair on the bridge and let out a breath she did not know she had been holding. "Very well, Major. If you are content the area is secure, please inform the XO to begin his survey."

"Understood. Egnorov out." Egnorov turned to Hopkins, who was kneeling in the center of the inner perimeter, "Captain says we have a green light, Ronald."

Hopkins nodded in understanding. "OK, people. Let's get started. Remember, no movement outside the marine perimeter without my express permission. And stay in your pairs." Man's first exploration of an alien occupied world began.

#

"So," began Ruth, looking across the table of the *Vasco de Gama*'s Briefing Room at Major Egnorov and Commander Hopkins, "you are sure of your results?"

"I don't think there is any room for error, ma'am," Hopkins replied confidently. "The samples we recovered have been tested thoroughly. There is no doubt the Saiph visited this system. All the samples recovered leave me in no doubt the indigenous species are products of the Saiph DNA manipulation."

Ruth sat still for a moment, considering her options. "Well... now we have a decision. Do we make our way back to Earth with our findings? On the other hand, do we spend more time in this system gathering as much information on the Baldies as we can before returning home? Thoughts gentlemen."

There was silence for a few seconds before Egnorov said, "I'm a Force Recon Marine and it's my job to gather as much intelligence on a target as possible..." Egnorov paused. "Despite this, our discovery here – another spacefaring species – Earth needs to know about this ASAP."

Ruth turned to Ronald. "Ronald?"

"Ma'am, the major is correct. We need to get this ship and the information home. Let the Admiralty get a proper first contact expedition set up and return here. We completed exactly what we set out to do – albeit," Hopkins grinned, "a bit beyond the intended target system."

Ruth and Egnorov both let out a short laugh.

"Ronald, your irony never ceases to amaze me. Very well, Ronald. Get together with the chief engineer and let's get started on our way home."

CHAPTER NINE

LIFE NO MORE

TDF JACQUES CARTIER - DELTA PAVONIS
19.92 LIGHT YEARS FROM EARTH

Captain Christos Papadomas sat alone in the briefing room of the TDF *Jacques Cartier*. He stared at the image of Planet III, spinning slowly in the holo cube. Dark clouds completely covered the planet, broken only by the occasional flash of lightning in the upper atmosphere. It seemed to promise so much, but the chance of life had been snuffed out by nature — wiping the slate clean ready to start again.

He touched a control panel and a small net of flashing lights began to surround the planet. A still functioning satellite network. Another touch of the panel and the image zoomed in, passing through the clouds, down even further until it reached the level of the ocean, and then carried on until it reached the ocean floor.

There, on the ocean bed was a massive crater some 600 kilometers across. A stream of data appeared on the right of the image: carbon dioxide (CO_2), soluble in seawater, was present in very large quantities. It mostly reported the bicarbonate radical ($-HCO_3$) stable at temperatures below fifty degrees Celsius – the normal sea surface temperature – but sea surface temperature could easily exceed this if or when an asteroid struck the ocean, inducing a large thermal shock. He understood in those circumstances very large quantities of CO_2 would erupt from the ocean as a heavy gas, and the CO_2 could quickly spread around the world in concentrations sufficient to suffocate air breathing fauna and animals. Asteroid impacts with the ocean might not leave obvious signs, but these impacts had the potential to be far more devastating to life on a planet than impacts with land.

He pulled the view back, and with a flick of his fingers sent it flying through the atmosphere over the nearest land – over the ruins of cities lying on the coastal region, struck by tidal waves up to a mile high, the damage subsiding the further inland he viewed. Even though the physical damage lessened, the result was the same, he noted. Everything requiring oxygen to breathe was dead.

His geologists put the impact at less than twenty years ago. Only twenty years ago and he would have seen a living, breathing planet with a world civilization who had put artificial satellites into orbit. But no more. The best he could do for them was to ensure at least some memory of them lived on. He shook himself out of his melancholy, touching a control. The image of his XO appeared where the dead planet had been. "Robert, could you round up Major Draper and join me in the Briefing Room at your earliest convenience?" It was a rhetorical question.

Robert Ranking guessed at the purpose of the meeting with his captain. "Would you like me to bring Doctor Gunnerman?" Doctor Rudolf Gunnerman was TDF *Jacques Cartier*'s xenobiologist and a history buff.

"Good idea, Robert. As soon as you can, please."

"Yes, sir." Ranking signed off.

Christos sat back in his chair and began to put together a plan to save as much of this dead civilization as his small ship could hold before returning to Earth with his solemn news. Life no longer existed in Delta Pavonis.

#

CHARON BASE - ORBIT OF PLUTO - SOL SYSTEM

Lieutenant Commander Elizabeth Wilson once again found herself in the office of Admiral Aleksandr Vadis, Commander of Operation Minerva on Charon Base, orbiting Pluto.

The solemn mood of the base reflected its commander. TDF *Vasco De Gama* had not made contact confirming its safe arrival at Gama Leporn. Vadis had authorized the dispatch of two courier drones to the system to make contact with the missing ship. Both had returned intact and reported there was no indication of either the ship or the communications buoy it should have released on its arrival in the system. Vadis was only delaying the inevitable by not declaring the ship lost but, Elizabeth reflected, he was the admiral and it was his decision.

Vadis turned from the Holo Cube image of Gama Leporn to face Elizabeth. "So, Commander. Give me some good news."

"Sir, Captain Radford has safely arrived in the Sol system and is due to dock within the hour. We have received a courier drone from Captain Papadomas. He requests he be allowed a further seven days in Delta Pavonis to secure as many facts as possible on the indigenous civilization."

Vadis nodded. "Granted. Inform him as to the current situation with TDF *Vasco De Gama*. Make it clear he is to leave Delta Pavonis at the first indication of any trouble. We still do not know what happened to Captain Witsell and her crew. I don't want to lose another ship."

Elizabeth made the annotations on her PAD before continuing, "As for TDF *James Cook*, Captain Lewis reports safe arrival at 31 Aquilae. That is all at this time." Elizabeth keenly felt a sense of relief at this particular news. She and Robert Lewis had enjoyed each other's company while preparing for the survey missions and she missed being able to talk to him. Elizabeth shook herself internally. *Robert is old and bold enough to look after himself without you worrying like an old woman,* she thought, and promptly halted her pondering as she waited for Vadis to reply.

"Very well, Elizabeth. Inform Captain Radford I expect a full briefing from him two hours after he docks, and please ensure the yard gets TDF *Henry Hudson* turned around as quickly as possible for redeployment."

"Yes, sir." Elizabeth stood to leave then paused. "Sir, if I may?"

Vadis broke his gaze away from the image of Gama Leporn in the Holo Cube. "Of course, Elizabeth."

"Sir, as you have pointed out, we have no idea what has happened to the *Vasco De Gama*, so maybe we should wait for a little while longer before we write them off?"

Vadis considered for a moment. "As always, Elizabeth, you know what to say and when to say it." Vadis gave her a small smile, the first she had seen since TDF *Vasco De Gama* had failed to make contact. "Maybe a few days more before I make any calls to the families." Vadis' eyes turned to reflect on the image of Gama Leporn. Elizabeth left the room.

CHAPTER TEN

TRIP WIRE

TDF JAMES COOK - 31 AQUILAE

TDF *James Cook* arrived at the pre-planned distance of 52 AUs from the primary star 31 Aquilae, some 49.41 light years from Earth. 31 Aquilae could be seen by the naked eye from Earth. The star was some 116 percent of the mass of Earth's own star and some 138 percent of its size. Spectrograph readings showed it as surprisingly rich in elements, with the exception of hydrogen and helium, for its age, some five billion years old – which put it about half a billion years older than our own sun. A blink of the eye on a cosmic scale.

Captain Robert Lewis viewed his bridge with paternal pride. His people were going about their jobs with the utmost professionalism and if truth were told, he felt outright redundant. Robert had been, perhaps, more surprised than the other captains on hearing of their selection to command Earth's first extra-solar survey ships. Robert was only a few years from retirement and had already been planning how he was going to spend his free time – commuting between his home on the south island of New Zealand and his daughter's home on the north island. He had gone as far as considering selling his place and moving lock stock and barrel to be closer to his daughter. However, his home on south island was where he and his late wife, Colleen, had lived, raised a family together and where, if it had not been for the cancer, they had planned on growing old together.

Robert shook himself out of his reverie. It was not to be. In any case, he had found a resurgent interest in his career. On receiving the briefing by Admiral Vadis and Lieutenant Commander Elizabeth Wilson on Operation Minerva at Charon Base, Robert had found himself spending many hours with Elizabeth going over details of the operation. Not only during work hours but also over the odd late dinner. Robert had been surprised to hear Elizabeth too was a widow, her husband had died in service early in her career. Lewis still thought he made a mistake in not inviting her to see New Zealand with him. Perhaps when this mission was over...

"Captain!" Commander Torrance, his XO, called and attracted his attention.

"Yes, XO?"

"Sir, if you would care to view the Holo Cube, astronomy have finished their plot of the system and have confirmed their findings." Robert spun his chair to get an unobstructed view of the central Holo Cube. As it sprang into life, Torrance continued. "As you can see, sir, the system consists of nine planets. Two are gas giants, three are effectively balls of ice, being too far from the system primary to receive anything in the way of heat, and another two are so close to the primary they make our own Venus seem a nice place to vacation. One is just outside the Goldilocks Zone and this one is just right," Torrance paused.

Robert interjected, "This sounds like the story of the three bears, Bruce."

Refusing to acknowledge the pun, Torrance carried on. "So far, sir, spectral analysis of the atmosphere has a high amount of carbon dioxide, methane, nitrous oxide and halocarbons."

Robert raised a finger to stop Torrance in mid brief. "XO, are you going where I think you are going with this?"

Torrance let a small smile reach his lips. "As usual, sir, you are a step ahead. I'm saying what you've already guessed — that these are four of the principle greenhouse gases which accumulate in the atmosphere, causing concentrations to increase with time. On our own planet, levels of this sort occurred in the industrial era."

"No sign of artificial power generation?" asked Robert.

"None, sir." confirmed the XO.

Robert sat back in his seat and involuntarily began to stroke his grey goatee. Torrance remained silent, allowing his captain to mull over the information.

"Very well," announced Robert, turning to face his navigator, Lieutenant Ash. "Mr. Ash, please plot us a spiral course for Planet IV. I want to survey the outer planets on the way in, no sense in taking any chances."

"Aye aye, sir."

"Lieutenant Marcks. I want passive sensors only, but get as much information as you can."

Marcks, the tactical officer nodded, "Yes, sir."

"XO, I shall leave the bridge in your capable hands. Download all our information to a courier drone and get it away please. Ensure the deployment of the communications buoy."

"Understood, sir."

"I'll be in my quarters, taking my pensioner's half hour. We of the older generation require our midday snooze, you know."

Torrance allowed himself another smile. After watching how Captain Lewis had driven the crew in preparation for this mission, he had more stamina than half the crew put together and could give the marines a run for their money as well. Instead he replied, "I'll be sure to wake you for dinner, sir," before turning to carry out his orders.

#

Robert was fast asleep when his Comm buzzed urgently. Without even opening his eyes, he had hit the accept button. "Captain. Go ahead."

"Sir, Lieutenant Ash. Could you come to the bridge, sir? Passive sensors are detecting what Tactical are classifying as an artificial power source on or near Planet V. Approximately two point eight AU from our current location."

The request brought Robert to full wakefulness. *How could it be? There should not be an artificial power source out here.* "Signal all stop, Mr. Ash. Rouse the XO and get him to meet me on the bridge."

"Aye aye, sir."

Robert swung his legs out of bed and dressed while ruminating the implications of an artificial power source in the system. Well, no need to over think until he received more information, he would just have to wait.

On reaching the bridge, Robert took his center seat just as Torrance came through the bridge hatch, slightly out of breath, and talking into his wrist communicator. Lewis smiled at him, "A little out of shape, XO?"

"Running and talking at the same time, sir. Need to get to the gym more, I think."

As Torrance moved to his console, Robert noted more harried, out of breath officers were arriving. Torrance had been rousing the senior bridge staff to replace the night crew. *Better to have the A Team on duty, good idea Bruce*, thought Robert. For a few minutes, Lewis let his team get themselves up to speed before getting down to business, "OK, XO. What do we know?"

"Captain, approximately..." Torrance took a quick look at the bridge clock, "seven minutes ago, Tactical detected an artificial power source emanating from the general location of Planet Five, which has now been narrowed down to a point approximately point five AUs from the planet. Although the power source is quite weak, Tactical are positive it is artificial, and having looked at the data so am I. Until now, we have not detected any attempt to sweep for us using active sensors."

"Can you be certain we remain undetected, XO?"

"I cannot guarantee it at this point, sir. Whatever is the source of the energy signature may have capabilities we cannot detect."

Food for thought, Robert agreed, *well, we can not just sit here.* "Recommendations, Bruce?"

Now it was Torrance's turn to take a breath. Robert waited patiently as his first officer ran through the various options in his mind, calculating what was best for the ship and the mission.

"Sir, I recommend holding station. We can observe the location of the power source with our onboard passive optical equipment. Whatever it is, its twenty-two point four light minutes from us. There are no detected aggressive moves we can get a good look at it before deciding on a course of action."

"Sounds good, XO, make it happen and let's see what we're really dealing with here. How long before we get results?"

"I'll meet with Lieutenant Curran from Supply and get the required equipment broken out of stores. Ensign Yamata has a first from MIT in Astrography and is my choice for setting it up."

Robert could see the cogs turning in his XO's head.

"Say three hours to locate, track, image and be ready to present the findings, sir."

"Make it happen, Bruce. Tactical, I want a permanent passive weapons lock on the source, but do not power anything up without my express permission. And notify me the second we have any change in either its output or aspect."

"Aye aye, sir," said Marcks at Tactical.

"XO, I also want everyone fed and watered. I fear we may have a long day ahead."

"Yes, sir. I'll see to it."

Robert left the bridge and headed for his cabin for what, he had no doubt, would not be his first mug of coffee this day.

#

Three hours later, Robert sat in his chair in the Briefing Room of the TDF *James Cook* with the rest of his command team and a seemingly aloof Major Karen Mills, the CO of the *James Cook*'s Marine detachment. All were eagerly awaiting the XO's presentation.

Robert found it hard to relate to Major Mills. She was obviously competent or she would not be here, but she kept herself and her marines apart from the rest of *James Cook*'s crew. Robert did not like this aloofness, however, he understood his officers had their own command style. Until it became an issue, he did not feel the need to interfere. Robert looked across at Torrance, "XO?"

"Sir, the last three hours have been very productive. We can now confirm the source of the energy readings is in fact from an artificial object which is station keeping at that point." Torrance activated the Holo Cube. There was a small and, what appeared, quite battered object. It looked remarkably like an old style communications satellite without the solar panels – a large box, roughly the size of a ground car, with two long antennas protruding from it and a large dish mounted on it. As the image rotated, one side of the box appeared covered in glass lenses and, as the image rotated further, Robert could see on the opposite side of the lenses there was an even larger dish, which covered one side of the box.

As the image rotated, Robert asked, "What is your assessment, XO?" A darker patch on the object had caught Robert's eye.

"Without stating the obvious, sir, we believe this object is not the product of any civilization in this system. Our analysis of the capabilities of Planet IV show no sign of space travel at their current level of development. It leads us to conclude it must have been placed by some other, unknown, nonindigenous civilization."

Silence descended on the table as people assimilated what Torrance had said: a civilization on Planet Four at a level of technology equivalent to Earth during the industrial revolution and, somewhere else, there was another civilization. This civilization not only had the technology for spaceflight, but also must have the technology for interstellar flight to travel to this system from which they did not originate. A sobering thought – man was not the only species currently traveling the stars.

"Going back to the object, XO. What are your thoughts?" asked Robert.

"If I were to equate it with our own technology, sir, I would say it was some form of surveillance platform. My best guess is the glass side of the box are the lens for some form of high definition space telescope. The protruding antennas gather any electromagnetic transmissions, the larger dish shape to the rear is a broadcast array. The platform is situated in a position where the lens is always pointed at Planet IV and, at this distance from the planet, even if the inhabitants were to develop the technology to put their own satellites in orbit, this platform would remain undetected, possibly for decades to come."

"Well thought out as usual XO. It leaves only the questions of who is watching Planet Four and how do they collect data?"

"One other thing, sir"

"Yes, XO?"

Torrance fiddled with the controls for the Holo Cube and the image of one side of the platform enlarged. "If I could point out this particular image, sir…" It was the darker patch Robert had seen earlier. "This would appear to be a jagged hole in the structure of the platform. It is my belief something struck the platform causing the damage."

Robert regarded the image. "We have no way of knowing how long ago the damage was inflicted, XO?"

"We think we do, sir. Tactical noticed a slow, but steady, reduction in the power output of the platform. Now we have taken the time to observe it more closely, it appears to have a slight wobble."

Lewis thought he could see where this was going, "Do you have a proposal, XO?" Out of the corner of his eye, Robert was sure he saw the cool Major Mills turn her head microscopically toward Torrance.

"Sir, I would like to propose we close with the platform. Do an onsite inspection, and if deemed safe recover it, return it to Earth."

Robert regarded Torrance for a moment. It was obvious the XO had thought this through at length, "What you are proposing is very risky, XO. If whoever placed the platform here comes back looking for it to make repairs and it's simply vanished, it could prompt them to ask the same questions we are: Is there someone else out here?"

Torrance looked steadily at Robert. "Understood, sir. But I think the risk outweighs the gain on getting our hands on this technology."

Robert still was not convinced. At the end of the day, the

decision lay with him. "Major Mills." If a marine could come to attention in a seat then Mills did so. "Get together with the XO and sketch out a plan to approach the platform, inspect it and, if possible, recover it. Cover all our bases here, Major. If you consider the plan unworkable, then we leave the platform where it is, understood?"

Mills looked from Captain Lewis to the frowning XO and back to Lewis, "Sir! Yes sir!"

Robert stood up. "OK people. We have a lot to think over. Communications. Get a courier drone away with images of the platform and a summary of my intentions. The rest of you are dismissed." Robert left the Briefing Room but not before noticing, astonishingly, what appeared to be a smile on the lips of Mills as she approached a still frowning Torrance.

#

The plan Bruce Torrance and Karen Mills developed was as straightforward and uncomplicated as they could make it. Karen was a firm believer in the KISS principle – Keep It Simple, Stupid. The more complicated the operation, the more chance there was Murphy's Law would come into play. This operation was too important to give Murphy any chance of screwing it up for them.

TDF *James Cook* hiding itself on the far side of Planet V was the basic plan. From there, a Tanto shuttle would launch with a joint Navy/Marine recovery team on board. They would approach the alien platform with the planet at their back so the natural electromagnetic radiation, generated by the planet, would help hide the miniscule amounts escaping from the covert insertion shuttle on the off chance the platform had the ability to detect objects approaching it. On arrival at the platform, the recovery team would perform an extra vehicular activity (EVA) – Navy speak for going out in spacesuits – and get a closer look at the platform after the Marine Explosive Ordnance Disposal (EOD) had cleared the platform of any self-destruct mechanisms.

To Robert Lewis the plan was good one. The only problem was after the Tanto moved beyond the radio horizon of Planet V, he would have no contact with the recovery team until it broke the radio horizon on its return journey to TDF *James Cook*. Nevertheless, moving the *James Cook* behind the planet was the only way to get as close as possible to the platform without putting the ship within any possible detection zone of the platform. *No plan is perfect*! Thought Robert. From his seat on the bridge Robert watched the Tanto move away from the *James Cook. Good luck and safe journey, Bruce.*

Bruce sat in the troop/cargo area of the shuttle, completely enclosed in his armored spacesuit. Not as good as the Marine issue Wraith suits, but good enough for him to survive and fight in a hard vacuum environment. Bruce looked for the hundredth time at the display in front of him as the Tanto made its stealthy approach to the alien platform. "Still no change in the power output, Gunny?"

Gunnery Sergeant Hazon was the Marine EOD and he had constantly monitored the platform's energy readings since the Tanto had started detecting them when it had broken the radio horizon of Planet V and begun its approach. Now only 100 meters from the platform, the Tanto sat stationary while Hazon confirmed there were no unexpected power spikes that might be a telltale signal of the Tanto's detection. Hazon took one more look to confirm his readings. "Still looking good, sir. I'm happy to say we have a go."

Bruce switched across to his private link. "Well, Karen?"

"I'm with the Gunny, Bruce," replied Karen over the link. "If he's happy to deploy, it's his call. He's the one who has to approach the thing first, after all."

Bruce had not been happy with this part of the plan, but Karen insisted. The platform had to be checked for self-destruct mechanisms. Bruce knew it was the gunny's job, but Karen had insisted the remainder of the team stayed within the added protection of the Tanto's hull until the gunny cleared the platform. It simply went against the grain with Bruce to send a man into potential danger while he sat in the relative safety of the Tanto. "OK Gunny. You have a go."

Hazon released his seat restraining ties with practiced ease and moved to the troop hatch on the side of the Tanto. He operated the hatch mechanism, stepping into the air lock and closing the internal hatch without even a backward glance.

Over the team link, Karen called Hazon. "Gunny, no chances here. If anything looks even slightly wrong, back away and return to the shuttle. Communications by whisker laser only, let's do this thing by the book."

"Understood, Major. Just a walk in the park." Hazon activated his pusher pack and a small blast of high-pressure gas moved him in the direction of the platform. Hazon stopped at ten meters from the platform, and then using the pusher pack he performed a complete three sixty degree check of the platform. "Nothing obvious on an initial visual survey. I'm going to move closer"

"Understood, Gunny. Still looking good from here: no signs of any unusual activity on the platform," Bruce acknowledged.

Hazon moved in closer and found what he was looking for "OK, I have found what looks like an inspection panel. Are you getting a good visual?"

"I see it, Gunny." Bruce could see on his display a rectangular panel roughly a meter by half a meter with what looked like retaining lugs spaced equally around it, securing it to the main body of the platform.

Hazon reached to his tool belt and lifted off a small handheld laser cutter, "I don't have anything which will fit the lugs, so I'm just going to go for a straight cut to remove the lugs and then lift the panel free." Hazon started cutting away at the lugs, knowing any one of them could be attached to enough explosives to destroy the platform and spread him over this entire area of space.

Karen noted a rise in his respiration. "Everything OK over there, Gunny? Your respiration and heart rate are up."

Without pausing in his work, Hazon replied, "I think I have a cold coming on, Major."

Karen had to fight to control her laughter before activating the link again, "That explains it, Gunny. Make sure you visit sickbay when we get back, I don't need you spreading it to the rest of the detachment."

Listening in, Bruce could not believe what he was hearing. She was berating the man for having a cold and not going to sickbay all the while he was cutting away at a potential bomb. He would never understand marines. Torrance failed to notice the slight shoulder movements of the Wraith suits of the remaining Marines as they laughed heartily, ensuring not to activate their own Comm links.

With the last of the retaining lugs removed, Hazon lifted the panel clear and secured it to the side of the platform. He was able to get his first clear look inside. A complex looking set of boards were joined by what looked like thick plastic strips to a central hexagonal shaped object about the size of a soccer ball.

"Hold there, Gunny. Zoom in on one of the connections to the object directly in front of you," Bruce ordered. As the Gunny zoomed in, Torrance looked at the connection more closely. "Gunny, run your PAD over one of those connections for me. I want to check something." Hazon did as instructed and fresh data appeared on Torrance's display. "OK, Gunny, confirmed. There is an electric current emanating from the central object. I think it's a safe bet this is the platform's power source. Unless there's a backup, we should be able to deactivate the platform by removing the source."

"Just give me a minute here, sir." Hazon removed his monomolecular blade from its scabbard at his shoulder. No marine went anywhere without a knife and the monomolecular blade was the ultimate knife. It could cut at the molecular level, carving through virtually any known material as easily as a hot knife through butter. Not something for the uninitiated to play with, but Hazon handled it with skill, giving not a second thought to the fact it could cut through his suit and expose him to vacuum. Hazon twisted his body to get into a better position and began slicing through the connections, careful not to touch the suspected power source itself, ever hopeful Commander Torrance was right about these connections and he was not about to be adjacent to a fatal, loud bang and expanding ball of gas. The last connection was severed. Hazon secured the blade in its scabbard and ran the PAD over the object again. No power readings. It looked like Torrance was right. "Are you getting this, Commander?"

"I see it, Gunny. OK standby. I'll get the remaining team to you and we'll get this thing in the hold and secured." As Bruce turned to the rest of the team, he heard Karen over the link.

"And don't forget to report to sickbay when we get back, Gunny."

Keep me safe from marines! Thought Bruce. *Does that woman never lighten up?*

#

Robert and the rest of the crew of TDF *James Cook* let out a collective sigh of relief when the Tanto, carrying the recovery team, finally made contact to report mission success. They had the alien surveillance platform on board and would shortly be docking with the *James Cook*. Onboard techs could not wait to get their hands on the platform and, if he was honest with himself, it had taken a conscious decision not to get his own hands dirty in the lab with them. Sometimes you just have to take a step back and let the experts get on with it.

The time had come to hear what they had discovered. Robert sat in the Briefing Room, with his command staff, all-anxious to hear the results. "XO, if you please."

Bruce stood and regarded the waiting, expectant faces. "Captain, our initial premise for the purpose of the platform appears to have been correct. It transpires the optics we assumed to be a sort of telescope are in fact a high resolution thermal imaging system."

Robert was confused "A thermal imaging system, XO? To what purpose?"

"If I could pass to Ensign Yamata, sir, she has a theory on it."

The diminutive ensign, like the rest of the crew, had only joined TDF *James Cook* at Charon Base. Where everyone else on the crew had at least one tour of duty under their belts before selection for Operation Minerva, Shizuko Yamata was fresh from the Naval Academy. Glowing progress reports had singled her

110

out, and Admiral Vadis, who had free rein with Personnel, directed her posting to Charon Base. Robert read the same reports and slotted the freshly commissioned ensign into a lieutenant's post, his faith in her had so far been fully justified. Bruce obviously felt the same way or he would not allow her to brief the command staff.

"Captain, ladies and gentlemen. Prior to the wars which nearly destroyed Earth, some of our larger nations engaged in various ongoing programs, the aim of which was to detect planets orbiting stars. What was known as Direct Thermal Imaging had an advantage over Direct Observation. Detecting an exoplanet using visible light as the detection mechanisms in the near and mid infrared are of utmost importance for characterizing the physical and chemical properties of any exoplanets and their atmospheres. I believe this was the purpose of the alien surveillance platform. But with a twist."

"A twist, Ensign?" asked Robert.

"Yes, sir." Shizuko paused, gathering herself to extol a theory, the reception for which she was unsure. "When employed by the larger nations, the system was used to detect exo-planets in orbit around distant stars. In this case, the system is within the same star system as the planet it is observing." Yamata took a breath. "Sir, I hypothesis the system was employed as a tripwire. If I could explain, sir?"

Robert nodded. "Please do, Ensign. Although I don't think I'm going to like it."

"Sir, as a civilization progresses, it expands its industrial base and population. As we observed on our arrival, Planet IV has detectable levels of the greenhouse gases in its atmosphere, all of which generate heat. If I could draw your attention to the Holo Cube…" Shizuko indicated two circular images which appeared side by side in the Holo Cube. "As you can see, the image on the left is significantly dimmer than the one on the right. The one on the left is a thermal image of Planet IV, which we took on our arrival in the system and we used to make our initial analysis of its atmosphere, the one on the right is an image of Earth."

There was a moment of silence in the room, the significance

of what the young ensign was showing them sank in. A gradual realization dawned.

"Sir," Shizuko continued, "if I was looking to identify an up and coming civilization, identify when it was becoming a potential threat, then place a surveillance platform in system with the ability to detect when it reached the equivalent of our industrial revolution – then this is how I would do it."

I knew I did not like where this was going, thought Robert. "Thank you, Ensign and good work." Shizuko bowed slightly and retook her seat.

"Unfortunately, your hypothesis may be correct." Robert came to a decision. "XO, let's get us moving back to Charon Base. We need to make the Admiralty aware of our findings as soon as possible." He paused, then continued, "Dismissed, people. Once again, good work."

Bruce stood, as did the rest of the staff, and left Robert alone in the Briefing Room. Robert contemplated the images of Planet IV and Earth side by side in the Holo Cube. Shizuko's hypothesis of the platform acting as a tripwire placed by an alien race to alert them of a key advancement in a civilization's industrial progress was indeed worrying. What would their reaction be when the wire was tripped? Would they just come and observe the planet's progress? Alternatively, would there be a more sinister purpose for their visit? The images of the nuclear-scarred surface of Rubicon, where the Saiph database was discovered, arrived unbidden into Robert's mind.

CHAPTER ELEVEN

LETTERS UNWRITTEN

CHARON BASE - ORBIT OF PLUTO - SOL SYSTEM

Admiral Aleksandr Vadis sat in his office on Charon Base. He contemplated the old style paper in front of him. If he were aware of time passing, he would have realized he had been staring at the paper for ten minutes. Sitting perfectly still, the pen in his right hand having only touched the paper once in those ten minutes: 'Dear Mr. and Mrs. Yamata'.

TDF *Vasco De Gama* was now two weeks overdue, courier drones sent to the Gama Leporis had returned without any successful contact with the ship. Lieutenant Commander Elizabeth Wilson had urged him to delay informing the crew's family of the probable loss of their loved ones, but the time had come. It was not the first time Vadis had sent young men and women into danger, he knew it would not be the last. No matter how many times he had to write to the families of those who had died or simply disappeared, presumed killed in service, it still took a little more out of his soul. Get on with it, Aleksandr! Vadis urged himself. The demanding tone of his Comm stayed his pen on the paper. Vadis pushed the accept symbol. The face of a smiling Elizabeth Wilson appeared above his desk.

"Admiral, I have the pleasure to report TDF *Vasco De Gama*

113

has arrived in system, and Captain Witsell reports all hands safe. And apologizes for her tardiness."

Vadis felt his own face break into a smile. "Inform Captain Witsell her apology is accepted and be sure to inform her she is responsible for adding years to an already old man!" He cut the link and his eyes fell to the letter in front of him, he reached down and ripped it in half before depositing it in the waste.

#

Vadis, accompanied as always by Elizabeth Wilson, sat in the main Briefing Room of Charon Base surrounded by the captains of the four survey ships and their Marine majors.

Only a scant seven months had passed since they had first arrived here at Charon Base and learned of their impending mission to take their Vanguard class ships to distant stars and look for evidence of the Saiph. What they had brought back! It caused the hairs on the back of Vadis' neck to stand up.

TDF *Henry Hudson* and Captain. Radford had found a life-bearing planet in 70 Ophiuchi. No sign of an intelligent species there yet, but analysis showed indications of Saiph meddling. Then there was the appearance of those Alcubierre driven ships identified by the Saiph database as having belonged to the Others. Not forgetting what appeared to be the establishment of some form of base on Planet II, the beginnings of a colony or perhaps a military base? The arrival of a second ship had caused Radford to make the prudent decision he had possibly pushed his luck too far and it was time to come home. Vadis would have done the same thing in his position.

TDF *Jacques Cartier* and Captain Papadomas discovered the remains of a freshly extinct civilization on Planet III in Delta Pavonis. The DNA extracts the *Jacques Cartier* returned with proved positive for Saiph intervention. From the crew's findings, it put the inhabitants of Planet II at the technology level of pre-World War 3 Earth, before their decimation by an asteroid which snuffed out all life on the planet.

Captain Lewis and TDF *James Cook* returned with, not only the news of a living, breathing world around 31 Aquilae but news of the inhabitants of Planet IV reaching the level of pre-industrial revolution by Earth standards. The discovery of the surveillance platform brought all further observation of Planet IV to a grinding halt. It proved beyond any doubt, Man was not the only one exploring the stars and looking for new life.

Ensign Yamata's hypothesis, now backed up by Vadis' own experts on Charon Base, was worrying. The surveillance platform would only trigger a message to its makers when the atmosphere of 31 Aquilae showed signs of large-scale industrialization on the planet. The question now was, what would be the reaction of the makers of the platform? His technicians had taken the platform apart and found symbols all over the inside. The linguists determined it was a language dissimilar to those found in the Saiph database. It led them to believe neither the Saiph nor the Others built it. So who had constructed it?

Finally, TDF *Vasco De Gama* and Captain Witsell. They may have missed their objective by a few thousand light years but what they had found was remarkable. A spacefaring civilization in Messier 54 had begun to colonize a neighboring planet within its own star system. Vadis was unsure the politicians back home would permit the nickname the crew of the *Vasco De Gama* had devised to describe the indigenous race, 'The Baldies', to stand. Vadis also gathered Doctor Jeff Moore was screaming for the return of George Lee, the Chief Engineer of TDF *Vasco De Gama*. Moore demanded his help to improve the current Gravity Drive, after Lee's modifications without a doubt had returned Captain Witsell and her crew home safely after a 50000 light year detour.

Overall, Vadis thought they had achieved the aim of the Vanguards mission. The Saiph had indeed interfered with the natural progression of life, within the star systems the Vanguards visited. Unfortunately, they had to weigh the fact the Vanguards had also encountered the Others against the successful mission. God only knew the implications.

"Ladies and gentlemen! If I could have your attention please!" The gathered captains and Marines simultaneously ceased their small talk, turning their full attention to the Admiral. "The information you have returned is remarkable and I thank you and your crew's for your efforts. However, it also brings troubling news. The Others are still out there. For the time being, I am halting all further survey missions. Until the threat is properly assessed by the Admiralty and the government back on Earth." Judging by the assembled faces, Vadis could see this news did not go down well. As each Vanguard returned to Charon Base there had been a mad scramble to turn the ships around, ready to head out to their next destination amongst the stars.

"On the plus side, I am authorizing shore leave on Earth for all crew members. I think two weeks should be sufficient, effective immediately." Everyone around the table smiled at this news. "Dismissed!" Vadis turned and made his way toward the hatch leading to his private office, only to stop as Wilson made to follow him. "Shore leave includes you, Elizabeth. You have been stuck on this rock with me for long enough. Go and visit the family or take a break somewhere warm."

"Why, thank you, Admiral. It has been some time since I was home."

Vadis noticed behind Elizabeth the Briefing Room was emptying, except for Robert Lewis waiting patiently. "I think Captain Lewis wants a word with you."

Elizabeth turned around and faced Lewis, who was rubbing his hands nervously.

"Commander Wilson, as the Admiral has authorized shore leave for you as well, I was wondering if you had ever visited New Zealand?"

Elizabeth felt her cheeks reddening like a schoolchild. *Control yourself,* she thought. *You are a grown woman, for Pete's sake.* "I can't say I have, Robert. But it's a place I always meant to visit."

"Perhaps we could discuss it some, over coffee," said a smiling Robert as Elizabeth led them out of the door.

As the office door sealed behind them, Vadis regarded the seated figure of Admiral Jing. He moved across the room to join him, "So what do you think, Ai?"

Vadis and Jing had been friends for as long as either of them could remember, but where Vadis had moved in the shadowy circles of intelligence, Jing had always been in the command line. He had progressed up the chain of command in the relatively small Terran Navy, with turns at the Naval Academy teaching tactics, until he found himself as head of the Naval Strategy Board. And, if what Vadis was hearing on the grapevine was correct, Ai was to be the next head of The Joint Chiefs on the retirement of General Joyce.

Jing leaned forward, placed his elbows on the table, and interlocked the fingers of both hands, a position Vadis remembered as Jing's thinking pose from the many occasions the two young officers sat late into the night discussing the strategic and tactical problems set by the instructors at the Naval Academy.

"All the data from the Vanguards is being collated and analyzed by the Strategy Board. I think I can safely say there will be a good many worried people back home. The existence of another spacefaring civilization in 'The Baldies' at their current level of development poses no immediate threat to Earth, but the fact remains we now have irreconcilable proof. The Others are out there and are capable of traveling between the stars. A worrying development," Jing stated.

Vadis nodded his head slowly in agreement. "So do we move forward with phase two of Chrysaor?"

"I think it would be only prudent, Aleksandr. The initial planning is in place. General Joyce has given his blessing for me to start scouting for a suitable base of operations in nearby star systems. If you could attach two of your Vanguards to Chrysaor then I'll get to work"

Vadis thought for a moment. "OK. When Captains Papadomas and Lewis return from shore leave, you can have TDF *Jacques Cartier* and TDF *James Cook*. Now, perhaps we can discuss how we are going to sell Chrysaor to the politicians back in the Senate."

Jing looked at his friend with a wrinkled brow, "By telling them the truth."

CHAPTER TWELVE

FULL DISCLOSURE

OFFICE OF THE PRESIDENT OF THE TERRAN REPUBLIC
GENEVA - EARTH

Rebecca Coston sat at the head of the conference table in her private office with an air of apprehension. Arrayed around the table were Senator Gillian Rae, Chairman of the Science and Technology Committee, Senator Geoffrey Rawson, Secretary of Defense, Senator Thomas Crothers, Secretary of Finance. General Joyce, Chairman of the Joint Chiefs was accompanied by Admirals Vadis and Jing. Doctor Jeff Moore and finally Doctor Patricia Bath, Head of Linguistics at Stickney Base, made up the group.

This select gathering had been at the request of General Joyce. It was he Rebecca turned to first. "General, I and my staff have had the opportunity to review the information brought back by Admiral Vadis' survey missions. I can tell you it has the top echelons of the government frightened. The discovery that 'The Others' are still out there, the possibility of another star traveling race, and another race are beginning to colonize planets within their own system, who may be on the verge of discovering star travel for themselves, and yet another race who are at the brink of their own industrial revolution."

Rebecca indicated Jeff Moore. "When Doctor Moore invented the Gravity Drive some seven years ago, we thought it promised us the means to explore the stars at our leisure. Who could have thought we would find the Rubicon Cave and all that followed from there?" Rebecca paused for a moment. "The discovery of the Saiph changed our understanding of not only the universe around us, but of ourselves and our own origins. It came as a huge mental blow to the general population. I now understand more than ever why President McMullen urged me to keep Operation Minerva a secret for as long as I could. Once it was general knowledge, I was surprised at the reaction from the public. Yes, they were annoyed we kept the operation secret, but there was also a groundswell of support for the operation and its goals. The public wanted to know if any of the other planets the Saiph visited had survived and prospered as we have."

Rebecca now settled her gaze on Joyce. If he expected to railroad her into silence then he had another thing coming.

"So before you begin, General, you need to know I have no intention of keeping the results of Admiral Vadis' surveys secret. The people have the right to know, and it is my intention to go onto the floor of the Senate tomorrow and inform them of the survey findings."

General Keyton Joyce had been a marine for nearly thirty-five years and in all that time he could not remember anyone who had a more resolute look in their eyes than Rebecca Coston at this moment. "Madam President, this is exactly what I and The Joint Chiefs want you to do."

Rebecca opened her mouth, ready to argue with her top general, when she realized what he had just said. "Excuse me, General. You want me to tell all?"

Joyce smiled. "Yes, ma'am. It's important the citizens understand the full nature of the threat we face and the actions we must take to counteract that threat."

Rebecca had not expected this reaction and was momentarily dumbstruck. With the poise of an experienced politician, she recovered quickly. "What actions would they be, General?"

"The reason I asked for this meeting today, Madam President,

120

was to go over an operation Admiral Vadis and Admiral Jing conceived and have been running in conjunction with Operation Minerva. We call it Operation Chrysaor."

Rebecca looked accusingly at Secretary Rawson. "Where you aware of this, Geoffrey? And if you were, you better have a very good reason for not telling me!"

Geoffrey Rawson was a career politician and knew how to play the blame game. "I was aware of the operation, Madam President, but I was assured by General Joyce it was only a planning exercise. I had no idea it was anything more." He redirected the president's anger onto the military men.

"Well, General?" demanded Rebecca.

Joyce took a second to look at Geoffrey, as if he were something unpleasant he found stuck on the bottom of his shoe, before turning back to the president. "Ma'am, the aim of Operation Chrysaor is four fold: firstly, to analyze the information returned by the survey ships. Secondly, to identify any threats to Earth from the analysis. Thirdly, to devise a strategy to counter these threats and finally to implement that strategy." Joyce nodded to Jing. "Admiral Jing, and this is difficult for the marine in me to acknowledge, is the foremost tactician of the Terran Defense Force. He has been running Operation Chrysaor."

"Thank you for your confidence in my abilities, General," Jing said.

"I ask him to review his findings, Admiral?" Joyce sat down as Jing stood to address the group. Jing could feel the eyes of all present focus on him.

"Madam President, ladies and gentlemen. If I could take the first and second aims of Operation Chrysaor in conjunction. In analyzing the information returned by the survey ships and employing the work of Doctor Bath in decrypting the Rubicon Saiph database we were able to compare the two and look for either similarities or discrepancies. As far as the threat posed by the civilizations in 31 Aquilae and Messier 54 are concerned, without further intelligence it cannot be fully assessed, however, the fact neither have star travel leads me to categorize any threat they may present to Earth at present as minimal."

"Reassuring at least," said Rebecca.

Jing nodded. "Agreed, Madam President. Unfortunately, the same cannot be said of whoever built the surveillance platform found in 31 Aquilae. It proves they are capable of star travel, and yet we have no idea as to their intentions. It would be prudent to take what precautions we can, although, on the other hand, we have yet no reason to believe they are hostile. As to the confirmed existence of the Others it, to use a sporting analogy, is a game changer."

"In what way, Admiral?" asked Rebecca.

"If I could ask Doctor Bath to explain, ma'am."

Rebecca looked down the table at the linguist. "Doctor?"

Doctor Patricia Bath cleared her throat before continuing. "Madam President, as you know the Saiph database provided us with a massive amount of information, so much so we were forced to prioritize. Our first priority was to discover the fate of the Saiph and find out why they lost their conflict with the Others."

"But I thought it was because they were simply vastly outnumbered?" interjected Senator Rawson.

"True," agreed Patricia. "But what we discovered during our research explains why they were so outnumbered."

"Go on, Doctor," urged Rebecca.

"Although the Saiph were able to travel between the stars, it seems they did not have any colony worlds. Yes, they visited other worlds and established research bases on some, but the vast bulk of the Saiph population remained on the home world. They had a stable population and saw no need to invest in colonies. The Saiph had been at peace with themselves for thousands of years. Add to the fact they had never come across another star traveling civilization since they began to explore the nearby stars and you can imagine how much of a shock it was when a fleet of warships, warships we now know belonged to the Others, arrived in the Saiph home system. The Saiph attempted to establish contact but the warships remained silent. They moved into orbit and began bombarding their home world. After so long at peace, the Saiph had no significant weaponry to fight back and the bombardment survivors headed for the research bases. The Others simply followed them and destroyed them as well. A few Saiph ships managed to escape. It was they who planned to tailor the DNA in the seventeen star systems listed in the database. They knew with their limited numbers, their race was doomed to extinction. They did what they could to make sure some part of them survived. Scattered around the star systems they visited, they left databases, like the one we found on Rubicon. Hoping, one day, one of their protégés would find it and use it to defend themselves from the Others."

As Patricia retook her seat, Jing stood.

"Madam President. This brings me onto the third aim of Operation Chrysaor: to devise a strategy to counter the perceived threats. If the Others were to appear in the Solar System tomorrow we would find ourselves in the same position as the Saiph. We have no established colonies outside our own star system." He indicated the Chairman and Vadis. "Our main goal must be the survival of the human race. We see the easiest way to do this, in the short term, is the immediate establishment of self-sufficient colonies outside our own solar system. We already know there are planets out there, such as Planet II of 70 Ophiuchi, which will sustain human life and have no indigenous intelligent species of their own."

"But Admiral, isn't Planet II where Captain Radford encountered the Others?" interjected Rebecca.

"Yes ma'am but they can't be everywhere. The Baldies of Messier 54 are such an example." Jing activated the Holo Cube and a star chart appeared hovering over the center of the table. "This is a diagram of what's known as the Local Bubble, a region within sixteen point three light years of Earth. Within this bubble, in addition to our own solar system, there are fifty-five stellar systems. Within these systems, there is a total of fifty-six hydrogen-fusing stars. Despite their relative closeness to us, only thirteen percent can be viewed with the naked eye. Besides the Sun, only three are first magnitude stars: Alpha Centauri, Sirius and Procyon. Admiral Vadis has already consented to two of the

Vanguard survey ships being seconded to Operation Chrysaor. It is my intention, at the earliest opportunity, to send them as a pair, in case of mishap or an encounter with the Others, to scout these three systems for a suitable world on which to establish a human colony."

Rebecca caught the eye of Gillian Rae, who nodded her approval. "OK Admiral. I can see the sense in your approach. I thereby approve the sending of the two survey ships. But the logistics behind establishing a colony are massive, never mind the expense." In her peripheral vision, she saw Thomas Crothers' gaze fixed on the image in the Holo Cube. The president could also see the financial planning involved in the establishment of the colony running through his mind. A plan began to form in her own head as to whom she should entrust with the planning for the colony. *The party leaders are not going to like it*, she thought. She could see Jing was waiting for her permission to continue. "Please go on, Admiral."

"Yes, ma'am. Secondly, in conjunction with Science and Technology, we need to begin a crash program into weapons research."

Senator Rawson tried to hide a grin at the news as he considered the extra power and influence he was about to gain. Jing chose to ignore him.

"The designs held in the Saiph database are untried in real life. They only exist as technical drawings. With their main industrial base destroyed on the home world, the Saiph never got a chance to build them, let alone try them. We need to incorporate their technology into ours – faster than we have been doing. Doctor Moore and his team have been working miracles but we need to expand his team, as rapidly as possible, to exploit the advantages of the Saiph technology."

Rebecca turned to Senator Rae. "Well, Gillian? Can we do it?"

Geoffrey Rawson made a small coughing noise. "Madam President, surely the exploitation of the Saiph weapon technology would best be handled by Defense?"

Rebecca was beginning to regret allowing the party to force

Rawson on her as Secretary for Defense.

"May I suggest a joint research and development team: Science and Technology to do the research and building while Defense review and prioritize the research and carry out testing," suggested Senator Rae.

"Sounds like a good plan," said Rebecca, smiling at Senator Rae and realizing the good senator had not lost her head for politics.

Senator Rawson looked rather crestfallen. "Yes... Madam President."

"Good, that's that sorted. Anything else, Admiral?"

"Just three more things, ma'am. We need to halt forthwith the surveys being conducted by Admiral Vadis and Operation Minerva."

Rebecca's eyes widened with surprise. "But why Admiral? Surely it's more important than ever to find out what happened to the remaining worlds the Saiph visited?"

"True, Madam President, however, sending survey ships to known star systems the Saiph have visited increases the chance of an encounter with the Others. In turn, this increases the chance they discover Earth's location, and, as I discussed earlier, we cannot afford for that to happen until we are sure we can handle them."

Forced to agree, Rebecca reluctantly nodded and replied, "Understood and agreed, Admiral. Next?"

"If we are to assess the full threat the Others pose to us, we require good, sound intelligence. Currently, all we have is the contents of the Saiph database. Having discussed it with The Joint Chiefs, we are in agreement we should employ the two remaining Vanguards to insert a Marine Force Reconnaissance team onto Planet II of 70 Ophiuchi to observe and report back on the Others base there."

"A big step, Admiral, are we sure the Marines can get in and out undetected?"

General Joyce spoke up. "There are no guarantees with this sort of thing, ma'am. Nonetheless, those marines are the best at what they do. I have every confidence in their ability to complete the mission."

Rebecca was the first to admit the reputation of the Force Reconnaissance Marines was the best, but still... "I don't know if I'm comfortable with the suggestion."

Joyce answered for the military men. "We don't see any other way to get the intelligence we need, ma'am,"

Rebecca was still unsure. However, sometimes you have to take a leap of faith. After a thoughtful pause, she said, "OK General, Admiral. I bow to your superior knowledge on military matters. And your final request, Admiral?"

"This is more to prepare you for what may be coming than for immediate implementation, Madam President."

Rebecca did not like the sound of this. "Stop beating about the bush, Admiral, and get on with it please."

"Very well, ma'am. We must consider there will be a requirement for a massive increase in the size of the Terran Defense Force in the near future. At present, we are little more than a coastguard and if, and I do say *if*, we are to face a conflict, we simply do not have the strength to fight more than a skirmish before our enemy, if they are of any significant force, brush aside our forces. The numbers are against us, Madam President. Our standing forces need to be increased, and these things take time. We have a solid core of experience to build on, but to build any sort of fighting force we need time and manpower and, to be blunt, the money to pay for it all."

Rebecca looked over at Senator Crothers. "Well, Thomas? How to pay for things is your area. So what do you think?"

Thomas Crothers looked around the table uncomfortably. He did not like being in the spotlight, despite being a politician. "Madam President, our current standard of living is higher now than it's ever been in our recorded history. Our population is rising at an exponential rate and, to be honest with you, if we want to avoid overcrowding and keep the standard of living at its current level we would soon have no choice but to look for planets to colonize anyway. The threat from the Others is only making our decision to colonize come faster. Our excess industrial capacity could very quickly be converted to military use and with some time we would be quite capable of building dedicated production facilities for the military with minimal effect on civilian output." Thomas paused and regarded those around the table and shrugged his shoulders. "The only thing I can't help you with is the manpower."

"Thank you, Thomas. Well, gentlemen, it would seem Thomas has a point." Rebecca looked from Joyce to the other two Admirals. "Do you have an answer to the personnel issue?"

Joyce met his president's eyes steadily. "Madam President, ever since the human race almost caused its own demise, we've been ingrained with the importance of the continued existence of the race as a whole. Maybe it's time to tell the people what we face and see if we really are ready to put the greater good before the good of the individual."

#

OFFICE OF THE CHAIRMAN OF THE JOINT CHIEFS OF STAFF GENEVA - EARTH

General Keyton Joyce let out a non-committal sound as he placed his coffee down on the table in his private office and turned off the sound on the Holo Cube on which he'd watched President Coston make her address to the Senate. He, Admirals Vadis and Jing had looked on in silence as President Coston outlined the survey ships' findings and then went on to explain the government's response. The Senate had sat in polite silence up until the point where the president had announced the immediate expansion of the Terran Defense Force, and then the Speaker of the House had no choice but to intervene and restore order. It had taken nearly ten minutes before the Speaker reinstated calm, allowing the president to continue. Now with her speech over, it seemed every Senator in the House clamored to speak.

Keyton turned to his two guests. "Well, gentlemen, it looks like the proverbial cat is out of the bag. I think it's safe to say we are about to live out the ancient Chinese curse."

Aleksandr chuckled. "I hope you live in interesting times," he quoted.

"Exactly," answered Keyton with a short laugh of his own before becoming serious again. "The plans for the future structure of the Defense Force, with emphasis on the Navy and Marines, Ai has come up with will be implemented forthwith. We will deal with the manpower shortfalls as and when they arise. I intend to create a post of Special Inspector with the rank of Rear Admiral working directly from this office. Their job will be to handle any problems arising from officers who become, how should I say? An obstacle to progress. We do not have the time to pussyfoot around, gentleman. Not with the fate of the human race at stake. You either get with the program or you will find yourself unemployed." Aleksandr and Ai both understood what was about to happen to the Defense Force was a necessary evil and found themselves agreeing it needed to happen as quickly as possible. The threat the Others presented was too great. Keyton could see the agreement in the faces of the two Admirals. "Unfortunately, Aleksandr, the first casualty comes from your command. With immediate effect Lieutenant Commander Wilson is promoted to Rear Admiral and transferred to this office." Joyce grinned. "She's my hatchet man now, Aleksandr."

Aleksandr grinned in return. "Only if I get to tell her she's just skipped three ranks and got her flag."

"Deal," said Keyton. "Now, back to business. Ai, what about fleet construction?"

Ai touched a control and the scene from the Senate floor changed to a warship. "This is the design from the Deimos Yards I prefer. They named it the Talos class cruiser. 452 meters long, fifty-seven meters at the beam, weighing in at 24400 tonnes. It carries three Tanto shuttles and has a crew complement of 710."

Above the table, the image of the warship rotated giving Keyton and Aleksandr a good look at the first true warship Earth had built to fight amongst the stars. "As you can see, sir," continued Ai, "the designers at Deimos have combined as much Saiph technology R and D can reverse engineer with the latest version of the Gravity Drive from Doctor Moore's research, to produce the Talos class. Starting with the known capabilities of

128

the Others' ships, we tasked the designers to develop a hull which could defeat an Others' ship in one to one combat and operate as part of a combat group.

They factored in speed, maneuverability, survivability and lethality. The Talos class mounts the same twin turret particle cannon as the Vanguard class but it has twenty-four such turrets spaced around the hull in five rings giving the Talos a three sixty degree arc of fire with a minimum of ten turrets being able to engage at any one time."

Aleksandr let out a low whistle. "A lot of fire power in a small package, Ai."

Ai nodded. "True, and there's more! We noticed the Others use bombardment to reduce any ground based target, so the Talos class will be fitted with a limited number of experimental High Velocity Missiles, or HVMs. They use a miniature Gravity Drive, similar to our courier drones, to deliver a small fusion device to a target. As it stands, the mathematics involved in using the Gravity Drive in such a tactical role is causing a few headaches, but Doctor Moore assures me his team are nearly there. To be honest, I'd rather have the HVMs as they are, than wait for a perfected version."

"OK makes sense." Keyton gave Ai a knowing look. "But you still have something up your sleeve. So what is it?"

"I never could keep secrets," said Ai. "May I draw your attention to the bow of the Talos. See the two, large projections side by side?" Keyton and Vadis both nodded. These projections had prompted Keyton's query in the first place. "You are looking at the largest grazers ever mounted on a human warship."

Aleksandr let out an excited "Surely not! The power requirements alone when coupled with the rest of the weaponry must be staggering!"

Ai now smiled openly. "True, but those smart designers at Deimos have used Saiph technology to build in four separate and independent power sources. One for the Gravity Drive, one for general ships systems, one for all the other weapons systems and one for the sole use of the grazers – giving them a rate of fire of three shots per minute. The test firing resulted in a million watts

129

per square centimeter, or put into perspective, one shot from the grazer will pass straight through the best armor on any ship we can produce, without even slowing down. And the ship will be left an expanding ball of plasma from the energy transfer."

"Very impressive, Ai," commented Keyton. "How quickly can we get a Talos from the drawing board through construction and into operation?"

Ai consulted his PAD for a moment. "For the first Talos, simply because it's a prototype, Deimos are currently estimating about ten months on construction. The Admiralty estimate three months for trials. So for the first ship to come on line, thirteen months in total. But..." as Ai's smile widened, "due to the modular construction employed in the Talos, Deimos are estimating their build time, when they start to benefit from the president's decision to expand our construction facilities, will eventually lead to a launch completed Talos every ninety days."

"My God!" exclaimed Aleksandr "Phenomenal!"

"The beauty of automated standardized construction," replied Ai, "The designers at Deimos have bigger and better things planned, and this particular design is only the first one to come off the production lines. The only problem I can envisage is one we have already identified – manpower."

Keyton changed the image on the Holo Cube back to a view of the Senate floor and pointed a finger in its direction. "That, gentlemen is a problem for the politicians. Our problem is this expansion, which must be handled well," gesturing at the Holo Cube and the still clamoring politicians. "We'll must head off anyone who thinks he can become a politician in uniform. There's going to be a lot of rapid promotions, and we need reliable people in command slots who can handle the pressure outside forces exert." Both the admirals understood what he was talking about – political interference in military decisions.

"If I may make a suggestion, sir?" interrupted Ai. Keyton nodded his assent and Ai continued. "We have a small pool of experienced flag officers, using Admiral Vadis as an example, some have been reactivated due to the exigencies of service. What I suggest is a board made up of a selection of these

130

officers, none of whom has any current political affiliations, as they are retired, and headed by an officer who we all know personally. And, if I may be so bold, scares the crap out of the Senate."

Keyton and Aleksandr looked at Ai before turning to look at each other and laughing aloud.

The three men held the mental image of the Senate faces when informed Admiral Helset was to be reactivated.

CHAPTER THIRTEEN

ENEMY

TDF HENRY HUDSON - 70 OPHIUCHI

Admiral Jing's brief to John Radford and Ruth Witsell had initially excited John. Excited by the prospect of taking TDF *Henry Hudson* and TDF *Vasco De Gama* back to Planet II of 70 Ophiuchi and inserting the Force Recon Marines onto the surface for a closer look at the 'Others'. However, as he had gotten to the initial planning stages with Ruth and the two Marine Majors, Alec Murray from the *Henry Hudson* and Vladimir Egnorov from the *Vasco De Gama*, it did not take long for John's excitement to wear off, replaced by an impending sense of dread.

Six months ago, on his last visit to the system, TDF *Henry Hudson* had detected the first ship belonging to the Others. From an undetectable position, the *Henry Hudson* observed the Others approach Planet II, begin shuttling equipment to the planet surface and start construction of some kind of base. However, a second ship had arrived only 275,000 kilometers to starboard. It changed course toward TDF *Henry Hudson* and powered up its weapons. If it had not been for the alertness of his Tactical Officer, Lieutenant Falconer, and the quick thinking of the Navigator, Lieutenant Danino, the *Henry Hudson* and her crew might not be here today.

John shook off his melancholic mood and returned his concentration to the present. On his tactical display, he could see the *Henry Hudson* approaching Planet II from the opposite side of the planet from where the Others had been establishing their base. TDF *Vasco De Gama* was in step, slightly behind and off to port. As John was senior to Ruth, the ultimate command of the mission had fallen on him. Communication between the two ships was strictly by whisker laser. Both ships were rigged for silent running with all electromagnetic emissions kept to a minimum. Both ships were employing the chameleon system to hide the ships from any prying eyes, both optical and electronic. John could only hope it worked as well as last time.

Lieutenant Cai at Communications interrupted his thinking. "Captain, Captain Witsell on whisker, sir."

"Go ahead, Ruth," said John as Ruth's face appeared alongside the tactical display in his Holo Cube.

Ruth looked as apprehensive as John. "Major Egnorov informs me he and his marines are aboard the Tanto and ready to go."

John glanced across at Tactical and got an affirmative nod from Lieutenant Falconer before addressing Ruth. "Major Murray also indicates ready. Best we get on with it then." John gave the order. "Tactical. Inform the marines to launch. I want a full passive lock kept on both Tantos until they cross the radio horizon."

"Aye aye, sir," replied Falconer.

John's concentration returned to Ruth. "And so the waiting begins."

Ruth gave him a small smile. "Don't sweat it, John. They know what they're doing." She cut the connection.

"I hope so," John said to himself, "Stay safe, Alec."

\#

Major Alec Murray, Marine Force Recon, Terran Defense Force, was forced to admit, as he surveyed the Others' base, he loved his job.

What other job in the world sends you to a distant star system, occupied by potential hostile forces, with God only knew what capabilities while six, (yeah, count them *six!*) 1700 meter long alien ships held geosynchronous orbit above your head? All while you lay dug into a hillside, covered in sheets of chameleon material with only one other marine for company. Murray laughed quietly so as not to wake the sleeping form of Corporal Semple beside him.

Alec and Vladimir's plan for what was termed a Close Target Reconnaissance of The Others' base was straightforward. The two Tanto shuttles had approached the base from opposite directions, until they detected emissions from the base, at which point the Tantos immediately grounded.

Group One, the marines of TDF *Henry Hudson*, split into a rear party of six marines under Gunny Young, to protect the Tanto and to act as an extraction force if Alec got into trouble. Alec took the remaining twelve marines of Group One forward, five kilometers from the base, at the Final Rendezvous Point (FRV). He split them into six by two man teams to form a loose semi-circle around the base and find suitable hide locations from which to observe.

Vladimir did the same with his marines, Group Two. Both groups were to stay in position for three planetary days before extracting to their respective FRVs, then head for the Tantos to return to the waiting Vanguards.

The only drawback to the plan was that apart from the marine beside him, Alec had no knowledge of what was happening to any of the other teams. All the Wraith suits the marines wore were in strict emissions control mode to avoid any chance of detection. The marines were under orders to break radio silence only if they came into contact and needed to fight their way out. In which case, all bets were off. Each team of two marines was to return to their FRV ASAP, wait for thirty minutes and, no matter how many marines made it, the senior man was to take command to get the marines back to the Tantos at best speed. It might seem callous, but on receipt of the initial contact report the Tantos would only remain on the planet for twelve hours, if you were late, your ride home would leave you.

Over the past two days, Alec and Corporal Semple obtained valuable intelligence on the composition of The Others' base. Observing construction techniques, identifying personnel accommodation, power plants, communication centers and what looked like weapon positions. Murray instinctively ducked as a shuttle passed virtually directly overhead at an altitude of about 300 meters. The Others appeared to be clock watchers: every four hours another shuttle would approach the base from exactly the same direction and land at a large shuttle facility at the western edge of the base, then offload its cargo before leaving along the exact same route it had approached on two hours later. Semple had suggested either the Others were anal about traffic management or the route the shuttles were using was a cleared lane through an air defense zone. Murray was inclined to agree with the latter. Murray settled back down for his remaining hour on watch before waking Semple.

#

Alec woke to an insistent nudging in his ribs, a brightly lit landscape revealed itself as he opened his eyes. Something must be wrong, his next shift was to start on the approach of nightfall. Alec turned his head toward Semple, his straight arm indicated to a small bluff maybe 250 meters from their dug in hide. Semple then made a fist, inverted it and stuck his thumb out, the hand signal for enemy. *Crap,* thought Alec, *Had the Others detected them somehow?*

Alec looked back in the direction of the bluff, as he watched two, what Alec could only describe as hovering sleds appear from around the bluff. Alec had observed the sleds moving around the perimeter of the base for the last couple of days but they had never ventured more than a kilometer from the perimeter. The sleds were rectangular, about three meters long and maybe a meter across with a bubble shape just short of a meter high toward the rear of each machine. Protruding from each side of the sled was the unmistakable shape of weapons pods. The sleds were flying maybe three meters apart and they were headed away at an angle from Alec's position. Neither

135

appeared to have noticed the marines. There was no doubt in Alec's mind the two sleds were some sort of The Others' clearance patrol sent out to sweep the area within line of sight of the base. Granted, this was the first patrol of this type they had seen since they had arrived, but it would probably not be the last. Alec came to a decision. As soon as the sleds were out of sight they would pack up their gear, make for the FRV and await the rest of the Marines before heading back to the Tanto.

Ten minutes later, with all their gear stowed, Alec and Semple were on the move. Alec's worst nightmare played out as the shrill tone in his helmet informed him one of his teams was in contact. Semple immediately went to ground scanning the area for threats, knowing Murray would be preoccupied trying to sort out what was happening. Murray's heads-up display flashed the names of two Marines in contact: Baker and Rodriguez. The display listed the distance and bearing to their location. Unbidden, Alec's head turned to the bearing, as if he could see the two marines.

What he did see was a large black cloud mushroom into the air, closely followed by a loud boom. The marines' names began to flash red in the heads-up display. The warning tone started up again. Alec cancelled the tone and cleared the display. He could do nothing for them now. Semple tapped his arm and indicated The Others' base. Alec used his helmet optics to zoom in. He could see more sleds moving from the base in the direction of the explosion, this time accompanied by larger hovering vehicles – troop transports if Alec was to make a guess. *From bad to worse,* thought Alec.

Alec gave the clenched fist jerking motion to Semple, indicating they were to double time it. Both men set off at a run, their Wraith suits building up to a steady and sustainable forty kilometers an hour. They covered the distance to the FRV in seven minutes and settled into firing positions to await the arrival of the remaining marines. They did not wait long. Alec was just catching his breath when his Wraith suit warned him a whisker laser, using the correct Identify Friend or Foe (IFF) challenge, had hit him. Murray ordered his suit to acknowledge and two

Marines appeared, as if out of nowhere, slotting themselves into firing positions expanding the perimeter of the FRV. Quickly, three more pairs of Marines arrived. IFF issued its challenge to each pair before Alec acknowledged and granted permission to enter the FRV.

Alec moved to the center of the marines and tapped Semple's boot. The Corporal turned to face him and Alec pointed a straight arm in the direction of the waiting Tanto. Semple gave him the OK signal, then tapped the marine to his right and moved off in the direction indicated by Alec. The marine Semple had tapped allowed Semple to get a few metres ahead before they, in turn, tapped the next marine to his right, stood up and moved off. Each marine repeated the action until all the marines were on the move. Third in line was Alec. Not a spoken word or an electronic emission made during the whole process. No need to give the Others a sniff of their location.

The marines had been moving at a steady rate for over an hour when Alec's suit buzzed for attention. The heads-up display indicated a low threat warning. It detected an increase in electromagnetic radiation. The onboard computer classed the source as a ground search radar of unidentified class off to the right of his line of march. Alec kept an eye on it but the source did not grow in intensity. He kept the marines moving. After a few minutes, the suit buzzed for attention once more. On the display, Alec saw a second source appear, this time off to his left. Alec did not like what he was seeing, he had an enemy contact on his right and now another on his left, time to step up the pace. Alec tapped the marine in front of him and indicated for him to double time it. Turning, Alec made sure the marine behind him got the same message.

Semple waited a few seconds to ensure the message reached the last man, then set off at double time. Alec's suit buzzed for attention a third time. He saw a third source appear on the display, this one behind him. The Others were boxing him in. It was still over fifty kilometers to the Tanto. *Forget covert!* Murray thought. He activated his Comms, keeping the power low so it only broadcast to the marines with him. "The enemy have us on three sides, they either haven't got a blocking force into position in front of us yet or the blocking force is in position and we're going to run right into them. Unfortunately, they are between us and our ride home. Keep your eyes open and watch each other's backs — this could get messy very fast. None of the marines replied, they had all seen the same thing on their own display and were all experienced enough to read the signs.

Alec's suit buzzed and on the heads-up display, the blocking force appeared 300 meters ahead of them. The Marines went to ground as Alec used his optics to scan the small ridgeline concealing the enemy. There! A slight movement in the vegetation. Alec switched to thermal imaging and the shapes of twenty or so Others were clearly outlined. The darker shape of long weapons they were aiming in his direction stood out in the display. Alec checked the groups to his left and right. They seemed to be holding position, as was the group to the rear, not wanting to walk into the crossfire from their own ambush, no doubt. Alec sent the information to his marines' suits so they could see what they faced, before opening his Comms link.

"OK marines. Here is the plan. We move forward in a skirmish line, using the chameleon units in the suits to get as close as possible. On either effective enemy fire or on my command, we break into our pairs and fire and maneuver through the enemy line. Once you are through, you hightail it to the Tanto and tell Gunny Young he is to run for the *Henry Hudson* at the slightest sniff of the enemy or at his own discretion. The intelligence is more important than any of us, understood?" A line of green lights on his heads-up display acknowledged his orders. "On the count of three, cross deck all the information you have to every suit. Stand by. One, two, three." Again, a line of green lights illuminated in his display as his suit acknowledged receipt of the data from the other marines. "OK marines. Let's move out."

The marines shook down into a skirmish line, each marine advancing up the ridgeline a few meters apart, with Alec in the center. The marines slowly approached the enemy position with their suits set to thermal vision. The Others' position was clearly visible to their front still with no indication they had detected them. Only twenty meters from the enemy, Alec's suit screamed at him as something his suit classified as a low intensity laser designator struck him. Somebody was pointing something nasty at him.

Alec swung his plasma rifle around and fired a short burst in the direction of the source of the laser. There was a satisfying scream, quickly cut off, a strike from a plasma rifle tended to kill quickly.

Alec's marines interpreted his action as their queue to break into fire and maneuver. One marine in each pair would provide covering fire while his partner moved a few meters forward, he would then fire while the first man advanced. It was an effective way to cover ground quickly while laying down constant fire. The marines advanced onto the ridgeline like the wrath of God, anything moving instantly received fire. The marines moved through the enemy position and broke for the waiting Tanto.

Alec looked into his heads-up display as it called for his urgent attention. His heart sank. The three remaining enemy forces were closing on his position. The suit projected all three would combine and intercept them while the marines were still fifteen kilometers short of the Tanto. Alec activated his comm link. "Corporal Semple. You plus Marine Chin, will continue to the Tanto. The rest of us will go firm here and attempt to delay the enemy."

Semple knew better than to argue. Instead, he grabbed Alec by the hand and shook it as he said, "Aye aye, sir. Good luck."

Alec watched as Semple and Chin ran, at the suits' best speed, for the waiting Tanto, carrying the precious information bought by the lives of his men.

The Marines set themselves up ready to receive the oncoming enemy force. Alec's suit was telling him it estimated nine sleds and three troop carriers. If the enemy forces he had faced on the ridge were of a similar makeup, then he should be facing upwards of sixty troops. Alec looked around at his seven marines. *Yeah!* He thought and a smile creased his face. He had them outnumbered!

The enemy forces came on at speed with the sleds in the lead. Alec let them close to within 100 meters before opening fire. The concentrated fire of Marine plasma rifles cut through whatever armor the sleds had. Within seconds, there were seven smoking craters in front of the marines' position, the surviving two sleds searched for cover, to no avail. The marines switched fire and brought the two sleds crashing down. Thick black smoke from burning sleds now obscured the area in front of the marines, the heat from the fires interfered with the suits' thermal imagery. The marines resorted to the Mark One Eyeball. The second the marines opened fire on the sleds, the troop transports went to ground, there was no sign of the troops Alec was certain they were carrying.

A series of explosions, just short of the marines' position, warned Alec of advancing troops. They were firing what seemed to be some kind of kinetic energy weapon from a small roof mounted turret. Fortunately, the fire was not accurate, but it was enough to keep the marines heads down, sufficiently distracting them for a few seconds —all they needed. A cry from a marine at the far left of their fire position enlightened Alec as to what had happened to the enemy who had been on the troop transports. They had left their transport behind and were attempting to outflank him. The telltale red in his display advised Alec, sadly, the marine's fight was over.

Alec quickly determined he had to swing his position or the enemy would roll him up. Just as he was on the verge of giving the order, his helmet filled with the voice of Gunny Young.

"Marines! Danger close! Get small!"

Alec curled into the smallest ball possible and hugged the ground. The entire world around him shook. Buffeted by explosions, flying fragments impacted his suit. The noise seemed to go on for an eternity but Alec knew it could only have been a few seconds, and then all was quiet.

The commanding voice of Gunny Young came through the comm link again. "Marines, count off."

Alec heard himself say "Murray here," and listened as his six surviving marines called in. Alec got to his feet and looked at the

140

devastation around his position. The enemy troop transports were burning shells, the dismounted troops cut down where they had stood by the now grounded Tanto. The troop hatch opened, Gunny Young stepped down and walked toward Alec as the marines Alec had left with the Gunny fanned out eagerly seeking new targets.

Young stopped in front of Alec. "Heard you needed a lift, sir."

Despite himself, Alec smiled. "Appreciate it, Gunny. I take it you have Semple and Chin on board?"

"I do, sir. Although Corporal Semple is in restraints at the moment."

"Dare I ask why, Gunny?" asked Alec

"He was very insistent on returning for you and the others, sir, after he ensured Chin's suit had all the data and it was good to be transferred to the Tanto. Went as far as using bad language to me, sir. You know I cannot abide bad language. I was forced to persuade him to remain on board. Medic says his teeth can be put back in when we get back to the *Henry Hudson* and the bruising should clear up nicely."

Alec could not help but let out a small laugh. "What can I say? He appreciates a good officer."

It was the Gunny's turn to smile. "Well, if I ever find one, I'll let you know, sir. Now, if you want to get yourself and the boys aboard, I'll give the area a quick once over and see if we can recover anything useful. Then I suggest we beat a hasty retreat for the *Henry Hudson* and get the hell out of this system – before the big boys up there make their presence felt."

Alec took a moment to look around. His gaze fell on a body of one of the Others and he moved closer to get his first good look at the enemy. The body looked to be about two meters tall and was covered head to toe in body armor, not dissimilar to the marines' own Wraith suits. Pale, almost translucent skin peaked out through a hole in the chest armor, penetrated by the impact of a Marine rifle. Alec used his boot knife to unseal The Others' helmet and opened it to reveal a broad face with two large eyes mounted further apart than a human. There was no appearance of a nose, and then Alec noticed what looked very like fish gills on either side of the neck. The mouth was more rounded than a human and contained an impressive set of razor sharp teeth. Any further examination of the body would have to wait. The Others' ships in orbit had already demonstrated they could lay waste to vast areas of a planet's surface if they so wanted.

"Let's get to it, Gunny, and make sure we secure some of the enemy remains and equipment, then we're out of here."

"Aye aye, sir." Gunny Young started passing orders to the marines while Alec headed for a seat on the Tanto. They were not clear of this yet.

#

John Radford was asleep in his quarters when the urgent comm tone woke him, he was up and dressing as he pressed the accept button. "Captain."

The face of Lieutenant Falconer his tactical officer appeared in the Holo Cube. "Sir, passive sensors have picked up the returning Tantos. They're coming in at full speed, even a blind man could see their emissions."

Not good, thought John, *They must be in trouble.* "Contact the *Vasco De Gama* by whisker laser and tell them both ships are to make for a shortest time intercept with the Tantos. Sound battle stations. Full emissions protocol remains in place till we know what we're dealing with here." The wail of battle stations erupted throughout the *Henry Hudson*. The automated computer voice called the crew to their stations as John ran for the bridge.

John entered the bridge, immediately calling to Lieutenant Falconer. "Update please, Tactical." His Holo Cube sprang to life, displaying two Tantos moving at speed toward them. John wondered what spooked Alec and his marines so much they were throwing all caution to the wind, running at full speed. A fresh icon, circled in red, appeared in his display, promptly followed by another and then another.

"Computer is designating the new ships as Bogies One, Two and Three. They match the size and shape of The Others' ship we ran into last time we were here. Power output shows their

142

weapons are hot," reported Falconer. Now John knew why the Tantos were running. The Others' ships were monsters compared to the lightly armed shuttles.

"Time till Bogey One can take the shuttles under fire?"

Falconer did some quick calculations. "Sir, our best guess at their armament would put the shuttles in weapons range of Bogey One in... eleven minutes with Bogies Two and Three entering weapons range in... sixteen minutes. Sir, if the computer's reading on the Others' weapons power output is even half right, a shuttle would not survive a direct hit."

John looked over at Lieutenant Danino, "Navigation. Time till we intercept the shuttles?"

Danino turned to look at his captain, "Fourteen minutes, sir."

Too late, thought John, *and there is nothing I can do about it.*

"Captain,"Lieutenant Cai's voice at Comms cut into John's thoughts. "I have Major Murray for you."

The face of Alec Murray appeared in John's Holo Cube. *What do I say to him? I cannot get to him in time...*

Alec spoke before John could say anything. "Captain, we've run the numbers here. We know you won't get to us before we enter their firing range so I'm transmitting all the intelligence we gathered to you now."

John got a nod from Cai. "We've got it, Alec. Tell your pilots to go to evasive maneuvers, just buy us a few minutes. We can get to you."

Murray smiled at him. "Captain, you know the *Henry Hudson* has as little chance of taking on one of those monsters as we do in a shuttle. You have the intelligence. Get it home. Don't let our lives have been for nothing." The signal cut off. John stared at where the face of his friend had been. *There must be something he could do?*

Cai called for his attention, "Sir, *Vasco De Gama* for you."

A view of the bridge of TDF *Vasco De Gama* appeared in front of John. There was a bustle of activity around the navigator's position as Chief Engineer, Taylor, worked on a PAD and entered data into the navigation console before turning to Ruth Witsell. "Yes, I can do it, ma'am."

"Thank you, Chief." Ruth turned to the pickup. "John, we think we can buy you some time."

"Tell me! I only need a few minutes and we can recover both shuttles," demanded John.

Ruth gave a small shrug. "By doing what needs to be done." She paused and looked down for just a moment before taking a deep breath and looking John square in the eye. "Get my people home John." She was gone.

"Captain, the *Vasco De Gama* has activated her Gravity Drive. She's gone," said a stunned Falconer. "No. Hold on... I have her again. She's dropped back into normal space. My God, sir! She's directly behind Bogey One, range 30000 meters," Falconer said in disbelief.

John spun to Cai at Comms. "Get me the *Vasco De Gama* now!"

Falconer began a running commentary. "*Vasco De Gama* is firing her particle cannon. Direct hit on Bogey One's drive. Bogey One is slowing."

"Get out of there, Ruth," John heard himself shout.

"*Vasco De Gama* is ignoring our hails sir," said Cai.

Falconer continued her commentary. "Bogey One is returning fire. Computer is designating the return fire as a Q Switching laser. *Vasco De Gama* is taking hits but the ablative armor appears to be holding. Attitude change from Bogey One: she's turning broadside on. Multiple separations from Bogey One. Computer is designating them missiles. *Vasco De Gama* Laser Area Denial Systems are going active and engaging."

John turned to Danino "Our time to shuttle intercept?"

Danino did not need to check. "Ten minutes, sir."

John calculated the math in his head. "Comms! Raise the *Vasco De Gama*. Tell them to get the hell out of there, now! They've bought us enough time." John saw a glimpse of light at the end of the tunnel. Maybe *Vasco De Gama*'s gamble would pay off.

A shout from Tactical. "Bogey Two is engaging the *Vasco De Gama*!"

John looked into the Holo Cube, just in time to see an energy beam cut the *Vasco De Gama* cleanly in half. Shortly after, the remains exploded as containment failed on the drives and weapon systems.

There was a deathly silence on the bridge of TDF *Henry Hudson*. The stunned crew stared, in shock, at where their sister ship had just perished along with 135 men and women. John broke the silence, trying hard to keep his anger in check. "Snap out of it, people! We have two shuttle loads of marines who still need us and we're short on time. Let's not waste it."

The bridge crew moved to carry out his orders. There would be time to mourn their dead later. For now, the living took precedence.

CHAPTER FOURTEEN

CHANGES

ORBIT OF PLANET II - ALPHA CENTAURI B
4.37 LIGHT YEARS FROM EARTH

"Well? What do you think, Captain?" asked Bruce Torrance from his seat on the bridge of the TDF *James Cook*.

Robert Lewis regarded the light blue and white planet centered in the Holo Cube as he contemplated the enormity of the decision resting on his shoulders. This was the third star system the *James Cook*, accompanied by the TDF *Jacques Cartier*, had visited in its search for an Earth like planet to be man's first colony outside his home system.

The first, Sirius, some eight point five eight light years from Earth, had proved to be a dead system. Any planet capable of bearing life became desolate when Sirius B had lost its outer layers when it had collapsed and became a white dwarf, the star's outer layers spreading through the star system like an unstoppable tidal wave of star plasma and radiation scrubbing clean all before it. The second, Procyon, some eleven point four six light years from Earth was deemed unsuitable as none of the system planets were found to have a stable orbit, almost certainly due to the main star's white dwarf companion, which was close enough to the orbit of the planets to influence them.

This led the search to Alpha Centauri. One of the brightest stars in the southern skies, it is the nearest stellar system to our own solar system, only four point three light years away. Alpha Centauri is actually a triple star. It consists of two stars, similar to the Sun, orbiting close to each other, designated Alpha Centauri A and B, and a more distant and fainter red component known as Proxima Centauri, where almost a decade ago, humans discovered the Rubicon Cave. Since the nineteenth century, astronomers have speculated about planets orbiting the stars which make up Alpha Centauri. The invention of the Gravity Drive meant Man at last was capable of travel and could observe for himself. The recent clashes in the 70 Ophiuchi system, the loss of TDF *Vasco De Gama* and all on board and the threat posed by 'The Others' to humanity all increased the impetus to settle beyond the home system. Alpha Centauri B is very similar to the Sun, but slightly smaller and less bright, with four planets orbiting it. One was so far from the star it was a frozen snowball, another was a gas giant, one orbited so close to the star its surface was molten, and then there was Planet II. The newly discovered Planet II the *James Cook* and *Jacques Cartier* were currently orbiting had a mass of a little more than Earth. The planet orbited about 106,000,000 kilometers away from the star, closer than Venus to the Sun in the Solar System. The orbit of the other bright component of the double star, Alpha Centauri A, keeps it hundreds of times further away, but it would still be a very brilliant object in the Planet II skies.

"The geologists say the planet has just come out of a period of glaciation?" asked Robert.

"Yes, sir. It's all in their report. Current surface temperatures are equivalent to just south of the Arctic Circle on Earth, at this time, but they will slowly rise in time," answered Torrance while, he too, regarded the blue and white marble in the display. So reminiscent of Earth. "The scientists tell me, using the same techniques we used to successfully grow crops during the cleanup of Earth after the wars, the planet should be self sufficient in food, dependent on population size, in no time. Native life appears to be limited, on land masses, to small mammals not much bigger than rodents, with the largest life forms detected in the oceans, some of them as large as our own whales."

Robert came to his decision. "Very well, Commander. Please inform Captain Papadomas to remain in this system and continue to survey the remaining three planets. We shall return directly to Earth. I need to speak to Admiral Jing so we can inform The Joint Chiefs I think we have found a suitable planet."

Torrance looked across at the lieutenant at Communications and could see she was already transmitting the instructions to TDF *Jacques Cartier*.

Torrance's attention returned to Robert as he asked, "One more thing, Commander."

"Yes, Captain," replied Torrance

"Your watch discovered the planet so you get to name it. Have you given it any thought?"

Torrance had not... at least not till now. He looked again at the blue and white marble, hanging there looking so pure and untouched he smiled slightly, "Janus, sir, after the Roman god of beginnings. Hopefully, we can tend to this world better than we have Earth."

"Janus," Robert repeated and gave Torrance a smile of his own, "I like it. Very well. Let's be on our way."

Torrance gave an affirmative "Aye aye, sir. Navigation! Plot us a fold for home and engage when you're ready."

TDF *James Cook* disappeared from the Alpha Centauri system leaving TDF *Jacques Cartier* to stand watch over the system.

#

STICKNEY BASE - PHOBOS - ORBITING MARS

A harried Patricia Bath was busy having a short lunch when a beep from her wrist Comm demanded her attention. With a wearied sigh, she wondered why she had ever let Senator Rae talk her into taking on the directorship of the newly founded Office of Research and Development. It may have given her control over all the ongoing research into the Saiph but she could not remember the last time she had taken a day off. Her wrist Comm beeped again, this time louder. *Oh well,* thought Patricia, *there goes lunch.* She activated the link. "Doctor Bath."

"Director, sorry to bother you over lunch. It's Doctor Fredericks. Could I have a moment of your time?"

Patricia thought Doctor Fredericks did not sound the least bit sorry for interrupting her lunch. "How about in my office in twenty minutes or so?"

"Would it be possible for you to come down to the lab as soon as you can? It is rather important," asked Fredericks.

Patricia looked at the salad, which was to be her lunch, and stood up. "I'm on my way, Bath clear." She cut the link and threw the remains of the salad in the recycling.

Ten minutes later, all thoughts of lunch had vanished as Patricia looked at the two DNA profiles displayed in the Holo Cube. She looked at Fredericks and said in a disbelieving, questioning tone. "Doctor, this can't be right?"

Fredericks stood shaking his head. "I know what you mean, Director. Nevertheless, I have double and triple checked the samples. The one on the left is from the Saiph database and is verified as the Saiph. The one on the right was taken from the remains of one of the Others returned by TDF *Henry Hudson.* I have taken samples from each of the remains and they all show the same results. The Others also show signs of Saiph DNA interference."

Patricia incredulously said, "There must be some mistake. Our searches of the Saiph database tell us the Saiph only began to meddle with the DNA on the seventeen planets after they were attacked by the Others millions of years ago."

Fredericks looked at Patricia, as a professor dispensing a lecture to a wayward student. "Director. Science does not lie. The Others incorporate the DNA of the Saiph. Now, I am the first to admit when it comes to weapons technology and engineering I am but a layman, but has it never occurred to anyone else, if the Others have been around for millions of years, why is their technology not so far advanced beyond ours as we are from the amoeba? It appears what you thought you knew for fact may not be true at all."

Patricia sat and stared at the comparative DNA profiles. How could this be? Her brain refused to digest this new information. The scientist in her eventually kicked in. They had to review everything they had extracted from the Saiph database with a fine toothcomb. This could set them back years. Shaking herself mentally Patricia brought herself back to the problem at hand.

"Is there anything else Doctor Fredericks?"

With a few taps on his PAD Fredericks changed the image in the Holo Cube, it displayed the neck of one of the Others. Patricia could just make out a dark image at the base of the skull.

"What... is... that?"

Another few taps of the PAD and the image enlarged. In front of Patricia was a rectangular box approximately two centimeters by four centimeters by four centimeters with a dark circle on the surface. Fredericks face settled into a puzzled frown.

"To be honest with you Director it has us all baffled here. We took samples of it and determined it was made of some type of metallic plastic composite."

It was Patricia's turn to look puzzled. "What do you mean it was made of? It's still there I can see it."

"That's the puzzling bit. According to the tests we ran, the object seems to have suffered a complete melt down and I mean literally. Whatever it was, was subjected to an intense heat source, which destroyed the inner workings of the object but left the flesh and muscle surrounding it completely untouched. Even more inexplicably we found microscopic tunneling along the spinal column and into the brain, all centered on the object."

Fredericks shrugged his shoulders and let out a sigh.

"Our best guess is The Other this object was retrieved from suffered from some form of spinal damage and the box was a kind of amplifier for the subject's own thoughts. Researchers have long tried to perfect a similar system to allow prosthetic limbs to be controlled directly by the user but so far they have only had limited success. Perhaps the Others had greater success. The tunneling extends as far as the limbs and vital organs on one side of the object and into what may be the movement control areas of the brain."

"Have you found any more of these objects in the other recovered remains?"

Fredericks shook his head. "Unfortunately all the other remains have been too badly damaged for us to substantiate our conclusions."

Patricia looked at the image for another few moments trying to puzzle out its purpose but nothing came to mind.

"OK Doctor type up your report and forward it to my office as soon as you can. I'll send it on to Canberra and we'll see what they can come up with."

Patricia turned on her heel and headed back to her office thoughts of her failure rebounding in her head.

#

Patricia sat at her desk with her head in her hands. How could she have been so wrong? It was more of a statement than a question. Following Fredericks' revelation she had tasked Vince Kealey, her colleague who had worked with her originally to decode the Saiph database, to take her work apart a piece at a time.

Vince had found the mistake quickly. A simple substitution in the decryption algorithm had completely changed the interpretation of a section of the Saiph language. Where the Saiph had indeed experimented with DNA on other worlds millions of years ago, they had, in fact, written the experiment off as a failure. It was not until the Others turned up in the sky, above their home world, they realized something productive had come from their meddling on other worlds. It was this final revelation that had Patricia sitting alone in her office. The Others had not destroyed the Saiph all those millions of years ago. The Others had rained destruction down on the Saiph less than 1000 years ago. A blink of an eye as far the cosmos was concerned.

Patricia thought of all those men and women who had relied on her interpretation of the Saiph database. Those sailors and marines who ventured out into the far reaches of space sure in the

151

knowledge those who had destroyed the Saiph were more than likely dust in cosmic history by now and not actively traveling the space between the stars.

When Valerie Hayes had plucked Patricia out of obscurity and placed her in charge at Stickney Patricia had been young and arrogant. A real fire breather as some of the older researchers had referred to her. Others were not so kind, they wondered who this young upstart, Hayes forced on them, thought she was. Vince had every right to be one of those whose nose was out of joint by Patricia's arrival, instead he sat back and allowed her full rein, helping her when she struggled to cope with researchers who were more senior and encouraging her when she doubted herself.

She felt she had let them all down, Vince, Valerie Hayes, the president and most importantly the men and women who flew amongst the stars. All those who had held faith in her.

Patricia touched a control and her Holo Cube sparked to life with the face of the duty officer in communications. "Yes Director?"

Patricia Bath took a deep breath, knowing this would be her last action as director. "Get me a secure link to the Office of the President."

#

OFFICE OF THE PRESIDENT OF THE TERRAN REPUBLIC - GENEVA - EARTH

The news from Stickney Base had been less of a surprise to some than others. The military had questioned amongst themselves why the Others' technology had not given them an insurmountable edge, but they simply got on with their task and did not count their chickens. Many a politician attempted to lay the blame strictly at the door of the now Ex Director of the Linguistics and Cryptology Division at Stickney Base, Doctor Patricia Bath as the media whipped the public into an unnatural fury at the desk jockey who had endangered the lives of those brave sailors and marines. The opportunists had jumped on the bandwagon and the broadcasts were filled with paid mouth

152

pieces spouting their version of the truth and pointing out in retrospect Patricia Bath's mistakes. *Hindsight is a wonderful thing*, thought Rebecca.

Valerie Hayes had pleaded with her to refuse Doctor Baths resignation but unfortunately the political heat was just too much and as much as her old friend liked the youthful Bath, Rebecca, with regret, would accept her resignation with immediate effect.

Not for the first time Rebecca reminded herself how much she hated politics. She genuinely liked Bath it was such a pity. Maybe when the media furore subsided she could quietly kick start her career again.

#

Rebecca turned to face the only other two people in her spacious presidential office, admiring the blue and white rotating ball that was the planet Janus. "So, General Joyce, how are we coming along with the refit of TDF *Ferdinand Magellan*?"

"Exceptionally well," replied Joyce. "The yards at Deimos are expanding as fast as they can and, with the added slips, the builders were able to basically redesign the *Magellan* and employ the modular construction we're beginning to see in all our ship construction. The basic dimensions of the ship have remained the same, 1300 meters long with a beam of 250 meters but we have managed to increase the gross tonnage to 250,000 tonnes. The reduction in size of the Gravity Drive engines is freeing up more space for cargo and a crew of only 130 with 6500 colony personnel. The Admiralty's plan is to have ten of this type of colony ship shuttling between Earth and Janus to enable the colony to be self-sufficient as quickly as possible. The ships would then be available for use, should we discover further suitable colony worlds."

Rebecca gave a small satisfied "Hmm... and when are we likely to deploy?"

Without the need to refer to the PAD in front of him Joyce answered, "The equipment is arriving steadily and being shipped directly into the cargo areas of the *Magellan*. The necessary foodstuffs, seeds and the minutia required to build a startup colony have been in planning and development since the decision to execute this phase of Operation Chrysaor. I estimate they should all be aboard in the next thirty days."

Rebecca gave a nod of approval, "Very impressive General. That only leaves the trivial issue of personnel."

"If you remember, Madam President, The Joint Chiefs raised the problem of insufficient personnel prior to your decision, which we fully endorsed, to announce the findings of our initial Vanguard surveys. This led to a surge in volunteers for government service, from colonists to the military, and…" Joyce cast his eyes to the ground in a momentary gesture of respect, "with the loss of the *Vasco De Gama*, we expected this initial enthusiasm to dry up. However, the opposite has happened. The ranks of potential colonists and military personnel have continued to swell, to such an extent I have had to make more than a few calls to certain key members of industry to reassure them our automation program to replace skilled workers will bear fruit in the near future."

"Good to hear, General. How is said industry holding up, Thomas?" Rebecca addressed the only other person in the room,

"Remarkably well, Madam President," replied the Secretary of Finance, Senator Crothers. "With the increase in construction and the shrinking base of available, experienced personnel, you would think it would leave industry in a bit of a jam. Nevertheless, the promised mass automation is coming online. The various industries have noticed how the machines, in comparison to human personnel, are cheaper to run, never tire, never argue about wages and don't get sick. All in all, the heads of industry are happier now than I have seen them in a long time."

"So, we are on the verge of establishing our first colony." Rebecca looked again at the planet Janus in the Holo Cube, soon to be the home to thousands, and one day millions, of humans. "Can you gentlemen think of anything else we may have missed which could assist the growth of the colony?"

Senator Crothers cleared his throat. "If I may make a suggestion, Madam President?"

154

"Go on," permitted Rebecca.

Crothers pointed at the image of Janus. "I have never pretended to be a military man," he said with a slight nod in the direction of Joyce, "but I am a man whose job it has been his whole working life to make things work while making a profit."

"Janus is not about making a profit, Senator. It's about the survival of the human race," interrupted Joyce angrily.

"I understand, General. Nevertheless, humans being humans always perform at their best when there is something in it for them. In the case of the men and women who head our industry – they want profit." Crothers paused to collect his thoughts, "Our aim is for the colony we propose to establish to be self-sufficient in the shortest time period, but, as it stands at the moment, the government has to pay for everything the colony needs and eventually transports. Our finances are finite in any given year. I have been floating the idea with certain trusted friends in industry that the government would be willing to give massive concessions to any cargo line who would be inclined to build ships with Gravity Drives and haul goods to and from Janus. Further, the main contractor at Deimos has suggested, using the new automated construction techniques, he builds a second yard in the Alpha Centauri system, doubling our construction facilities at a stroke and providing redundancy in the event the Others locate our solar system and destroy our only means to mass produce warships." Crothers sat back and waited for the president and Joyce to reply.

"Well," said a very impressed Rebecca, "I see you have given this a lot of thought, Thomas. I have to admit we never thought of this before now. Why? I do not know. This lack of forethought, on my part, smacks of foolishness." Rebecca looked across at Joyce who seemed to be equally impressed.

"Don't take this the wrong way, Senator. But I never thought you had it in you," said Joyce.

Crothers smiled at him, as a teacher to a pupil who had just independently figured out a lesson he had been tutoring for months. "I'll take that as a compliment, General."

Joyce went on. "Admiral Jing raised concerns over us having

only one production facility. He has looked at the raw economic data and figured the construction of a separate shipyard for Janus was at least five years away."

"On the contrary, General." Crothers was warming to his subject. "Taking into account industry financed participation, my projection shows we could have a viable, completely self-sufficient colony on Janus within two years."

Crothers' last sentence clinched it for Rebecca. "Well, Senator, it would seem the only thing left for you is to resign."

Crothers looked aghast, stumbling over his words "But... eh... why... Madam President...? Eh... I am only trying to improve the colony's chance of success."

Rebecca paused for a moment. "I understand completely, Senator. However unfortunate, I cannot have you double jobbing as Secretary of Finance *and* Governor of Janus. I accept your resignation forthwith."

Crothers' mouth hung open, like a fish. He wanted to say something but no words were forthcoming.

Joyce stood and stuck out his hand. "Congratulations, Governor!"

CHAPTER FIFTEEN

A NEW BEGINNING

JANUS COLONY - ALPHA CENTAURI B
4.37 LIGHT YEARS FROM EARTH

Thomas Crothers, Governor of Earth's first extra solar system colony of Janus, looked out through the clear steel window of his office on the fourth floor of the Terran Republic building, in the center of the capital of the colony. A capital which by popular demand had been named Witsell after the captain of the TDF *Vasco De Gama* who had sacrificed herself and her crew to save the marines fleeing from 'The Others' during the fighting in 70 Ophiuchi a year before.

Only a year? Thought Thomas as he looked out at the bustling streets. The Magellan class colony ships had been shuttling people from Earth as fast as the expanding colony could take them. The current population was now over 1.5 million on just the surface of Janus. In orbit and in the asteroid belt, another 500,000 humans labored to supply the needs of the flourishing colony with its fledgling shipbuilding yards. If the projections were correct, given another year Janus would have a population of five million and be completely self-sufficient.

A descending shuttle caught Thomas' eye as it headed for the landing pads – that would be his visitors. With a sigh, he turned from the window and returned to the waiting, seemingly endless bureaucracy that came with the job, in a vain attempt to empty his inbox before their arrival.

Half an hour later, Thomas stood as the entry chime sounded on his office door. It swung open and allowed Fleet Admiral Jing, newly named Commander of First Fleet in the rapidly expanding Terran Navy, and a vice admiral he did not recognize into the office. The Governor walked around his desk to greet the Navy men. "Good to see you again Admiral Jing, and...?"

The unnamed admiral smiled and shook the Thomas' proffered hand. "Vice Admiral Robert Lewis, Governor."

The name was familiar to Thomas and then his memory placed the name, "Of course, Captain of the *James Cook*. A well-deserved promotion if I may say so, Admiral."

"Please don't, Governor," interjected Jing with a chuckle. "Since being appointed my deputy at First Fleet, he has become insufferable. In fact, my trying to get rid of him is what has brought us to Janus."

Thomas indicated a group of comfortable chairs and the three men sat before Thomas asked, "And how do you intend to rid yourself of poor Admiral Lewis?" as he gave Lewis an apologetic look.

Jing pulled a PAD from his case and pressed his thumb against the DNA scanner to activate its secure contents. "It has been noted by many back in Geneva, Governor, Janus is well ahead of schedule and, without sounding like a sycophant, nobody back home is fooling themselves the success is down to anything other than your hard work, Governor."

"And many others who have put more blood and sweat into the building of the colony than I, Admiral," added Thomas.

A politician willing to put others before himself? Thought Jing. *How novel!* "Well your combined efforts enabled the TDF to bring forward its schedule by nearly ten months. The shipyards, here in Janus, have reached a level at which The Joint Chiefs believe a percentage of their production may now be dedicated to the production of military hardware."

"What sort of percentage are we talking, Admiral," asked

Thomas apprehensively. "We still have a lot of work to do in the asteroid belt and the orbital habitats."

Jing consulted his PAD before answering. "Based on your own figures, we would be looking at switching over twenty-one percent at this stage, growing to thirty-five percent by the end of the year."

Thomas opened his mouth to protest, but Lewis got in first. "Governor, if I could explain?"

"Please do, Admiral Lewis," said Thomas unhappily.

"The speed with which the colony expanded beyond our planning has meant The Joint Chiefs feel the resources of the Sol system are being stretched to provide adequate defenses for both the home system and Janus. And, to be blunt, if you don't start to provide the material to defend yourself, then everything you are building here could be for nothing if the Others come calling."

Thomas paused for thought, the admirals had a point. Everything the population of Janus had worked so hard to build could be taken from them if the Others stumbled on Janus. After all, the whole idea of Janus was if, God forbid, some disaster befell Earth, then mankind would be able to continue. Was it not his duty as governor to ensure the safety of the colony?

"My apologies, Admirals. Of course Janus must assume the burden of its own defense. Please continue."

Both admirals let out a small sigh of relief. They had expected a harder fight for the resources they needed.

"Governor," continued Admiral Jing, "it is the intention of The Joint Chiefs to expand the TDF's forces here at Janus. System defense needs to be brought up to par, and to do so the Navy intends to build a fleet base here for what will eventually become Second Fleet, and Admiral Lewis has been chosen as its commander."

"Ah," said Thomas with a slight smile toward Admiral Lewis, "This would be Admiral Jing's cunning plan to get rid of you."

Lewis gave a small shrug of his shoulders. "So it would seem, Governor."

"So, down to brass tacks gentlemen. What sort of forces can I be expected to provide?" stated Thomas, all business now the decision for Janus to build its own units had been taken.

Jing indicated for Lewis to continue. "In broad brush strokes, the first thing we need to establish is a sufficient defensive capability to ensure Janus can fend off any initial attack and buy enough time for forces from First Fleet in the Sol System to respond and come to our assistance. Once I believe our defense units are sufficient to secure Janus, we will switch production over to offensive units, which is where the main power of Second Fleet will be. It gives us the capability to respond to any calls from First Fleet for assistance as well as to go on the attack independently if needed. We plan to initially bring manpower from Earth to form a core of experienced crew for the ships but Janus will be expected to provide what it can."

"I don't see it being a problem, Admiral," said Thomas. "The people are proud of what they have achieved here and will want to protect it and their families who have settled here."

Lewis nodded his understanding. "People will always protect their families and what they have built themselves. We project the mainly automated orbital defenses should be fully operational in six months with the first fleet units operational between twelve and eighteen months from now."

Thomas held a hand up to stop Admiral Lewis "A suggestion, Admiral."

"Of course, Governor." Lewis looked across at Jing. Was the Governor going to change his mind in supporting their plan?

"If I were to reduce your percentage of yard production from twenty-one percent to say, eighteen percent, how would this reduction impact on your production of the automated orbital defenses?"

Jing did some quick calculations on his PAD. "It would extend our orbital defense completion by a month or so."

Both admirals sat waiting patiently. The Governor appeared deep in thought before his eyes refocused. "If I use the three percent to build additional yard units and build the Navy its own dedicated construction facility, it could be incorporated into your fleet base. And means you roll out the first fleet units in eight months."

160

The admirals regarded Thomas in amazement.

Thomas went on, seemingly ignorant of the admirals' expressions, "Of course you would need to step up your personnel movements, but I'll have a word with the colony construction teams. I'm sure we can sort something out in the short term until your fleet base is up and running. Is there anything else I can do to help?"

Jing shook himself. "No, Governor, everything is covered."

"In that case, I shall organize a meeting with Admiral Lewis and the colony planning board for tomorrow and we can get things rolling." Governor Crothers stood.

The admirals stood and shook hands with a man who had just changed their perceptions of a politician's behavior.

#

OFFICE OF THE PRESIDENT OF THE TERRAN REPUBLIC - GENEVA - EARTH

Rebecca Coston walked through the entrance of her private conference room stopping the ongoing, quiet conversations as the gathered men and women turned, looking at her expectantly. Rebecca recognized most of those in the room but was surprised to see Edward Munro, Director of the Federal Investigation Bureau, Carol Manning, Secretary of Finance and Edvard Dietel, the Attorney General, present. "Please take your seats," said Rebecca.

Rebecca took her seat at the head of the table. "Ladies and gentlemen, I must assume this is an urgent matter or I would not have agreed to this meeting on such short notice. Would someone like to tell me what is going on?"

General Joyce, cleared his throat nervously. "Madam President, as you are no doubt aware, we have been building warships and expanding our military forces as rapidly as possible in the face of the perceived threat from the Others."

"General I am well aware of this," said Rebecca with some exasperation. "Has something changed that I am unacquainted with, for you to ask for this meeting so urgently?"

Joyce looked across the table at Vice Admiral Wilson, before continuing. "When the decision was made to begin the expansion, I put in place certain measures in the hope of containing any internal or external interference in it." Joyce nodded toward Wilson, "If I may introduce Vice Admiral Elizabeth Wilson, who works directly for me. Her job is to overcome any such obstacles."

Rebecca regarded Wilson. "You mean she's your hatchet man, General," she stated.

Joyce allowed a small smile to appear on his face. "Hatchet man is a fair description, Madam President, and due to Admiral Wilson I asked for this meeting."

Rebecca looked toward Wilson quizzically. "Surely you have not found some obstacle within the military the chairman of The Joint Chiefs cannot deal with? Surely you do not require presidential intervention?"

"The issue, Madam President," replied Wilson "isn't within the military per se."

Rebecca was becoming a little irritated with all the pussyfooting around, "Please get to the point, Admiral."

"Very well, Madam President. Your secretary of defense, Senator Geoffrey Rawson, has been selling contracts for bribes and has been embezzling funds on a huge scale," Wilson said matter-of-factly.

Rebecca stared at the Admiral for a few moments. *That weasel!* She thought. *Curse the day I ever agreed to him getting the post!* She took a deep breath and steadied herself before asking. "How much Admiral and for how long?"

It did not occur to Wilson the president had not questioned the validity of her claim for a second. "I first had an inkling something wasn't quite right when I compared the costing and output of the yards at Deimos with the yards at Janus. The discrepancy was nearly ten percent per unit, and even though they were using virtually identical equipment Deimos' construction time was fifteen percent longer than at Janus. Now we all know Governor Crothers has a knack for efficiency and cost cutting but the discrepancy was too much to be ignored so, with General Joyce's permission, I began an off the books investigation using outside agencies, investigators from the Federal Investigation Bureau and auditors from the Department of Finance..."

Rebecca was finding it difficult to remain calm. "I shall ask one more time, Admiral. How much and for how long?"

The room became very still. No one present had ever seen President Coston as aggravated as this before.

To her credit, Secretary Manning spoke up. "Madam President, my auditors discovered a trail which leads us to believe Secretary Rawson has been lining his own pockets since his appointment as secretary of defense. Our current estimate is approaching eight-three million credits between skimming the budget and bribes."

Rebecca let out a gasp. "Eighty-three million! How the hell did no one notice?"

"When Secretary Rawson took over at Defense, he brought a lot of his own people with him and it would appear many, if not all, are implicated. To be honest, we just have not had the time yet to go over all of their finances. Remember, Madam President, we have been flinging money at Defense hand over fist for the past three years and it would appear, according to Director Munro's people, anyone Rawson couldn't pay off was pushed out of Defense or an excuse was found to sack them."

Rebecca pointed at Director Munro. "I want rid of him! Not tomorrow, not at the end of the day. I mean right now. That man has not only stolen money from the Republic, but by slowing construction of our defenses he has put the lives of the people of the Republic at risk."

Director Munro hesitated. "Are you sure you want this done publicly, Madam President? I could have agents arrest him at his home this evening and give you time to prepare a press statement."

Rebecca fixed him a look to wilt a lesser man. Without taking her eyes from him, she addressed the Attorney General. "Is there enough evidence for a charge of Treason, Edvard?"

The Attorney General struggled to keep his voice calm and

level. Treason was a crime which still carried the death penalty within the Republic. "Yes, Madam President. I believe the evidence I have seen is enough to justify the charge of treason."

Rebecca's eyes had not strayed from Director Munro. "Well, Director?"

Director Munro tapped his secure wrist link. "This is Director Munro. Inform the protection detail for Secretary Rawson, on the President's order, they are to secure the Secretary immediately and await the arrival of agents from my office. The Secretary is to have no contact with any person or access to any electronic system."

Rebecca stood abruptly. "I think that will be all for today, ladies and gentlemen. Thanks to you, I can pretty much guarantee the rest of my day is shot to hell."

As the people gathered in the room began to leave, Rebecca called, "General Joyce, a moment please."

The General halted and returned to stand by his seat at the table. Rebecca indicated for him to retake his seat as she sat herself.

"So how long have you suspected Rawson?" asked Rebecca in a tired voice?

"Admiral Wilson came to me about a year ago with her concerns and I trusted her instincts enough to let her run with the investigation," replied Joyce.

"And you didn't trust me enough to let me know of your suspicions?"

"Madam President, with all due respect," replied Joyce, "when Admiral Wilson came to me to tell me she suspected the secretary of defense, a secretary you had appointed, what would you have done?"

For the first time in the day, Rebecca smiled wryly. "I would have trusted no one General. You did the right thing. My problem now is when this scandal breaks, who will the people trust enough to be secretary of defense? And how quickly can we undo the damage done to our military buildup caused by Rawson?"

Joyce sat back in his chair and ran the numbers in his head for a few seconds, "The damage caused is mainly in production schedules at Deimos. The efficiency of the Janus yards goes part way to offsetting the delays, in fact, if we were to introduce the same procedures Janus employs at Deimos, we should be back on schedule within the year."

At least there is some good news, thought Rebecca.

"As far as a new secretary of defense goes, well, who takes up the post is a political issue, Madam President."

Rebecca knew the General was right. The people had to have confidence in its political leadership. Ever since the threat from the Others had become known, the citizens of the Republic had recognized their duty and had joined the military in their millions. They had complete faith in the generals and admirals to do their duty. The politicians will be distrusted, unless... An idea came to Rebecca.

"So, General, how goes the senior officer selection boards?" Rebecca asked conversationally.

Joyce, somewhat thrown by the president's sudden change of tone, could smell something brewing. "Ah, very well, Madam President. The board, run by Admiral Helset, has appointed the required number of senior officers, and the promotion requirements for further advancement of junior officers is in place and working well." With a small chuckle, Joyce carried on. "To be honest with you, it's working so well the Admiral may find himself out of a job soon."

As soon as he said it, Joyce could have kicked himself. The crocodile smile spreading across the president's face told him he had just been played.

Rebecca knew Joyce now realized what was going on, but carried on with the charade regardless. It was not every day you got one over on the chairman of The Joint Chiefs, "Oh well, I suppose it rests with you to let Admiral Helset know he is once again facing retirement."

Joyce was virtually squirming in his seat. Rebecca could have sworn he was mumbling a few choice words. "Yes, Madam President. I suppose that duty does fall on me. Perhaps you could suggest some gainful employment for him?"

165

With difficulty in keeping a straight face Rebecca replied, "I believe the position of secretary of defense has just become vacant."

#

OFFICE OF THE SECRETARY OF DEFENCE - GENEVA - EARTH

Secretary Olaf Helset sat behind his desk in the office, his for the past month, looking across at General Joyce and Admirals Jing and Vadis. Men he had served alongside for more than thirty years. "Well, tell me the bad news."

Joyce spoke for the military men present, "Well, Admiral... apologies, Mr. Secretary!"

Secretary Helset looked down his barrel like finger, now pointed at the chairman of the joint chiefs. "You, Mr. Chairman, serve at the pleasure of the President, and in this room I act in her stead. If you continue in your disrespectful tone, I shall summon your own marines and have you escorted from here and keel hauled until you begin to show the degree of respect I require," before breaking into a large grin. "Now get on with it Keyton."

Joyce bowed deeply at the waist. "Of course, your majesty. Although there is significant damage to production, it is repairable. And with the able assistance of men lent to us by Governor Crothers, we are nearly back on track."

Joyce regarded the display on his secure PAD for a moment then touched a control and a Holo Cube sprang into life, he began to explain what he saw. "As you can see, Mr. Secretary, our current strength is broken into three areas, the first of those being planetary defense." The display changed to show Earth and Janus side by side. "Over the past three years, our priority has been planetary defense of, firstly, Earth and secondly, Janus. As it has expanded, so have our defenses there. The Army has expanded and been shaped into a heavily armored reaction force to respond to any threat of actual planetary invasion. The Army also has responsibility for the ground based Planetary Defense Centers." Pin pricks, spread out over Earth and Janus, became animated on the display. "Installations scattered around the surface of both

166

planets are armed with particle weapons and High Velocity Missiles. They can reach out to geosynchronous orbit."

The display changed. This time it showed two seemingly innocuous boxes. The box on the left, on closer inspection, consisted of an L shaped body on which was a pallet with nine square openings on one end. The main body had Laser Area Denial clusters on each of its four sides. The right hand box also displayed had the same L shaped body, but the pallet attached to it had only a single round protuberance set at its far end.

Joyce indicated to the first box. "Mr. Secretary, what you see here is a multi-functional disposable point defense platform. We call it Viper. The left hand Viper is armed with nine HVMs, each with a megaton nuclear warhead. The Viper on the right is armed with a single grazer with an integrated power supply. It's good for 100 shots. Each Viper, as you can see, has its own Laser Area Denial System for its own defense and can be controlled by a local Planetary Defense Center or it can be allowed independent action within a given engagement zone."

Helset let out a low whistle, "A lot of firepower, Keyton."

"Yes, sir," agreed Joyce. "Combined with the Planetary Defense Centers it gives us a layered defense capability with the ability to engage any ship, in theory, as far as it can be detected."

"In theory, Keyton?" asked Helset.

"Yes, sir. As you know, the HVMs have a limited amount of fuel. They can boost only so far and change direction only so many times until they exhaust their onboard fuel supply, then they either carry on in the direction they were traveling or self-destruct. The particle weapons have, in theory, an unlimited range. In reality, the range is restricted by the fact we have to be able to detect a target for our weapons systems to engage it."

Olaf could see the problem. "Am I to assume, then, you have a solution, Keyton?"

The Holo Cube image changed. Now, there was a third platform. The same L shaped body but this time the box on the pallet had an array of antennas protruding from it. "We call this Sherlock, outfitted with our best detection and target identification systems, it can update the Planetary Defense

Centers or cross deck its information directly to the Viper units."

Olaf was suitably impressed. "So would it be safe to say Earth and Janus have enough of these units to defend against the Others tactic of bombardment?"

Joyce took a moment to look at the two admirals with him. "Mr. Secretary, nothing is a sure bet, but with what we have seen of The Others' tactics, we consider the Viper units to be our best defensive strategy."

Olaf held Keyton's eye for a moment. "Very well Keyton. If it is the considered opinion of The Joint Chiefs. How long before you can begin deploying them to protect our habitats throughout the Solar and Janus systems?"

"Production of the required Viper units is in full swing." Keyton consulted his PAD briefly. "At current rates of production, another six months should be enough to provide sufficient cover for any strategically valuable asset in both systems Mr. Secretary."

Satisfied Earth and Janus were adequately protected from any immediate danger, Olaf turned to Jing, "So, Ai. How goes things with First Fleet?"

Keyton turned his PAD over to the Admiral who, with a few touches of the controls, changed the display in the Holo Cube.

"Mr. Secretary, on the display is the completed Order of Battle for First Fleet. The fleet will be broken into five parts, three battle forces, BatFor 1, 2 and 3. Each BatFor will consist of three battleships, four heavy cruisers, two light cruisers and ten destroyers. A Marine assault division of some 19000 marines consisting of four regiments, a tank battalion, a reconnaissance battalion, two light armored reconnaissance battalions, two combat engineer battalions and one orbital assault battalion. The entire division is lifted in ten assault ships and has a dedicated light cruiser and destroyer escort. And, as of zero eight hundred hours this morning, First Fleet is active."

"And what of Second Fleet, Ai?" asked Olaf.

"Admiral Lewis assures me Second Fleet, minus its Marine contingent – who are still forming up on Earth and awaiting transport to Janus – will be up to strength within the next twenty-eight days."

Helset gave Ai a knowing look as he nodded slowly. "Very impressive work, gentlemen. Very impressive indeed. But there is something else, isn't there?" pointing a lazy finger at Vadis. "Otherwise, Aleksandr wouldn't be here, would he now?"

Vadis smiled slightly. "We never could get anything past you, sir."

Olaf regarded the three senior officers as a disproving schoolteacher. "No you couldn't, could you? So let me guess. You got Keyton here to wax lyrical about the strength of the defenses and then poor Ai about how First Fleet has been activated and then how Second Fleet will be activated within the month, because you have some cunning plan up your sleeve and you want me to take it to the President for approval."

Vadis leaned forward in his seat and said flatly, "We want to go back to Messier 54 and 31 Aquilae."

Olaf did not even flinch. "I was beginning to wonder when you were going to ask."

CHAPTER SIXTEEN

IN TO THE FIRE

TDF JACQUES CARTIER - 31 AQUILAE

Commodore Papadomas sat in his chair on the bridge of TDF *Jacques Cartier* and regarded the Holo Cube to his front, it displayed three blue icons representing his survey flotilla.

A smile crossed his lips as he realized he considered the Vanguard survey ships as his. TDF *Jacques Cartier*, TDF *James Cook* and TDF *Henry Hudson* had been dispatched to 31 Aquilae under the newly promoted Commodore's command. His mission, as outlined by The Joint Chiefs was simple enough: enter the system and deploy surveillance platforms to observe not only the pre industrialized civilization inhabiting Planet III (or as some researcher had dubbed it, Garunda, apparently after the Hindu name for this constellation), but to deploy a shell of surveillance platforms around the system looking outwards. Research and Development assured him each of these new style surveillance platforms could detect 'The Others' Alcubierre drive out to a distance of a light year.

He turned to the duty communications officer. "Please signal the *James Cook* and the *Henry Hudson* I am beginning deployment of the planetary surveillance platform and they may begin their own deployments when ready and we shall meet them at the rendezvous point in three days."

The young lieutenant at communications replied, "Aye aye, sir," without turning around.

"Commander Ranking, the bridge is yours. I'll be in biosciences if you need me." Without waiting for a reply Papadomas got up from his chair and headed for biosciences to see for himself the initial take from the planetary surveillance platform which they all hoped would bring them a greater understanding of the life on Garunda.

#

TDF HENRY HUDSON - 31 AQUILAE

Captain Bill Talbot was enjoying a late lunch alone in his small cabin when the urgent chiming from the intercom demanded his attention. Bill reached over and activated the small Holo Cube, which sprang to life with the head and shoulders of his new XO, Commander Euan Campbell. "Problem, XO?"

The XO was concise and to the point. "Captain, approximately ten minutes ago platform twelve picked up indications of an Alcubierre drive. I ordered platforms nine and eleven re tasked to the same area. They confirm not only one, but six drive sources headed for this system. Tactical identifies them as the Others. They have the same drive signature as those designated Buzzard class from 70 Ophiuchi."

"ETA XO?" asked Bill.

The XO looked down at something out of the pickup's range, then back at Bill. "At current rate of advance Tactical estimates fourteen hours till they enter the system."

Bill's mind began to race. "OK, this is what I want to happen: download all our current data to four courier drones. Dispatch two to First Fleet and two to Second Fleet and launch when ready."

Bill could see his XO typing furiously and then felt a small lurch as the drone bays beneath the *Henry Hudson* came open and the four drones where launched.

The XO looked up. "Drones away, sir."

"Good. Is the *James Cook* still within whisker range?"

Without needing to check, the XO was able to answer, "Negative, sir. They completed the nearest portion of the surveillance shell a few hours ago and have moved to their next deployment area."

Bill thought through his options for a moment. "Very well, launch a drone to the *James Cook* and one to the *Jacques Cartier*. Inform them it is my intention to go to silent running and continue to monitor the surveillance platforms in real time for as long as I remain undetected by the Others, unless the Commodore orders otherwise. Then I want the crew placed on mandatory rest and get them all fed and watered, XO. The next few hours could be tricky."

In the Holo Cube, Euan Campbell nodded his agreement. "Understood, sir. I'll get right on it."

"That order applies to you too, XO. I'll come up and relieve you in two hours," said Bill.

"Aye aye, sir," acknowledged the XO.

As Bill cut the link, he wondered how the authorities back on Earth would react to the news of the Others heading for 31 Aquilae.

#

OFFICE OF THE PRESIDENT OF THE TERRAN REPUBLIC
GENEVA - EARTH

It was the early hours in Geneva when one of her aides wakened Rebecca Coston. The secretary of defense and the chairman of The Joint Chiefs were on a secure link requesting to speak with her urgently.

In all her time as President, not once had she answered a call with such a feeling of dread as she activated the link, the faces of Secretary Helset and General Joyce appeared on the split screen in front of her. Rebecca did not like the look of worry etched on both men's faces. "Gentlemen, by the hour of the day I take it this is not a social call."

Olaf Helset shook his head slowly. "No, Madam President

I'm afraid not. An hour ago First Fleet received a courier drone from the Vanguard survey ship, TDF *Henry Hudson* which, as you are aware, along with TDF *James Cook* and TDF *Jacques Cartier*, was tasked to the 31 Aquilae system to place surveillance platforms around the planet now known as Garunda and a detection shell around the system."

Rebecca's sense of dread deepened. "What have they found, Olaf?"

"Madam President, there are six Buzzard class Others ships headed for the system. The captain of the *Henry Hudson* stated his intention was to remain on station and monitor their approach. Commodore Papadomas confirmed this decision in a second drone received by First Fleet fifteen minutes later. I estimate the Buzzard's arrival at just over twelve hours."

Both men waited patiently as Rebecca fought her drowsiness to understand the implications of this information. After a few seconds, the president asked, "Do we have any idea of their intentions, Olaf?"

Olaf shook his head and a frown appeared on his forehead. "Impossible to tell, Madam President. They could be coming to survey the system as we have done. On the other hand, I would remind you what happened to the Saiph home world. The Others arrived in orbit without a word and began to bombard the planet. The civilization on Garunda are pre industrial revolution." Olaf shrugged his shoulders. "They would have no defense against an orbital bombardment."

"What are our options, Olaf?" asked Rebecca.

The secretary of defense shifted in his seat and replied in a flat, neutral tone. "Option one, we sit back and allow the Others to enter the system and, if their plan is to carry out a survey, our ships sit in stealth and get as much intelligence about their tactics as possible." Olaf continued, his face contorting as if he had eaten something particularly distasteful. "Option two, they enter the system and begin to bombard Garunda and we watch the extinction of a civilization."

In her mind's eye, Rebecca could imagine the inhabitants of Garunda going about their business on just another day as, without warning, a fiery rain of destruction begins to fall on their homes and their lives are cut short. Rebecca cleared the images from her mind as she looked back at Olaf with steel in her eyes. "Not good enough, Olaf. I will not stand by and allow the extermination of an entire race. I want another option."

Olaf gave the only other answer he had. "We intervene, Madam President."

Rebecca regarded her two closest military advisers and could feel a momentous decision bearing down on her. Taking a deep breath, she asked, "How?"

Joyce broke his silence. Until now, he had said nothing to allow his lord and masters to come to the decision he knew in his heart was the only viable one. "BatFor 1 is ready for immediate deployment, as is BatFor 3 from the Janus system if required. It is my recommendation that the deployment of one battleship force is required in this particular scenario."

Rebecca was well aware a deployment of human forces could well be a slippery slope. "And what would be their orders?"

"BatFor 1 would deploy to the edge of the system and observe the Others. They would only move to intervene if they believed the Others were about to attack the planet. If the Others simply carry out a survey mission and then leave, BatFor 1 would return to its base."

Rebecca had once spoken to her predecessor, President McMullen, about his decision to keep the existence of Operation Minerva secret. He remarked it was not the fact he kept Minerva a secret that was the hard part, it was the fact he realised when he made the decision it was his and his alone. President McMullen had told Coston about another leader from the time before the wars who had had a sign on their office desk, which read "The Buck Stops Here." Now President Coston knew what he had meant.

"Very well, General. Deploy your forces."

#

TDF CARTAGENA - 31 AQUILAE

From the Flag Bridge, Rear Admiral John Radford looked at the Holo Cube, which displayed the 31 Aquilae system before him. The blue icons of BatFor 1, First Fleet, Terran Defense Force surrounded his Nemesis class battleship, TDF *Cartagena*, in a layered globe. Destroyers formed the outer shell, cruisers a mid-layer and the battleships at the heart.

Compared to John's last command, the Vanguard class survey ship TDF *Henry Hudson*, TDF *Cartagena* was nothing less than a monster. The Nemesis class battleship had been designed with only one thought in mind, to defeat anything the Others had so far fielded in a toe-to-toe stand up fight. It was 980 meters long, 120 meters at the beam and weighed in at 52000 tonnes. The Nemesis was not designed to hide from the enemy. It was designed to close with and destroy him, using the most efficient particle weapons, grazers and missiles which mankind, utilizing Saiph technology, could devise. The *Cartagena* was not alone. Two more Nemesis battleships, the *Lagos Bay* and the Fort Royal, four Vulcan class heavy cruisers, two Talos class light cruisers and ten Agis class destroyers rounded out BatFor 1. For this mission, it was decided, BatFor 1's Marine element was not required.

As John continued to watch his display, it split and the face of his flag captain, Joshua Ward, appeared.

"Admiral, I see we have customers," said Ward grimly.

In the display, the red icons of the Others' six ships moved past the outer surveillance shell in three groups of two ship formations and the lonely blue icon representing the *Henry Hudson*. "Well, Captain. There's the first good news of the day. The Others have either not detected or have chosen to ignore the *Henry Hudson*. The bad news is the Buzzards are still making a best time course for Garunda." Without taking his eyes from the display, John called, "Tactical, estimated time till the Buzzards reach Garunda?"

The lieutenant at Tactical checked her readouts before answering. "Current rate of advance would put Buzzard One's arrival in orbit around the planet in fifty minutes, Admiral."

The clock is ticking, thought John. "Project phase line

Trafalgar onto the tactical display and give me an ETA for the Buzzards breaching the line."

A red globe superimposed itself around Garunda. Phase line Trafalgar – an imaginary sphere, which was the scientists' best guess using references from the Saiph database at the maximum of the Buzzards' planetary bombardment range. To John it marked his decision point.

"Forty-five minutes till phase line Trafalgar is breached by Buzzard One," called the lieutenant at Tactical.

John thought this could be the longest forty-five minutes of his life. With a voice calmer than he felt, John ordered, "Communications, signal to the fleet: All ships to battle stations."

John looked back to his display and the waiting face of Captain Ward, "Captain, I believe I may have some business for you shortly."

#

All conversation on the flag bridge of the *Cartagena* slowly tailed off as Buzzard One inexorably closed on phase line Trafalgar. John found himself staring intently at his tactical display. The Buzzards had retained their three two ship formations as they closed with Garunda. Then it happened: the leading Buzzard passed the red line.

"Phase line Trafalgar breached by Buzzard One, Admiral!" came the confirmation from Tactical.

Now we find out if all our hard work pays off, thought John as he gripped the sides of his chair that little bit harder. "Communications, signal to fleet: We will go with ops plan Nelson Two."

The communications officer transmitted the pre-arranged signal. Just as quickly, the ships of the fleet replied. "Fleet acknowledges, Admiral. Nelson Two on your command."

John waited a heartbeat before ordering, "Execute!"

BatFor 1, Terran Defense Force disappeared from the outskirts of 31 Aquilae only to reappear a split second later barely 1000 kilometers from the leading two ship Buzzard formation.

John leaned forward and quickly studied his tactical display. BatFor 1 had reemerged from fold space, not in the globe it had entered in, but now arrayed in a conical formation with the three battleships at the point of the cone and the cruisers spreading out on the flanks. Of the destroyers, there was no sign. John shifted his eyes closer to the planet and was relieved to see the blue icons of the destroyers forming up as a shield between the Buzzards and the planet. They were John's last line of defense against any missiles fired at the planet which leaked past his cruisers.

Well, phase one worked, thought John. The micro jump first performed by the *Vasco De Gama* in 70 Ophiuchi to get into a firing position behind another Buzzard had been repeatedly practiced as the tactical advantage it gave was now fully recognized.

Now for phase two. Without another word of command from John, all three Terran battleships fired their main grazer armament. The targeted Buzzards had no time to react: by the time their light speed sensors told them BatFor 1 was there, the light speed grazers were only seconds behind. As John watched, the grazers of *Cartagena* and *Lagos Bay* (four of the heaviest grazers ever mounted on a Terran ship) struck the flank of Buzzard One. They passed through the battle armor like it wasn't even there, taking off the rear third of Buzzard One and leaving the remaining two thirds to begin a steady tumbling motion in the same general direction the Buzzard had been originally headed on.

"Communications! Inform the nearest cruisers to engage what remains of Buzzard One with HVMs," ordered John without taking his eyes from his display. Damn! Buzzard Two had been lucky, only one of the grazers from Fort Royal impacted, but the bow of the Buzzard was now an expanding ball of plasma.

The gunners of Buzzard Two were quick off the mark and Q laser fire began hitting the armored hull of the Fort Royal. But this was what the Nemesis class of battleship had been designed for. Fort Royal shrugged off the hits as her forward particle cannon opened fire and she maneuvered to bring her grazers bear. As the particle cannon impacted on Buzzard Two, John saw in his display Buzzards Three and Four slowed to allow Buzzards Five and Six to catch up, and their formation was changing.

John's tactical officer saw it too. "Admiral, aspect change of the remaining Buzzards. They're maneuvering broadside onto us, I would suggest to deploy missiles and to clear as many weapons as possible to engage us."

As the tactical officer finished, a fresh set of red icons appeared on the display and began speeding in the direction of the Terran ships.

The tactical officer reacted immediately. "Vampire, Vampire. Enemy missile release. The fleet now has weapons free for anti-missile assets. The cruisers are engaging."

Compared to the near light speed grazers and particle weapons, missiles might seem slow, but the anti-ship HVMs BatFor 1 carried moved at 60000 kilometers per hour and had a powered range of 300,000 kilometers. They carried either a nuclear or a conventional warhead controlled from the firing ship or by the missile's onboard computer. The anti-missile HVMs could accelerate up to 100,000 kilometers per hour but had a much shorter range, only 1000 kilometers. Again, they could carry either nuclear or conventional warheads controlled by the firing ship or onboard computers.

John watched the display as a shoal of anti-missile missiles flew from the cruisers of BatFor 1 as the battleships held their missiles in reserve. John knew this was the first major engagement between the Others and the Terran Defense Force and, although John would have loved to engage with everything at his disposal, this fight was a chance to learn how effective the Terran tactics and weaponry were, so, despite himself, John held back from committing his battleships fully.

"Second missile separation from the Buzzards," came the call from Tactical. "Fewer in number this time but with a larger energy reading."

As John continued to watch the battle develop, Q lasers continued to strike out at *Fort Royal*, but the Nemesis battleship seemed unaffected by the strikes. *The Fort Royal's* particle cannon were taking large bites out of Buzzard Two and as the *Fort Royal's* grazers came to bear, they fired in tandem, striking the Buzzard dead center. With a blinding flash, the Buzzard simply ceased to exist. Where a 220,000 tonnes starship had once been, there was now only an expanding cloud of debris.

Out of the corner of his eye, John could see the tactical officer, whose fingers had so far throughout the battle been flying over his controls as he coordinated the actions of the whole of BatFor 1, had paused and was looking intently at his repeater display. "Problem, Commander?"

In reply, the second volley of missiles from the Buzzards lit up in John's display. The commander at Tactical spun his chair to face John with a look of puzzlement on his face. "Sir, it appears this second volley of missiles, our count is twenty from each Buzzard, are on course to clear our engagement envelope. They won't come anywhere near our ships."

John looked again at the display, trying to discern the enemy's intention. Why fire sixty missiles in the middle of a firefight when all sixty head off at a tangent from the enemy? John started and sat bolt upright in his seat hoping to God he was wrong. "Tactical! Have the destroyer screen around Garunda shadow the trajectory of the second wave of missiles. I believe they're not aimed at us at all – they're going for the planet! They're just completing a dog leg course to avoid us intercepting them."

The battle continued to rage around John. His battleships had, so far, taken only minor damage, and John could feel a growing sense of confidence emanating from the flag bridge. The Others did not appear to have an answer to the heavy grazers mounted on the TDF ships, and the particle cannon, although not as effective, was still able to inflict significant damage. Anti-missile HVMs from the cruiser screen easily defeated the missiles fired at BatFor 1. John involuntarily relaxed a little in his seat. Maybe this was not going to turn out so badly after all. A call from Tactical changed his mind in an instant.

"Aspect change on the second flight of missiles we've been tracking." The commander paused checking his data. "Looks like you were right, Admiral. The missiles have changed course and are now heading for the planet and are increasing speed. The enemy missiles are now traveling at 75000 kilometers per hour."

Damn! Thought John as his eyes moved across the display to focus on the missiles closing with Garunda. The missiles had formed into three distinct waves. The first wave consisted of thirty missiles, followed by two further waves of twenty missiles each.

John looked at the blue icons of his ten Agis class destroyers which had interposed themselves between the oncoming missiles and the planet. The Agis class were designed as fleet protection ships. They mounted a complex Fire Control system, which allowed them to integrate their defensive fire with other ships. Their firepower was distinctly skewed toward the role of long-range anti-missile pickets specifically tasked to kill any missile threat to the fleet. Were John's ten Agis ships going to be enough against sixty incoming missiles?

John ran a quick scenario through his head, then turned to his tactical officer, "Tactical, re task the cruisers closest to the enemy missiles. I know it's a long shot and the chances of hits are minimal, but they are to engage the enemy missiles heading for Garunda with their particle cannon. I think the Agis can do with all the help they can get."

On John's display, he saw the re tasked cruisers shift position slightly to bring their weapons to bear on the new threat, and then all hell broke loose.

Three of the Buzzards slipped into a tight triangle formation and slowed noticeably. Before John or anyone else on the flag bridge could react, a bright blue beam shot out of the bow of each of the Buzzards and all three beams connected with the *Lagos Bay*. The sidebars on John's display had difficulty keeping up with the thermal blooming recorded from the battleship.

There was a stunned silence on the flag bridge. In the main Holo Cube, the blue icon representing the *Lagos Bay* changed to a blinking red, after only a moment, the red held solid. The *Lagos Bay* was gone... along with 2000 humans.

John shook himself. He was still in a firefight and the

Buzzards were lining up for another shot, "Tactical, *Fort Royal* and the heavy cruisers are to concentrate fire on a single Buzzard. I want *Cartagena* and the light cruisers to swing around for a flanking shot. Let's give them two distinct targets and see if we can't split their firepower."

As BatFor 1 maneuvered to come at the Buzzards from two sides, the first wave of missiles headed for Garunda were engaged by the Terran destroyers in their desperate attempt to stop them reaching the planet. The command and control of the Agis ships was second to none: enemy missiles began to fall victim to coordinated anti-missile fire. The first wave was reduced to just eleven survivors. The Others sprang their next surprise.

At a range of only 50000 kilometers from the Agis destroyers, all the remaining eleven missiles detonated. A single bomb pumped x-ray laser shot from the nose of each missile and impacted on an Agis. Each x-ray laser beam was barely ten centimeters in diameter. It struck the hull of an Agis and blew chunks off the ablative armor where it hit a weak point. It penetrated deep into the core of the ship, destroying everything it touched until it reached the outer hull on the opposite side of the ship, where the armored hull halted its deadly path.

Chance is a fickle thing. Of the eleven surviving x-ray lasers targeting the Terran destroyer's, six shots were clean misses. TDF *Conquerant* and *Venomous* took one hit a piece, causing minor damage, but TDF *Oberon* was struck by three: one penetrated her forward missile magazine. The result was immediate and catastrophic. Megaton range nuclear weapons exploded before the crew of *Oberon* had an inkling something was wrong. *Oberon* died, along with 250 of her crew, in all-consuming nuclear fire.

Oberon's sister ships could not spare the time to mourn her passing as the dispassionate computers compensated for the hole left in the anti-missile net by *Oberon*'s passing. The second wave of missiles was upon the destroyers and the space around them filled with HVMs, particle beams and laser defense cluster fire as computers on board the destroyers took over from their human operators – for only they were quick enough to prioritize and engage targets as the Others' missiles swept over the little destroyers.

The third wave arrived quickly on the heels of the second. Space filled with the defensive fire of the nine remaining Agis destroyers as they struggled to cope with the onslaught. TDF *Venomous* found itself rocked to the frame by the explosion of a fifty-megaton missile as it died under the fire of one of the *Venomous'* laser defense clusters. The shock caused the command and control system to go off line for a fraction of a second, and yet more time was lost as the system re booted itself. It was enough. Two of The Others' missiles made it cleanly past the destroyers and began their final plunge toward the surface of Garunda.

A shout from Tactical alerted John to the impending destruction on Garunda. "Leakers! We have leakers. At least two missiles moving beyond the engagement range of the destroyer screen and headed for the planet surface. Time to impact two minutes."

John knew in his heart he could do nothing to stop the two remaining 'Other' missiles. He could only pray whatever their target, it was a thinly populated one and the attack resulted in minimal casualties.

John pulled himself back to his current predicament – the remaining Buzzards. *Fort Royal* and the heavy cruisers succeeded in destroying another of the Buzzards from the group of three that had killed the *Lagos Bay*. From the readings on his display, it appeared they had badly damaged another. That left only two to deal with. The remaining Buzzard from the three ship formation and the single Buzzard that had, so far, hung back from the main battle.

As the *Cartagena* and her two Talos light cruiser escorts swung around, it brought the Buzzard broadside onto the *Cartagena's* grazer. As John watched, the grazer fired, striking the Buzzard amid ship and cutting it cleanly in half. The smaller grazers mounted on the two Talos light cruisers fired, and the remains of the Buzzard were wiped from space.

John was staring intently at his tactical display, plotting his next move, when the icon for the Agis destroyer TDF *Dagger* vanished, only to reappear virtually touching the planet Garunda. It hung there for a few seconds before again disappearing and reappearing in almost the exact location within the tactical display from which it had vanished. John rubbed his eyes quickly, it must have been a brief fault. Dismissing it, John still had the last Buzzard to worry about.

"Aspect change on Buzzard Six Admiral!" called the tactical officer. "She's reversed course and is moving away."

John's reaction was immediate. "Communications! Signal all ships: Engage the remaining Buzzard immediately." The information the Buzzard contained was priceless. The Others had already witnessed the effectiveness of not only the Terran weapons but of their own weapons on the Terran ships. John had to stop this precious knowledge from getting back to them.

The commander at Tactical was fully engrossed in his display as he reported to John, "Direct hit on the rear quarter of Buzzard Six, Admiral. Her speed is dropping, looks like complete engine failure."

The Other's ship was dead in space and John paused for a moment with his steepled fingers in front of him. He realized a golden opportunity presented itself. It would have to wait though for the time being – the Other's ship was not going anywhere any time soon.

John regarded the floating image of Garunda in the tactical display and felt the heavy burden of responsibility weigh on his shoulders. He wondered at the destruction caused by the two surviving missiles that had somehow avoided the destroyers' desperate attempts to protect the planet.

"Communications! Signal the destroyers to move into low orbit and compile a damage assessment of Garunda."

The commander at Tactical turned to John with a wide smile on his face. "The missiles didn't impact the planet, Admiral."

John looked at him incredulously as he felt the weight lift from his shoulders. "Explain, Commander,"

"Sir, on his own initiative Captain Engel carried out a micro fold and placed TDF *Dagger* just outside the upper atmosphere of Garunda where he proceeded to engage and destroy the two remaining missiles before returning to his place in the destroyer screen."

To say John was astonished by one of the gutsiest maneuvers he had ever heard of was an understatement. It would only have taken the slightest of miscalculations to place Engel and his ship in the atmosphere of the planet – no place for a ship designed to be operated in space. Yeah... gutsy was the word.

"Communications! Signal to *Dagger*: You and your crew have the personal thanks of the fleet commander for your actions this day."

John returned to his display. His fingers called up a more detailed image of the Buzzard and an idea began to take shape in his head. "Tactical. Have you enough data on the Buzzard to ensure you cleanly disable her engines permanently and identify all her exterior weaponry?"

The commander at Tactical turned slowly in his chair as he began to understand what his admiral was asking of him. "Sir, would I be right in assuming you wish to ensure Buzzard Six remains dead in space and you wish me to remove her ability to fire upon us but you don't want me to destroy her?"

John smiled and pointed a finger in his direction. "I believe, Commander, you may have read my mind."

The tactical officer frowned as he thought over the complex task Radford had set him. "I can certainly use surgical strikes from our particle weapons to do as you want, Admiral. But may I ask, why?"

John's smile broadened as he turned back to the image of the Others ship. "Because Commander, I intend assaulting that ship with marines and taking it intact."

#

As the battle raged around Garunda, a small surveillance platform sitting motionless high above the ecliptic plane and identical to that found around Planet V used its passive sensors to record the unfolding events and safely store them away. Its internal clock told it to expect the signal to download its take to the next visiting ship in just over three months.

CHAPTER SEVENTEEN

BOARDING ACTION

TDF CARTAGENA · 31 AQUILAE

To John Radford's surprise his request for marine support to carry out a boarding action of the remaining Buzzard was answered within the hour by the appearance of the marine assault ship TDF *Saint Nazarene*.

Based on the Vulcan class heavy cruiser TDF *Saint Nazarene* was an Excalibur class assault ship, carrying little in the way of offensive armament she relied on her extra armor to survive in battle. What she did carry was a marine assault battalion of 510 fighting men and women. Ten Buffalo assault shuttles to carry twenty wraith suited marines into a hot landing zone. Five heavy lift Gigant shuttles to carry the marines' heavy equipment and five Reapers to provide close air support on a planet's surface. The Reapers were a small, two man, highly manoeuvrable and lethal craft equipped with rapid-fire plasma cannon and HVMs. All in all, *Saint Nazarene* carried everything a marine battalion needed to carry out independent actions like the one John had in mind.

"*Saint Nazarene* is hailing us Admiral."

"Put her through Lieutenant" replied John as he spun his chair to face his personal Holo Cube. John felt his face break into a grin as the smiling face of Alec Murray appeared.

"Well, well, well. Look what the cat dragged in. Good to see you Alec. I see you didn't waste any time getting here."

Alec shrugged his shoulders in his typically nonchalant manner.

"I hear the navy couldn't finish the job without us marines coming to the rescue… again."

John let out a short snort of laughter before getting straight to the point.

"That Buzzard out there could be a wealth of intelligence Alec. Just the chance to get our hands on one of their ships, a look at their technology. Maybe even the opportunity to secure their navigational data, find out where they come from and the extent of the area under their control. It could lend us insight into what we are facing in this war."

John's voice took on a somber tone. "And make no mistake Alec, this is a war now. We may have won today but we have no idea of what we truly face."

In the Holo Cube Alec's life like image nodded its head in understanding.

"Time is of the essence here, Alec, The Others have a two hour head start and if I were in command of their ship I would demolish anything and everything I thought useful to an enemy. We must get aboard that Buzzard and secure as much as we can before they destroy it."

John paused and Alec saw a frown appear on his friend's brow. "To be honest with you Alec, I don't understand why they haven't abandoned ship and scuttled her already."

"It occurred to my planning team as well, Admiral. We came up with only two options: one - for whatever reason they can't scuttle her or…" any trace of a smile left Alec's face, "two - they're waiting for us to board her, then scuttle her and take us with them."

Taking a breath John looked resolutely into the disembodied face of his friend, before he gave the order he knew could be condemning Alec and his marines to death.

"It's a risk we have to take Alec. The prize is simply too big to pass up."

From the Holo Cube, Alec's eyes steadfastly held John's. It was not the first time John had sent men and women under his command into danger and Alec knew his friend would not do it lightly.

"You of course have my full support for your plan Alec…" the grin slowly returned to John's face. "You do have a plan don't you?"

This time it was Alec's turn to let out a short laugh. "It may not be pretty but I reckon it will do the job." Alec's gaze flicked out of the holo cube's field of view for a moment before returning to fix on John. "My marines are boarding the shuttles now. We launch in ten minutes."

"Good luck Alec."

With a quick nod from Alec the connection terminated. John sat back in his chair and quietly said a prayer for the marines.

#

Aboard his command shuttle Alec Murray remained outwardly calm. To any observer everything was under control. The operation will run as smoothly as a Swiss watch… Alec reassured himself, so why was his stomach doing flip-flops and his brain running at a thousand miles per hour?

"Five minutes 'til contact Colonel." The warm, honey like southern accent of the female marine pilot called as if it was just another training flight.

Alec pulled up a real time flight plot on his Wraith suit's heads-up display. Nine Buffalo shuttles were formed up into three flights of three shuttles. Each flight of three performed an intricate weaving pattern designed to fool any enemy gunners as they approached the 1700 meters long, 220,000 tonnes enemy ship from the rear. The navy assured him by using pinpoint energy weapon strikes on the Buzzard's outer hull, they turned anything resembling detection equipment, anti-ship or anti-missile systems into worthless scrap metal. All the same Alec saw no reason to take life threatening risks. He was not complacent, although no enemy fire had been directed at his

188

shuttles, it could mean the enemy were simply waiting until the shuttles reached point blank range before opening fire.

Alec's plan was simple, as he mulled on it a worried frown crossed his forehead. The plan was stripped back as he had no idea what he and his marines were going into. There was no intelligence to indicate the internal layout of the Buzzard. The crew estimate of 1400 was exactly that. Based on Intelligence's guesstimate on crew requirements for a human ship the size of a Buzzard. Alec had no idea whether his marines would face the Others version of themselves once they entered the Buzzard or whether it would just be armed ships' crew. Assuming of course they were able to actually enter the ship.

The Buffaloes were headed for what Intelligence had identified as airlocks spread along the hull of the Buzzard. Alec let out a sigh of resignation, they thought they were airlocks, they could be waste disposal hatches for all they knew. The thought of his marines blowing their way into the Buzzard only to be confronted by a mountain of rubbish was one which in any other circumstance, would bring tears of laughter to Alec's eyes, but not today. Intelligence rationalized the ports were spread evenly around the hull of the Buzzard and were roughly equidistant along its length.

Alec divided his initial assault force into three sub units: 'A' Company under Captain Brandon, the bow where all things being equal they would locate the bridge. 'C' Company under Captain Alonso, the stern where they should find the engineering spaces. 'B' Company under Captain Tanaka, with Alec's small headquarters element attached amidships where on human ships you would expect to find the computer core.

Of the three marine companies initially employed in the assault 'C' Company had, perhaps, the easiest yet most crucial task. Human warfare was governed by The Rules of War, it stated an enemy should be given the opportunity to surrender. In drawing up his assault plan Alec recognized he had no choice but to breach this rule, he could not afford to give anyone in the engineering spaces the opportunity to set off scuttling charges. 'C' Company were ordered to give no quarter, they were to secure the engineering spaces at all costs and hold until relieved. Captain Alonso's stoic look when he received said order indicated he understood tough calls had to be made at times and this was one of those times.

Following the initial insertion the Buffaloes were to return to TDF *Saint Nazarene* and pick up the second wave of marines who would then insert through the breaches made by the assault force to reinforce as Alec deemed necessary. This was guesswork on Alec's part but it was all they had to work with.

#

"One minute… doors opening. Gravity off." The command came in the same calm voice. The loadmaster pressed a control and Alec felt the bottom of his seat retract until his legs dangled below him. The marines were now secured only by the magnetic shoulder harness as the emptiness of space sped past below. Alec took a sharp intake of breath as, not ten meters below his feet, the scarred and gouged battle armor of the Buzzard suddenly appeared. Damn that hull was close! Alec hoped the pilot did not have to make any radical maneuvers. She had not left herself much wiggle room.

The shuttle came to a halt directly over a three by three meter hatch with what looked like a locking mechanism off to one side. Alec assumed a rigid vertical position as the loadmaster touched the control activating the pusher system. The shoulder harness dropped explosively downward before disconnecting from the marines suits, shooting the marines out of the shuttle bay akin to a cork exploding from a bottle. Twenty marines spat out of the shuttle bay doors at a speed only the integral Wraith suit computer could compensate for. The marines' shoulder harnesses were still retracting into the shuttle bay as the shuttle was piloted back to TDF *Saint Nazarene* for her next load. Alec felt his legs bend slightly at the knees as his suit automatically prepared to take the impact with the hull. With a jolt Alec's feet contacted the hull and his suit activated its magnetic boots to secure him in place while he oriented himself.

With no word of command the two marines carrying the

breaching charges moved to the airlock doors and placed their cargo. The remaining marines stacked up a few meters clear, ready to enter once the charges went off. In Alec's helmet display a small clock appeared and a warning tone sounded in his ear. Five… four… three… two… one… flash! The helmet filters automatically dimmed what Alec knew was a blinding explosion, he felt a slight vibration through his body and knew the initial breach was successful. A marine moved forward and without exposing himself stuck his rifle barrel into the hole. Alec's heads-up display was filled by the image, courtesy of the marine's barrel camera of a room four by three by two meters with a second bulkhead at the far end. It was indeed an airlock.

"That's a beer I owe Intelligence," Alec muttered as his marines were occupied with the next stage of their assault. A marine maintained an over watch on the inside of the airlock while another, with a second breaching charge dropped in, his feet found the deck inside. "Internal gravity is on" Alec noted out loud.

The marine approached the inner airlock door and placed a second breaching charge before beating a hasty retreat to the outer hull. Five… four… three… Alec watched the countdown on his heads-up display as the warning tone sounded, two… one… Flash! Another successful breach. The airlock gushed atmosphere as the corridor beyond was subjected to explosive decompression. Atmosphere was not the only thing to rush out into the cold darkness of space. At least half a dozen unsuited crew were dragged through the airlock and ejected into space. They may be the enemy but Alec hoped the merciful embrace of death came quickly to them.

The marines surged through the airlock, into the now empty corridor beyond and took up covering positions.

"Williams! Scan!" Ordered Tanaka. Marine Williams produced a handheld device from a leg compartment of his suit and slowly turned in a circle.

The Buzzard's armor had previously defeated the TDF's scanning equipment. The layout of the Buzzard could not be determined without a navy ship closing with it and using a powerful penetrating radar which would have damaged any computers and storage devices onboard and irradiated the crew. The decision to carry out a manual scan after the breach was not really a decision, it was the only choice. Williams was doing a sterling job and within moments Alec's suit indicated it had begun receiving the data to build into a complete schematic of the Buzzard. Alec took the opportunity to check the progress of his other assault teams.

The other two 'B' Company teams amid ship had successfully gained entry and had as yet met no opposition. On the other hand the three 'A' Company teams in the bow were meeting stiff resistance by space suited crew armed with laser rifles.

Alec's suit was having difficulty getting a solid link with 'C' Company. He was not unduly concerned as communication difficulties were to be expected. The engineering spaces on any ship were heavily shielded and would, no doubt, cause interference. Alec keyed his radio and called Captain Brandon as Williams finished his scan. A ship's schematic appeared in Alec's display containing the marines known positions.

"Sitrep Captain Brandon."

"Team One is pinned down in the corridor adjacent to the airlock. I have three KIA and two walking wounded. Without using something heavier I will be unable to make progress. Team Two met minimal resistance and are advancing to what they believe to be the main missile bays. I prioritized that task and have sent Team Three in support. I believe we have identified the bridge.

Our scan shows what appears to be a mass of command and control lines running to an area two decks above my current position, it's more heavily shielded than any other section in the bow. I intend to break through current enemy resistance and make our way to that section." A clear concise report, a sure sign Brandon was an experienced combat leader. Alec's own experience led him to read between the lines. Brandon's professionalism and dedication to his men prevented him from spelling out his worst fears, his marines would continue to die without the release of heavier weapons.

192

Alec unconsciously worried his bottom lip, a habit he developed in childhood which reappeared whenever he had a tough decision to make. He was sympathetic to Brandon's position but using heavy weapons on board brought with it collateral damage and the possibility of destroying exactly what they had come to secure.

His marines though where taking casualties. Alec came to his decision. "Heavy weapons at your discretion Captain but don't get all John Wayne on me understood?"

"Aye aye Sir."

"On 'D' Company's arrival in…" Alec quickly checked the progress of the second wave of marines. Damn! They were still sixteen minutes out. "Sixteen minutes I shall chop two teams to your command. Your mission is to secure the bridge ASAP."

"Roger that Sir. I'll use explosives to blow upward through the deck plates which should side step their defenses."

"Sounds good Captain. Let's make it happen!" Alec cut the link and gave the sub vocal command "Suit, call Alonso." A pause followed by a double tone informed Alec his suit could not establish a link to Alonso, instead it automatically searched for the next active ranking marine.

"Go for Semple." The voice sounded strained and distracted. Alec's face paled as he did a quick mental calculation. Semple was something like tenth in the chain of command.

"Sitrep Sergeant?"

"The situation is… let's call it fluid at the moment Sir… Wait. Jonas on your six! Two enemy on… Shit!"

On Alec's display Marine Jonas' name flashed red then disappeared as Semple came back on the link.

"Sir I have fifty-three KIA and virtually everyone else has an injury of some sort. The initial entry went as planned but as soon as we cleared the airlocks we were assaulted by enemy marines in full up armor. They were using some sort of plasma grenade. The suits can take a lot of damage but plasma in a confined space you can imagine…" Semple paused, Alec could hear the stress in his voice.

"Sergeant! Can you hold?"

"We've killed all the armored marines and secured all the entrances into engineering by bodging the breaching charges and using them to warp the bulkheads. If they want back in here they'll have to either blow or cut their way in. I'm sweeping the area now for anything that looks like scuttling charges and enemy stragglers. They seem to be mostly suited crew armed with nothing more than improvised weapons but they'll attack a suited marine with whatever they can get their hands on. It's like they have some form of death wish or something."

Alec felt a surge of pride. 'C' Company had suffered fifty-three dead from a fighting force of eighty marines. According to Alec's readouts the remaining twenty-seven had all sustained injuries to varying degrees. With all his officers and senior NCOs dead, Semple had assumed command continuing the mission until its successful conclusion.

Alec checked the arrival time of the second wave again. The clock was not going fast enough for Alec's liking and not for the first time that day he wished he could control time.

"Sergeant. You'll have a team from 'D' Company with you in twelve minutes. Murray clear." A flashing icon in his display told Alec Captain Tanaka was waiting to speak with him.

"Go for Murray."

"Sir. If you'll check your schematic it looks like we've identified the computer core."

Alec scanned the schematics now showing in his display. An area highlighted in yellow was located at almost the center of the ship. It appeared heavily shielded, one small area at the heart, seemingly constructed of the same type of battle armor as the ship's hull.

Alec's brow furrowed in thought, it seemed to be overkill. If a deep penetrating weapon such as this struck, surely the ship would be lost. Why bother protecting a comparatively tiny area to this extent. Alec mentally shrugged, there was only one way to find out. Alec pulled up his marines positions. His display showed Teams Five and Six, the other two amidships teams, were making their way horizontally along their respective decks, away from the computer core.

"OK Captain that looks like our objective. Order Teams Five and Six to make their way there now." Tanaka cut the link to pass the necessary orders while Alec contemplated his next problem.

The Buzzard's battle armor was blocking all communication with anything beyond the hull, he couldn't talk to either the Admiral or the shuttles carrying the second wave. At least this comms problem had an easy answer. Alec punched in the link for his two-man security/headquarter team. Gunny Wanderman and Corporal Fredricks.

"Gunny. You and Fredricks remain here. We'll use your suit's comms units to act as a relay for the marines inside the hull to the outside world. I'll stay with Captain Tanaka."

With a curt "Aye aye, sir" the Gunny and Fredricks moved into the cover of the inner airlock and almost immediately the icon for the flagship began blinking.

"Go for Murray."

"Thought we'd lost you there for a minute," came the concerned voice of John Radford before turning business like, "Sitrep?"

"Admiral we're taking casualties but we believe we have secured the engineering section. We are confident we have identified the missile bays, the bridge and the computer core and I have teams moving to secure them now. The Buzzard's crew are putting up stiff resistance in places but on the deployment of the second wave I am sure I can secure our objectives."

"Understood, Alec. Keep your head down."

"That's one thing you can be assured of. Murray clear."

Changing channels Alec stood up. "Let's go, Captain."

#

Gunny Wanderman followed the progress of the various teams and the imminent arrival of the reinforcement shuttles with one eye while keeping a wary lookout for the enemy with the other. He clocked Corporal Fredricks bracing herself in the upper corner of the airlock with her head poking out of the jagged remains of the outer airlock door, presumably to allow her suit's

195

surveillance systems to get a clear image of the outer hull until its curved shape took it out of line of sight. Wanderman's thoughts were interrupted by a call from Fredricks.

"Gunny I've got movement on the hull."

Wanderman brought the image up on his display. Sure enough he made out at least four space suited figures cresting the curve of the hull about twenty meters from the airlock. None of the suits were transmitting an IFF code. Wanderman's heart rate rose several beats per minute, what were the enemy doing on the hull? He did not have to wait long for an answer. Two of the enemy figures raised a long tube onto their shoulders. Missiles!

Wanderman activated the emergency link on his suit, automatically overriding all other broadcasts on the marine net. "Vampire. Vampire. Enemy soldiers on the hull with missiles. Location twenty meters ship north of airlock four I am engaging with small arms. Wanderman clear."

Fredricks had already swung her whole body up through the outer airlock and was firing at the enemy soldiers. As Wanderman pushed himself upwards to join her he saw Fredricks' shake then, in gruesome slow motion he watched her lower half, neatly cauterized just above the pelvis, fall backwards into the airlock. Fredericks' remains hung, suspended by the suit's magnetic boots. Of her upper torso there was no sign.

Wanderman stuck his rifle up through the airlock and used his suit's targeting system to show him the enemy soldiers. Fredricks must have downed two before her demise there were only two left. One had taken cover behind a large section of damaged hull denying Wanderman a clean shot. The other, however, was advancing toward his position as fast as his magnetic boots would allow, he made no attempt to move from cover to cover. *More fool you*, thought Wanderman as he fired off an aimed shot which struck the advancing soldier squarely in the chest. The plasma round was traveling at a significant portion of the speed of light and went through the soldiers armored chest like it wasn't even there. Exiting through the back of the suit it carried on into the infinity of space. Wanderman was contemplating moving onto the hull to get a clean shot at the remaining soldier when the shrill tone of a proximity warning sounded in his ear, interrupting his thought process. The starlight around him disappeared as a Buffalo shuttle came to a stop not two meters above him. The nose of the Buffalo was pointed at the section of damaged hull behind which the enemy soldier was hiding and as Wanderman looked on the nose mounted rapid fire plasma cannon discharged. The section of the hull and the soldier vanished in a brilliant flash. Twenty fully armed and Wraith suited marines dropped beside him and headed through the airlock to join the fight. The blinking icon of an incoming call caught Wanderman's attention.

He activated the link. That warm, honey like voice said "Thank you kindly for the heads up Gunny. The other Buffaloes are reporting missile teams were waiting for them at each of the airlocks. Could've been a nasty surprise if you hadn't got that warning out"

Despite recent events Wanderman smiled. "My pleasure Ma'am."

"I think maybe we should hang around for a while in case you need any more flies scratched off your back."

"I'm obliged. Wanderman clear."

#

Deep in the hull Alec Murray and Team Four were closing on their objective. The suspected computer core. During a natural pause between tactical bounds Alec took a minute to check on the progress of the teams in the forty minutes since the initial breaching action.

What appeared to be the main missile magazine had been secured with the minimum amount of casualties by Teams Two and Three. The lieutenants, in charge of each team, got their heads together and came up with an idea, which was quickly adopted by all Team Leaders, of using a small charge on every bulkhead door they came across. The ones on either side of their route of advance got a charge large enough to buckle the frame making the doors inoperable. The ones on the actual route of advance were blown open and left that way. The net effect was that the entire line of advance was left in hard vacuum trapping the ship's crew in the areas which still retained atmosphere. On reaching the missile bay the marines had simply blown the bulkheads and allowed the atmosphere to escape before entering to minimal opposition. It may seem cruel to some but it kept marine casualties and collateral damage to a minimum. A good thing too as Team Two reported the crew had been in the process of rigging some of the nuclear missiles with dead man switches which would have allowed them to be detonated by hand rather than electronically. The detonation of a few nukes would have destroyed the ship, the crew and the marines.

Captain Brandon had managed to circumvent his immediate opposition by blasting his way through the deck plates but Brandon reported stiffening opposition from armored soldiers as he approached the bridge area but he was confident with the imminent arrival of reinforcements he could take the bridge in short order.

Sergeant Semple held the engineering spaces with the arrival of fresh marines he was in the process of evacuating his wounded, although he refused to leave himself. Memories of 70 Ophiuchi came to mind and Alec wondered if he was going to have no choice but to send Gunny Wanderman to Engineering to remind Semple of the consequences of refusing to obey orders.

"Moving."

The call on Team Four's net brought Alec back to his current position. By the schematics reckoning Team Four was less than twenty meters from the area which showed the heaviest shielding. The lead marine made his way to the corner of the corridor and went to one knee as he extended his rifle in front of him giving it, and by extension, his suit which passed the image to the other suits of the team a clear look along the marines' line of advance. Alec had the fleetest of moments to identify a barricaded position as the entire corner where the lead marine was kneeling exploded outward flinging the marine clear across the corridor where he bounced off the far wall and lay still. The red blinking name Morales appeared then disappeared in Alec's display.

The marines around him hugged the corridor walls for cover as two small, round, black objects rebounded off the corridors wall and fell by Morales' still form.

"Grenade!" screamed Alec as he fell to the deck. The world around him rocked and his suit filters blackened as the first wave of superheated plasma passed over him. Alec sensed rather than felt being violently beaten onto the deck. The beating seemed to last forever. Alec prayed for his suit to maintain its integrity and spare his life.

The detached, rational part of Alec's mind knew only a few seconds had passed, not a lifetime, but a few seconds in combat was the difference between living and dying. He knew if he was in command of the enemy soldiers he would order a follow up charge on the heels of the explosion.

Alec struggled to his knees as the first armor clad enemy soldier came around the corner. A lethal looking rifle in his hands was swinging in Alec's direction. Alec tried to raise his own weapon but his brain was finding it difficult to coordinate. Alec realized he was not going to make it and resigned himself to his fate... What the hell? Alec shook his head to clear the fog... he saw the hand of God pluck the soldier off the corridor floor, throw him high in the air before returning him as a million shredded pieces. Something tapped Alec's shoulder, he turned toward it. All external sound practically muted by the ringing in his ears, Alec concentrated on the moving lips he saw, and the muffled noises coming from them

"Sir! Can you hear me? Sir! Are you all right?" Alec strained to hear the marine.

"Captain" Alec struggled to get the word out as he re oriented himself.

Muqimi repeated "Sir! Are you OK?"

Alec shook his head to clear it as his suit systems began injecting pain numbing medication, enough to keep him mobile. He nodded in assent and Muqimi helped him to his feet, urgently grabbing at his arm and pulling with great strength while maintaining possession of his own weapon. Now on his unsteady feet, Alec looked around him and snorted at his own stupidity, it had not been the hand of God to the rescue, it was his reinforcements.

He sobered immediately on the realization that Team Four had ceased to exist. Twelve fellow marines gone in an instant. The survivors had sustained severe injuries.

"Muqimi, it must have been the plasma grenades," Alec gestured toward the destruction. "Semple came up against them in the engineering spaces," Muqimi nodded his understanding, "around the corner are the enemy who've just wiped out your fellow marines I want them to understand that killing a marine is a bad idea." Alec was almost running on a full tank of gas now, "Do you understand me?"

Muqimi, a marine for the guts of fifteen years, understood his commander perfectly. "Message received and understood Sir!" He switched to his team channel. "Marines covering fire on my command. Breaching charges forward. Standby. Standby. Fire!"

The wrath of God rained down fire, engulfing the enemy position as Team Fourteen poured plasma fire onto the killers of their fellow marines. Under this cover two breaching charges were launched, their magnetic hooks held them fast against the enemy barricade. A heart beat later their shaped charge heads exploded, reverberating throughout the ship. The barricade and its defenders ceased to exist. The marines charged through the cloud of debris. A still shaky Alec with them. No quarter was asked for nor given. The marines cleared the position leaving only death and destruction in their wake.

Before them lay the bulkhead leading to the computer core. As Alec approached the bulkhead he felt, just for a moment, an unusual tingling. He checked his suit readouts, he had not imagined it. Then through the deck plates beneath his feet he felt a deep rumble. "Suit, analysis!"

A male un intoned, synthesized voice replied, "Systems show a three hertz ultra-low frequency signal. Duration two seconds. Generated from indeterminate source located seven meters beyond the bulkhead. One second later there was a thermal baric explosion. There is no electrical activity from that section, further I detect the only life signs aboard this vessel are those belonging to Terran Defense Force personnel."

CHAPTER EIGHTEEN

FIRST CONTACT

OFFICE OF THE PRESIDENT OF THE TERRAN REPUBLIC - GENEVA - EARTH

Rebecca sat alone in her office as she contemplated the events of the past couple of weeks. Since the battle in 31 Aquilae, the press had been full of praise for the members of BatFor 1, especially one Captain Engel, who was swiftly becoming regarded as some form of hero for his actions in stopping the missiles which would have wrought so much destruction on the defenseless planet Garunda. There was even a suggestion he should be awarded the Terran Medal of Honor, one which if put forward officially Rebecca would only be too happy to agree to.

A flash of lighting made Rebecca look out the windows of her office, a wry smile crossing her lips as she regarded the gathering storm clouds as they blew over the mountains. The first rain spoiled the mirror perfect surface of Lake Geneva.

A soft knock on the door drew her attention back into the room as the door opened and Secretary Helset and General Joyce entered the room. Rebecca came around her desk to greet them.

"Gentlemen. Glad you could make it." Rebecca shook both men's hands warmly as she indicated for them to take a seat around her private briefing table. "I'm eager to hear what progress the team from Research and Development are making on the captured enemy ship."

"Madam President, with your permission…" began Joyce. Rebecca nodded her ascent and Joyce inserted a secure chip into the Holo Cube concealed in the table. It sprang to life on command and displayed the interior of a ship, similar to a human ship but undoubtedly alien.

"Madam President, as you know, following the arrival of extra Marine elements, Admiral Radford began a boarding operation of the last surviving Buzzard. During the operation, marine casualties were high. They were restricted in the weaponry they could employ on board without destroying the very thing they had come to capture and the crew of the ship fought tooth and nail for every meter of the ship." Joyce's voice faltered as he continued, "By the time the marines secured the ship, they had sustained eighty-four killed in action and 142 seriously wounded."

Rebecca shook her head slowly. "Any update on enemy casualties?"

Joyce paused and composed himself. "No living crew members have been located. It appears those who weren't killed fighting the marines committed suicide when it became obvious they were about to be captured."

Rebecca forced down a shiver. She had hoped, with the fight for the ship over, the search teams would find some of the crew alive. All of them dead? Some at their own hand? What sort of people are they? "Excuse me, General. Please continue."

"Colonel Murray's decision to seize the engine room and the missile magazines first undoubtedly saved lives. His marines found the crew in the missile magazines attempting to detonate the warheads and the engine room crew trying the same thing with the engines. If either group had succeeded, it would have destroyed the ship and killed our boarding party."

"Colonel Murray is to be commended, General." A furrow appeared on Rebecca's brow. "Murray. The name seems familiar."

Helset leaned forward. "Colonel Murray was promoted

following the operation in 70 Ophiuchi where he commanded the marines who carried out the reconnaissance of 'The Others' base there, Madam President."

"A well-deserved promotion then, Olaf," commented the president. "Please go on, General."

Joyce manipulated the Holo Cube controls and a schematic of the Buzzard appeared in the air above the table, a forward section highlighted. "The team from R and D identified this as the source of the weapons fire which managed to destroy the TDF *Lagos Bay*. Initial analysis by the team leader states the weapon is a large x-ray laser similar to those the Others had deployed on their missiles used against the destroyer screen."

Rebecca held up a hand to stop the General. "Didn't the initial brief state those lasers were powered by a nuclear detonation? Surely, General, the Others don't detonate a nuclear device on board their own ships every time they fire that thing?"

In response, Joyce manipulated the controls once more and a line appeared on the schematic, weaving its way from one end of the ship to the other. "The R and D team believe the weapon is tied directly into the ship's engines, which might explain their sudden drop in speed just prior to the weapon being fired. It's slow firing and leaves them at a small tactical disadvantage as they lose speed but, as the destruction of the *Lagos Bay* shows, if it hits its intended target the effects are devastating."

The room stilled. The loss of the *Lagos Bay* and its crew of 2000 had been the largest single loss of life the Terran Defense Forces had ever suffered, but everyone in the room realized it would not be the last.

With a small sigh of resignation Rebecca went on. "Have we learned anything more I should know about, General?"

"Yes, Madam President. The team have identified what they believe to be the main computer core. It's not completely intact, but fortunately the marines got to it before it could be wiped. We're hoping it holds vital intelligence. Rather than try and work on it in situ, the whole section containing it is being removed from the ship and will be taken back to Stickney Base for analysis there."

"That's the best news I've heard all day, General. Our lack of knowledge about the Others is our biggest handicap by far."

Joyce nodded his head in agreement. "I couldn't agree more, Madam President, although I must remind you to be realistic. Deciphering the computer core will undoubtedly take time."

Rebecca gave a small chuckle. "I understand, General. I'll try not to get my hopes up too high. Now, is there anything else?"

With a sound like a grunt, Helset cleared his throat.

Rebecca spared him a smile. "Olaf, you would never have made a good politician."

Helset returned her smile with one of his own. "Thank you for the compliment, Madam President."

Rebecca emitted a laugh. "You're welcome, Olaf. Now, how may I help?"

Helset sat a little further forward in his seat. "Madam President, the decision to intercept the Others and defend Garunda, while undoubtedly the right thing to do, has left us in a bit of a precarious position."

Rebecca could feel the involuntary frown on her brow forming. "How so, Olaf?"

Helset glanced at Joyce before continuing. "Our plans have always been centered on defending Earth and Janus, but with our action around Garunda I feel it has committed us to the defense of a third star system – a system containing a native civilization for which we are now responsible, for better or for worse."

Rebecca could feel the anger rising in her. "Are you suggesting we abandon Garunda to its fate, Olaf, after the sacrifices made in its protection?"

Helset raised both hands as if to ward off a physical attack from the president. "No, not at all, Madam President. Please don't misunderstand me. I am as committed to defending Garunda as you are. Please accept my apology if that is how my words were interpreted."

By the look of shock on the Secretary's face, Rebecca realized she may have over reacted a little. Getting control of her anger, she continued in a more even tone, "Apology accepted, Olaf. Please accept mine in return. I should know you would never leave those people defenseless."

Helset looked relieved. "Thank you, Madam President. My point is our current force deployment does not take into consideration the defense of a third star system." Helset touched the controls in front of him and the Holo Cube displayed three star systems, with a list of TDF assets displayed under each.

"Madam President, as you can see, the TDF have First Fleet in the Sol system securing Earth and Second Fleet to secure Janus. The assets in 31 Aquilae protecting Garunda are currently drawn from BatFor 3 of Second Fleet as BatFor 1 has been withdrawn to Deimos for repairs and refit. As things stand, it is The Joint Chiefs' intention to continue to rotate a BatFor into 31 Aquilae until such time as construction of new hulls and training of personnel allows for 31 Aquilae to have its own dedicated BatFor."

Helset gave Joyce a quick glance, one not missed by Rebecca. "Olaf, am I to take it you and The Joint Chiefs are in disagreement?"

When Helset did not offer an immediate reply, Rebecca became apprehensive. "Olaf, would you like to tell me what is going on?"

Unbidden, Helset stood, took a few steps away from the table and stopped with his back to the president, looking out of the wide windows being rain lashed by the approaching storm. Helset turned to face Rebecca and stood a little bit taller. "Madam President, when we discovered the Gravity Drive, it opened the stars to humanity and what we have found in the Others could destroy us all. But not only us. We have found three other civilizations out there, one populating Garunda, for which we have intervened and saved from destruction and another, Messier 54, which has, as far as we know, no idea either we or the Others exist. The third, the builders of the surveillance platform observing Garunda, we have no idea whether they are friendly or not."

Helset began to pace up and down as he spoke. "The problem as I see it cannot only be solved by military means. In the longer term, the Others will want to know what happened to the ships it

206

sent to destroy Garunda. It makes more sense to build a fleet base in 31 Aquilae which will become the home to what I envisage will become Third Fleet. However, we can't just go building fleet bases in other people's star systems, even if they have no clue we exist. The problem needs a political solution."

"And what is this problem you're eluding to, Olaf?" asked Rebecca.

Helset stopped his pacing and looked directly at the president. "We need to make first contact with the indigenous populations of both planets, Madam President. Garunda first because we're already there, followed by Messier 54."

The silence in the room was palpable and seemed to stretch for minutes, even though Rebecca knew it was only a few seconds. "You always come to me with the hard ones, Olaf. I'll give you that."

Haslet let a smile escape his lips. "If they were easy, Madam President, I would sort them myself."

Rebecca chuckled. "Indeed, Olaf."

It was Rebecca's turn to pause and think. The two men in the room waited patiently, knowing the importance of the decision the president faced.

Rebecca refocused her attention into the room. "I'll need to put this before the Senate, but I see the merit of your argument, Olaf. Leave it with me."

Both men stood to leave, but Rebecca stopped them. "One more thing, Olaf. If we are to make contact with the people on Garunda and in Messier 54, it would appear prudent that more research into them is carried out prior to first contact. Could you get together with R and D and have a working group set up before the Senate decides to do it themselves and lumbers us with a bunch of politicians looking to make a name for themselves?"

"Yes, Madam President. I'll get right on it." Haslet turned to leave but Rebecca stopped him with a touch to the elbow.

"Oh and one other thing, Olaf. I would like Doctor Bath on the group."

Both Helset and Joyce looked skeptical.

"Everybody deserves a second chance," said Rebecca, by way

of reply to the unasked question. They left to carry out their president's orders.

#

Aaron Beckett, a career diplomat, had spent over fifty years traveling around the world and the various human habitats dotted throughout the solar system. He had acted as a troubleshooter for eight different presidents, negotiating everything from trade disputes to calls for more autonomy amongst the asteroid belt habitats.

Four years previously, as he turned seventy, Aaron had decided it was time to retire permanently. He moved from the hustle and bustle of Geneva to a small log cabin in the Rocky Mountains. Aaron's wife, Margaret, had died the year before in a freak transport accident, they never had children, Aaron was always too busy. Now he faced a life alone, a life which modern medical science promised would keep him active well into his early hundreds.

Aaron was sitting on his porch, reading a book in the late afternoon sun, when he heard the unmistakable sound of a hover jet approaching from across the lake. He remained seated as the sleek transport had landed on the shoreline and a single passenger disembarked, their face hidden in shadow by the slowly sinking sun behind them. Aaron was unable to make out the face of the visitor until she was nearly at the cabin. Recognition brought him out of his chair in a hurry and his book fell to his feet.

"Good... eh, morn... I mean... afternoon... Madam President." The words tumbled out as best as Aaron could manage through his confusion.

A smiling Rebecca Coston reached forward, brushing away his outstretched hand, instead giving him a kiss on the cheek and a small hug. "It's been too long, Aaron. How have you been?"

Aaron gave a small shrug and a lopsided grin. "Good, Madam President. Thanks for asking. I've been catching up on my reading and just enjoying the quiet life."

"So what does a girl have to do to get a coffee around here?"

208

Aaron cleared some books from a bench seat, next to his own. "If you'd like to take a seat, I'm sure I could rustle up something."

While Aaron made the coffee, Rebecca took a moment to admire the view. A gentle downward slope to the shoreline, the lake water reflected the setting sun as it sank slowly behind snowcapped mountains. Beautiful, simply stunning.

Aaron returned with two mugs of piping hot coffee for them and set them on a small table. "I suppose this isn't really a social visit, Madam President."

Rebecca picked up her mug and blew on the hot coffee before taking a sip. "No, Aaron, it isn't. To be honest, I have a problem and there isn't anyone else I could think of could solve it for me."

With a deep sigh, Aaron took in the view for what he knew would be the last time for the foreseeable future. "How may I serve, Madam President?"

#

ORBIT OF PLANET GARUNDA - 31 AQUILAE

Two months on and Aaron found himself leading Earth's first diplomatic mission amongst the stars. The president's decision to include Patricia Bath, seen by many as controversial, was the key to unlocking the more commonly used languages on Garunda. The highflying stealth drones, employed to gather them from the different nations living on the planet, had unobtrusively recorded Garunda's languages.

Aaron looked again at the distinctly reptilian shaped form in the Holo Cube. The stump of what had been, in its genetic history, a tail was still obvious as was the elongated face covered in overlapping scales and the protruding pink eyes. Aaron's attention, as always, was drawn to the hands. Five fingers with opposable thumbs, the unmistakable sign of Saiph DNA intervention.

The decision on how best to approach first contact rested with Aaron. After all, he would be the one on the ground, so to speak.

The sheer number of identified nation states ruled out the feasibility of visiting each in turn. After many hours consultation with the leading lights in the field of sociocultural anthropology, Aaron concluded the easiest way to reach the majority of the population was to identify the state that appeared to control the greatest land mass in proportion to population. Surprisingly, it turned out to be a relatively small island nation in the southern hemisphere. It appeared to be in control of over one third of the planet. Many of the anthropologists drew on the similarities between that small nation and Britain in the late nineteenth and early twentieth centuries. Aaron inwardly laughed. He just hoped they were not as stuffy.

The beeping of his wrist comm interrupted his thoughts, Aaron touched a control on his desk. The face of Rear Admiral Analisa Chavez, Commanding Officer BatFor 3, Second Fleet replaced the native Garunda.

"Ambassador, your shuttle is prepped and ready for launch."

Aaron had come to know the Admiral over the past couple of weeks spent aboard her flagship, he could see concern lurking behind her calm exterior. Aaron stood a little bit straighter. The decisive moment had arrived. "Thank you Analisa. I'll be along shortly."

Chavez paused as she reached to disconnect the link, "Good luck Aaron." Her face disappeared.

Good luck indeed, thought Aaron. *I'll need it.*

#

As the shuttle dropped from the Nemesis class battleship TDF *Mishima*, Aaron Beckett threw a furtive glance across the aisle at Patricia Bath sitting opposite him. Aaron saw the whites of her knuckles she gripped the side of the seat tightly.

Like many others, Aaron had his doubts when informed Doctor Bath was his official translator on this mission. He too had heard the media reports from the previous year, how her mistake in the translation of the Rubicon database led to an almost disastrous misjudgment by the military of the threat the Others posed to Earth.

Calculations corrected, after the discovery of Patricia's error, revealed the Saiph home world had been destroyed by the Others around the year 1187 AD and not millions of years previously as estimated. Patricia's detractors pointed to the Roman Empire, they existed on Earth for at least 1200 years before their eventual demise. There was, therefore, no reason to believe the Others were extinct, however, there was *every* reason to suppose they were still out there amongst the stars... waiting for a human ship.

Yes this mistake could have held huge consequences, but aside from it Patricia Bath had shown to be a remarkable interpreter. Aaron was no fool. He knew many of Patricia's critics begrudged her successes, after all, she'd been selected by Valerie Hayes.

Valerie was notorious for finding exciting young talent to bring a fresh perspective to problems. She plucked Patricia from virtual obscurity at the ripe old age of twenty-two to heads-up the Linguistics and Cryptology Division at Stickney Base on Phobos. Unfortunately, Valerie also collected political enemies. Her promotion to Special Science Adviser to the president meant many disgruntled colleagues. These colleagues saw protégé Patricia's mistake as an opportunity to damage Valerie's reputation... ending Patricia's career was simply collateral damage.

They took advantage, created a media storm, made Patricia the scapegoat and achieved their aim. Patricia Bath's resignation was reluctantly accepted by President Coston.

Aaron understood the president presented a hard political shell to the world, but having known her for most of her adult life he also knew that underneath was a warm beating human heart, so when the media storm died, Rebecca made a point of giving Patricia a second chance by ensuring a place for her on Aaron's staff.

So here they were, about to initiate man's first contact with another sentient species and the majority of the groundwork had been completed by this slim, auburn haired thirty-one year old. Patricia had spent the last two months either locked away in her office or sleeping in her accommodation aboard the *Mishima*. It had not escaped Aaron's notice that she'd eaten all her meals solo in either her office or accommodation, politely refusing all staff invitations to share a meal, particularly avoiding any young males.

Aaron was concerned Patricia was distancing herself, until now he'd kept his worries to himself in the hope she would come out of her shell but now with no change in her distant behavior and the fact first contact was imminent he was left with no choice but to intervene... somehow.

He reached across and tapped Patricia lightly on the arm, "Doctor Bath." Patricia's head snapped around to face him, shocking Aaron with what he saw in her frightened childlike eyes, he quickly decided on a gentle approach and said softly, "Are you alright Doctor? I'm sure the shuttle will be landing soon and we'll all be back on firm ground."

Patricia slowly shook her head. "Believe me Ambassador it's not the flight I find bothersome. I've been working on the language program for nearly eight weeks and you've based your decision on where to make first contact solely on my interpretation of the available data. I..." her eyes watered and her body began to shake almost imperceptibly, "I just don't want to let you down."

Aaron felt anger well in him as he realized her meaning. The media had not only almost destroyed this young woman's career but had quite clearly obliterated her self-confidence. All this time, working day and night on board TDF *Mishima*, she had been in constant fear of failure, fear she would disappoint Aaron. He closed his eyes briefly, kicking himself with guilt he had failed to cottoned on to the underlying issues behind Patricia's behavior. Well he could solve this problem.

"Doctor Bath... Patricia, the president herself came to me and personally recommended you for this mission. If she has such faith in your abilities then who am I to question them?" Aaron reassured her. "When we land I expect you to stand by my side as my personal aide de camp, not just an interpreter. You have carte blanche to intervene and make any suggestions you feel appropriate." Aaron smiled at the open-mouthed dumbfounded look on Patricia's face. "Close your mouth Patricia, you'll catch flies." Patricia closed her mouth with an audible click.

Aaron reclined with a contented smile on his face, he considered what the media would say about his choice of aide de camp... Screw them!

#

Patricia's head was spinning. Chief Aide and Adviser to Aaron Beckett? Me? The repeater display in front of her sprang to life and halted her whirling thoughts. She got her first good look at the destination she had chosen as man's first meeting with an alien species... Oh God, let it all go as planned! Patricia offered her silent prayer as the shuttle cleared the upper atmosphere and the electro optical systems threw their destination into stark relief.

She had chosen a relatively small island nation in the southern hemisphere located just off the coast of one of the three major landmasses. At first glance there was nothing special about this island. The reconnaissance probes had flown over it and other more populated areas of Garunda but flags only began popping up with the analysis of the compiled data.

While the neighboring continent appeared to be in the throes of what human history characterized as the first industrial revolution: chemical manufacturing, iron production processes, improved efficiency of water power, increasing use of steam power and the development of machine tools. This little island displayed signs it was already well into the period of a second industrial revolution. Technological and economic progress continued with the adoption of steam-powered boats, ships and railways, the large-scale manufacture of machine tools and the increasing use of machinery in steam-powered factories. Analysis showed a much more dense population than its neighbors and reconnaissance probes captured images of seagoing vessels flying the emblem of the island nation in various ports around the planet in a much higher proportion than any other. Taking all these factors into consideration Patricia concluded this small nation was a major planetary power, if not

213

the major planetary power on Garunda.

Patricia wrinkled her forehead… Garunda. Humans had dubbed the planet 'Garunda' soon after their arrival in the system but through research it seemed the planet had been given many different names by its various nations and religious groups. She decided it was an issue best dealt with at a later date, Aaron Becket had much bigger fish to fry than identifying the indigenous population's name for their world.

The shuttle levelled out and the display filled with views of well-defined fields of crops being worked by small groups of farmers. Their faces turned skyward at the unfamiliar noise of the shuttles screaming aero engines before Patricia saw them begin to run in all directions in what she could only assume was panic. Not one of the reconnaissance probes had shown evidence any Garundan nation had yet developed flight, not even rudimentary hot air balloons had been recorded so it was reasonably safe to assume the human shuttle was the first flying machine the Garundans had ever seen.

The rolling fields soon gave way to a more built up area of scattered houses which within a few more kilometers thickened considerably. Large factories belching smoke into the sky were now mixed in amongst the dwellings. The pilot banked the shuttle into a large lazy turn and the extent of the city was fully revealed. A wide river ran through the middle of the city with numerous bridges spanning it and as far as the eye could see there was factories and homes. Near the center of the city lining the river was a large dock area with dozens of ships gathered along it.

Then, as the shuttle began to level out once more Patricia caught sight of their final destination. A large group of overly ornate buildings set in what on Earth would be a large park. This was the only part of the city not covered by buildings and stood out like a sore thumb in the reconnaissance imagery. Patricia was convinced this cluster of buildings was the seat of power for this small nation and, as the shuttle came into to make a landing, she could make out dozens of figures scurrying away but more importantly she saw others dashing toward the site of their landing. All of them dressed in a similar fashion and taking up what even a novice of military tactics could see where defensive positions between the shuttle and the buildings.

The shuttle rocked slightly on its landing gear as it touched down a few hundred meters from the largest of the ornate buildings and Aaron released his restraints and stood. The two marines detailed as his close protection team were resplendent in their dress blues which only served to draw the eye even more to the dull black pulse pistols secured at their waists. Pausing to straighten his jacket cuffs before taking a step toward the shuttle hatch he paused again and, without turning his head said "Are you coming Doctor Bath?"

It had been agreed only Aaron and his two marine escorts would disembark the shuttle until the friendly status of the locals could be determined but obviously Aaron had decided to fling that plan out of the airlock. Patricia fumbled with her restraints as she rushed to join him at the hatch and she swore she caught the sound of a subdued chuckle.

The shuttle hatch opened and the ramp extended until it touched the grass. The marines moved down the ramp and took up positions on either side of it at the position of parade rest. Bodies locked rigidly in place, hands clasped to the rear, heads up and eyes forward.

"Now for the moment of truth." Whispered Aaron as he stepped off down the ramp followed closely by Patricia. As he reached the marines at the bottom of the ramp, they snapped to attention in unison and gave a parade ground salute any drill sergeant would have been proud of. Aaron acknowledged the salute with a polite thank you as he moved past them a few paces and halted facing the buildings. The marines resumed the position of parade rest as Patricia passed them and took her place beside Aaron.

"You were right about the marines Ambassador. They're very impressive."

"That they are Doctor Bath but their purpose is twofold. Firstly they saluted me and not you which identifies myself as a person of importance which, if you look at the number of

215

Garundans in uniform currently arrayed in front of us and the fact we have no way of identifying their rank structure at the moment, gives them a polite advantage."

Patricia could not help but notice the numbers of uniformed Garundans which had formed a loose circle around the shuttle. Their numbers seemed to swelling by the minute and the majority of them had a very ugly tri-barrel rifle aimed at her.

"Secondly. The marines are in an obvious uniform whereas you and I are not. I hope it indicates to whomever is in charge over there that we are civilians and not military. A distinction enforced by the marines saluting a civilian, I hope to show that although we do have a military capability it is subordinate to civilians."

A commotion interrupted any reply that Patricia was about to make, it came from the rear ranks of the Garundans located near the building. Patricia made out three Garundans making their way through the soldiers toward the shuttle. At last the front row of soldiers parted and the three Garundans approached the waiting humans. Patricia noticed they seemed to have a slight side-to-side motion as they walked, no doubt due to their tail stump. The group stopped only a few meters from Aaron and both sides regarded each other for a few moments before a particularly well dressed Garundan stepped forward and began to speak. The interpretation program took a few seconds to catch up before Patricia clearly heard his voice through her ear bug.

"I am Prime Minister Bezled of the Yeut Confederation. This is Governor Tzir of Makol and Chancellor Rol of Esper." On being introduced each of the Garundans gave a curt nod to Aaron.

"I am Ambassador Aaron Beckett of the Terran Republic and I come to you in the spirit of friendship and cooperation."

The voice of an alien coming out in their own language made quite a few of the Garundan soldiers take a wary step back accompanied by a few gasps of surprise. Prime Minister Bezled and his companions hardly batted an eyelid. Aaron recognized the signs of skilled politicians when he saw them. Aaron indicated his wrist comm. "This device interprets my voice and yours so we may understand each other."

"A useful machine indeed, Ambassador. May I suggest we continue our conversation inside I feel we have much to discuss."

#

OFFICE OF THE PRESIDENT OF THE TERRAN REPUBLIC
GENEVA - EARTH

Winter had descended on Geneva and snowflakes coated the ground as Aaron Beckett was ushered into the president's office.

"Welcome back, Aaron," said Rebecca with a warm and welcoming smile. After all, what he had achieved in less than a month was nothing short of miraculous.

He bowed his head slightly. "Madam President."

Rebecca ushered him into one of the comfortable informal chairs as a steward brought them both coffee.

"I've read the reports, but I'd like to hear a summary from your own lips to be sure there's no misunderstandings. It seems to me there is something missing from them."

Aaron put his elbows on the arm of the chair, steeple hands in front and a smile creased his face. "To put it plainly, Madam President, they were expecting us. They may not be as advanced as us, but they do have optical telescopes and more than one had witnessed the battle between us and the Others. In the time it took us to get my team together, get a handle on the main languages and make landing, they had already been in frantic communication with each of the other major nations and had decided to fight us as one if we invaded."

Rebecca was shaking her head in disbelief, which made Aaron chuckle. "You may find it hard to believe, Madam President, but imagine my surprise when instead of speaking to one national leader I was confronted by representatives from all the major powers."

This time it was Rebecca's turn to chuckle. "So how did you persuade them we weren't about to invade?"

Aaron looked at her a little sheepishly. "Ah, well, you see, Madam President, I may have slightly overstepped my authority there, which is why I thought it would be better if you heard this from me and didn't read it in a report."

Rebecca placed her coffee cup down on the table and sat back in her chair, looking at Aaron warily. "Go on."

Even after all his fifty years negotiating on behalf of presidents, Aaron knew this was the biggest gamble he had ever taken of his own accord. "Madam President, I knew going into this my actions would set the standard for every first contact we make from hereon in. I decided to be completely honest with the Garunda." Aaron took a deep breath. "I explained how we had found the Rubicon Cave and what we knew of the Saiph and their experiments in different star systems with indigenous life forms' DNA and how we came into conflict with the Others."

"Sounds reasonable so far, Aaron. But there's something else isn't there?"

"I offered them full access to the Saiph database and promised assistance in bringing their technology up to a level where they could defend themselves without our help."

Rebecca jolted out of her seat as if she had suffered an electric shock. She looked at Aaron disbelievingly. "You did what? My God! Aaron do you realize what you have done? The information in the database is priceless. We've still got no idea what else remains to be discovered in it."

"Madam President," Aaron pleaded. "We needed the people of Garunda to trust us, and I think my openness did the trick."

Rebecca attempted to rein in her anger. "How so, Aaron?"

"For their entire recorded history, the people of Garunda have fought with each other, either as tribes or cities or as nation states like they are now. For God's sake, they couldn't even agree on a name for their own planet and they ended up adopting the name we dubbed it!"

"Our arrival has changed Garundan dynamics. The fact I met representatives from all the major nation states proves it. They also insisted on sending a small team of representatives back with me, to see how we came together as one planet. They realize as single nations they stand no chance against the Others."

The president stood perfectly still, "You mean – they are here

218

now?"

Aaron nodded his head. "On board the same ship that brought me back."

"You could have given me a bit more warning we are about to hold an interstellar conference, Aaron."

Aaron simply shrugged his shoulders. "They insisted. And I thought it would be impolite to say no."

Rebecca gave him a withering look, but then a small smile appeared on her face. "Well, if I am to meet with them, I'm not going to do it on my own." The president pressed a control on her wrist Comm and the disembodied voice of her personal assistant came into her ear.

"Yes, Madam President?"

Rebecca looked at Aaron and her smile widened. "Jim, please inform the Vice President, the cabinet and the leaders of both houses we will be hosting a full state dinner tomorrow evening for a delegation from Garunda."

"Of course, Madam President."

"Thank you, Jim." As Rebecca signed off, she turned to Aaron, shaking her head. "You know, Jim has served three presidents and I have yet to hear of him ever being fazed by any presidential request. The man must have ice water running through his veins. Now you!" She pointed at Aaron like a schoolteacher berating a misbehaving pupil. "Get out of my sight! You have work to do. I want a detailed paper on Garunda etiquette with Jim before the end of the day so I don't make any major cock ups tomorrow, or I will have your head on a block. Is that understood?"

Aaron stood and bowed his head in a newfound respect for his president. "Yes, Madam President. And thank you for trusting me."

Rebecca walked him to the door. "Aaron, if I hadn't trusted you to do the right thing, I would never have sent you."

#

Rebecca looked around the spacious reception room as she awaited the arrival of the delegates from Garunda. The balmy

219

room was set to a temperature of twenty-six degrees centigrade, with a humidity of sixty-five percent, to better suit her guests. Rebecca could not help but scratch her left ear, where the ear bug protruded slightly. Doctor Bath assured Rebecca the translation program preset into her wrist comm would successfully translate the Garundan language and she would hear the standard English output via the ear bug. The Garunda delegation had been similarly equipped. At least they should be able to talk to each other.

A low chime sounded throughout the room. All eyes turned to the entrance doors. They swung slowly open. The Master of Ceremonies announced the arrival of the Garunda delegation. *Well here goes nothing!* Thought Rebecca as she moved to the head of the reception line.

The first person through the door was Aaron. He was chatting amiably with a Garunda, resplendent in a light green uniform with a gold sash across the right shoulder. Apart from the sash, the only other decoration appeared to be a small diamond encrusted star on the left side of his chest.

The Ambassador came to halt in front of Rebecca. "Madam President, may I introduce Prime Minister Bezled of the Yeut Confederation who has, by agreement with the other major powers of Garunda, been chosen as their representative."

Rebecca regarded the Prime Minister for a moment before turning her back on him. She could hear the sudden intake of breath from the humans in the room as Rebecca carried out what any human could only describe as a calculated insult. To the human watchers' amazement, the Prime Minister waited a few seconds before saying, "Please turn, Madam President. Your faith in my honorable intentions is appreciated. And I offer you my back in return." As Rebecca turned to face him again, the Prime Minister turned and presented his back to Rebecca.

"Your honorable intentions were never in doubt, Prime Minister." Relieved she had performed the ritual correctly, Rebecca continued. "If I may introduce the other members of my government." Rebecca worked her way down the reception line, each person introduced gave a slight bow to the Prime Minister, as they completed the ritual of honorable intentions.

On reaching the end of the line, they came upon a very uncomfortable naval captain in his dress whites. He appeared to prefer to be anywhere else than in this room full of dignitaries at this moment in time. On the captain's chest was a small blue and white ribbon, the Terran Medal of Honor.

"Mr. Prime Minister, I believe you especially requested to meet the captain of the destroyer *Dagger*." Rebecca noticed the entire Garunda delegation tense slightly as they turned in the captain's direction. "May I introduce Captain Engel?"

"Captain Engel, when Ambassador Beckett came to us and told us of these... Batha!" the Prime Minister said in a tone which no human or Garunda in the room could mistake as anything but a term not to be used in polite company, "these Others had come to destroy our home, we were skeptical."

With a raised arm, he gestured around the room. "After all, how were we to know you were not just fighting the Others for control of Garunda, and after defeating them you would not invade us yourselves?"

Rebecca could feel this spiraling out of her control and began to protest. "Mr. Prime Minister, I can assure you that was never our intention. We –"

Prime Minister Bezled raised his hand and Rebecca fell silent as Bezled went on in an even and quiet tone. "Madam President. I am a politician as are you and words are just that. Words. But Captain Engel's actions in putting the lives of his crew and himself in jeopardy to stop those last two missiles, which I now know could have killed so many of our people, say more about your intentions toward us than any mere words could say. Your decision to send humans into battle knowing some could, and indeed, did die to protect Garunda speaks volumes for you and your people. If it was possible, I would thank each and every family who sacrificed a loved one that day so my people could live."

Bezled reached up and removed the small diamond encrusted star from his chest looking at it fondly. "Captain Engel, this is the Star of Yeut, it was presented to me many years ago by a grateful nation. I now ask *you* to accept it on behalf of your fallen comrades as a gift not only from my nation, but from all the people of Garunda."

Engel reached out and took the star from the Prime Minister. "I accept your gift on behalf of all those who cannot be here today, and I shall wear it proudly in their memory."

"I have no doubt, Captain. Now, Madam President..." The Prime Minister turned his attention back to the waiting president. "Shall we continue?"

Shaking herself, Rebecca said, "Of course, Mr. Prime Minister."

It did not escape the president's notice as each Garunda passed Captain Engel, they came to their version of attention and placed their hand flat on the center of their chest. *One to ask Aaron later,* she thought, wondering what further surprises were in store tonight.

#

Rebecca sat in a comfortable chair in her private living room, lit only by a solitary table lamp and the flickering flames from the wood fire burning in the hearth. Her shoes lay where she had kicked them off and she sat with tucked legs underneath her. She savored the smell of the brandy in the glass Aaron handed her.

"Aaron, did you know what Bezled was going to propose tonight?"

He sat in the chair opposite Rebecca and contemplated the flames for a moment before answering. "No, Madam President. It came as much of a surprise to me as to you."

Rebecca chuckled "Aaron, I've known you over twenty years, so when we're in here and alone, please call me Rebecca."

Aaron felt his cheeks redden slightly. "Of course, Madam... Rebecca."

Another chuckle escaped Rebecca's lips. "That's better. Now what about this proposal from Bezled?"

Aaron closed his eyes and rubbed the bridge of his nose as he thought through his answer. "To be honest with you, Rebecca, I still don't know what to think of it." Aaron shook his head

222

slowly. "As it stands, Garunda is broken into a number of nation states, each with their own military forces. But the threat of the Others has made them realize for all their differences they are all Garundans."

"You mean in the same way our own near self-destruction made us realize we couldn't go on killing each other?"

"Exactly. Prime Minister Bezled is offering as many Garundan military and scientific personnel as we can train, each will give up their individual national identity and swear allegiance to a pan-national Garundan authority." Aaron felt a smile tug at the corners of his mouth. "I think we have just witnessed the birth of a planetary government."

Rebecca Coston raised her glass with a smile. "Then let's be the first to wet the baby's head. Cheers!"

CHAPTER NINETEEN

FRIEND OR FOE?

31 AQUILAE

High above the ecliptic plane, the stealthy surveillance platform finished downloading its data to the ship keeping station alongside. On entering normal space, Sub Leader Verus was shocked to find the whole system, especially the area around Planet IV, teeming with energy signatures, which were unmistakably spacecraft.

It could not be right! The population of Planet IV could not possibly have developed space travel in the three years since the last ship had downloaded the surveillance platform's memories. The fact Sub Leader Verus could not establish contact with the other platform closer in system was also disconcerting.

To add to his confusion, the energy signatures did not match anything held in his ship's database, so unless the old enemy had developed a completely new form of space drive then it could not be them. Who were these people?

Scratching the short fur behind his right ear, in a motion his crew knew displayed his puzzlement, he called to the navigator, "Plot a course for home. We'll let the Council decide what to do about what we have found here." The navigator started the calculations as the captain sat back in his chair and wondered if he had discovered a new enemy or a new ally.

"Course plotted, Sub Leader."

Sub Leader Verus had one more look at the mass of energy signatures moving about the system while again stroking the fur behind his right ear. *We had best be on our way,* he thought. "Execute!" he said.

The navigator's index finger, in a hand comprising five fingers, pressed down on the control panel in front of him, and the ship entered fold space.

#

The lieutenant at Tactical on the Flag Bridge of TDF *Mishima*, in orbit around Garunda, stiffened as the console he was operating let out an urgent beep. "There it is again, Admiral!"

Rear Admiral Analisa Chavez, commanding officer BatFor 3, Second Fleet stood up from her command chair and crossed her flag bridge to stand behind the lieutenant at Tactical. Chavez's one meter thirty centimeters height, slight frame and long black hair had lulled many a recruit at the naval academy, who did not know her, into believing she was a little girl playing at being a naval officer. Until she beat them hands down at nearly everything on the syllabus, graduating top of her class. Behind those soft brown eyes, there was a mind as sharp as a razor and as cunning as a fox – the reason she was still on her flag bridge at half past three in the morning

It followed a report from Tactical, just after midnight, they had the merest sniff from a Sherlock platform of an unknown energy signature well above the ecliptic plane. The signature, put through their database, was too weak for the computer to identify. If it had been 'The Others' then surely the Sherlock platform would have detected it further out and not as a stationary point above the ecliptic.

Chavez chose to wait rather than send her force to battle stations and possibly scare off her quarry. It looked like her gamble had paid off.

"Well Lieutenant. Has the computer got a better reading this time?" asked Analisa patiently.

The lieutenant did not answer immediately, Analisa allowed a little impatience to enter her tone. "Lieutenant?"

The lieutenant spun in his chair to face her and she could see the confusion evident on his face. "Ma'am, I've run the energy signature through the computer twice." The lieutenant swallowed. "We don't have an exact match in the database but the computer is giving an eighty percent probability match."

"Spit it out, Lieutenant."

"Ma'am, the closest match is a Saiph star drive."

#

PLANET PARS - PERSEUS ARM
6,400 LIGHT YEARS FROM EARTH

The room fell into silence as the Chairman of the Council of Twelve called for order. Chairman Tarrov was the longest serving chairperson in the 242 years of the council's existence. He was also the oldest serving member of the council at 163 years of age. His fur may have lost the moonlight black of his youth, replaced steadily by fine silver, but his mind was still as sharp as in his youth, even if it was now tempered with the experience his fellow younger council members still had to learn.

"My fellow councilors. By now we have all had a chance to review the data Sub Leader Verus recovered from our surveillance platform. I think the time we all knew would come eventually is upon us."

Tarrov looked slowly around the table at the other council members. Some signaled their agreement, others stayed perfectly still, not committing themselves, but not one disagreed with him.

"When our forefathers left the original planet Pars, in the first wave of three colony ships, and headed out amongst the stars for a new home, they had no idea what they would find. Not all the probes deployed to the nearest stars had returned when the decision was taken to launch the first of the colony ships. How impatient we were."

Tarrov went on retelling the history every living Persai knew by heart. "Our forefathers made planet fall here. Ten years after

226

leaving home. As planned, the colony ships were broken into pieces to form the basis of the new colony, knowing all the time the following ships would bring the parts and personnel required to expand the fledgling colony." Tarrov's tone became bitter. "But the ships never arrived. Two years after landing, we found out why."

The images of the ships appearing in orbit around the home planet, the frantic attempts to establish contact and finally the nuclear death that rained down, all transmitted to the stranded colonists with a final message. Save yourselves, for we are lost. You are all that remain!

"Between them, the three colony ships carried 12000 colonists along with everything needed to establish a viable colony. That is what we did. We named the colony Pars so we would never forget our home world." Tarrov looked around at the rough cut stone walls of the council chambers. "But the threat from this unknown enemy still exists, so we decided to hide all signs of ourselves on this world, moved everything underground. That was when we discovered the true nature of our enemy."

Unbidden, all eyes in the room were drawn to the dais on which stood the raised lectern in the corner of the room.

"Our miners, looking for minerals stumbled on the cavern containing the Saiph library. Although it took us years, we decoded the information contained in them. We learned the truth. We are the descendants of some long lost Saiph experiment, which means nothing to us for we are our own people. Our only true link to the Saiph is our common enemy. The Enemy!

"As they have hunted down and exterminated the Saiph, so they might hunt us. The last of our people. We would simply cease to exist. A footnote in history." Tarrov's voice became hard edged "But we survived!" Around the table, the council members' heads rose proudly and they each had a glint of defiance in their eyes.

The entire room reverberated to the banging of fists on the council table, the feeling of intense hatred filled the room for those who had destroyed their home was a living, breathing thing.

Tarrov allowed the cacophony to go on for a moment longer before raising his hand for quiet. "We learned from the library and, although we didn't have the resources to replicate exactly the ships from the library, we improvised and we overcame the technical challenges. The only thing we could never overcome was our need to husband our resources. For years now, we have kept our population artificially low, for any sign on the surface of organized farming could lead The Enemy to us. We looked beyond this star system. For the past twenty years, we have placed surveillance platforms in systems listed in the Saiph library, avoiding those which give off any form of electromagnetic signals, for fear they could be The Enemy. But now… now, my fellow councilors, we have seen The Enemy defeated."

Tarrov touched a control and an image of Radford's ship, TDF *Cartagena*, firing into the Others ship during the battle for Garunda appeared.

"Whoever these people are, the data clearly shows they have placed some sort of warning buoys around the system and detected the approach of The Enemy. But not until it became obvious The Enemy intended to close with the populated planet did they intervene and destroy The Enemy ships."

Tarrov rested his hands on top of the table. "The important thing is what happened next."

One of the junior councilors spoke up. "But Chairman, nothing happened next. The unknown ships made no approach to the planet."

Tarrov's lips curled back, exposing a vicious set of canine fangs. "Exactly, my young friend. Exactly."

The same junior councilor looked confused. "I'm sorry, Chairman. I admit to not understanding your point."

Tarrov touched another control, and the data ran forward until it showed the formation of the ships of BatFor 1 following the battle. "If these people had planned to take the planet following their defeat of The Enemy, then why are they forming a defensive shell around the planet?"

Understanding slowly spread through the room and Tarrov

gave it a moment to fully sink in. "Until Sub Leader Verus downloaded the data from the surveillance platform, it had recorded only the comings and goings of one small shuttle to and from the planet. Even after the original ships that had taken part in the battle departed and were immediately replaced by a force of similar makeup, no hostile move was made to either fire on the planet or invade."

Tarrov saw on the faces surrounding him the moment of comprehension. "Fellow councilors. For years, we slowly built a small but powerful fleet in the uncertain hope that one day we could have our vengeance on The Enemy. In our heart of hearts, we knew our fleet would be too small to take on the might of The Enemy." Tarrov pointed at the human ships "But these people stood up to The Enemy and defeated them."

Every Councilor in the room was looking at the image of the human ships. "I propose we return to the system in which the battle with The Enemy took place and offer an alliance with this unknown race."

There. Tarrov had committed himself.

The gathered leaders of the Persai spent a long moment looking from Tarrov and then back to the image of the human ships. One councilor began banging the table in a slow, methodical manner. One by one, the remaining councilors joined in until the entire room reverberated to a slow, methodical drumming.

#

OFFICE OF THE SECRETARY OF DEFENSE - GENEVA - EARTH

The weekly planning and coordination meeting with General Joyce was drawing to a close. With the rapid expansion the Terran Defense Force had overseen over the past few years, Secretary Helset had found that to stop himself being bogged down in all the minutia, it was easier for him to have Joyce brief him on a weekly basis. This allowed both men to raise any issues.

This week it was the planning of a timetable for the training and equipping of the Garundans. As Joyce had pointed out, although you could not fault their enthusiasm, it would simply take time to bring their basic understanding of the advanced human technology to a level where they could progress to and employ the same technology.

"So give me a ballpark figure then, Keyton."

Joyce leaned back in his chair. His face blanked for a moment as he ran numbers in his head. "Well, Mr. Secretary. If, for the sake of argument, we write off the current Garundan industrial base, start from scratch as we did for Janus, I would say we are looking at maybe two years before we have established sufficient in-system resources to begin constructing hulls. As far as training goes, the proposal is we introduce a tailored course at the Academy for Garundan officers, with an expanded syllabus to bring them up to the same level as our own officer corps. Other ranks will be treated in a similar fashion with extra classes added to basic training. We would look at moving them to the training fleet. It is felt, and I must agree, that hands on practical experience is more important than theory."

Haslet felt himself nodding in agreement. "It appears the Office of the Joint Chiefs has this pretty well in hand."

"Thank you, Mr. Secretary"

"Moving on. I read the proposal for the deployment of a permanent force to be based in the Garundan system."

"Yes, Mr. Secretary. Admiral Jing and the Strategy Board feel since we are now committed to the defense of Garunda, for at least the next two years, rather than rotate a BatFor every three months, our first order of business is to establish a fleet base under a Vice Admiral. He or she would oversee the buildup of our forces and the integration of Garundan units as they come on line."

"Sounds like a wise move, do you have anyone in mind for the post?"

Before Joyce could answer, the urgent beeping of his wrist Comm demanded his attention. Both men knew only something of the utmost priority permitted interruption to this meeting. With a look to the Secretary for go ahead, the General accepted the call.

"General, Commodore Riesling, Duty Watch Officer. A courier drone just arrived in system with a priority message from Rear Admiral Chavez in the Garundan system."

The General and the Secretary exchanged a worried look. Had the Others returned in force to finish what they had originally intended for Garunda?

"I'm in the Secretary of Defense's office, please patch the message through."

There was a brief pause before Helset's Holo Cube sprang to life and the face of Rear Admiral Chavez appeared. Helset touched the playback control and the message played,

"Central Command this is Admiral Chavez. At fourteen twelve hours, Terran Standard Time, an unidentified ship arrived in the Garundan system. The ship has made no attempt to progress any further in system as of this time. It is my intention to dispatch a flotilla of destroyers to investigate and report to me before any further action is taken. It should be noted, however, the energy signature is a match for the one which we detected three weeks ago in the same general area as this ship. I must remind you at the time the ship was tentatively identified as Saiph. I will report to you when I know more. Chavez out."

#

TDF MISHIMA - 31 AQUILAE

Analisa Chavez forced herself to relax as she contemplated the tactical plot displayed in the Holo Cube in her private briefing room. The plot showed the positions of all the ships constituting BatFor 3, but Chavez only had eyes for the three blue icons representing the destroyer flotilla she had dispatched to investigate the lone red icon which remained stationary some 39.4 AUs above the ecliptic plane.

Those three blue icons were now stationary and spread out in a line some 50000 kilometers from the unknown ship. Not for the first time, Chavez found herself cursing the huge distances involved in trying to retain command and control throughout an

231

entire star system. For a radio message to reach her from the destroyers it took nearly five and a half hours, for them to receive her reply another five and a half — eleven hours in total. A lot could happen in eleven hours. To combat this, courier drones were employed to make micro folds. Nevertheless, there was still a time delay as a message was downloaded, a reply composed and uploaded to the drone and sent on its way back to Chavez. Yes, it dramatically reduced the communications lag but, and not for the first time, Chavez wished it was she who was out there. However, she knew her place was here, in overall command of BatFor 3, not gallivanting all over the star system.

Analisa's Comm beeped. She touched a control and the Holo Cube split to show Lieutenant Kyle at Communications. "Ma'am, a courier drone from *Rhin* has arrived and the message downloaded."

At last! Thought Analisa. TDF *Rhin* was the lead destroyer of the formation she had sent to investigate the unknown ship. Louis Chesneau, formerly her own tactical officer before getting his own well-deserved command, captained *Rhin*. Analisa knew Chesneau to be cool and level headed under pressure, and Analisa had the utmost confidence in him. "Pipe it down to my briefing room, please."

The face of Chesneau replaced Kyle's and Analisa touched a control to allow the message to play. "Admiral, the flotilla is currently holding station 50,000 kilometers from the unknown vessel. As per your instructions, we are not using any active systems to scan the vessel in case they are misinterpreted as hostile. Our passive systems confirm your original analysis. The energy signature is an eighty percent match for a Saiph star drive. Now we are close enough for the passive systems to get a good look at the vessel, the computers are telling us, although not a perfect match for the Saiph designs in the database, many of the vessel's features are similar. In my opinion, they are too similar to be a coincidence."

Analisa paused the playback as she considered this new information. A ship emitting an energy signature virtually the same as that in the Saiph database? Now Chesneau was telling her he had identified design similarities as well. *The plot thickens,* Analisa thought, as she touched the control to allow the message to continue.

"It would appear the vessel has powered down all its systems except life support. Immediately upon our arrival, the vessel began to transmit a directional radio signal toward us. It was the same short message being repeated over and over. We ran it through linguistics and surprise, surprise, we found a match in the Saiph database. As best as we can tell, the message being transmitted is one word: 'friend'."

Anyone else in the briefing room would have likened Analisa's face to a goldfish – her mouth dropped open and stayed that way for all of five seconds. She regained control and her mouth snapped shut. Analisa's mind raced. Had they made contact with some remnant of what they all thought were the long extinct Saiph? The authorities gave an admiral wide-ranging powers of discretion, but any decision making here was well above her pay grade. This needed direction from not just the Admiralty but from the top levels of the Republic. They were light years away. Analisa was the one on the spot, but she was no diplomat. Then a light bulb lit up in the Admiral's head: Ambassador Beckett! He was back on Garunda as the Terran Republic's official ambassador to the new Pan Garundan Government.

Analisa touched a control and the face of Lieutenant Kyle appeared before her. "Lieutenant, download to *Rhin* they are to continue to hold position and take no action unless in defense of themselves. Then get hold of Ambassador Beckett at the Republic embassy and tell him I request his presence on board *Mishima* as a matter of urgency. And please attach the message from *Rhin*. Once the embassy confirms receipt of the signal, dispatch a shuttle to collect the ambassador. Lastly, send a copy of *Rhin*'s message back to Central Command."

Without waiting for confirmation, Analisa cut the link and sat back in her seat with a wicked grin, imagining the faces of the ambassador and those at Central Command as they watched the message from Chesneau.

CHAPTER TWENTY

MASSACRE

OFFICE OF THE PRESIDENT OF THE TERRAN REPUBLIC
GENEVA - EARTH

As she closed her eyes and used her fingers to massage her temples in a vain effort to ward off the oncoming headache, Rebecca understood why no president was permitted to run for more than three consecutive terms.

Rebecca put her burgeoning headache down to the latest message from Aaron. The Ambassador, accompanied by Doctor Bath, had been waiting for the shuttle sent for them by Admiral Chavez. They wasted no time, on their arrival on board the *Mishima*, to badger the Admiral into relocating her flagship to join the destroyers sitting off the unknown vessel which had been hanging in space broadcasting the Saiph word for friend.

Bath was an expert in her field of linguistics and at Aaron's direction began a tentative dialogue in the language of the Saiph with the unknown vessel, all the while believing they had indeed encountered the Saiph themselves.

The crew of the unknown vessel agreed to a video conference. The image as it appeared in the Holo Cubes on board *Mishima* quashed the hope that man had at last found the Saiph. The central being was tall, well built, with short, almost silver fur and faintly familiar canine features. Tarrov, Chairman of the Council of Pars, stared back at Aaron, in the background the leaders of a race calling themselves Persai could be seen. Aaron put a personal footnote on his message, Tarrov reminded him of an elderly werewolf. Rebecca smiled to herself as she thought the comment was certainly not politically correct, but the more she thought about it and recalled her first look at the images of the Persai she could see the resemblance.

Rebecca blamed her imminent headache on the rest of the message. Tarrov relayed to Ambassador Beckett the story of the destruction of their Persai home world, destroyed by 'The Enemy', or as it turns out, 'The Others'. Tarrov continued with his tale, describing The Enemy's sudden appearance in orbit around the original Persai home world swiftly followed by its wanton destruction – despite the population's pleas for mercy. They had received no reply from the silent enemy. Tarrov told of the establishment of the colony, naming it Pars after the dead home world and of the colonists' decision to secrete themselves underground for fear of discovery by the Others. Then the all important discovery of the Saiph library and the knowledge it brought. Armed with the knowledge the Persai had built starships and once more ventured out into the night sky in an attempt to discover the fate of the other worlds listed in the Saiph database. Caution tempered the Persai's curiosity. Deep down, they knew if the Others discovered the new Pars, then its fate would be as its dead namesake. The order went out, any system showing signs of artificial energy sources was to be avoided and would never be visited again.

Rebecca and her advisers thought the latter statement was possibly a little short sighted on the part of the Persai. However, when Tarrov explained the Persai had enforced an artificial ceiling on their population, a conscious decision made by them after taking into account their limited subterranean resources, Rebecca and her advisors began to understand their decision. The Persai made the conscious decision not to mine the asteroid belt of their system and take advantage of its abundant resources for fear of discovery by the Others. This led to the Persai's complete reliance on only what they could mine from the planet without leaving any telltale signs. Hence, the limited numbers of Persai ships.

The secretary of Defense and The Joint Chiefs had initially been disappointed when they had heard the Persai had only a limited number of ships available. The thought of having to stretch the already overextended Terran Defense Force even more thinly was not an appealing one. Jealousy soon replaced this disappointment. The Persai had had over 150 years to examine the Saiph database. As their understanding of Saiph technology grew, so had the sophistication of their ships. Joyce and Doctor Moore, representing Research and Development, had been practically drooling at the thought of getting their hands on one of the Persai ships.

That was exactly what Tarrov offered. Access to Persai technology. In return, an alliance. Unlike Garunda which was completely reliant on the TDF for defense from the Others until such time as its own forces were up to sufficient strength, Persai had a limited number of ships available with which to defend itself. In return for access to Persai technology, Tarrov wanted a guarantee, if the Others were to threaten Pars, then the TDF would come to their aid.

Rebecca felt she was being inexorably dragged toward an unknown fate. From the very moment of the Gravity Drive's discovery, to the revelations of the Saiph database and humankind's first clash with the Others, which led to the rapid expansion of human forces, and then her decision to commit those same forces to the defense of Garunda. Now the Persai had arrived on the scene with their offer of advanced Saiph technology and an alliance that would again commit human forces to the defense of an alien world.

She closed her eyes and resumed massaging her temples. The urgent beeping of her comm forced her tired eyes open as she accepted the incoming message. "Yes?"

The face of her personal assistant appeared above her desk. "I'm sorry to disturb you, Madam President, but we've just received news from Central Command the research ship dispatched to Delta Pavonis has come under attack from the Others."

#

DELTA PAVONIS - 19.92 LIGHT YEARS FROM EARTH

The insertion from orbit progressed quietly. There was no sign the Others had detected their arrival in the system, never mind their stealthy approach to the planet. Vladimir Egnorov looked at his rescue team. They were the best of the best, men who had been Special Forces for most of their adult lives. Not one had backed down when he had asked for volunteers for the mission. Each marine knew the risks of dropping into potential enemy held territory. The scientists had made no contact with Earth since the first report via courier drone of a single ship, identified as one of the Others Buzzard class, appearing in orbit. Of that research ship and her crew, there was no sign. Hopefully, the scientists who had been on the surface at the research base had followed Standard Operating Procedure, powered everything down and moved away from the main research buildings to the pre prepared extraction point to await rescue.

The tinny sound of the pilot's voice over Comms interrupted his musings. "Two minutes from the drop point!"

The drop point was the lowest the shuttle could come to the planetary atmosphere without leaving a visible indication of its presence. The marines decided on a high altitude, high speed insertion by exo-atmospheric jump. Risky, to say the least. The marines in their Wraith combat suits would jump in a cocoon of armor, which they jokingly called 'eggs', designed to get them onto the ground as quickly as possible.

Vladimir acknowledged the pilot's message and gave the thumbs up to the loadmaster, who passed the message to the company of marines to get into their protective cocoons. Vladimir's heads-up display told him all his marines acknowledged the instruction and sealed their eggs before he too sealed himself inside his and awaited the drop.

With a gut wrenching pull, the egg dropped from the shuttle.

237

He could see via his display the exterior of the egg heating up, its ablative armor burning away as it dropped into the atmosphere at supersonic speeds. Speed was life, the sooner he was on the ground the less time any enemy gunner had time to shoot him down.

The retro rockets firing forced him into his couch, and then the front of the pod blew off and he released his harnesses stepping out of the egg, bringing his rifle to the ready position as he checked 360 degrees around him for targets. None were visible.

Vladimir called up the location of his company's Eggs on the display and found all but two had landed safely. One had had a retro failure and had ploughed into the earth at a speed approaching Mach two, fatal for the marine inside. The other had not made it through the atmosphere and had broken up, spreading itself and its unlucky occupant over the upper atmosphere.

His heads-up display flashed a point on the map, the rally point, and he headed in its direction as fast as the Wraith suit would carry him. Better to clear the landing zone before the Others had a chance to bring fire down on it.

On reaching the rally point, Vladimir conferred quickly with his platoon commanders before they formed the troops up and began to move in the direction from where the scientists' beacon was located. Time was of the essence: the more time they gave the Others to gather their strength, the more chance the marines would be pinned down before they could link up with the scientists and the shuttles from the light cruiser TDF *Konigsberg* to lift them all to safety.

The landing zone was only a kilometer from the scientists' beacon and the marines made good time, covering the ground quickly but tactically, ready to react to any threat.

As the lead platoon reached the pickup point, they reported no sign of the scientists. Vladimir ordered the company on toward the main research base on the most likely route the scientists should have used to reach the pickup point.

The Marines did not have far to go. Vladimir got a call from the lead platoon commander to come forward. When he reached

238

their location, the sight of 264 dead scientists confronted him. Laid out in a line extending back toward the research station buildings, each scientist had a single, precise entry wound in their forehead, if he had to guess, from a handheld laser pistol. There was no sign of resistance on the scientists' part. No weapons in sight and each of the scientists had their hands bound behind their backs. the Others had executed them. Left their bodies laid out in a macabre message to whoever came to discover their fate. He struggled to keep his anger in check as he signaled the *Konigsberg* for pickup.

He understood the message. One day, he would make sure he replied in kind.

OFFICE OF THE PRESIDENT OF THE TERRAN REPUBLIC - GENEVA - EARTH

The news of the massacre on Delta Pavonis spread like wildfire. Somehow, the press had gotten hold of the grisly video footage, which showed the neatly laid out bodies of the scientists with their hands bound behind their backs and the single hole in the center of each man and woman's forehead.

Maybe it was because the images evoked memories of humankind's own terrible past, that the reaction of the general population was so strong. The memories of the barbarism of the Nazis, the ethnic cleansing in the Balkans and throughout Africa. The religious wars of the mid twenty-first century had led to the near extinction of mankind in World Wars Three and Four. This was something humanity thought consigned to history. But no, here, once again was an example of an evil man thought would never revisit him.

It was not that the people did not recognize the Others caused the extinction of the Saiph, or that they nearly caused the extinction of the Persai and the attempted extinction of the Garunda. It was not the losses BatFor 1 had taken in defending Garunda. This time, it was the coldblooded execution of unarmed men and women.

239

It must not happen again!

In the weeks following President Coston's office had been strangely quiet. Yes, immediately after the news broke, the president addressed the people and there had been the normal denunciations of the Others actions along with the government's promise to take whatever steps it deemed necessary to protect the Republic. Apart from that, the president refused all other requests for interviews. Unsurprisingly, her opponents in the Senate had pounced on her silence as a sign of weakness and were attempting to make what political capital they could from it.

Two months to the day after the massacre, President Coston's office contacted all the major broadcasting outlets and informed them the president requested airtime the same evening for an announcement. As news of the request spread, many a senator wondered if the president was about to announce her resignation, but try as they might to garner details of the address none of the president's staff were talking.

All around the world and on human habitats throughout the solar system, men, women and children watched as the face of President Rebecca Coston appeared in their Holo Cubes.

"My fellow humans. The events on Delta Pavonis have shaken us all to the core. It has wakened in us memories of days gone by, days we prayed we would never see again. Mankind saw so much pain and anguish at his own hands and in the end, you, the people, joined together to say *no more*! No more death and destruction at our own hands. No more senseless slaughter of the innocent. Out of that time of sadness we forged a new beginning. We came together as one and the Terran Republic was born. We rebuilt our shattered world and brought peace and prosperity to all. As man has travelled amongst the stars, we have discovered many new wonders and, following the discovery of the Saiph database, have been forced to reassess our place in the universe. Our travels have also brought us new friends."

As the camera pulled back it showed on Rebecca's right, Prime Minister Bezled, now head of the Garundan Pan National Government and, on Rebecca's left, Chairman Tarrov of the Persai.

"But what we have also found is a race, the Others, whose only objective seems to be the destruction of everything they find to be alien. I am sure Prime Minister Bezled, Chairman Tarrov, you the people and I, agree the Others are a threat to us all. It is something we cannot and will not tolerate!

"During the past two months, my office has been working frantically behind the scenes on a project I wish to reveal to you now. I believe neither the Republic, Garunda nor Pars have the resources individually to tackle the threat from the Others. Garunda, with our help, is still over a year away from the ability to resist any attack from the Others. The Persai are more technologically advanced than the Others but they find themselves in the same situation as the Saiph found themselves in. They are numerically inferior to the Others and would be simply swamped by greater numbers. Although we have defeated the Others in battle, we still have no idea of their total strength."

Rebecca took a deep breath and pushed on. "In consultation with my esteemed colleagues from Garunda and Pars, I am proposing we establish a Commonwealth Union of Planets incorporating our three civilizations. Together this Commonwealth would abide by a Commonwealth Charter which would establish a common foreign and defense policy, enshrine our belief in free trade and travel between worlds. A right to democracy, human rights and the rule of law. Each member planet would retain its own independence within the Commonwealth but every individual would have dual citizenship of their own planet and of the Commonwealth and would be afforded the same protection under law as any other citizen no matter where they are."

In millions of homes around the solar system, the silence was tangible.

"There is nothing really new in these proposals. When the Terran Republic was founded, these principles I have outlined to you were the same ones which allowed mankind to live in peace and harmony for hundreds of years, so why should they not allow the Garundan, the Persai and ourselves to do the same? We know from the Saiph database they visited at least seventeen worlds

241

where they dabbled in the indigenous life form's DNA. Who are we to say in the future we may not come across other civilizations on these worlds from whom we, and they, may benefit from being a part of this Commonwealth Union of Planets?

"What of the spacefaring civilization found by our survey ships in Messier 54? We know, for a fact, they are a result of Saiph intervention. But what of our own colony world of Janus? Is it not realistic to think, as its population grows and humans are born and raised on Janus that they grow up considering Janus not Earth to be their home? I foresee a day, in the not too distant future, when Janus will want to be its own world and not simply a colony. Rather than lose them, let us embrace them as an equal into the Commonwealth Union.

"As you can see Prime Minister Bezled and Chairman Tarrov stand by my side. They have agreed in principle to the establishment of this Commonwealth. At the end of this broadcast they will return to Garunda and Pars to seek the approval of their people. I have ordered a plebiscite to be carried out on Earth and Janus thirty days from today. It will ask one question... Do we form this Commonwealth Union of Planets?

"In the meantime, I ask you to consider this question: Do we face the future together? Or do we struggle on by ourselves and hope we can overcome whatever else the universe decides to fling in our path?"

The camera zoomed in to show only the face of President Coston. "I have faith you will make the right decision. Thank you for your time and goodnight."

#

KUIPER BELT - 31 AQUILAE

the Others ship slipped into the Kuiper Belt of the 31 Aquilae system, home to the Garunda, and came to a halt. It used a small body approximately 100 kilometers across to mask its presence from the many energy signatures it identified as spacefaring vessels closer in system.

When the six vessels dispatched to erase the alien species detected on the fourth planet had not returned this single destroyer deployed from the nearest fleet base to find them. It had taken two months at maximum cruising speed for them to reach the system.

On its approach to the system the destroyer detected no signs of the ships it was sent to find, so the captain decided to drop back into normal space further than normal, just beyond the system's Kuiper Belt, about sixty AUs from the system's star. It allowed his ship to coast in unpowered. Covering the distance had taken his small ship nearly three weeks but it had been worth it.

The Kuiper Belt, surrounding the 31 Aquilae system, extended from around thirty-eight AUs from the star to around sixty AUs. Similar to the Sol System's asteroid belt, but far larger, it was composed of mainly small bodies left over from the formation of the 31 Aquilae system. Although circular in shape, the belt actually extended approximately ten degrees below and above the ecliptic which made the belt actually more donut shaped than circular.

The destroyer captain used the ten degree angle above the ecliptic plane to his advantage. He positioned his ship to look down into the solar system to get a clear look as to what lay in system. The presence of so many spacefaring vessels had surprised the crew. This system was supposed to be incapable of spaceflight, this incapability was the reason only six ships were dispatched to ensure its destruction, obviously a mistake.

It was obvious to the captain the race from the fourth planet had already been conquered by a technologically more advanced race, a race his people had not yet met. From his ship's readings of the inner system, there appeared to be heavy inter-system traffic indicative of mining operations in the asteroid belt and, if he was not mistaken, the beginnings of construction of ship yards in orbit around the fourth planet. He had seen enough. The fleet must know of this new threat.

With the same alacrity as he had used to get his small ship into the system, the captain edged his ship away again.

CHAPTER TWENTY-ONE

PARS

PLANET PARS - PERSEUS ARM
6400 LIGHT YEARS FROM EARTH

As TDF *Northern Lights* smoothly entered orbit around Pars its crew hastily prepared its single shuttle for departure. *Northern Lights* was one of the new fast courier ships, designated Clipper class, entering service and was specifically designed to get a small number of passengers from one planet to another as quickly as possible. The ship was designed around its Gravity Drive. Engineers fitted the biggest and most efficient drive into its small hull, then squeezed the most accurate navigational computer into it. This allowed it to make longer jumps in fold space and to make micro jumps, thereby dispensing with the need for the normal reaction drives, which other larger vessels needed to use within a system.

With the successful formation of the Commonwealth Union of Planets the month before, the need for small courier ships of this type to shuttle diplomatic missions around the new Commonwealth had already risen exponentially, and they would see a lot more of these little Clippers in the future.

On board today, the *Northern Lights* carried a very impatient Doctor Jeff Moore and a small, handpicked team from Research and Development eager to take up the Persai invitation to share their insights into Saiph technology. Accompanying them was Ambassador Aaron Beckett and his assistant, Doctor Patricia Bath, who had come to Pars to establish Earth's diplomatic presence along with a group of diplomats from Garunda with the same intention. Last, but not least, was Rear Admiral John Radford, tasked by The Joint Chiefs to assess the Persai military strength.

John was a last minute addition to the team after Admiral Wiggans from The Joint Chiefs' personal staff fractured his leg in a skiing accident. It was felt that John's input, as the only flag officer to have actually met and defeated 'The Others' in a fleet engagement made him an ideal replacement.

Standing around the boat bay on the *Northern Lights*, John found himself disagreeing strongly with The Joint Chiefs' assignment of him to the Pars mission. BatFor 1 was due to return to Garunda in a week's time following its stint in the hands of the shipyards which had been repairing the damage from the battle with the Others. As its commanding officer, John felt his place was there, ensuring it was at its peak performance and ready to deploy – not light years away inspecting Persai ships which, from what he had gathered from the briefing pack, represented the equivalent of a small Terran battle force.

Sure, the additional ships would always be helpful, but could not some staffer from The Joint Chiefs' staff have been assigned instead of him? John thought irritably.

Since arriving on the *Northern Lights*, John had had his head stuck in the briefing pack and had only managed to catch glimpses of his fellow mission members as they had boarded. The Terran delegates he had only previously seen pictures of.

John sighed as he waited impatiently for the civilians to board the shuttle. The Garundan delegation was already aboard and had been chattering away like a bunch of excited schoolchildren. John felt a smile grow on his face. Who could blame the Garundans? Less than one year ago, they thought they were alone in the universe and were still using primitive steam engines. Now, they were an equal part of a multi star system

Commonwealth which jumped their technology forward at least 300 years.

John's train of thought was broken as Beckett and Bath entered the boat bay, accompanied by a very animated Moore. John felt the smile return to his face as he watched Bath, whose pictures, he had to admit, did not do her justice, pretend she was interested in whatever Moore was talking about. Bath noticed John watching her and rolled her eyes at him. Caught unawares, John let out a small laugh, which he managed to cover with a not very convincing cough.

"Something caught in your throat, Admiral?" asked a smiling Patricia as she walked past him and entered the shuttle.

For the first time in a long time, John did not know what to say. So he just shook his head and followed the small group into the shuttle. Maybe this mission was not going to be as bad as he thought.

#

As the shuttle descended through the atmosphere John got his first proper look at Pars, the home of humanity's latest ally in the struggle against the Others. The shuttle pilot had piped into the passenger area the feed from the nose camera. John had to admit he was not overly impressed so far. Speeding past below the shuttle John could only see kilometer after kilometer of rolling grassland and every now and then a herd of large herbivore which scattered in all directions as the shuttle shot past at almost tree top height. There were no signs of any buildings or even crops anywhere to spoil the completely natural look. Any passing survey ship would take the planet to be uninhabited. It reminded John of the veldts of southern Africa except the green of the grass was slightly off.

"The grass doesn't look right." Commented John more to himself than anyone else and immediately regretted opening his mouth.

Jeff Moore lent forward in his seat behind John so his head was protruding between the headrests.

"Oh that's probably because of the slightly different shift in the yellow light emanating from the local star. We see because light bounces off things and then into our eyes, the colour that bounces off is what it looks like. Chlorophyll looks green because it stores the red and blue light and bounces off the green and yellow light which go to our eyes..."

John turned in his seat and gave Jeff Moore a look which cut him off midsentence.

"Thank you Doctor for your succinct explanation."

As Jeff's mouth was left hanging open in midsentence, John could make out a muffled laugh from the seat across the aisle from him. Turning his head John regarded the source of the laughter. Patricia Bath was trying her best to fain interest in her PAD she was holding up at eye level. Noticing John's attention she tried to regain control of herself but continuing shaking of her slim frame gave her away.

John set his face in his best admiral's scowl and returned his attention to the passing terrain.

The shuttle was following a Persai ship, which met them as they had entered the upper atmosphere. John read the scrolling read outs along the bottom of the image when he noticed that both ships had slowed significantly. Perhaps they were at last approaching their destination.

With a small bump not completely cancelled out by the compensator, the shuttle crested a small rise and without warning dropped like a stone into a wide canyon. John heard a short gasp from Jeff Moore and for once John had to agree with him. Laid out before him was a canyon the like of which John could only equate to the Valles Mariners on Mars. The shuttle continued to drop as the canyon walls towered above the shuttle. John's repeater showed him the extent of the canyon as the shuttle levelled out after a descent of nearly eight kilometers. The canyon was only two kilometers across at its widest point, narrowing to under a kilometer in places and it ran for over 3000 kilometers. A massive, jagged scar ran across the equator of Pars.

John felt pressure on his headrest again as Jeff used it to pull himself forward.

"This canyon was probably formed by some massive tectonic

247

event in the crust of the planet millions of years ago…"

John tuned him out as Jeff continued to wax lyrical about similar events scientists had discovered in the solar system. Johns full attention focused on the scrolling read outs in his display and he brought up the virtual keyboard and began to tap away frantically. This got the attention of Patricia Bath and she unlocked her restraints and stood in the aisle so she could better see what had so interested the admiral that even the incessant lecturing of Jeff Moore had failed to distract him. As Patricia lent over to get a better view of John's display he sat back with a satisfied grunt. On his display a series of red blocks began appearing.

"What are those Admiral?"

John let a small smile appear on his face. "Those Doctor Bath…" As John extended a long finger and pointed at the red blocks. "Are weapons emplacements. Damn well shielded from electronic and optical sensors but definitely there and, from the sniff at the power readings I can get, I'd say that they'd give even the batteries on our most powerful warship a run for its money. These people are serious about protecting wherever we are headed."

Without warning the shuttle rapidly decelerated and made a radical left turn. The compensator's failed in their attempts to keep the turn smooth for the passengers. Patricia, standing in the aisle leaning over John's seat to view his display, tumbled head long into his lap in a flurry of arms and legs saved from any serious injury by the simple expedient of John wrapping his arms around her and holding her close to him as the shuttle once again regained level flight.

For the first time John became aware of the faint smell of her perfume as he looked into her wide emerald collared eyes and felt the warmth of her body next to his. In an instant the moment was gone as Patricia's face flushed scarlet with embarrassment and she struggled to her feet and attempted to regain her demeanor flicking her hair from her face.

"Thank you Admiral and my apologies for my clumsiness."

John felt his face break into a wide grin. "My pleasure

Doctor. And please call me John, after being so close I feel it's only right we call each other by our first names don't you?"

If Patricia's face could have gone even more scarlet it did. "You may call me Patricia. Not Pat or Patty I am not a pet or a small child." She said in a stern voice as she sat back into her own seat and secured the harness while John looked on, a ludicrous childlike grin on his face.

"Patricia it is then."

As Patricia looked away she caught the smiling face of Aaron Beckett regarding her from the seat diagonally across the small aisle. Fixing him a look a scolding parent gives their wayward child, she said "And you can take that smile off your face too."

Chuckling softly Aaron could only comment "A good politician should retain their composure no matter the circumstances Patricia."

In reply Patricia stuck her tongue out briefly in a most unladylike manner before closing her eyes and wishing this flight would come to an end before she could embarrass herself even further.

It seemed Patricia's prayers were to be answered as the shuttle came to a stop at the entrance to a large cave entrance. The Persai vessel led the way as the human shuttle followed closely behind, its external lights casting strange shadows across the walls of the cave. Jeff Moore let out a low whistle as the extent of the cave was revealed on his display.

"When nature wants to remind us we are only a small part of the cosmos it does it in style. According to the radar returns the cave is 270 meters high, 160 meters wide and extends for approximately five kilometers. Some of the stalagmites are over seventy meters tall. This place even has its own river running through it."

The next five kilometers passed in near total silence as the each of the shuttle occupants marveled at the beauty of nature passing by above, below and on both sides of the slowly coasting shuttle. The shuttle came to a halt again as it reached the end of the cave, hovering in place in front of what appeared to be an implacable stone wall. As John looked on a sliver of light fractured the wall top to bottom, gradually the sliver widened to reveal what had to be the biggest airlock John had ever seen.

"Now that's impressive. Although I don't see any landing pads." John altered his display to show the pilots display and now it was his turn to let out a soft whistle.

Aaron turned to John. "Perhaps you would like to enlighten us Admiral?"

Touching a few controls John sent the information he was reading to Aaron's display. "We're not seeing any landing pads as we still have something like two kilometers to travel."

The shuttle glided forward and the massive cave doors sealed behind it. An equally large set of what looked like battle armored doors began to open in front of the shuttle revealing a sharply sloping shaft. This shaft had not been naturally formed. As the shuttle moved along the shaft its smooth sides were indicative of very intense heat, probably from a powerful mining laser which had simply melted its way through the natural rock.

The Persai do not do things by half, do they? Thought John. Even with the best equipment available it would have taken human engineers years to build something like this. The shuttle passed through another two of the massive armored doors before finally passing through into what was unmistakably a major shuttle bay which, although not as big as the natural cave at the start of their subterranean journey certainly gave it a run for its money. Shuttles easily the size of the one carrying the delegation were parked around the bay. The scurrying figures of their crew and maintenance personnel allowing John to use their known size to judge the true extent of the bay.

The shuttle made its way an oversize pad located near one corner of the bay where John could see a small crowd gathering. *Well,* thought John, *time to meet the locals. Let's just hope they're as friendly as I've been led to believe.*

The shuttle bounced lightly on its extended landing gear, the entire delegation released their restraints as the shuttle passenger door opened with a slight hiss, and John could feel his ears pop as the pressure equalized. This being a primarily a political mission Aaron Beckett led the way out of the shuttle and down the steps onto the bay floor and toward the welcoming party.

This was John's first meeting with the Persai. Of course he had seen images of them in the briefing packs but meeting one in the flesh, so to speak, was something else. Whoever had compared them to werewolves had got it spot on. Even down to the slightly bent spines which led to their heads being carried less upright on their necks than a humans would be.

John hung back as Aaron was approached by a Persai with more silver in his fur than the moonlight black of his obviously younger entourage. This older Persai stopped in front of Aaron and raised his right arm and extended it out with the hand/paw facing the ground showing the exposed palm.

Through the translator bug in his ear John heard the Persai address Aaron. "I am Tarrov, Chairman of the Council of Twelve and I welcome you as comrades in arms and hope that together we may vanquish our enemy."

Aaron extended his right arm and mimicked the pose of Tarrov. "I am Aaron Beckett, sent by the President of the Terran Republic as a sign of friendship and trust and in the hope we may become allies in our struggle against evil."

A Persai elicited what John could only describe as a low growl. The source of the growl stood slightly apart and exuded a sense of aloofness from the main welcoming group. Chairman Tarrov's mouth dropped open in what John later learned was the Persai version of a laugh. "May I present Force Leader Taminth? The Force Leader will be your military liaison for the duration of your stay. Taminth has viewed your fleets' destruction of the enemy with relish and keenly awaits his opportunity to fight alongside you."

Aaron turned and beckoned John forward. "In that case the Force Leader may wish to speak to Admiral Radford. Admiral Radford was the commander of the human fleet which was victorious that day."

Taminth took a step forward and presented his hand in the same manner as Tarrov had. "An honor Admiral."

Not missing a heartbeat John repeated the gesture. "The honor is mine Force Leader."

Taminth stepped back and resumed his position as John did the same.

"May I suggest the remaining introductions be completed en route to your accommodation? I'm sure you could do with some time to relax and freshen up before we begin our various meetings." Tarrov indicated toward a bulkhead set into the wall of the shuttle bay.

"An excellent idea Chairman." Replied Aaron smoothly. "It has indeed been a long trip to get here and perhaps a few hours to recuperate would be more than welcome."

As the group made its way toward the bulkhead doors John found himself walking beside Taminth. The Persai said nothing but John had the feeling Taminth could not wait to hear all about the battle around Garunda. A distracted John nearly walked into the back of Jeff Moore as the scientist came to a dead stop a few steps through the bulkhead doors.

John was about to berate the scientist when the words died in his throat. The doors had opened to reveal what John could only describe as the most amazing thing he had ever set eyes on. Extending into the distance was a vast subterranean city, complete with parks, rivers and skyscrapers. As John took in the view his eyes were drawn up the skyscrapers sides as they disappeared through… clouds! Clouds within a cave. Impossible!

Taminth came to a halt beside John and his mouth formed into the shape of a Persai laugh. "This is the place where my ancestors found the Saiph blockhouses. My people spent decades expanding this cave to hold our capital city. Everything we need to survive is here. Homes, power generators, hydroponic gardens, industrial plants. All concealed below the surface so our enemy will never find us."

"Amazing."

"And with your help Admiral perhaps it is time for us to come out of our caves and finally face the enemy who has haunted my people for so long."

John looked up into the face of Taminth. "You have my word Force Leader."

#

A vaguely canine face smiled and exposed its short fanged incisors. "Well, what do you think, Admiral?"

"I'm suitably impressed, Force Leader Taminth," nodded John Radford from his seat at the rear of the bridge of the Persai battle cruiser *Vitaros*. In the nine weeks John spent with the Persai, Force Leader Taminth acted as his guide. Taminth was second in command of what John thought of as the Persai Navy. The battle cruiser *Vitaros* was its flagship. Although around the same size as the Terran light cruisers of Talos class, the *Vitaros* was a pure beam weapons platform carrying no missile armament at all. What it lacked in size it made up for in punch. Utilizing Saiph technology, the Persai equipped the *Vitaros* and her sister ships with a main armament of a single, high-energy plasma cannon which, Doctor Jeff Moore had assured John, was at least twice as powerful as the TDF's current heaviest grazer weapon. A similar, though less powerful, plasma cannon provided secondary armament, and finally close in defense was provided by a series of quick firing x-ray lasers – powered independently from the other weapons systems to ensure its survivability as a last line of defense. Well not quite a last line.

On discovering from the Persai the Saiph had been working on a form of energy shielding using exotic matter as a power source, John thought Moore's face was the picture of a schoolboy in a sweet shop. The Persai had been working to perfect it and actually had had success in generating an energy shield in the laboratory but their need to stay hidden from the Others had precluded their search for the right materials to make the energy shielding work on a practical basis. John had left Moore deep in discussion with Persai scientists about Bose–Einstein condensates and Quark—Gluon plasma. It all sounded very boring to John.

John's nine week mission had culminated in the last two days of fleet maneuvers. The fifteen Persai ships had simulated an incursion into the Pars System by a force of forty Buzzard class Others ships, whose aim had been to close with Pars and launch on the planet. Having detected the Others approach using the

Persai equivalent of the Terran Holmes platforms seeded throughout the system's asteroid belt, the Persai ships had ambushed them as they entered the system and using micro folds had out maneuvered the Others as they pressed on toward their objective of Pars. The Persai constant hit and run tactics had allowed them to attack and destroy the Others fleet a few ships at a time, and then micro fold away before suffering any significant damage themselves. The Persai had repeated the process without a break for two days until the Others fleet had been reduced to manageable numbers before confronting them in a full fleet engagement, leading to the inevitable total destruction of the Others fleet while the Persai suffered minimal losses.

John had to admit, the Persai ship handling and tactics impressed him. Although their lack of missiles limited the offensive range of their ships, the devastating main plasma cannon ensured any hit by it was a kill shot. If the TDF could re-equip its ships with the Persai plasma cannon, it would significantly increase its firepower.

Moore had assured John the Persai Gravity Drive, although differing from the one he had developed independently of the Saiph, was only slightly more efficient and not worth introducing to the TDF but the fusion generators the Persai used were smaller and more efficient and they were well worth adopting into TDF service.

The other part of the Persai Navy John had been impressed with was its small fleet of survey ships, like the one commanded by Sub Leader Verus who had first discovered the Terran intervention in Garunda. These ships had all the properties of the TDF's own Vanguard class survey ships but reflected the Persai fixation with remaining hidden from the Others. They were equipped with superior stealth technology. They also reflected the Persai issue of depth of trained personnel, due to their population limits. The Persai were forced to heavily automate ship's functions and relied on advanced computer systems, just one more thing Moore drooled over.

John stood and walked to where Taminth sat in the middle of the flag bridge. "A good day's work, Force Leader Taminth. And

254

now perhaps we should return to Pars for a well-deserved rest and to allow me to compile my report for The Joint Chiefs." *And, John thought, a chance to see more of Patricia Bath.* He found Patricia increasingly in his thoughts, he hoped he was in hers too.

Taminth turned his head at John's approach. "With you and your kind by our side, Admiral, I think the time of our revenge on The Enemy is getting closer." Taminth smiled and bared his incisors, slightly disconcertingly John could sense the intense need for revenge. As he looked around the bridge, he felt it radiate from every Persai present. It was a feeling John hoped would not consume the Persai if they ever came into conflict with the Others.

CHAPTER TWENTY-TWO

RETURN TO MESSIER FIFTY-FOUR

CHARON BASE - ORBIT OF PLUTO - SOL SYSTEM

Commodore Christos Papadomas had been expecting the call from Admiral Vadis ever since he was informed a Persai survey ship and two of their battle cruisers had arrived in orbit around Charon Base. Once the home to the secretive Operation Chimera, it was now the base for the Survey Command arm of the Terran Defense Force. The pace, of late, for Survey Command had slowed as the TDF recovered from the battle with 'The Others' around Garunda and the discovery of the Persai. To Papadomas and the leaders of the TDF, it became apparent that despite the fact the Vanguard class survey ships successfully avoided contact with the Others, if the Vanguards had been detected and come under fire, they would not have the necessary firepower to overcome the Others. The TDF could not rely on catching the Others out with a micro fold as Captain Witsell had done in 70 Ophiuchi.

Now he found himself waiting patiently in Vadis's briefing room accompanied by Captain Bruce Torrance of TDF *James Cook* and Captain Bill Talbot of TDF *Henry Hudson*.

Keeping his voice at a low conspirator's level, he said to Torrance and Talbot, "Well, gentlemen. Do you get the feeling they may at last have found a job for us poor relations in Survey Command?"

Talbot let out a little chuckle as he replied in a similar way. "Best keep your comments to yourself, Commodore. You know Vadis hears everything, he used to be a spy, you know."

The other two men laughed and quickly stifled it as none other than the said Vadis entered the briefing room, followed by a Persai who was deep in conversation with a human in smart civilian attire and a Garundan in what passed as their version of a suit. *Politicians...* Christos thought, as he and the other survey officers brought themselves to attention.

Vadis smiled his usual fox's smile as he walked to the head of the table and took his seat. The human suit and the Garundan sat without invitation while the Persai remained standing and gave the two politicians what Christos could only assume was a look of disdain highlighted by his revealing one bared incisor and a low one word mumble. Christos attempted to hide a grin as he realized the military's dislike for all things politic appeared to cross all species boundaries.

Vadis indicated the vacant seats before his officers. "Please, gentleman. Take your seats and let's begin." Vadis touched a control and the image of the Messier 54 system appeared above the center of the table. "This, gentlemen, is why we are gathered here today."

Christos felt a nudge at his elbow as Talbot leaned his head toward him. "Told you."

Vadis ignored him as he went on with the briefing. "It has been decided the time has come for us to return to the Messier 54 system and attempt to make friendly contact with its inhabitants." Vadis smiled his smile again. "The Baldies."

The human suit coughed quietly. "Admiral, must you call them that?"

Vadis regarded the politician with a playful glint in his eye, "My apologies, Ambassador Schamu. I never was very good at political correctness."

Christos could see out of the corner of his eye the Persai giving the ambassador a look of distain again as he struggled to keep a grin from appearing on his own face.

Back to the briefing, Vadis continued, "The plan is relatively simple: three Vanguard class survey ships will accompany a Persai survey ship captained by Sub Leader Verus."

The Persai gave a small nod in the direction of the human officers.

"The Vanguards will carry out reconnaissance of the outer system and Sub Leader Verus will use his ship's more advanced stealth technology to get as much information on the two occupied planets as possible without being detected. The Ambassador and his party will then assess the information and formulate a plan to approach the Baldies."

At the use of the slang word, again, the ambassador cringed. Christos was sure the Admiral had done it on purpose.

Vadis went on as if he had not noticed the politician's reaction. "The joint chiefs have decided, although there is no indication of a presence of the Others in the system, from now on all Survey Command missions of this nature will be accompanied by warships to provide the mission with some teeth in case they run into any trouble. To that effect, two Talos class cruisers and two Persai cruisers have been attached to this mission."

Ambassador Schamu lent forward and interrupted Vadis. "May I point out this is the first mission to consist of representatives of all three Commonwealth Union members and I have been selected to lead our political representatives?" He sat back with a very smug look on his face.

Vadis continued as if he had not heard the ambassador. "As such, the flotilla will come under command of the ranking Commonwealth Union officer, who will take into account the suggestions of the ambassador. This officer will ultimately have command of the mission."

Schamu looked crestfallen at the announcement of the chain of command to everyone in the room.

Vadis smiled again as he turned to face Christos. "That would be you, Rear Admiral Papadomas."

It took a moment to register what Vadis said but a hearty slap on the back from Talbot brought him back to his senses.

"Congratulations, Christos – sorry Admiral Papadomas."

After a moment Vadis continued. "Indeed, Admiral Papadomas. Congratulations. Now I would suggest your first order of business is to let Commander Ranking, your XO, know he is now Captain Ranking, then get together with your other captains and Sub Leader Verus and familiarize yourself with the Persai ships' capabilities and formulate a plan. I expect your ships to depart for Messier 54 within the week."

#

Rear Admiral Papadomas looked around his rather spartan flag bridge on TDF *Cutlass*. Not designed to house admirals and the staff which inevitably came with them, the Talos class Cruisers had simply had the marine areas converted for the Admiral and his hangers on use. A temporary measure until the shipyards built the new survey support cruisers.

Unashamed pride is what he felt. He found himself not caring one iota how his flag bridge looked because the important thing was, it was all his to command. This last week had been a busy time for the Admiral and his new staff. Aside from getting to know how each other operated, he had the added burden of having to listen to the insufferable Schamu's incessant complaining – about everything: from his quarters to the quality of food... The sooner the ambassador had something else to occupy him and his party the better.

Now the time had come. He and his newly named Survey Flotilla One were formed up and ready to depart. "Communications has the flotilla signaled to the flag it is ready to depart?"

"Signal has been received and acknowledged, Admiral," replied the Communications officer.

"Thank you." He activated his link to Captain Mkhize whose face appeared in the Admiral's Holo Cube.

Mkhize was from the Natal Province of Earth. With his striking ebony features, deep bass voice with its easily identifiable accent and seemingly irrepressible sense of humor, he and Mkhize found themselves drawn into a natural working partnership, where it appeared Mkhize occasionally had the uncanny ability to predict his Admiral's intentions without a word being said. Qualities an Admiral needed in his flag captain.

"Vusumuzi, I believe it is time we were on our way."

Mkhize smiled at his Admiral. "Your wish is my command Admiral."

He could not help but smile as Mkhize's infectious good nature took hold. "Then the command is let's be on our way to Messier 54, Captain."

"Aye aye, sir," replied Mkhize.

Papadomas cut the link and noted with satisfaction the flotilla moving as one, and quickly picking up speed as it cleared Charon Base.

His excitement grew as the commander at Communications called out to the bridge in general, "Fold in three, two, one." Survey Flotilla One disappeared from Terran space.

CHAPTER TWENTY-THREE

STEALTH ATTACK

KUIPER BELT - 31 AQUILAE

TDF *Aurora* ran silently through the darkness of space, every active system on board shut down as she flew on a ballistic course through the outer reaches of the 31 Aquilae system. Her mission was simple: attempt to penetrate the system without detection by any of the watching Sherlock platforms or the patrolling warships of BatFor 4. The joint chiefs would periodically run these exercises to test unit readiness. The unit in question, the newly arrived BatFor 4, had no foreknowledge the destroyer *Aurora* was coming. If a unit commander was aware an exercise was scheduled, they may increase their operational tempo in response. It was their normal operations the joint Chiefs wanted to test.

Aurora had been selected for this mission as she was equipped with the latest chameleon stealth systems which, it had been promised, would raise the TDFs stealth ability to a level that should give it parity with the Persai. Right now, *Aurora* was fast approaching the Kuiper Belt circling approximately fifty AUs from the system primary which Captain Francis McNamara intended to use to mask his approach.

McNamara had been busily planning his next move after

clearing the Kuiper Belt when a call from Tactical interrupted him.

"Captain, I'm picking up something odd on the passive sensors."

"Throw it up on the main Holo Cube and let me have a look please, Guns." The Holo Cube sprang to life with a view of the approaching Kuiper Belt. The Kuiper Belt comprised the bits and pieces left over from the formation of the system, which normally were reasonably small. Some pieces could be as big as 100 kilometers across and some even large enough to qualify as dwarf planets with a diameter around 1600 kilometers. Centered in the image, McNamara was looking at, was exactly that – a dwarf planet. Scattered across it was a dusting of twinkling lights, like the stars on a cloudy night obscured and unobscured by the moving clouds.

McNamara's gut told him something was not right. "What am I looking at, Guns?"

"Captain, the light points you are seeing are computer generated renditions of fleeting energy signatures the passive sensors have detected but are having difficulty locking onto."

McNamara hated it when he was right. "Could they be ships running their power at minimum levels just like we are?"

The lieutenant at Tactical's forehead frowned as she considered the possibility. "If I were to take a guess... I'd say that is exactly what they are. It's hard to get a firm read on their numbers, but I guess at least thirty ships are out there. BatFor 4 only has twenty-two ships in its current order of battle including its resupply, fast replenishment ships. Could The Joint Chiefs be running some sort of major fleet exercise we're unaware of?"

McNamara felt his gut tightening. His mind raced as he tried to muster up an explanation as to why so many ships would be hiding out here in the Kuiper Belt. No matter how hard he tried, there was no alternative. There could only be one reason why those ships were here: 'The Others' had returned to 31 Aquilae, and this time they had come en masse.

McNamara hit the recessed control in his chair arm and the bone penetrating wail of the battle stations alarm reverberated throughout the *Aurora*, urging the crew to their posts. McNamara gave rapid-fire orders in succession. "Guns! Bring the weapons on line and go active on all your sensors. Get as much on those ships as you can, then download all your data to the courier drones and append our current location and logs. I want the drones constantly updated and programmed to fold for Garunda on my command."

The young lieutenant spun in her chair as she went to her task. McNamara hardly noticed as he continued his orders. "Engineering! Standby the Gravity Drive. Communications! Hail those ships, identify us and request their identities and intentions."

"My God!"

McNamara looked across to Tactical where the unbidden remark originated "Guns! What are you seeing?"

A very pale faced lieutenant turned to face her captain, her fear evident in her voice. "Captain, those ships are powering up. I now make... forty-two ships. The computer identifies at least thirty as Buzzard class and," the lieutenant swallowed hard, preparing the delivery vehicle for bad news, "the remaining twelve... the computer puts at fifty percent larger than the Buzzards. Somewhere in the 330,000 tonnes range. Their power readings are at least twice the Buzzards."

Those on the bridge who overheard the conversation between the captain and his tactical officer stopped whatever they were doing, momentarily, in mid flow. All eyes turned to McNamara, pleading with him to order a fold jump, to let them escape from the nightmare the ships in front of them represented.

McNamara saw the anxious faces of his officers but knew if a force of this size caught BatFor 4 unprepared then it would be a slaughter. "Navigation, flight time for a Buzzard at maximum known speed to Garunda?"

Fingers flew over controls. "I make it seven hours from a standing start to insertion into Garundan orbit, sir."

Only seven hours, thought McNamara. Seven hours for Rear Admiral Thapa and BatFor 4 to prepare for the Others onslaught. McNamara said decisively. "Communications! I want a flight of eight drones launched as quickly as you can get them away, two each for Garunda, Earth, Janus and Pars."

"Aye aye, sir."

"Navigation! Plot us a fold back to Garunda. Let's get the hell out of here." McNamara felt the *Aurora* shudder as the courier drones began launching in rapid succession. He counted them off. One, two, three, four, five...

The near light speed energy weapons fired at them by the nearest Others ship guaranteed neither McNamara nor his crew saw home again. As the weapons connected with the small destroyer, the ablative armor held for a moment before the sheer volume of fire blew its way through it. TDF *Aurora* and all her crew had no chance of survival.

As the *Aurora* died, the Others' fleet formed itself up and moved toward Garunda.

#

As the Others advanced in system toward their ultimate goal of the planet Garunda, BatFor 4 raced to battle stations. On receipt of the devastating message alerting him to the massive enemy fleet heading toward him from the *Aurora*'s courier drone, Rear Admiral Thapa dispatched his own drones to Earth, Janus and Pars. He requested any and all available ships to make their way to Garunda.

Thapa was no fool. He knew his BatFor were in for the fight of their lives. The Others fleet outnumbered him and this new type of Others ship, his tactical officer had designated them Vulture class, outweighed his own TDF *Richelieu*, a Nemesis class flagship by four and half to one. Even if it had comparable weapons to the Buzzard class, he knew he could do little but slow the Others down and hope the cavalry arrived before the Others managed to range on Garunda and obliterate all life on that world.

The only way Thapa could see to buy time was with the lives of his own brave men and women. Thapa looked slowly around the flag bridge of the *Richelieu* and steeled himself for what was to come.

"Communications! General fleet signal: Ships are to form up on the battleships as per Case Yellow."

Without turning, the lieutenant at Communications acknowledged the order with a tense "Case Yellow. Aye aye, sir."

As Thapa watched, a sidebar on his Holo Cube listing the names of the ships of BatFor 4 highlighted in turn as each ship acknowledged the order.

Case Yellow planned for this very scenario facing BatFor 4, an attack by overwhelming numbers on a shortest time course for Garunda. The plan was simple: BatFor 4 would place itself between the attacking Others and Garunda and fight a long range missile duel with BatFor 4 attempting to slow the Others progress to the planet and gain time for the reinforcements to arrive. Unfortunately, Case Yellow was conceived on the premise BatFor 4 would face Buzzard class ships only, not these new Vulture class ships. The readings gained by TDF *Aurora* had allowed Tactical to make a best guess at the range of the Vulture's weapons. It was exactly that – a guess. Thapa would not know for sure until his ships closed with the Others and engaged them.

As Thapa watched his display, he noted with satisfaction Commodore Nikulin and his three Ragusan class fleet replenishment freighters were already moving off with their escort of two Agis destroyers, while six of his remaining destroyers broke into pairs and moved to either flank of his three Nemesis battleships. Specifically designed to be anti-missile platforms, the Agis would augment each battleship's own anti-missile defenses. The four heavy cruisers positioned themselves two above and two below the line of battleships to protect against any attempted pincer movements by the Others. Many civilians did not know a space battle was fought in three dimensions, so protecting the space above and below you was just as important as your sides, front and rear. The two Talos light cruisers would fold to a position to the rear of the Others and use hit and run tactics in an attempt to cause as much damage to the enemy's drive systems as they could.

One lone destroyer left – TDF *Comanche*. Thapa watched it blink out of existence and only a moment later it reappeared high above the ecliptic plane, far from any danger. *Comanche* had the unenviable task of being the messenger to inform Earth of the seemingly certain death of BatFor 4 and the destruction of Garunda and her hundreds of millions of inhabitants. *Comanche* would hold her position and record the impending clash until BatFor 4 and Garunda's fate was decided.

#

Ensign Roawan looked around him in a state of mild confusion as the human crew of the Ragusan class fleet replenishment ship TDF *Wayfarer* seemed to move around him, as if he were a lonely outcrop of rock in a sea of people. Roawan was one of the first native Garundans to graduate from the Joint Naval Academy. He had specialized in communications and the *Wayfarer* was meant to be his maiden cruise where he would apply all the lessons he learned in the classroom in the real world. But right now, as he watched the humans around him move with a purpose, he felt like a spare cog in a very large machine. He knew he should, no, he knew he needed to be doing something. The Others were attacking his planet and he couldn't leave the humans to shoulder the burden of its defense. He was now a naval officer and it was his duty to do whatever he could to protect his people. With a new found purpose, Roawan headed for Comms and hoped he could be of some assistance.

He entered the Communication Center, a very grand name for a very small room holding two naval ratings and a chief petty officer who monitored the flow of traffic to and from the *Wayfarer*. Most of the traffic on the *Wayfarer* was generated from the bridge where the duty Communication's officer was stationed. Roawan had been working here since his arrival on board the *Wayfarer*. He found humans always treated him with the respect his status as an officer deserved, even if he was only an ensign and straight from the Academy.

The CPO heard the hatch open behind him. On the realization Roawan had entered the room, he quickly brought him up to

266

speed. "Sir, we have established solid whisker locks on the escorting destroyers and *Splendid*. The *Maverick* has reported a fault with her forward whisker mount but we have a solid lock on her stern mount." TDF *Splendid* and TDF *Maverick* were the *Wayfarer*'s sister ships. "We have six courier drones prepped and ready for launch awaiting any downloads from the bridge and we are currently running health checks on our remaining ready couriers. I have also ordered a health check on all the courier drones we are carrying in the cargo holds." The CPO quickly checked his PAD. "Our current stock is forty-seven ready for immediate off-loading with eighteen down for essential maintenance."

Impressed by the CPO's comprehensive report, Roawan could not help but feel, again, he was excess baggage. "Thank you, CPO. What of the fleet's current status?"

The CPO touched another control and a small Holo Cube sprang to life in the corner of the room. The blue icons representing the fighting ships of BatFor 4 had folded away to a point approximately 200,000 kilometers from the oncoming enemy ships, and had begun to engage them at long range using anti-ship missiles in an obvious attempt to slow their progress toward Garunda. On a sidebar, Roawan saw the list of damaged and destroyed TDF ships growing slowly but surely.

These new Vulture ships of the Others might be slower than the Buzzards, but their weight of firepower was telling. Thapa was forced to continually maneuver to avoid the waves of anti-ship missiles being launched by the Others. These new Vultures carried a more powerful version of the Buzzard's x-ray laser which, if it struck a TDF ship, invariably caused massive damage or outright destruction. The Admiral was forced to maneuver and keep the Others within his own weapons effective envelope. Roawan noted so far in the battle, BatFor 4 had been unable to cause any significant damage to these new Vulture ships. Tactical had identified another new type of Others' ship, designated Goshawk. The Goshawk was similar in size and construction to a standard Buzzard but it appeared to be an anti-missile ship designed to protect the larger Vultures. Similar to the role of the Agis destroyers within the TDF but on a much bigger scale.

So far, in battle, the Goshawks were very effective. TDF reports indicated only the standard Buzzards were taking casualties. No TDF missile had gotten close enough to the Vultures to cause any damage.

"How are communications with the fleet, CPO?"

"We are maintaining a steady stream of courier drones back and forth to the fleet. The bridge is having us launch drones back to Earth, Janus and Pars with status reports every thirty minutes."

Roawan's face contorted into the Garundan equivalent of a frown at the news. "We must be burning through our drones quite quickly then, CPO?"

Without consulting his PAD, the CPO answered. "With our current rate of expenditure, our stocks will be dry in nine hours." With a shrug, the CPO added in a quiet, resigned voice. "No matter, sir. It will all be decided by then anyway."

There was a moment of silence in the room. Even with the valiant efforts of BatFor 4, the Others were making steady progress through the system. At their current rate of advance, they should be within weapons range of Garunda in five hours.

Roawan could feel something nagging at the back of his mind, even as he contemplated the destruction of his home. Then it came to him. "CPO, you said at our current rate of expenditure we would be dry in nine hours."

Now it was the CPO's turn to be slightly confused. "Yes sir. Nine hours is what the numbers are telling me."

"Are we not losing any drones to enemy fire as they arrive at the fleet?"

A large grin appeared on the CPO's face. "Well, sir. Before I moved over to communications, I used to be in navigation. I'm pretty good at calculating fold jumps." The CPO indicated the Holo Cube again. "As you can see, the Others and our fleet are moving at a relatively steady rate toward Garunda – almost a predictable rate. I have programmed each drone to emerge 30000 kilometers to the rear of our ships, redefine its location and identify the flagship and its current speed, then micro jump to within a kilometer of the ship. The drone is then shielded from enemy fire by the ship while it transmits its data, gets a reply and then micro folds away a safe distance and repeats the process in reverse to arrive back here."

Roawan was looking at the CPO in amazement. "How many drones have we actually lost to enemy fire?"

The CPO's chest puffed out with pride. "I lost two drones while I refined the computer programming. But since then? Not one has been lost." The grin on the CPO's face faded as he realized Roawan was no longer listening to him. An unusual blank expression fell over the ensign. "Sir, sir… are you alright?"

Roawan ignored the concerned CPO. He pushed past him to a computer terminal and began typing in commands as fast as he could.

The CPO watched over his shoulder as the load manifest of each of the replenishment ships was called up. Roawan became very still as he leaned on the terminal for support as if drunk. The CPO was forced to take a step back as the young ensign spun round to face him and grab him by the shoulders.

"CPO, do you know what you've done? You have given me the means to save my people!"

The CPO and the two ratings could only stare at the young ensign in bewilderment.

Roawan was making for the door, shouting orders excitedly over his shoulder. "CPO! I want those drones downed for maintenance online as quickly as possible. Inform *Maverick* and *Splendid* to conduct health checks on all their available drones, ASAP."

Roawan stopped and turned at the entrance to the Comms Center to face its confused occupants. His joy replaced by determination. "Now we will see how well they die."

#

Radford looked across the table directly into the eyes of Patricia Bath and for just a moment held her gaze longer than he should, before Patricia broke contact. Her cheeks flushed slightly in embarrassment. When John first arrived on Pars, it had quickly become the norm for John, Aaron Beckett, Patricia Bath and Jeff Moore to meet for either dinner or a late supper and update each other on the events of the day. As the weeks passed and the humans became more and more pressed for time in their daily routine, it had left only John and Patricia to carry on the ritual.

John admitted to himself he was actually quite glad Aaron and Jeff could not make it anymore, for it gave him more time to spend talking to Patricia. Yes, the conversation always started about work, but recently work talk quickly tapered off. Each talked about their personal lives, their families and friends, personal likes and dislikes. John found himself wanting to know everything there was to know about Patricia.

The urgent tone of John's wrist Comm brought his attention back to the present. "Radford. Go ahead."

"Admiral." John immediately recognized the gruff tones of Force Leader Taminth in his ear bug. "We have received a courier drone from Garunda with some disturbing news."

John felt his whole body stiffen. Patricia must have sensed it too. Without thinking, she reached across the table and took John's hand in hers.

"The courier was from the TDF *Aurora* which has been trying to penetrate the 31 Aquilae system as part of a readiness exercise. It reports at least forty-two ships, identified as The Enemy, hiding in the Kuiper Belt of the system. From the *Aurora*'s sensor data it appears The Enemy have twelve ships of an unknown type at least fifty percent larger than their Buzzards. No more information is known at this time, but I feel certain The Enemy have come with the intention of destroying Garunda."

"Well, we thought it would happen eventually. I just wish we had had more time; the fleet base isn't even fully operational yet. Thank God, the first phase of the Viper defense platforms are in place, it should at least give Garunda a decent chance of defeating any missile bombardment of the planet." John knew the Viper defense platforms with their two variants, one armed with nine high velocity missiles and the other with a powerful grazer good for 100 shots and the same ones Earth and Janus trusted with their defense. It was just a matter of how many had been deployed around Garunda.

"Admiral, Chairman Tarrov has activated our defense agreements under the Commonwealth Union Charter and the Persai will immediately dispatch units to the aid of Garunda. I would request you join me on my flagship as quickly as possible." As second in command of the Persai Navy, John knew Taminth's request was more of an order than a request.

"Of course, Force Leader. I shall be with you as quickly as possible." Taminth cut the link and John went to stand, only to find Patricia still held his hand. John looked down at her and thought he could see a small tear running down her cheek. He picked up a napkin and went to wipe it away but Patricia stopped him and gave his hand a small kiss.

"You come back to me, John Radford. Do you hear me?"

John could hear the strain in her voice and realized he had fallen head over heels in love with this woman. "I promise," he said softly, hearing the strain in his own voice. He slowly pulled away from her, turned and headed for the shuttle pad.

Patricia sat alone at the table and stared after him, the tears she tried to hide from him now running freely down her face.

#

Admiral Jing regarded the faces of the three men and one Persai floating in the Holo Cube before him from his seat on the Flag Bridge of TDF *Reliant*. "Are you certain the automated drones are up to the task, Commodore?"

Without hesitation, Commodore Nikulin answered the ranking officer of the combined Commonwealth fleet, hastily cobbled together and now sat in hiding in the shadow of the only gas giant in the 31 Aquilae system. "I have complete faith in the system Ensign Roawan devised, sir."

Jing's fingers formed a steeple in front of him and he pursed his lips in his trademark pose. Jing knew time was of the essence. The Others were now only ninety minutes from being able to fire on Garunda. To commit his forces to a battle plan, which was ultimately reliant on an untested weapon, designed by an ensign, from a people who two years ago were still on the cusp of their

271

own industrial revolution, was a big ask.

Around the *Reliant* floated the biggest fleet ever brought together by the Terran Defense Force. When the call for help arrived from Admiral Thapa and he stated he was initiating Case Yellow, Jing knew time was short. He organized his ships on the fly. Jing brought with him BatFor 2, which had been the alert BatFor, ready to respond to any incursion into Earth space, and the parts of BatFor 1 and 3 with enough men on board to fight. He stripped Earth's defenses to the bone. The politicians howled their disagreement as he ignored their calls and folded out for Garunda with seven Nemesis battleships, five Vulcan heavy cruisers, six Talos light cruisers and seventeen Agis destroyers.

Vice Admiral Lewis had not had to overcome the same whining politicians. Thapa and the men and women of BatFor 4 were based in Janus, and Governor Crothers had immediately given Lewis his blessing to take whatever he needed to come to their aid. Governor Crothers and the population of Janus felt a deep affiliation with the men and women of the TDF. In fact, a large percentage of the crew operating the ships of BatFor 4 had already applied to become citizens of the colony when they left the services. Lewis had arrived with two complete BatFors: six Nemesis battleships, eight Vulcan heavy cruisers, four Talos light cruisers and twenty Agis destroyers.

What was unexpected was the speed with which the Persai had reacted. When Jing arrived at the rendezvous point, behind the gas giant, he found ten Persai cruisers waiting for him. Force Leader Taminth had not hesitated in placing his ships under the command of Jing and Jing decided to leave Radford where he was on Taminth's flagship, *Vitaros*, as his liaison officer.

Jing caught the eye of Lewis in the Holo Cube and Lewis gave him a curt nod. Jing made his decision.

"Admiral Lewis, you will immediately fold with BatFor 5 and 6 and join with Admiral Thapa and bolster his defenses. Your aim is to slow the Others as much as possible. Try to keep them at arm's length, they are not permitted to enter weapons range of the planet at any cost. Commodore Nikulin, continue to deploy as many weapons as possible. You will launch only on my command but you can work on me giving that order…" Jing check the time displayed at the bottom of the Holo Cube. "Twenty-six minutes from now."

Jing turned his head to regard Radford and Force Leader Taminth, the last two members of this council of war. "Force Leader, for this to work I need those Goshawks providing anti-missile defense for the Vultures to be put out of action. Can you do it?"

Taminth's ears went back and his lips curled back to display his incisors, his voice in the Admiral's ear was cold as ice. "Admiral Jing, my people have waited a long time for this moment. Again, The Enemy come to butcher the innocent, but this time they have met peoples who will not succumb without a fight. We of the Persai will do our duty or die trying."

"Very well, gentlemen. You have your orders. Admiral Thapa's people are dying out there, so let us get to it. Dismissed." The four faces vanished from the Holo Cube and as Jing watched, the tactical display changed as Lewis's ships folded away to join their comrades in BatFor 4, while the Persai ships left to begin their attack runs. Commodore Nikulin and the *Wayfarer* returned to Garunda to supervise the final deployment of the weapons the plan hinged on. Jing sat back in his chair and without thinking his fingers formed a steeple, fervently he hoped this was the right decision.

#

John gripped the arms of his seat on the flag bridge of *Vitaros* a little harder. For the first time, the *Vitaros'* sensors got a good look at the battle raging between the Others and the human ships defending Garunda. In the five hours since the Others began their attack, BatFor 4 had virtually ceased to exist. As John watched, a Vulture fired its main x-ray laser and the TDF destroyer *Black Skull*, which had strayed into the Vulture's weapons range, vanished in a blinding flash.

The arrival of Admiral Lewis and his reinforcements had been in the nick of time. BatFor 4 was critically low on missiles – both anti-ship and anti-missile. If the Others had managed to coordinate their fire properly, they would have swamped BatFor 4's meagre defenses and ensured its destruction. For whatever reason, they had not yet managed to do so. Now the twenty Agis destroyers of BatFor 5 and 6 brought their own highly coordinated anti-missile systems into play, and the number of the Others' missiles getting through their orchestrated fire was slowing to a trickle as the battered remnants of BatFor 4 retired behind Lewis's fresh ships and full magazines.

Taminth gestured for John to join him. John left his seat to stand by the Force Leader's side as he regarded the main tactical plot. "Admiral, from the information supplied by BatFor 4 we have identified the twelve Vultures and their escort of two Goshawks apiece. My command will break into five pairs and we will attack as one wave with each pair assigned to engage the escorting Goshawks. I intend to attack the Goshawks protecting the Vultures closest to Admiral Lewis first, in an attempt to relieve some of the pressure on the Admiral, then sweep through the remainder of The Enemy fleet until all the Goshawks have been destroyed or until we have sustained sufficient critical damage which precludes any further offensive action."

Taminth's plan was simple in concept. John had seen the effect of the *Vitaros'* main high energy plasma cannon in action. Unless the Others had another surprise up their sleeves, then the cannon should be sufficient to deal with the Goshawks. John's only worry was how the *Vitaros* and her sister ships' x-ray missile point defense lasers were going to hold up. *Vitaros* had to get within 10000 kilometers of the Goshawks to ensure a one shot, one kill ratio. If the Others got a lock onto the *Vitaros* while the Persai were getting a firing solution then their point defense x-ray lasers would be pushed to breaking point.

Well, John thought, *We'll just have to wait and see.* "Force Leader, I concur with your plan."

Taminth let out a short grunt as he put one hand on John's shoulder and turned to address the Persai on the flag bridge. "Let us send The Enemy to hell. Attack!"

The *Vitaros* winked out of existence only to reappear a moment later less than 9000 kilometers off the starboard side of a

Goshawk.

The Persai at Tactical shouted, "We're being hit with rapid, high band radar, Force Leader! The computers are calling it targeting radar. Four seconds until main weapon is ready to fire. Targeting solution looks good. Firing now."

John stared at his readout as the invisible x-ray laser reached out, at nearly the speed of light, and touched the hull of the Goshawk dead center. John mouthed a silent prayer, hoping the Persai weapon proved effective on the Others' ships as all the simulations had said it would be... It was.

Before his very eyes, a large plume of escaping gases and debris exploded from the far side of the Goshawk, seconds later it exploded into a million pieces.

A jubilant cry went up from the bridge crew and Taminth had to shout to be heard. "Navigator! Get us out of here before they target us."

"Yes, Force Leader." And the *Vitaros'* Gravity Drive took it away from the Others without suffering a single hit.

As the *Vitaros* reentered normal space, Taminth requested a status check on all the Persai ships.

The Persai officer at Tactical carrying out his order paused and became still. "Burrav disobeyed your orders, Force Leader."

Taminth struck the arm of his chair with his hand with such force John thought it would break. "What did that impetuous fool do?"

Taminth's tactical officer turned to face the force leader. His voice was hollow at the dishonor and needless sacrifice disobeying the Force Leader's orders had caused. "After engaging and successfully destroying his assigned Goshawk, Burrav attempted to engage the Vulture it had been escorting. By the time Burrav had a lock on the Vulture, he had come under fire from other Enemy ships. His ship simply couldn't stand up to the massed Enemy fire and it was destroyed."

Taminth bowed his head low for a moment. John thought he heard a mumbled prayer for the dead Persai before Taminth told the tactical officer to continue with his report.

"We have confirmation all ten intended targets are destroyed,

Force Leader."

Taminth nodded slowly and turned to John. "It would seem our plan is working. We will immediately re engage the remaining Goshawks."

"They'll be expecting us this time, Force Leader," said John cautiously.

Taminth nodded again. "Agreed, but time is running short and if Admiral Jing's plan is to succeed we must press our attack."

This time it was John's turn to agree. "True. By my calculations the Admiral should be launching his attack in twelve minutes."

"Then we have no time to waste, Admiral Radford." Taminth spun in his chair. "Communications! Signal the ships to begin their second attack and continue until all Goshawks are destroyed."

Vitaros once again entered fold space and, as it emerged into normal space, John's repeater display filled with the bulk of a Goshawk. John's readout told him it was 4850 kilometers away. Damn! Spitting distance in a space battle. The *Vitaros'* navigator was good.

The tactical officer was watching his display intently as the computers worked frantically to get a lock on the Goshawk. "Target locked. Firing in three, two –"

The Persai never got to say 'one' as the *Vitaros* was rocked by the impact of a Q Switching laser fired by the Vulture on the port quarter. The tactical officer's station took the brunt of the impact as the laser penetrated the *Vitaros'* hull and entered the flag bridge. His voice cut off as his station exploded, his body shredded by deadly fragments.

John could only watch as the horror unfolded in slow motion. Taminth became the next victim. His chair was ripped from its mount and flew across the flag bridge to be stopped by an unyielding bulkhead. The sound of escaping atmosphere filled John's ears. He reached for the emergency helmet mounted in a rack at the side of his chair, secured it in place and said a silent prayer as all the telltales turned green. At least he did not have to worry about the lack of oxygen killing him. John punched up the weapons control on his repeater and was astonished to see the green ready light of the main armament still flashing its ready signal. John doubled checked to see the weapon was still locked onto the Goshawk and pressed down on the firing stud with all his might.

4850 kilometers away, the Goshawk that killed Taminth expired itself.

The remaining Persai on the flag bridge were struggling to come to terms with the sudden violence and the death of their commanding officer. John had to act and act quickly before another of the Others ship started using the *Vitaros* for target practice and they all died. John worked furiously at his terminal, fully expecting the next moment to be his last.

"Navigation! Fold us to the coordinates I've just sent you. Damage Control! Get the hull breach sealed. Communications! Slave fire control to your terminal and be prepared to fire on our next target." John barked his orders.

The *Vitaros* folded to the coordinates John had supplied and as it entered normal space, another Goshawk appeared in John's display. John bared his teeth behind the protective faceplate of his helmet. "Lock on and kill that son of a bitch."

The Persai at communications did not hesitate. "Yes, Force Leader." As the fire ready light turned green, the *Vitaros* fired and another Goshawk was guided into oblivion. John did not have the time to gloat, he punched another set of coordinates into his terminal and sent them to the navigator.

The *Vitaros* rocked as another laser hit her but she folded away only to reappear directly behind a Goshawk. John did not need any words of command. As the fire ready light turned green, the Goshawk joined its companions as rapidly expanding clouds of wreckage.

A red zero began flashing in John's display. *Time's up,* thought John, hoping they had done enough for Admiral Jing's plan to work. "Fold for the rendezvous point, Navigator."

"Yes, Force Leader." That was the second time a member of the bridge crew addressed him so. Maybe they had forgotten he was a human admiral and not a Persai.

Admiral Jing watched the clock inexorably counting down to zero. On his tactical display, the Others fleet was approaching a line which represented one hour's Buzzard flight time from Garunda. The time at which they would reach maximum launch range for any missiles targeted on Garunda. His display was constantly updated by the information arriving by courier drone from Admiral Lewis. Drones were arriving every five minutes now as the battle reached its most critical phase.

As the clock touched zero, Jing turned to his waiting Communications officer and uttered a single word. "Execute!"

#

Commodore Nikulin could cut the atmosphere on the bridge of the *Wayfarer* with a knife. Mad panicking over now. Either the plan would work or it would not. Nikulin could not help but smile as he watched Ensign Roawan nervously hopping from one foot to the other, as he lent over the shoulder of the *Wayfarer*'s tactical officer.

When Roawan had ran onto the bridge demanding to speak to him. Nikulin put it down to fear, fear he was about to witness his planet die before his eyes. Nikulin was wrong. Roawan explained his idea, flabbergasting Nikulin with its simplicity.

Take all the available courier drones on board the three replenishment ships. Remove the seeker heads and replace those with megaton range nuclear warheads from the anti-ship missiles Nikulin's ships were carrying, and finally load the software CPO Higgins had devised. And hey presto – immensely accurate, Gravity Drive-equipped, nuclear tipped, ship killers. Something R and D had been working on for what seemed like an age, a lowly Garundan ensign and a human chief petty officer had solved in a matter of a few hours.

"Commodore, courier drone from Admiral Jing. Download is one word: 'execute'."

Nikulin addressed the young Garundan. "Ensign Roawan, if you would do the honors."

The *Wayfarer*'s tactical officer pushed his chair back from his terminal and stood up, inviting Roawan to assume his post. Roawan sat, lent over the terminal and let his finger hover over the flashing red light, savoring the moment for just a brief second before pressing down with all his strength. "Weapons away sir."

163 nuclear tipped courier drones picked up speed and vanished as their Gravity Drives engaged.

#

"Drones arriving 300 kilometers to our stern, Admiral!" Lewis rocked in his seat as another near miss shook the hull of the *Reliant*. His ships had only engaged with the Others for a little over half an hour but his list of casualties in ships and men filled the display.

Unlike BatFor 4, Lewis was forced to close with the Others as the distance between the enemy fleet and Garunda shrank. With the reduced gap, the Others brought their powerful main armament into play and increased the number of hits his ships took.

Now the decisive moment. "Tactical! Update your plot and prepare your strike package. I want ten drones assigned to each Vulture. It may be overkill but let's make sure of a kill. We only get one chance at this. The remainder at your discretion."

Reliant's tactical officer's hands flew over his keyboard as he prioritized his target list and entered the latest location data. "Targeting package ready, Admiral."

"Send it!" Lewis said with a sense of satisfaction.

The drones disappeared into fold space, only to reappear a second later, less than fifty kilometers from their intended targets. No living thing could react quickly enough. Computers on board the targeted ships tried. But on locking onto their targets the drones accelerated as hard as their drives would go. Two seconds after lock on, twelve Vultures and five Buzzards were racked by multiple megaton nuclear explosions. When the blast clouds dispersed not even wreckage remained to show where millions of tonnes of starships had once been.

The flag bridge of the *Reliant* broke into spontaneous

applause and cries of delight, no doubt mingled with a sense of relief as they realized the untried weapons performed exactly as anticipated. All twelve Vulcans destroyed, along with five Buzzards. Add the twenty-four Goshawks the Persai killed prior to the launching of the weapons and the four Buzzards destroyed by BatFor 4 in their long retreat toward Garunda. Leaving only two Buzzards suddenly alone and facing the might of the combined Commonwealth fleet.

The Others beat a hasty retreat, their remaining ships reversed course, only to find Admiral Jing blocking the Buzzard's escape route after moving his ships from behind the gas giant.

The remaining two Buzzards did not even slow down or attempt to change course. They accelerated headlong toward Admiral Jing's waiting seven Nemesis battleships, five Vulcan heavy cruisers, six Talos light cruisers and seventeen Agis destroyers. The human ships ensured the Buzzards joined their recently departed friends in short order.

CHAPTER TWENTY-FOUR

UNEXPECTED GUESTS

TDF CUTLASS - MESSIER 54 CLUSTER

Survey Flotilla One, in the Messier 54 Cluster for only twelve days, received the news of the second battle of Garunda. Rear Admiral Papadomas fleetingly considered halting his expedition to make contact with the inhabitants of Planet A and their colony on Planet B, and return to Charon Base, but could see no real purpose in doing so. Instead, he continued on his mission with his small survey flotilla of three Vanguard class survey ships, one Persai survey ship, two Talos light cruisers and two Persai battle cruisers.

Christos was in his private quarters, perusing the information his flotilla had thus far gathered on the Baldies and their civilization. A smile appeared on his face. He really should stop calling them 'Baldies', but every time he mentioned it in the presence of Ambassador Schamu it made the ambassador physically wince, it was so worth it!

Back to work, he chastised himself. Twelve days of frantic work had produced some solid results. He amended his initial plan slightly. He had two of the Vanguards, TDF *James Cook* and *Henry Hudson*, work over the asteroid belt and outer planets. The remaining Vanguard, TDF *Jacques Cartier* would provide over watch for the Persai survey ship, commanded by Sub Leader Verus, as it moved in close to first Planet B, then the Baldies' home world of Planet A. He held his own cruiser, TDF *Cutlass*, and the Persai battle cruiser, *Vitachi*, in geostationary orbit around the outermost planet of the system. He remained ready, at a moment's notice, to come to the aid of either pair of survey ships if they ran into something they could not handle.

The reports from the two Vanguards showed the Baldies had begun mining operations of the system's asteroid belt, but apart from what looked like smelters and other limited industrial habitats with limited populations there was no form of militarization present and no indication the Baldies were worried about visitors from other star systems skulking around.

On the other hand, the report from Sub Leader Verus in relation to his close approaches to Planets A and B made fascinating reading. When Captain Ruth Witsell and the TDF *Vasco De Gama* arrived in the Messier Cluster five years or so ago, following a fault in their navigation computer, they found Planet B in the initial stages of colonization by the inhabitants of Planet A. Eavesdropping on electromagnetic transmissions had produced an image of what are now known as the Baldies. Approximately 168 centimeters tall, wearing a tan and brown uniform with emblems at the waist. A small circular mouth with what appeared to be three slits on either side of where a nose should be. Two eyes set widely apart above the slits, with no apparent ears on the head. Two arms with double jointed elbows and shortened forearms, and no visible body hair – hence the term the crew of the *Vasco De Gama* came up with, Baldies. What sealed Saiph DNA tampering was the fact the Baldies had five fingers.

At the time of the *Vasco De Gama*'s visit it was estimated the Baldies were at a level of technology roughly equivalent to Earth prior to World War Three. Their ships were powered by a low power ion drive which meant a one-way trip between Planet A and Planet B took around eleven months. Using similar propulsion methods meant a trip between the inner planets and the industrial habitats in the asteroid belt could take up to anywhere in the region of three years. Planet B's estimated population was at the time in the low thousands, which was why it was chosen by Captain Witsell as the site for a landing by her marines and a survey party which had taken soil and plant samples, confirming Saiph interference in the natural progression of life. Captain Witsell never visited Planet A, preferring not to risk contact with the Baldies without the nod from the politicians.

Sub Leader Verus had been able to use his highly stealthy survey ship to slowly close with Planet A, until he reached a point where he could launch small reconnaissance drones to better observe the planet and its surrounding space. What his drones had discovered was a flourishing artificial orbiting network of space habitats, serviced not only by ships moving back and forth from the surface of the planet but two space elevators. Massive constructions, which were anchored to the surface of the planet by immensely strong nano fiber cables, which reached up into orbit and connected with a large cargo handling facility, located in one of the planet's Lagrange points, a point where the gravitational pull of the planet was cancelled out by its orbiting moon. These space elevators had been theorized on Earth, but with the disruption caused by the third and fourth world wars they had never been built, even with general agreement it was probably the cheapest and quickest way to get large payloads to and from orbit.

As far as population and governance went, current estimates put the planetary population at around the eight billion mark, which was probably why the Baldies were beginning to establish colonies on Planet B. From what was known of the political setup, it appeared there was a centralized planetary government but, and he found this next point rather unsettling, it would appear to be a very militaristic one. All news broadcasts were made by Baldies wearing the same brown and tan uniform and all the broadcasts ended in the same way. An image of an elderly Baldy, in uniform, accompanied by what he could only assume was some form of national anthem. Until the translation computers could provide accurate interpretations of communications, he could only guess and he was not willing to bet the success of this mission on guesswork.

All this information was passed to Ambassador Schamu and his staff. If the ship scuttlebutt was to be believed, then the ambassador was as worried about the Baldies being a militaristic society as Christos was.

The urgent beeping of his terminal and a flashing red light interrupted him. He reached over to accept the emergency signal. The unsmiling face of Captain Mkhize appeared.

"Admiral, we've just received a courier drone from the *James Cook*. Captain Torrance states while conducting operations in the asteroid belt he has come across a vessel in distress. He states it appears to have suffered micro meteor damage to its engines and is venting atmosphere. The vessel is transmitting a repeating message in what has been identified as the language of the Baldies, but Captain Torrance believes the message is so weak it has little chance of reaching one of the Baldy installations before the vessel's atmosphere is completely vented into space."

He could tell by the look in Mkhize's eyes that Mkhize was thinking the same thing he was. A spacer's worst nightmare. A long, slow, cold death in space as the air in the suit ran low, the batteries supplying heat beginning to fail and the cold chills the body to its very core, before eventually the carbon monoxide scrubbers fail, darkness closes in and the body slips into unconsciousness. No life form, with a conscience, could allow that to happen to another.

"Send to the *James Cook*. You are to move to intercept the vessel in distress and render any and all assistance which in your view is required. Any surviving crew of the vessel are to be treated with the utmost respect and brought aboard the *Cutlass* at the earliest opportunity."

The relief on Mkhize's face was obvious. "Thank you, Admiral."

"And oh, Vusumuzi, could you inform Ambassador Schamu we may be having extra guests for dinner this evening."

Mkhize let out a loud belly laugh which took him a few seconds to get control of. "My pleasure, Admiral."

#

Christos and Ambassador Schamu stood together in the small, but well equipped, medical bay of TDF *Cutlass*. They watched Doctor Richards fuss over the three patients, each lying in beds surrounded by medical equipment. The beds were occupied by surviving crew of the Baldy ship, the same ship TDF *James Cook* had aided. The bodies of the other eight crew were currently in the *Cutlass'* makeshift morgue. Christos caught the Doctor's eye and she came to stand beside him while keeping her eyes on the patients.

"You asked to see us, Doctor?" said Schamu in a way which could only be interpreted as he had better things to do than stand in the medical bay.

Doctor Richards let out a small sigh. "The Baldy..." Christos noted a frown appear on Schamu's forehead at the Doctor's use of the slang term, he tried to hide his smile. "My apologies, Ambassador... The patient on the far left is recovering from his ordeal well. He is awake, our advanced translation program has told him he is in no danger and where he is. He should be fit enough to be discharged by the end of the day. Unfortunately, the other two are in a bad way. I'm keeping them sedated. They suffered severe lung and brain damage. I simply don't know enough about their physical make up to do much more than keep them alive."

Ambassador Schamu gave the doctor a stern look. "Not acceptable, Doctor."

"Acceptable or not, Ambassador, it is a fact. Unless those two patients get medical attention from their own people within the next twenty-four hours, their chances of making a full recovery are slim at best."

Christos looked from the doctor to her three patients and then back to the doctor. "Is it possible for us to speak with the patient who is awake without overtaxing him?"

Richards folded her arms and regarded the Admiral and the ambassador like a primary school teacher. "I don't see why not, Admiral. As long as you understand if he does show signs of stress, I may have to intervene."

"Thank you, Doctor. That will be all for now." With a nod,

Richards left Christos and Schamu alone and returned to her patients.

"Well, Ambassador. I suggest you begin questioning our visitor as soon as you can, for in twelve hours the *Cutlass* will be in orbit of Planet A and these patients will be off loaded to receive the medical attention they need."

To Christos' surprise, the ambassador did not seem fazed at all. "I may seem a bit stuffy at times, Admiral, but even I would not let harm come to anyone for the sake of political expediency. If you'll excuse me, I have a lot of work to do and little time to do it."

Christos was left standing on his own as the ambassador made his way over to the conscious Baldy. A large smile appeared on the ambassador's face as he stretched out his hand in welcome to the confused Baldy. Christos shook his head in amazement at the change in the politician's demeanor as he turned to leave the medical bay and make his way back to his quarters. He had work to do as well if he was to be ready in twelve hours.

CHAPTER TWENTY-FIVE

THEY'RE COMING

OFFICE OF THE PRESIDENT OF THE TERRAN REPUBLIC
GENEVA - EARTH

Rebecca Coston entered her office to find her invited guests already waiting for her. "My apologies, ladies and gentlemen. But for some reason some senators believe the longer they go on, the more likely I am to give them what they want. They obviously don't know me very well." That got a smile and a few chuckles from Rebecca's guests. "Please sit. We have a lot to get through, so I suggest we just hit the high points."

As Rebecca took her seat at the head of the small conference table, she regarded each of the invited guests in turn.

Secretary Gillian Rae, Head of Research and Development. With the sharing of technology between humans, Garundans and Persai, her department was expanding every day and some of the technology being shared, such as the Persai shield initiative and nano technology, could change the way humans lived their lives.

Secretary Olaf Helset. The Terran Defense Force had expanded steadily for the past five years, but with the latest Others attempt to destroy Garunda it left the First and Second Fleets weakened, however, the main point to come out of the attack on Garunda was the determination of the new

Commonwealth Union of Planets to act to protect its members. The size of the Vulture ships had been a shock – but as Rebecca understood, the hybrid courier drone/anti-ship missile had evened out the firepower imbalance and Research and Development were already rushing through a tailored design for mass production.

Ambassador Aaron Beckett, the man who helped her design the framework for the Commonwealth Union and was instrumental in its success, was convinced by Rebecca to retire from retirement and be her messenger to both the Garundans and the Persai

Governor Thomas Crothers, Governor of Janus. Rebecca's one time Secretary of Finance in whom Rebecca had entrusted the establishment of mankind's first colony world, Janus. In under five years, Crothers had taken it from zero to a colony with a population of over 20,000,000. A thriving, industrial world which now had its own shipyards, producing starships for trade and commerce and of course was home to Second Fleet under Vice Admiral Lewis.

Rebecca could see the day fast approaching when Janus would be independent and she would be addressing *President* Crothers.

"So to business, ladies and gentlemen. Aaron, I've managed to catch some of the reports coming back from Messier 54 so why don't you bring us up to speed on Ambassador Schamu's progress to date."

Aaron cleared his throat as at the touch of a control the Messier 54 system appeared in the Holo Cube in the center of the table. "Madam President, we now know Planet A is actually called Alona and Planet B is called Geta. Following a series of major wars on Alona, the military forces carried out a coup to stop further bloodshed. Military leaders in each country then came together for the greater good, under the leadership of General Paxt, later declared Emperor of Alona. Every adult male and female must spend three years in a branch of the military performing tasks for the greater good of the people. If someone chooses not to join the military, then they are not considered a citizen of the empire and as such have no voting rights." The Ambassador took a breath then continued. "Although governed by an emperor, this position is not hereditary. On an emperor's death, their successor is elected by the governors of each District. The governors are elected by the citizens of their respective Districts and local law is decided by the governor and his advisors, only national law and policy is decided by the emperor. The system has been in place for 300 or so years and the people seem content. Alona began to explore Geta eighty-five years ago but serious colonization is only now beginning. Ambassador Schamu puts that down to population expansion."

A loud "hmm…" came from Gillian Rae. "So the military runs things in the name of an emperor. I don't know if I like the sound of it."

Aaron nodded his head in agreement. "If that was the way it actually was I would agree with you. However, over the years, society on Alona has developed to such an extent the military is not what we would regard as a military at all. It has diversified so it is responsible for everything from education to health to industry. If it's a dictatorship, it's a very benign one."

Rebecca interrupted him. "What progress has the ambassador made in securing political links with the Alona?"

"So far, Ambassador Schamu has gotten agreement for a single embassy to be established to look after all the concerns of the Commonwealth Union. It is my understanding this has been agreed to by both Garunda and Pars."

Olaf Helset raised a finger and Rebecca nodded for him to go on. "For them being militaristic, according to the dispatches I have read from Admiral Papadomas, they appear to only have a small number of in-system gun boats which are used for anti-piracy operations. Papadomas reports there does not appear to be any form of sensor network in operation to alert them to the presence of any alien ships entering the system. Do I take it then the Alona are not aware of 'The Others' or of the Saiph?"

As Aaron started to reply, Rebecca raised a hand to stop him. "I'll answer that, Aaron." Rebecca touched a control and the image in the Holo Cube changed to show the Earth at the center and two lines reaching out. One line ended with Garunda and the second line ended with the Pars.

"At this juncture I, in consultation with the other leaders of the Commonwealth have decided not to alert the Alona to the fact that sometime in their past their planet was visited by the Saiph. As far as any potential threat from the Others is concerned, Messier 54 is 50000 light years from Earth. The Others attacked Garunda which is 49.41 light years from Earth and the original Persai home world which was 34.36 light years from Earth."

Two more lines appeared in the Holo Cube. "We have encountered the Others in 70 Ophiuchi, 16.59 light years from Earth and at Delta Pavonis, 19.92 light years away. The Persai are 6400 light years away and have had no contact with the Others." Rebecca looked around at the others in the room, meeting each person's eye before going on. "This has led the leaders of the Commonwealth to the conclusion that the Others originate from one of the star systems listed in the Saiph database no more than 100 light years from Earth."

Olaf nodded slowly, "The Joint Chiefs have come to the same conclusion, Madam President. According to the Saiph database, not counting Earth, they visited eleven star systems. We can discount four of those systems as being the home of the Others because we have either run into them there or, in the case of the Garundans, it's a home planet of a Commonwealth member. That leaves us with seven systems. If I may, Madam President?"

Rebecca nodded her consent and Olaf added the seven systems to the display. "Gamma Leporis, 29.25 light years away, the original destination for the Vasco De Gamma, and which we have not gone back to. Tau Eridani, 45.58 light years. 16 Cygniz, 70.5 light years. 23 Librae, 83.7 light years. Algol 3, 92.8 light years. Regulus 4, 77.5 light years and last, but not least, 9 Ceti, 66.5 light years."

Olaf touched another control and a sphere ten light years in diameter appeared around Garunda. "This sphere indicates the distance a Buzzard at maximum speed can travel in six months – the maximum time we estimate the Others had to react to the destruction of its ships in the first battle of Garunda. As you can see, none of the seven systems are within that sphere. Our conclusion is the ships we engaged in the second battle of Garunda came from a naval base of some kind. Perhaps similar to the one we believe them to be constructing in 70 Ophiuchi."

Olaf could see he had the undivided attention of everyone in the room. "Using the information the Persai have gathered from their surveillance platforms, we have ruled out Tau Eridani and 9 Ceti." On the display, those two systems dimmed in response. "However the Persai platforms have shown artificial power generation in the remaining five systems."

"Are you saying the Others originate in one of those five systems, Olaf?" asked Crothers.

"It would certainly fit the facts as we know them, Thomas. What also concerns me is the fact The Joint Chiefs believe the ships we faced in Garunda the second time were only what the Others had to hand at the naval base at the time. And it took the combined strength of First and Second Fleets aided by the Persai to defeat them. If they were to arrive in the Sol system with the forces we believe them capable of, then the TDF wouldn't have enough strength to even slow them down – never mind prevent them from decimating Earth."

The silence Olaf's last statement brought to the room was tangible. After a few awkward moments, Rebecca broke the silence. "I take it The Joint Chiefs have a recommendation, Olaf." It was not really a question.

Olaf's expression was one of resignation as he shook his lowered head before looking up into the eyes of his president. "Madam President. For most of my adult life, I was a military man. That doesn't mean I am a believer in a large military machine. But, to be honest with you, the only way I can see of securing our own survival, and in turn the Commonwealths, is to continue, and if at all possible, speed up our current military buildup and that of our allies."

Rebecca looked to Aaron Beckett. "Do we have a feeling for what the Garundans and the Persai would think if we went to a full war footing?"

Aaron thought for a moment before answering. "Well, the Persai have essentially been on a war footing ever since they arrived on Pars, and since we came on the scene they have gone into overdrive, their main problem is workforce. Years of enforced birth control has left them short of personnel. We can supply equipment to build their own shipyards and, as Gillian will no doubt back me up, they are freely supplying us with as much of their technology as we can deal with."

Gillian was nodding her head in agreement. "The Persai are sharing everything they have developed with us. My teams are like kids on Christmas morning. I actually think Jeff Moore is looking at emigrating to Pars if they would take him." That got a laugh from everyone in the room.

Aaron went on. "The Garundans, on the other hand, are virtually the opposite of the Persai. They have more personnel than they know what to do with. The Naval Academy is pushing them through as quickly as they can, but the naval base in Garunda is just nearing completion and the shipyards will not be able to supply completed hulls for at least another six months."

Crothers spoke up. "What if I freed up some space in my shipyards? I could probably complete one Nemesis class battleship every ninety days for them."

"Every little would help, thanks," said Aaron. "But by the look on Olaf's face I think he would rather you concentrated on building hulls for use by the TDF."

Olaf's face reddened ever so slightly. "I hate to say Aaron is right. However, if The Joint Chiefs are right about the strength the Others may be able to field, I'm going to need every ship I can get my hands on. Besides, we'll need any spare yard space to carry out the retrofits of Persai weaponry on our existing ships."

"So where does that leave us, Olaf?" asked Rebecca from her seat at the head of the table.

Olaf touched another control and an order of battle in the Holo Cube replaced the image of the star systems. "This is The Joint Chiefs' preferred order of battle for the TDF. As you can see, the fleet has expanded to three times its current size. The Joint Chiefs envisage a force of eighteen BatFors equipped with the new Bismarck class battleships formed up in six fleets."

Thomas Crothers let out a low whistle. "That's a lot of ships and men."

Olaf turned to him. "We estimate a build and commissioning time of three years, at the end of which we should be in a position to carry out the next phase of The Joint Chiefs' plan." Olaf glanced in Rebecca's direction. "With presidential approval of course."

Why did Rebecca get the feeling she was about to be railroaded into something? "And what sort of plan do The Joint Chiefs have up their sleeve this time, Olaf?"

"Madam President, our biggest problem is intelligence. We have been able, with Persai help, to establish where the home system of the Others may be, but we have no idea how big an area they control. It may be just a couple of star systems or they may have a massive empire we have just touched the edges of. We simply don't know."

Rebecca gave Olaf a look of frustration. "Get to the punchline, Olaf, if you please."

Olaf brought the image of the five star systems that could be the home of the Others up in the Holo Cube. Leaning his elbows on the table, he lent forward in his seat and pointed at the display. "The Joint Chiefs want to initially beef up Survey Command and then send these ships to these five systems to establish which is the home of the Others. We'll do it as stealthily as possible to avoid any chance of detection, but I feel it's something we have to do. And in three years when the fleet is ready, we'll take the war to the Others."

Olaf sat back in his seat and awaited Rebecca's reply.

All Rebecca Coston could think of was hope. Hope the Others gave the Commonwealth the three years it needed so desperately to ready itself. Because three years or no... the Others were certainly coming.

###

Books by PP Corcoran

The Saiph Series:
Discovery of the Saiph, book 1
Search for the Saiph, book 2
Hunt for the Saiph, book 3
Legacy of the Saiph, book 4

The K'Tai War:
Invasion, book 1

Anthologies:
The Empire at War: British Military Science Fiction
Explorations: Through the Wormhole
Explorations: First Contact
A Fistful of Credits

Science Fiction (shorts):
Beyond Apollo

Ghost Soldiers (shorts):
The Province

Most books also available in ebook and audiobook.

Sign up at www.ppcorcoran.com and get 'Beyond Apollo' free!

The following is an excerpt from:

SEARCH FOR THE SAIPH

PP Corcoran

CHAPTER ONE

THE HAPPY WANDERER

"Chief Engineer Logan reports we're ready to fold, Captain. Port control has given us the green light and wishes us a safe journey."

"Very well, Robards, let's be on our way. 'Time and tide wait for no man.'"

Richard Boswell smiled at the quizzical look his young navigator gave him at his use of the ancient phrase before turning his attention to the controls.

The journey from Garunda to Alona was split into ten folds of 5000 light year legs each. As the ship emerged at the end of each leg, it contacted navigation buoys placed by the navy's survey command and verified its position. The whole trip would take around ten hours, incorporating the mandatory two hour shutdown for normal service, inspection, and any minor adjustments the gravity drive needed between such long folds.

The Happy Wanderer accelerated steadily under the push of its ion drive, its massive bulk of 1,800,000 tonnes picking up speed until it finally reached three quarters the speed of light.

"Three. Two. One. Fold!" Robards called.

They shifted into fold space with an almost imperceptible shiver that ran the length of the ship.

A second, stronger vibration indicated their return to normal space.

Alarm bells rang.

Throughout the ship, the "FIRE" alarm signs flashed, their urgent blinking mirrored in the captain's display, demanding Richard's attention.

What the hell! Richard quickly brought up the ship's schematic. Fire in the engine room. The sound of bulkhead doors clanging shut reached his ears and the normally constant hum of the air conditioning died as it automatically shut down to prevent the spread of smoke. Richard overrode the alarm on the bridge, silencing it.

First Officer Yoshi Marona turned to Richard. "No reply from the engine room, Captain. I think I should head down there."

Richard desperately wanted to go himself, but his place was on the bridge. He reined in his impulses and calmly released his first officer.

"Off you go, Yoshi. Scare up what crew you can along the way and give the chief all the help she needs."

The majority of functions on ships like the Happy Wanderer were fully automated. She ran with a skeleton crew of just fifteen. Most of this crew worked in Engineering, which just happened to be the seat of the fire.

Yoshi nodded and headed for the bridge exit.

"Yoshi!"

The first officer turned toward his captain.

"You be careful now. Take no chances, or your wife will never forgive me!"

Yoshi flashed Richard a toothy grin and disappeared down the corridor, heading for the engine room at a dead run.

Richard turned to his next order of business. "Sitrep, Robards!"

"Captain, on re emergence into normal space, we continued on course at just under a quarter the speed of light…" he tapped the controls as he spoke. "The engine controls are unresponsive and my board shows the engines went on automatic shutdown at the first indication of fire. My systems are running on emergency power and I have minimal active sensor systems."

"Kennedy," Richard addressed his young communications officer, who was busy tapping keys at her workstation. So focused on the screen she was studying, she seemed unaware of her surroundings. Richard raised his voice. "Kennedy!" Still he garnered no response.

"Lorna!" Richard shouted.

Lorna Kennedy jumped as if stuck with a cattle prod. "Yes, sir!" she squeaked.

"Take a deep breath and calm yourself. We have a job to do, keep focused. OK?"

Lorna's cheeks flushed with embarrassment, her first real emergency at the age of twenty-one and she was acting like a scared five year old. She shook herself. *Yes, it's my first deep space voyage, yes, I've only been here fourteen days and don't know the crew, but where did that bubbly, confident communications officer go!? Get a grip on yourself, woman, you're meant to be an officer!* In a stronger voice she replied, "Yes, sir. Sorry, sir. It won't happen again."

"I'm sure it won't. Now, lock onto the navigation buoy and download a message to it. Instruct it to launch its emergency communications drone back to Garunda and inform Port Control we have a fire in the engine room, we're currently adrift at the first way marker, and we're declaring an emergency and request assistance as soon as possible."

"That's the thing, sir. I've been trying to raise the buoy, but the rear whisker laser mount isn't responding to commands or any of my computer fault interrogations. The bow mount can't traverse far enough to see the buoy and get a lock."

Richard mulled the problem. Each of the navigation buoys contained a communications drone equipped with its own gravity drive. The drones on this run were programmed to head for either Garunda or Alona, whichever was the closest. Any ship in distress could download a message to the drone and launch it automatically, then sit back and await rescue. Now that wasn't an option.

"Kennedy, warm up the emergency drone. Download our current logs but don't launch until we hear back from the First Officer."

The *Happy Wanderer*, like every commercial starship, was required to carry at least one communications drone. After the incident with the TDF *Vasco De Gamma*, where it ended up 50000 light years from its intended destination, it seemed like a prudent requirement. *Well*, thought Richard, *how right they were*.

Lorna was tapping at her keyboard again, happy to have a purpose.

The attention tone beeped in the captain's display and Richard activated the pickup. It revealed the image of Yoshi in a hard vacuum suit. A sense of dreadful foreboding twisted his stomach. "Go ahead, Yoshi."

"Captain, I've reached the bulkhead at Engineering. The telltale signs on this side of the door show it's over 1800 degrees in there. I can't get a visual as the cameras are down. But…" Richard saw Yoshi's despair as he shook his head, "I'm sorry, sir, there's no way any of the engineering crew could've survived."

"No way?" Richard responded, rhetorically, as he processed the likely deaths of his crew.

Yoshi shook his head slowly, sharing his captain's pain. "No. I can't see it, sir."

Richard lowered his head, rubbing his forehead gently. Chief Engineer Michelle Logan and he had been friends for almost thirty years, since he had joined Zurich Lines. They had crewed the long haul cargo runs from the asteroid belt to the inner planets. They were godparents to each other's children. Now, in an instant, she was gone. How was he going to break the news to her husband?

Yoshi's tinny voice jolted his captain back to the present. "With your permission, sir, I'm gonna seal the next bulkhead back from Engineering and then pump out the air from between the two — use it like an air lock. If the fire's consumed all the oxygen in Engineering then there's no point in giving it the fuel to reignite."

"Sounds like a good plan, Yoshi."

"I'll enter Engineering and open it to allow the heat to dissipate before resealing it and re pressurizing before I do a proper damage estimate."

"How long do you think till you can get in and give me a provisional damage report?"

"Not long, sir. We're already suited up here. Give me twenty minutes and I should know what we're facing."

"OK, Yoshi. Permission granted and I'll expect to hear from you in twenty." Richard cut the link and turned to the waiting Robards and Kennedy. "We wait," he said simply.

It was the longest twenty minutes of his life. Richard alternated between hope and dread. Surely there was a chance someone could have survived? There were emergency suits stored in Engineering in case of a coolant leak or sudden depressurization. A suit's internal oxygen supply was good for up to an hour. Some of the crew may have reached them in time. Reality swiftly quashed these thoughts. There was no chance anyone could survive an 1800 degree fire that would have enveloped the entire space in seconds...

True to Yoshi's word, the captain's console beeped for attention just over twenty minutes later. At the touch of a control, Yoshi's face appeared, sweat streaming from his brow and a worried face. Richard steeled himself for the news he knew, in his heart of hearts, was coming.

"I take it the news isn't good, Yoshi?"

"I'm sorry, sir... We've failed to locate any survivors. The heat was too intense. It's horrific down here. Without proper forensic analysis, I can't even identify the remains of the crew."

Nausea welled in the captain as all hope for the missing men and women dissipated. Now his next priority was his surviving crew, and he pushed aside his queasiness. "What about the machinery, Yoshi?"

"To put it mildly, Captain, we're well and truly screwed. All the computer gel packs are destroyed. That wouldn't be too much of a problem as we have enough spares to replace the more important ones and get the engineering computers back up and running if only..." Richard frowned as Yoshi continued, "the heat from the fire has warped everything in here. I could probably cobble something together to get the control mechanisms working but the actual physical parts of the drive are damaged. I'm afraid there's nothing we have on board that could replace them... Sorry, sir."

"Understood, Yoshi. Get your men clear and seal the door."

"Yes, sir. And sir..."

"Yes, Yoshi?"

"I'm sorry about Logan."

The captain's vision blurred as tears filled his eyes. "Thanks, Yoshi."

Yoshi nodded curtly and cut the link.

Richard gave his eyes a quick rub, hoping neither Robards nor Kennedy noticed and if they did, they would politely ignore it. He still had a ship to get home.

He quickly glanced at the ship's clock, fifty minutes – on this course at a quarter of the speed of light. Richard calculated they'd traveled 225,000,000 kilometers from the position they'd entered normal space and with every passing second were moving a further 75000 kilometers from the shipping lane. As long as a rescue ship had his base course and speed they should still find him without too much trouble.

"Kennedy, please update the logs on our communications drone with our current position, heading and speed. Download the First Officer's report and request immediate assistance. Launch the drone as soon as you're ready, please."

Kennedy busied herself at her console and Richard sat back as he calculated how long a rescue vessel would take to reach their location. The shaking of Lorna Kennedy's head caught his attention.

"Problem, Kennedy?"

"Um… yes, sir. The drone accepted the downloads OK. And the command to launch. But my board shows a red light from the launch bay doors. They appear to be stuck."

Richard conjured an image of the launch bay doors in his mind. Positioned just forward of the rear whisker laser communications mount. The laser mount that also wasn't responding. Damn! What else can go wrong? The captain punched the link to Yoshi. The image of his First Officer halfway out of his pressure suit filled his display.

"Sorry, Yoshi, you're not finished yet. The launch bay doors for the Comms drone are stuck. Probably damaged by the fire. I need you and someone else to go free them so we can get the drone out and get some help."

Yoshi had paused while removing his bulky suit. He started shrugging it back on, his brow wrinkled in thought. "Either the hatch controls are fried or the hatch mechanism itself has been warped by the heat. I may have to cut the hatch away and release the drone manually, I don't see another way around it."

"Do whatever's needed, Yoshi, but the sooner we get the drone out, the sooner we get some help."

"Understood, Captain. I'll let you know what I find." Yoshi cut the link, thinking, *it never rains but it pours*!

#

On the exterior hull, Yoshi regarded the hatch in front of him and wished he wasn't always right. Just as he'd thought, the hatch covering the communications drone bay was partially opened and jammed. Most likely, the bay door rams had suffered catastrophic damage. The drone was intact, a minor miracle.

No sense hanging about out here, I may as well get to work, thought Yoshi, as he carefully held the plasma cutting torch at arm's length and ignited it. The flame was designed to cut through anything up to and including battle armor, any mistake and it would make very short work of his suit. That mistake would take Yoshi's day from bad to fatal in a heartbeat.

He'd only been working a few minutes and already the plasma torch had easily cut through one of the four rams operating the bay doors. Yoshi looked up to ensure the crewmember with him was safely out of the arc of the plasma torch while he moved to reposition himself to start on the next ram. He was confronted with the crewmember's back.

"Hey Browne, are you with me?"

Yoshi got no reply. He turned the plasma torch off and secured it to the hull, by the bay doors, using the magnetic strap. He walked over to Browne. As he edged closer, he noticed the small hole in the back of her helmet.

"Oh God, no!" Yoshi moved as quickly as he could in his cumbersome suit to check Browne from the front and was confronted by another neat hole in the faceplate. The suit encased a now dead Browne.

"No!" Despair filled Yoshi as the rational part of his brain tried to figure out what had happened. Had a micro meteorite hit her? If so, shouldn't the faceplate be completely or at least partially shattered? Movement over Browne's now stiff shoulder caught Yoshi's eye. What the…

The short laser blast from the rifle of the armored figure passed right through Yoshi's chest.

The shot destroyed the integrity of the suit, the electronics controlling the magnetic boots failed, the atmosphere rushed out, the sum result was that Yoshi was lifted clear of the *Happy Wanderer*'s hull. Yoshi's brain, thankfully, began to shut down just as he saw dozens of armored figures scurrying toward the open airlock and entering the ship.

#

The screaming alarm on Lorna's console drew all eyes to it. She silenced it and briefly interrogated the computer to confirm its readings. Without raising her head, she shouted: "Dutchman! Dutchman!" It was the call no captain wanted to hear. "I have a crew member off the hull and moving away at speed. Suit beacon is coming in strong and I'm getting good telemetry. Bio readings show…" Lorna's voice faded as her throat closed over. My God, no! Not Yoshi! She slouched in her seat, dropped her head into

304

her hands, and sobbed.

Richard left his seat and gently moved the sobbing young woman to one side. His worst fears were realized. On the display, a red circled icon with the name "MARONA" blinked.

The fire damage at the rear of the ship meant Yoshi had already been over 200 meters from the *Happy Wanderer's* hull and moving away at forty kilometers per hour when the mid-ship sensors picked it up. It didn't matter anyway, the suit's biosensors showed Yoshi was already dead.

Richard's eyes fixed on the flashing icon of his dead first officer as he addressed Robards. "Robards, suit up. Browne's still out there, and with the stern sensors down, we don't know her status, she may need your help."

As Robards stood to comply, the bridge doors opened. Richard looked up and the sight of a group of armored figures rushing onto the bridge confronted him.

Robards reacted faster than his captain, he lunged for the nearest intruder only to be viciously beaten into unconsciousness with a few swings of a rifle butt. As Robards fell to the deck, Richard instinctively placed himself between his Comms officer and the invaders. An uneasy standoff held for what seemed an age, it was broken only when a commanding figure entered the bridge.

This one was different. Red paint covered the entirety of the left arm of his armored suit and a strange symbol adorned his chest plate. Something like a black circle covered the entire chest and a red X the size of a man's hand overlaid the middle. The figure held an ugly looking pistol loosely in its right hand.

The other intruders parted like a wave in front of him. Could this one be the leader? Richard's brain finally caught up, and as he drank in the shape and colors of the armor, recognition slowly dawned. Images of these suits had been carried by every media channel throughout the Commonwealth.

Richard furtively glanced at the large red button protected by the clear plastic cover on the arm of his command chair. The button that would purge all the navigation computers aboard the *Happy Wanderer,* denying an enemy the locations of the

Commonwealth home systems. Richard tried to calculate the time it would take to get to the chair before the intruders either cut him down or beat him unconscious, like the bleeding Robards.

The alien commander caught Richard's gaze and followed its target, the captain's chair. It turned back to Richard, lifted its right hand, and without hesitation shot Richard and Lorna with two easy jerks of its armored fingers.

The Others were in command of the *Happy Wanderer* and its navigation computer. The Others' had every coordinate of every world known to man.

###

The K'Tai War Series
Invasion, book 1

The Carters have a past.

A secret past.

A past that the K'tai didn't reckon on.

Dave and Sue Carter have just moved to the frontier planet of Agate on the border of human and K'tai space. Tensions between humans and the K'tai are heightened over the discovery of large deposits of the precious mineral Redlazore on Agate.

Yet the Carter's new lives are peaceful, just as they hoped. Dave commutes daily to his mid-level exec post in the city and Sue counsels in their local suburban High School, much to their twin teenager's distaste. In the midst of diplomatic talks the K'tai invade Agate.

It's unexpected, it's violent and it's chaotic.

The Carters are separated by just eight miles, but it quickly becomes a battleground. The seemingly impossible mission to reunite this family through the bloodshed begins.

Order Now - http://smarturl.it/BuyKTaiWarSeries

Books by PP Corcoran

The Saiph Series:
Discovery of the Saiph, book 1
Search for the Saiph, book 2
Hunt for the Saiph, book 3
Legacy of the Saiph, book 4

The K'Tai War:
Invasion, book 1

Anthologies:
The Empire at War: British Military Science Fiction
Explorations: Through the Wormhole
Explorations: First Contact
A Fistful of Credits

Science Fiction (shorts):
Beyond Apollo

Ghost Soldiers (shorts):
The Province

Most books also available in ebook and audiobook.

Sign up at www.ppcorcoran.com and get 'Beyond Apollo' free!

Printed in Great Britain
by Amazon

31403622R00175